TRIPOINT

ALSO BY C.J. CHERRYH

CYTEEN:★
The Betrayal
The Rebirth
The Vindication

RIMRUNNERS

HEAVY TIME

HELLBURNER

Published by Warner Books

★Winner of the Hugo Award for Best Novel

C.J. CHERRYH

TRIPOINT

WARNER BOOKS

A Time Warner Company

ASPECT IS A TRADEMARK OF WARNER BOOKS, INC.

Warner Books, Inc., 1271 Avenue of the Americas, New York, NY 10020

W A Time Warner Company

Printed in the United States of America

ISBN 0-446-51780-1

TRIPOINT

Chapter One

— *i* —

Dream of an interface of energies above the Einstein limit.

Dream of a phase-storm skimming what it can't envelop—until the storm slides down, down, down the nearest gravity-pit—

In this case, E. Eridani. Viking, Unionside, with ties to Pell, on the Alliance side of the line.

Shipyards and industry. Trade. Mining.

Hydrogen glows in the bow-shock. The ship dives for thermonuclear hell.

The field re-shapes itself. Almost. Once. Twice.

Becomes *Sprite,* inbound for the habitation zone.

The ring engages.

Body settles to the mattress.

Breaths come Viking-time now, ten, fifteen to the caesium-timed minute. Heart fibrillates and finds its beat.

Right hand gropes after the nutri-pack, left hand flutters off-target, trying to pull the tab. Hand to mouth is another targeting problem.

God-bloody-awful, going down. But if a man lay very, very still for a few minutes, the luxury of the off-duty tech, he'd find he felt a lot, lot better for swallowing all of it.

And Tom Hawkins, at twenty-three, had made close to two hundred such system drops, a few of them before he was born. At twenty-three, he was a veteran of the Trade, the Fargone–Voyager–Mariner–to–Cyteen circle that had been *Sprite*'s routine.

Long time since they'd seen Viking—in a time-dilated childhood, longer since Viking had seen him.

Those had been the scary days, runs when you got into port and other ships told you you'd be crazy to go on as you planned . . . even as a kid, you caught the anxiousness in the seniors and heard the rumors. You knew, even as a kid, when a run was dangerous, and you heard, though the seniors were sure you weren't in earshot, about dead ships and Mazianni raids.

Mariner was all rebuilt now, modern and shining new. The pirates were mostly out of the picture. Pell resumed its role as gateway to ancestral Earth and its luxury trade. Cyteen and Pell had signed the long-negotiated trade treaty, with the final closing of the Hinder Stars, by the terms of which, Pell dropped its claim to Viking and agreed to tariff adjustments on haulers plying the Viking–Mariner run, thus promoting Viking commerce, since Viking hadn't much to sell *except* machinery, raw materials, and accommodations for the long-haulers.

But, bad news for the smugglers—by the treaty just signed, Viking became a free port, Union by government, tax-free for Earth goods, shipped through from Pell, and for certain Union goods, shipped through from other ports.

Big boost for struggling Viking, that was what Mischa-captain-sir had said when they'd drawn their fat government contract. Bigger boost for themselves—*Sprite* wasn't a warm-hold hauler, and only a few of her class had gotten into the lottery for the government contracts, though the Family hadn't even been in agreement at the outset to take the offer, being reluctant to fall out of their ordinary cycle, and miss their frequent rendezvous with decade-long friends on *Polly* and *Surinam;* but the figures had worked out, showing them how they were going to get back into the loop with their trading partners—make two tightly scheduled, fast transits between Viking and Mariner, and they'd be meeting *Polly* and *Surinam* on their trips back from Cyteen Outer Station, intersecting their old schedule for a loop out to Fargone once every other ship-year, making a literal figure eight with *Bolivar* and the Luiz-Romneys, who had likewise lusted after the contract and found the same objections. *Sprite* and *Bolivar* together could do what the big combine ships did, perfectly legal, if they met schedule.

So it wasn't goodbye forever to old friends, off-ship lovers and favorite haunts—just wait-a-while.

And hello to Viking. He'd not been here since he was six— since an unscheduled long layover had provided the kids' loft a rare permission for the middles and olders in the loft to go downside, right out the lock and down the dock, with a close guard, in those wild years, of armed senior crew.

That had been impressive—their escort of uncles and aunts and mothers carrying guns at the hip, his first-ever view of a station dock in all his young ship-born life, a memory of cold, frosty breaths, browned metal and huge machinery the seniors said would snatch strayed children up and grind them into the fishcakes Viking sold.

At that age, he'd believed it absolutely, had particular suspicions certain two cousins in the group would feed him to the machines, and held tight to the crocodile-rope, gawking about but being very wary of sneak attacks by cousins and rapacious robot loaders.

Warehouses, long, long areas of warehouses, huge cans waiting loading, that was what he remembered: vending machines where they'd all gotten soft drinks and chips—lousy chips, but they'd never seen food drop out of a machine and it was a marvel. He remembered a long row of bars children weren't supposed to go into, but the seniors had let them look into one, which was dark and loud and full of people who stopped drinking and stared at them, moment frozen in a kid's remembrances.

Thirty years ago, station-time, that was. He lived ship-years, his own biological years. The arbitrariness of outside time had confused him when he was six—and still, though computers and numbers were his job and his livelihood, he fell into that childhood misconception when he tried to *feel* the near forty years outsiders said he'd lived.

But that only mattered against history. He'd been six on that outing, not ten—body and mind, a staggering difference, but station officers always wanted your universal dates on the customs papers you had to fill out. To ship-dwellers, body-years mattered, and you knew those from Medical; computers calculated it by where your ship had been, what it hauled, and kept careful track all your life, never mind how long it took some long-ago planet to go around its star. Ship was your world. Ship was four hundred sixteen cousins and uncles and aunts, all Hawkinses, every one. Inside was Us, where you were born, where you had a ship-share and the freedom to come and go with the ship forever—a couple of weeks in any port and then out again, good-bye, see you next turn about, or never again. Spacers weren't in charge of sureties. It was always if, and plans changed, and ships went where the trade was.

Two hundred ship-years old, *Sprite* was. Not a big ship. Not as old as *Dublin* or *Finity's End.* Not a glamour ship, no long runs, no memorable action in the war, just a light-armed hard worker that kept the goods moving and delivered the heartbeat of civilization when she made port and the information of her last port flowed into the current ports. Data on banks, stock reports, trade figures, births and deaths, books, entertainments, news and inventions across the web of stars: the tick and pulse of everything human was in *Sprite*'s databanks when she docked. Some of it she was paid to carry; some was public information, obligatory for any ship that docked to carry, non-charge, to its next port. At Viking, *Sprite* would drink down an informational feed she hadn't had directly in years, the data of Earth-space and Alliance, such, at least, as Alliance was willing to spill to Unionside in this strange new era of peace.

That dataflood-to-come meant a lot of work ahead for *Sprite,* to make its own best use of what it learned—knowledge ultimately as valuable to the ship as the goods in her hold, data that was profit, and survival, for a ship that competed for its contracts and owned at least most of its own cargo. It took a lot of head-work and computer work to keep a small ship competitive in a market that saw new station-bound combines and cartels trying to tie up the trade and turn everything corporate. . . .

Though captain Mischa Hawkins had said that wouldn't go down: the Beyond had fought the War to get rid of the Earth-based corp-rats, and merchant spacers would never tolerate it. The starstations that had rebelled against Earth's governance might think they were going to play that game themselves. But if stationer governments built ships to compete with the Family ships that had helped them in the War, those ships would have small, expensive accidents, nothing to cost a life—unless they pushed back. If they hired crew, they'd not be quality, or reliable. The merchanter Families ruled commerce on both sides of the Union–Alliance boundary, disdaining permanent allegiances, and they'd shut every station down cold, if stations tried to dictate to them again.

Stations knew it. Stations kept one law on their upper levels, but the docks and the sleepovers were under separate rules; and on the deck of every individual ship was that ship's own law, at dock or in space.

So the law was the same. Still, it was a new concept to Thomas Hawkins—to go out on station docks with *no* ship he knew in port—like a first-timer, almost, which he assuredly wasn't . . . he'd been cruising the docks on his own since he was ship-wise eighteen, never gotten knifed, never gotten into anything he couldn't talk his way out of. Most often he scored with some spacer-femme likewise looking. . . .

Particularly with one dark-eyed *Polly* crew-brat, who he wasn't certain was using precautions, but, if you said you weren't and she didn't, that was entirely her business and *Polly's* business. A man just wondered . . . might he *have* a kid on some ship . . . somewhere . . . and he wouldn't see her for two years.

Mind was going random. He was sliding down into sleep again. There was a little sedative in his post-jump packet, aspirin, mostly. Didn't take much to send you under, after jump, and he wasn't scheduled for duty till next watch.

Busy time coming, then. Lot of equipment to check. Nav and cargo on their necks, meanwhile juniors got all the wonderful routine, the stuff that wasn't ops-critical, and there was always a pile of it, all the data storage, hard and matrixed. . . .

Load the chain of records, compare and check it off: if some subspace gremlin had bombed one file it wouldn't get the backup in exactly the same way. The operations computers checked themselves, monitored by Senior technicians. For all those datafiles not regularly loaded there were the junior techs to do the job, on the auxiliary boards, why else did lower lifeforms exist?

Load another record . . .

Log the check . . .

Meanwhile test all the systems.

Good reason for a nap.

"Thomas Bowe."

He blinked. Thought he'd dreamed it. Shut his eyes.

"Thomas Bowe, confirm."

Eyes opened. He *wished* they wouldn't call him that. He'd complained. That was a by-the-book tight-ass senior cousin on the bridge. He knew the voice: Duran T. Hawkins, senior Com, who didn't give a damn about his complaints.

But a by-name call, coming hard on system entry, scared him, once his brain cut in—as if—God—had somebody dropped dead on entry? They didn't call junior officers on the com for social chatter.

He rolled out of his bunk, ignored the pounding in his temples, and braced his arm on the opposite wall to push the button. "This is Tom B., confirming to com."

"Report to the captain, Thomas B., on the bridge, in good order, ship is stable, confirm."

"Confirm," he said, and heard the com click out without a window to query, and no patience if he called back to ask questions, not with Duran at the board.

Besides, they were legitimately busy up there—it *could* be they were calling computer techs for some kind of ops emergency, in which case it was a definite hurry. His heart had begun thumping with a stupid panic, the pain in his sinuses had grown acute, the result of going vertical in a rush, but they hadn't said *stat,* they'd given an *in good order,* which meant take time to clean up.

So his mother couldn't have had an attack or something. Marie was under forty, ship-time,—healthy as the proverbial horse. They'd had breakfast together before they jumped, she'd talked about something he couldn't remember. But they called you if a relative had taken ill. . . .

Or most of all they called you if you'd screwed something critical and they wanted to know exactly what you'd done to systems before Mischa asked you to take a hike in cold space.

But he hadn't laid a hand on the main boards since long before they left Mariner. He was absolutely sure of that.

Balance wasn't steady yet. He bashed an elbow, slid the bathroom door open—the whole end of the 2-meter-wide cabin on a circular track. He met his own confused, haggard face in the mirror, squinting at the automatic glare of white light. He peeled out of his clothes, set the shower on Conserve, for speed, slid through the shower door without losing vital parts and shut his eyes against the 30 second all-around needling of the cleaner-and-water spray. A quick, breath-taking blast sucked the water back again. The vacuum made his ears pop, and didn't at all help a nervous stomach or a sick headache.

But he was scrubbed, shampooed, shaved, and saner-looking as he shut the bath behind him. He struggled into clean coveralls, remembered the key-card while he was walking his boots on, went back and found it on his dirty coveralls, clipped it on one-handed as he opened the door onto the lower main corridor. *Ship is stable* meant no take-holds expected, no clip-lines required, and he made a dash down-ring to the lift. Crew was coming and going, likewise at speed when they had to cross the ship's axis. Somebody for sure had reported ill: he could see the infirmary lit and the door open, down the positive curve of the deck.

But Com had ordered him specifically to the bridge, see the captain, and bridge it was—he found the lift idle on rimside level and rode it up, a good deal calmer in that ride, now that he wasn't jump-rattled and half-asleep—but uneasy, still, mind spinning around and around the handful of guesses his experience afforded him.

The lift clanked into lock and let out into the dim grey plastics-and-computer light environment of the bridge. Heads turned, senior cousins interrupting their work to stare as he walked through, the way people stared at victims of mass calamities.

Which didn't help his nerves at all. But his first glance accounted for his whole personal universe of relatives he cared about: his mother, Marie, stood in the middle of the bridge, talking to Mischa. Mischa was sitting at the main console. Marie and the captain were sister and brother; and Marie was clearly all right—but what Marie was doing on the bridge during approach was another question.

God, what had he done that rated Mischa calling Marie up from the cargo office?

"Sir," he said, feeling like an eight-year-old criminal, "ma'am."

"Station schema just came in." Mischa tapped the screen in front of him, a schematic of Viking station and its berths, same as any such diagram the outsystem buoy delivered them when they dropped into system. He didn't understand at first blink, or second, since he had nothing reasonably to do with that input or the system that put it up.

Mischa said, *"Corinthian.* Austin Bowe's in port."

Hit him in the gut, that did. He couldn't look at Marie. Mischa pointed to a certain berth on the station schema. "They're scheduled for undock nine days from now, we're in for fifteen days' turnaround, and we'll make dock tomorrow morning. Figure right now that there'll be ample time after he's left to do any personal touring you want to do around that berth. I'm giving an absolute order, here, that applies to you, Marie, and you, Tom, and everyone in this crew. *No* contact, no communication with *Corinthian* in any way, shape, or form that doesn't go through me, personally. We can't afford trouble. I'm sure *Corinthian* doesn't want it either. I swear to you, I'm not going to look the other way on this, Marie. On government contract, we've no latitude here, none, do you read me clear on that?"

"Perfectly clear," Marie said. Too cheerful by far, Tom thought. Marie's calm ran cold fingers up and down his spine. "Bygones can be bygones—unless, of course, Austin Bowe comes onto *our* dock."

"I don't like that attitude, Marie. I've half a mind to hold you and him and the whole crew aboard until he's out of here. And *nobody's* going to be real damn happy with you if that's what I have to do."

"And how would *that* look? You want Viking saying we're afraid of him?"

"Viking, hell. I'll lay odds no stationer here remembers any problem between us and them."

"I'll lay equal odds that ships at dock remember."

"This is our business. And it *is* business, Marie. No personal vendetta of any member of this crew is worth our legal standing, and anybody sane is going to understand that. This isn't the War. The man's a senior captain now. We're talking about our entire livelihood at stake."

"I absolutely agree. I don't see a problem."

Lying through her teeth, Tom thought again, hands locked behind him, face absolutely neutral. Mischa knew Marie was lying, and couldn't get her to engage with him.

"Bygones, is it? You listen to me, Marie. You, too, Tom. You listen *up*. Government contract and government cargo means we've got clearances, we've got special ratings, we're in first on the port they've been negotiating for the last twenty years, and the Board of Trade isn't going to care about excuses. Neither is the rest of the Family."

"We're in the middle of the damn *bridge,* Mischa, why don't we just throw the com open so the whole Family can hear it? Send the kids to the loft and let's just tuck down and hide in our ship until *Corinthian* goes away, why don't we? We know we can't defend ourselves. Rape's a lovely experience if you just lie back and enjoy it. God, I can't believe I'm hearing this!"

"Quiet it down, Marie!"

"I'm going to do my job, Mischa! I'm not sitting in this ship. I'm not hiding. *I* didn't commit any crime. *I'm* not a rapist, in case you got it backwards at Mariner, and I've nothing to be ashamed of! If *Corinthian* wants trouble, they can come looking. If they don't—"

"—if they don't?"

There was quiet all around. Tom stood there remembering to breathe, and felt a tremor in his whole body when he heard Marie say, quietly, reasonably, "I'll do my *job,* Mischa. I'm not crazy," and heard the captain say to her, then,

"You do that, Marie, you damn well do it, and *nothing* else. That goes for every member of this crew."

Marie walked out. The captain's sister, cargo chief, Marie Kirgov Hawkins, challenged the captain to lock her in quarters for the duration—and walked out, with the whole ops section watching.

Mischa possibly could have handled it better—but you never knew where you were going with Marie. Mischa could have been easier on Marie—but she'd lied to him the minute she'd said bygones could be bygones with that ship. She'd lied to his face, and her brother, as ship's senior captain, had laid the law down.

Drawn a line Marie Hawkins shouldn't cross—and that was a mistake with Marie, on a *good* day.

Her son said, quietly as he could, "May I be excused, sir?"

"I want to see you. In my office. One hour. I've got my hands full right now. You leave your mother alone. You don't need her advice. Hear me, Thomas?"

"Yes, sir." At least, at twenty-three, he'd outgrown 'boy.' Other uncles managed to say 'son' to their sisters' offspring. Mischa never had. It was 'your mother' when he disavowed Marie, it was 'Marie' when they agreed, and 'Thomas' when *his* behavior was in question. "Yes, sir, I hear you."

"Go on." Mischa gave him a back-of-the-hand wave.

He walked back to the lift. Other heads averted quickly, back to business, except the most senior cousins, who gave him analytical stares, wondering, quite probably, whether Thomas Bowe-Hawkins was in fact part of the Hawkins family, or whether, because of that ship sitting at Viking dock, he was going to do something lethally stupid.

"Son."

Saja. Tech chief. Likewise giving him a warning stare, turning in his seat to do it.

But Saja was senior on duty right now and couldn't break away, so that was one heart-to-heart lecture he could duck, although if he had to choose, he'd take Saja's over the captain's, no question.

The lift came up from downside, where Marie had left it. He punched Down, hoping Marie had gone to her office, and left the corridor. She'd *be* working, after this, nonstop, and God help anybody in the Family who walked through her office door. He knew her fits: Marie worked when she was mad, Marie worked when she was upset, Marie got up for no reason at all in the middle of the night and went to the office, staying there nonstop, thirty-six, forty, fifty hours, when she got in a mood, and he wouldn't go near her now by any choice.

The lift stopped. The door opened. Marie was waiting for

him on lower deck, leaning against the opposite wall, arms folded.

"What did you say to him?"

"Nothing. I swear. Nothing."

Marie's eyes were grey, black-penciled like her brows; and cold, cold as a moon's heart when she didn't like you. In point of fact, she didn't always *like* her son. She was undoubtedly thinking about *Corinthian,* maybe seeing Bowe's face on him . . . he didn't know. He'd never known. That was the hell of it.

So now Austin Bowe was *Corinthian*'s senior captain. Mischa and Marie kept current using dockside sources he didn't have, clearly they did.

"I've done my job," Marie said, "I've *worked* for this ship. Where does he get off, calling me on the deck like that, in front of the whole damned crew?"

"I think he just wanted you to know, before the word got out—he couldn't leave . . . "

"The *hell* he couldn't! The *hell* he couldn't manage the intercom. Wake up, Marie, oh, by the way, Marie, could you come *up* here, Marie? *Damn* him!"

"I'm sorry." When Marie blew, it was the only safe thing to say. Teenaged cousins clustered in the corridor, now, down by the infirmary. Probably it was a shock case, some young fool cheating on the nutri-packs. Every half-grown kid thought he knew what was enough—at least once in his life.

"Mischa's going to be *talking* to you," Marie said. "I know his ways. He's going to be telling you all his good reasons why poor Marie can't be trusted outside. Poor Marie's just too emotional to do her job. Marie who got raped and beaten half to hell while her mother and her brother dithered about station law just might do something like go down the dock and take a cargo hook to the son of a bitch that did it, because poor Marie just never got over it. I chose to have you because *I* choose what happens to me, and Mischa doesn't trust poor Marie to manage her own damned *life!* Well, poor Marie is

going to go around to her office and study the market reports
and see if there's any way in hell to screw Austin Bowe's ship
in the financial market, legally, because that's my arena! So
when dear Mischa calls you in to tell you you've got to spy on
poor Marie, for the sake of the ship, you'll know just what to
tell him."

"He wants to see me."

"How could I not guess? Tell him to—" Marie shut her
mouth. "No, tell him whatever you want to tell him. But I'm
not crazy, I'm not obsessed. Motherhood's not my career, I've
always been clear on that, but you've turned out all right." She
reached—in teenage years he'd flinch—she'd fought that piece
of hair all his life. She brushed it away from his eyes. It fell.
"Tell Mischa he's an ass and I said so. —It was a long time ago
I told you kill that son of a bitch that fathered you. It was a
bad time, all right? I made some mistakes. But you've turned
out all right."

It was the first time Marie had ever admitted that. She paid
him a compliment, and he latched on to it with no clear idea
how much she meant by it—like a fool, he tucked it into that
little soft spot he still labeled mama, and knew very well that
Marie of all people wasn't coming down with an attack of
motherhood. She was absolutely right. It wasn't her specialty—
though she had her moments, just about enough to let on
maybe there was something there, enough to make you want
a whole lot more than Marie was ever going to give, enough
sometimes to make you feel you'd almost attained something
everybody else was born having.

She walked away, on her way to her office.

The general com blasted out the announcement that juniors
should be careful about the nutri-packs, and take their dosages
faithfully.

You could guess. Some kid down in infirmary had muscle
cramps he thought he'd die of and a headache to match.

Always a new generation of fools. Always the ones that
didn't believe the warnings or read the labels.

He'd trade places with that kid—anything but show up in Mischa's office and listen to Mischa's complaints about Marie. Mischa couldn't tell Marie to sit down and shut up. He didn't know why, exactly, Mischa couldn't. But something Marie had said a moment ago, about her mother and Mischa waiting for station law—that was another bit in a mosaic he'd put together over the years, right pieces and wrong pieces. Put them in and take them out, but never question Marie too closely or you never got the truth.

Sometimes you got a reaction you didn't want. His nerves still twitched to tones in Marie's voice, nuances of Marie's expression. Sometimes she'd strike out and you didn't know why.

Not a good mother—although he *liked* Marie most of the time. Sometimes he admitted he loved her, or at least toyed with the idea that he did, because there was no one else. Gran was dead at Mariner. He didn't remember her except as a blurry face, warm arms, a lap. Saja . . . Saja was solving a staff problem, by taking his side. And Mischa . . .

Well, there was Mischa.

— *ii* —

"How's your mother taking the situation?" Mischa asked, leaning back, with the desk between them.

That was a trap, and a broad one. Mischa, monitor the lower corridor? Spy on his own crew and kin?

Maybe.

"I don't know, sir. We did talk. She wanted to."

"She did." Mischa didn't seem to believe that, just stared at him a beat or two. "I don't know how much of the detail she ever gave you. . . ."

Plenty. Much too much, and he didn't want a rehash from Mischa, but he'd found out one and two things he'd not heard before in the last hour, just by listening, and he sensed a remote chance of more pieces.

He shrugged, nerved himself not to blow, and waited.

"We pulled into Mariner," Mischa said. "Like now, *Corinthian* was at dock. Ten other ships. It was the middle of the War, stations were jittery, you didn't know what side the ship next to you might be on. *Corinthian* was real suspect. Had a lot of money, crew throwing it around. The ship smelled all over like a Mazianni sellout, but you couldn't prove it. We had a caution on them. And my sister—" Mischa rocked the chair, regarded him a moment, frowning. "Austin Bowe's the devil. Granted. Marie was seventeen, sweet, happy kid—in those years nobody could know for sure who was running clean and who wasn't. You stayed close to kin and you didn't spill everything you knew in sleepovers with strangers. That was the atmosphere. And this was her first time cruising the docks, not sure she's going to do it, you know, but looking. 'Stay close to Family,' mama said. 'Stick with your cousins.' Two ships in port, we knew real well. We—Saja and I—tried to set her up with a real nice guy off Madrigal. We arranged a meeting, we were going to meet some of their crew in a bar, but Marie ducked out on us. Wouldn't go with us, no. We waited. We had a drink, we had two. Marie knew the name of the bar, she had her pocket-com, she didn't answer a page, I was getting damn worried, I was stupid—Saja kept saying we should call in, I figured Marie was doing exactly what she did, she wouldn't go with any guy her brother set up, oh, no, Marie was going to do things her way, and Heston—he was captain, then—was going to kill her, you know what I mean? I was covering for her. I figured she wasn't too far away. Wrong again. We started searching, bar to bar, quiet, not raising any alarm. Next thing I know I've got a call from the ship saying they'd had a call relayed through station com, clear around Mariner rim, Marie's in trouble in some sleepover she doesn't know the name of, she's crying and she's scared."

Marie didn't cry. Never knew Marie to cry. He didn't recognize the woman Mischa was telling him about. And he couldn't fault Mischa on what Mischa said he'd done.

"What we later reconstructed," Mischa said, "your mother'd hopped a ped transport that passed us. That was how she ducked out. She'd gone into blue sector—we were in green— pricier bunch of bars, not a bad choice for a kid looking for action, and here's this complete stranger, tall, good-looking, mysterious, the whole romantic baggage . . . *Corinthian* junior officer gets her drunker than she ought to be, talks her into bed, and it gets kinkier and rougher than she knows how to cope with. She gets scared. Guy's got the key—mistake number two. Mama—your gran—gets the com call. At which point I get the call, mama's on her way over to blue with Heston, and they've called the cops. At least Marie had the presence of mind to know the guy was *Corinthian,* she could tell us that. So the cops called *Corinthian, Corinthian* probably called Bowe—but Bowe's *Corinthian*'s senior captain's kid, so you know *Corinthian*'s not just real eager to see him arrested, and in those days, stations weren't just real eager to annoy any ship either. Supply was too short, they were scared of a boycott, the government wasn't in control of anything, and they assumed they just had a sleepover quarrel on their hands. Bowe took the com away from your mother, we didn't have any other calls, *Corinthian* was in communication with Bowe—we still didn't know what sleepover he was in. But *Corinthian* crew knew. They occupied the bar, maybe intending to get their officer out and back to the ship where the cops couldn't get him, maybe going to take Marie with them, we had no idea. We couldn't get any information out of station com, the police weren't feeding us *Corinthian*'s communications with them or with Bowe, ours were breaking up if we didn't use the station relay, but by now we had no doubt where Marie was—I was on the station direct line trying to get the stationmaster to get the police off their reg-u-lations to get in there, but nobody wanted to wake him up, the alterday stationmaster was an ass, insisted they were moving in a negotiating team. Meanwhile Heston and mama and some of the rest of the crew went into the bar after Marie. *Corinthian* crew had opened up the liquor— you can imagine. Things blew up. A *Corinthian* got his arm broken with a bar chair, the station cops got into it, *they* couldn't force the doors. By time we got the mainday station-master out of bed, a cop was in station hospital, six of your future cousins were in our infirmary, about an equal number of *Corinthian* crew were bleeding on the deck, and things were at a standoff, with station section doors shut."

Doors big as some ships. Stations didn't *do* that. Not since the War.

"—We had two ships calling crew from all around the docks," Mischa said. "Station central was refusing to relay calls, threatening to arrest *Corinthian* and *Sprite* crew on sight, *Madrigal* and *Pearl* crews were hiding some of our guys from the cops. I was in blue section, with about fifty of us. *Corinthian,* unfortunately, was docked right adjacent to blue. There were at least fifty of them holed up in the bar, about fifty more on deck, in blue, about that number of station cops and security, several hundred of our crew and theirs *and* cops stuck in sections they couldn't get out of. Forty-eight hours later, station agreed to total amnesty, we got Marie out, *Corinthian* got Bowe and the rest of their crew out, and the bar owner's insurance company and the station admin split the tab. We agreed to different routes that wouldn't put us in the same dock again, which is how, by a set of circumstances, we ended up Unionside. And your mother turned up pregnant. That's the sum of it."

Mischa left a silence. Waiting for him to say something. He wanted to, finally ventured the question he wouldn't ask Marie.

"Was Austin Bowe the only one?"

"As Marie tells it, yes."

"As she tells it?"

"The captain's son, and in a hell of a bind? He knew she was his best bargaining chip. Only thing that *might* get *Corinthian* out scot free was Marie, in one piece. She walked out of there.

Cut lip, bruises. Refused medical treatment, station's and ours. She was holding together pretty well for about the next twelve hours. She'd take the ordinary trank. . . . "

The picture snapped into god-awful focus. "You took her into *jump?*"

"By the terms, we agreed to leave port."

"Marie wasn't the criminal!"

"Station had a riot on its hands. Station wanted us on our way. *Marie* wanted out of that port. Medical thought she was doing all right."

"My God."

"In those days, the guns were live, all the time. *Heston* wanted out of there as soon as *Corinthian* jumped out. We weren't sure they weren't spotters, we didn't want them sending any message to any spotter that might be lying in wait out there in the dark—they did that, in those days, just lurk out on the edges, take your heading, meet you out at your jump-point—spotters didn't carry any mass to speak of. They'd beat you there. They'd be waiting. You'd be dead. We skimmed that jump-point as fast as we dared and we got the hell on to Fargone. It wasn't an easy run. We pushed it. You did things you had to do in those days, you took chances, the choices weren't that damn good, Thomas, it wasn't like today. No safety. When you were out there in the dark, you were out there with no law, no protection. We just *had* no choice."

"It's a wonder she isn't crazier than—" He cut that off, before it got out, but Mischa said,

"—crazier than she is. I know. You *think* I don't know. I knew her before."

"Why didn't somebody *order* an abortion? I mean, doesn't Medical just *do* that, in a case like that?"

"The captains don't *order* any such thing on this ship. Your mother said if she was pregnant, that was fine, she *wanted* . . . "

"Wanted what?"

Mischa had cut an answer short, having said too much about

something Mischa knew, about *him.* But if he chased that topic, Mischa might stop talking.

"She said it was her choice," Mischa said, "and nobody else was getting their hands on her. I'll tell you something, Tom. There's not been another sleepover. No men. She won't get help. Your aunt Lydia studied formal psych—specifically with Marie in mind. Never did a damned bit of good. Marie copes just real well, does exactly what she wants, she's damned good at what she does. I'll tell you something. She wouldn't have any prenatal tests, wouldn't take advice, damn near delivered you in her quarters, except your grandmother found out she was in labor. Marie was dead set you were a daughter, and when she gave birth and found out you weren't, she wouldn't look at you, wouldn't take you, wouldn't hold you, until three days after. Then she suddenly changed her mind. All of a sudden, it's—Where's my son? And your aunt Lydia tells me some crap about postpartum depression and how it was a traumatic birth, and a load of psychological nonsense, but I know my sister, I *know* the look she's got; and I'm *not* damn blind, Tom, I hoped to hell she'd turn you over to the nursery, which she did when she found out she really hated diapers, and being waked up at odd hours. I wasn't for it when she wanted you to come back and live with her. I really wasn't for it, but your grandmother always hoped Marie would straighten out, sort of reconcile things . . . small chance. I watched you and her, damned carefully. Mama did. I don't know if you were aware of that."

Blow across the face. Didn't know why. He didn't know why mama ever did things, one minute hit him, another held him, Marie had never made sense about what made her mad. Call her Marie, not mama, that was the first lesson he learned. Marie was *his* mother, and finally, finally she took him home to her quarters like the other kids' mothers—but if he made her mad or called her mama she'd take him back and the other kids would know. . . .

Which she did. More than once.

"Were you?" Mischa asked, and he didn't know what Mischa had just said.

"I'm sorry, I lost it."

Long silence, long, long silence in the captain's office, himself sitting in front of the desk, like a kid called in for running, or unauthorized access. Damn Mischa, he'd thought he understood, he'd thought Marie was right. Now he didn't know who'd lied or what was real or how big a son of a bitch Mischa was, after all.

"I can't control Marie," Mischa said. "Your grandmother might've, but she's gone. *I've* talked to her. Ma'am's talked to her. Your aunt Lydia's talked to her. Said—You're hurting that boy, Marie, he's too young to understand, he doesn't know why you're mad at him, and for God's sake let it *be,* Marie. Which did damned little good. Marie's not—not the kid that went into that sleepover. She'd hold a grudge, yes. But nothing like—"

Another trail-off, into silence. Maybe he was supposed to fill it. He didn't know. But he still had his question.

"Why didn't she abort? What was it you almost said she wanted?"

Mischa didn't want that question. Clearly.

"Tom, has she talked to you about killing Austin Bowe?"

"She's mentioned it. Not recently. Not since I moved out on my own."

"She ever—this is difficult—do or suggest anything improper?"

"With me?" He was appalled. But he saw the reason of Mischa's asking. "No, sir. Absolutely not."

"The answer to your question: she said . . . she *wanted* Austin Bowe's baby. And she wouldn't abort."

It rocked him back. He sat there in the chair not knowing what to say, or think.

Marie'd said, just an hour ago, she'd kept him because *she* chose what happened to her. Obstinacy. Pure, undiluted Marie, to the bone. He could believe that.

But he could . . . hearing the whole context of it . . . almost believe the other reason, too. If he could believe Mischa. And he did, while he was listening to him, and before Marie would turn around and tell him something that made thorough sense in the opposite direction.

"Wanted his baby," he said. "Do you know why, sir?"

"I don't. I've no window into Marie's head. She said it. It scared hell out of me. She only said it once, before we jumped out of Mariner. Frankly—I didn't tell your grandmother, it would have upset her, I didn't tell Lydia, I didn't want that spread all over the ship, and Lydia's not—totally discreet. I didn't even know it was valid in the way I took it. She'd been through hell, she never repeated it in any form—it's the sort of thing somebody might say that they wouldn't mean later."

"Have you asked her about it?"

Mischa shook his head, for an answer.

"Shit."

"Thomas. Don't *you* ask her. She and I—have our problems. Let's just get your mother through the next week sane, that's all I'm asking."

"You throw a thing like that at me, and say . . . don't ask?"

"You asked."

He felt . . . he wasn't sure. He didn't know who was lying, or if Marie was lying to herself, or if Mischa was deliberately boxing him in so he couldn't go to Marie, *couldn't* ask her her side.

"What do you want me to do?"

"Has she talked—down below—about killing anyone?"

"She said—she said she wants to get at him through the market. Legally."

"You think that's true?"

"I think she's good at the market. I think—there's some reason to worry."

"That she might pull something illegal? Damaging to us?"

If Mischa's version of Marie was the truth—yes, he could see a danger. He didn't know about the other kind of danger—

couldn't swear to what Marie had said, that she wouldn't take to anybody with a cargo hook, that it wasn't her style. Cargo hook was Marie's imagery. He hadn't thought of it.

"What are you going to do?" he asked Mischa.

"Put Jim Two on it—have him watch her market dealings every second. Have *you* go with her any time she goes onto the docks. And you remember what she pulled on me and Saja. You don't take your eyes off her."

"You're going to let her go out there."

"It's a risk. It's her risk. It's forty years ago station-time, like I said, probably Viking has no idea it's got a problem—but ships pass that kind of thing around. Somebody out there knows. Damned sure *Corinthian* hasn't forgotten it, and I'm hoping Bowe isn't as crazy as Marie is. He's got no good reputation, *Corinthian*'s still running the dark edges of the universe—damned right I've kept track of him over the years—and I don't think he wants any light shining into his business anywhere. If he's smart, and I've never heard he was a fool, he'll find reason to finish business early and get out of here. I'll tell you I'm nervous about leaving port out of here with him on the loose—war nerves, all over again. But there's nothing else I can do. We've got a cargo we've got to unload, we've got servicing to do, we just can't turn around faster than he can and get out of here."

"You really think in this day and age, he'd fire on us?"

"He didn't acquire more scruples in the War. Damned right he would, if it served his purpose. And if he hasn't tagged Marie as a dangerous enemy, he hasn't gotten her messages over the years."

"She's communicated with him?"

"Early on, she sent him messages she was looking for him. That she'd kill him. She's dropped word on crew that use his ports. Left mail for him in station data. Just casually."

"God."

"Dangerous game. Damned dangerous. I called her on it. Told her she was risking the ship and I told Heston. But stopping Marie from anything is difficult. I don't *think* she kept at it."

"And you're asking me to keep tabs on her?"

"You better than anyone. Take her side. There's nobody else she'd possibly confide in."

"Why, for God's sake? Why should she tell me anything?"

"Because you're Austin Bowe's son. And I think you figure somewhere in her plans right now."

"My *God*, what do you think she's going to do, walk onto his ship and shoot him?"

"If she's got a gun it's in spite of my best efforts. They're not that easy to get nowadays. And Marie may not have ever expected to have her bluff called. I haven't gotten information on Bowe's whereabouts all that frequently—frankly, not but twice in the last six years, and that had him way out on the fringes. I *didn't* expect to run into him here. No way in hell. But he is here. And even if she was bluffing—she's here, and it's public. This isn't going to be easy, Thomas. I may be a total fool, but I think she'll go right over the edge if she can't resolve it now, once for all. She's my sister. She's your mother. She has to go to the Trade Bureau like she always does, she has to do her job, she has to walk back again like a sane woman, and get on with her life. If *Corinthian* leaves early, that's a victory. Maybe enough she can live with it. But it's going to scare hell out of me."

"You think he will leave?"

"*I* think he will. I think he's on thin tolerance at certain ports. I think he's Mazianni, I've always thought so. His side lost. I don't think he'll want to do anything. Just her crossing that dock with you is a win, you understand me? Calling his bluff. Daring him to make a move."

"Does he know about me?"

"I think she's seen to it he knows."

That scared him. Anonymity evaporated, and anonymity was the thing he cultivated on dockside, for a few days of good times *not* to be Thomas Bowe, just Tom Hawkins, just a crewman out cruising the same as everybody else on the docks. He was famous enough on *Sprite,* with every damn cousin, and his uncles, his mother and an aunt hovering over him every breath, every crosswise glance, every move he made subject to critique, as if they expected he'd explode. And now captain Mischa was sending him out dockside with Marie?

Two walking bombs. Side by side. With signs on them, saying, Here they are, do something, Austin Bowe.

He sat there looking at Mischa, shaking his head.

"If she goes out there and she does something," Mischa said, "the law will deal with her. And do you want Marie to end up in the legal system, Tom, do you *want* them to take her into some psych facility and remove whatever hate she's got for him? Do you want that to happen to Marie?"

He couldn't imagine permanent station-side. Never moving. Dropping out of the universe. Foreign as an airless moon to him. And as scary. Mind-wipe was what they did to violent criminals. And they'd do that to Marie if she went for justice. "No, sir," he said. "But you're trusting *me?*"

Mischa said, "Who have I got? Who *will* she deal with? There'll be somebody tagging you. You won't be alone. You just keep with her. If you can't do it any other way, knock her cold and bring her back on a Medical, I'm completely serious, Tom. Don't risk losing her."

Nobody *trusted* Tom Bowe-Hawkins. Saja hadn't *trusted* him when he'd passed his boards, as if he was going to blow up someday and do something illicit and destructive to the ship's computers.

"You know," Mischa said, "if *you* did anything to *Corinthian* crew, you'd fare no better in the legal system. Station law doesn't know you. Station doesn't give a damn for ship-law. It's not a system you'd ever want to be part of."

"Yes, sir," he said. Mischa'd had to say that last, just when he'd thought Mischa might have trusted him after all. "I hear you. Does this make me one of you?"

Silence after that impertinence. Long silence.

"Where does that come from?" Mischa asked.

Didn't the man know? Didn't the man hear? Was the man blind and deaf to what he was doing when he pulled his psych games?

When the kids in the loft painted *Korinthian* on his jacket?

When the com called him to the bridge an hour ago as Thomas Bowe—the way Marie had enrolled him on the ship's list, three days after he was born?

"You're not the most popular young man aboard," Mischa said slowly. "I think you know it. I know you've had special problems. I know they're not all your fault. But some things are. You've got try-me written all over you. You're far too ready with your fists, even in nursery you were like that."

"Other kids—" —went home with their mothers, he started to say, and cut that off. Mischa would only disparage that excuse.

"Other kids, what?"

"I fought too much. My father's temper. I've heard it all."

"You got a bad deal. I'm sorry, but, being a kid, you didn't make it better. Do you know that?"

"I gave back what I got. Sir."

"You listen to me. You made some mistakes. I'm saying if you get through this situation clean, it could help Marie. And it could change some minds, give you a position in this Family you can't buy at any other price. For God's sake, use your head with Marie. She's smart, she's manipulative as hell, she'll tell you things and sound like she means them. Above all else, get that temper of yours well in hand. I can't control what everybody on this ship is going to say or do in the next few days. That's not important. Getting this cargo offloaded and ourselves out of this port with all hands aboard—is. Don't embarrass Marie. Let's get her out of here with a little vindication, if we can do that, and hope to hell we don't cross Bowe's path for another twenty of our years."

Mischa Hawkins gave good advice when he gave it. Didn't *do* much for him, the son of a bitch, but what did Mischa Hawkins actually owe him?

"I'll do my best," he said. "I'll do everything I humanly can."

Mischa stared at him a moment, estimating the quality of the promise, or him, maybe. Finally Mischa nodded.

"Good," Mischa said, pushed the desk button that opened the door, and let him out.

Do something to clean up *his* reputation. What in hell had *he* done?

God!

He didn't punch the wall. Didn't even punch the nearest cousin, who passed him in the corridor, with a cheery, "Well, what's the matter with *you*, Tommy-lad?"

He went downside to the deserted gym, dialed up the resistance on the lift machine, and worked at it until he was out of breath, out of brain, and draped completely limp onto the bar.

Things had been going all right until that blip showed up on the display.

Marie had been all right, he'd been all right, he'd gotten his certificate, grown up like the rest of *Sprite*'s brat kids, passed the point of teenage brawls, gotten his life in order. . . .

Go rescue Marie from blowing Austin Bowe's brains out? On some days he'd as soon wish her luck and hope they got each other. He didn't want to meet his biological father. There were days of his life he wanted nothing more than to space Marie.

There were whole hours of his life he knew he loved her, no matter what she did or how crazy she was, because Marie was, dammit, his mother—not much of one, but he was never going to get another one, and he always felt—he didn't know how— that somehow if he could grow smarter or act better, he could eventually fix what was wrong.

Take-hold rang. He went to the back wall of the gym and

stood there while the passenger ring went inertial and the bulkhead slowly became the deck. They were headed in.

One could walk about the walls during gentle braking, if one had somewhere urgent to be and a good idea how long the burn was going to last. Easier just to shut the eyes and lie on the bulkhead and let the plus-*g* push straighten out a tired, temper-abused back.

Fool to go at the weights in a fit of temper. Only hurting yourself, aunt Lydia would say. He was. But that was, Marie's own claim, at least his choice, nobody else's.

— *iii* —

PROGRAM CAME UP, PROGRAM RAN, categorizing and digesting the informational wavefront from the station, and Marie made a steeple of her fingers, watching the initial output.

She regretted the dust-up on the bridge, but, damn it, Mischa had known he was pushing. Mischa deserved everything he got.

Crazy, Mischa called her, in private and behind her back.

And so, so considerate of Mischa to spare her feelings . . . in public, and all.

Viking was at mainday at the moment, halfway into it, the same as *Sprite*'s ship-time. But *Corinthian* was an alterday ship. *Corinthian* ran on that shift. Her principal officers awake during that shift: that meant the juniors were on duty right now.

That suited her.

Rumor had always maintained that certain merchanters had close operational ties to Mazian's Fleet, back in the War. The Earth Company called them loyalists, Union called them renegades. Merchanters called them names of fewer letters. Most merchanters had taken no side during the early stages of the War—Earth Company, Union, it was all the same: whoever had cargo going, at first you hauled it—until the EC Fleet stopped ships, and appropriated cargoes as Military Supply and took young crew at gunpoint, as draftees. After that, most merchanters wouldn't come near the Fleet.

And when, at the end of the War, Mazian hadn't surrendered, but kept on raiding shipping to keep the Fleet alive, there were certain few ships who, rumor had it, still tipped him about cargoes and schedules—and picked off the leavings of the raids, pirates themselves, but a small, scavenging sort.

And, no less despicable, some ships still reputedly traded with the Mazianni . . . ships that disappeared off the trade routes and came back again loaded. The stations, blind to what happened outside the star-systems, were none the wiser, and with the Union and Alliance governments limited by the starstations' lack of interest in the problem.

But deep-spacers whispered together in the bars, careful who was listening. And *she* regularly caught the rumors, and sifted them through a net of very certain dimensions—since stations claimed they didn't have the ability to check on every ship that came and went . . . since stations were mostly interested in black market smuggling of drugs and scarce metals and other such commodities as affected their customs revenues.

Very well. Viking didn't give a damn until the mess landed on its administrative desk. Viking certainly didn't remember what lay forty years in the past as Viking kept time. Viking wasn't going to call *Corinthian* and say there was a problem. Oh, no, Viking, like every other station, was busy looking for stray drugs or contraband biologicals.

And the fact that particular ship was on alterday schedule might give *Sprite* that much extra time to get into port before senior *Corinthian* staff realized they had a problem: their arrival insystem had to come to *Corinthian* off station feed, since a ship at dock relied on station for outside information—and how often did a ship sitting safe at dock check the traffic inbound?

Not bloody often. If ever. Though *Corinthian* might. Bet there was more than one ship that had *Corinthian* on its shit-list.

She owned a gun—illegal to carry it, at Viking or in any port. She kept it in her quarters under her personal lock. She'd gotten it years ago, in a port where they didn't ask close questions. Paid cash, so the ship credit system never picked it up.

Mischa hadn't figured it. Or hadn't found where she kept it.

But it was more than Austin Bowe that she tracked, not just the whole of *Corinthian* that had aided and abetted what Bowe had done, and there was no more or less of guilt. Nobody got away with humiliating Marie Kirgov Hawkins. Nobody constrained her. Nobody forced her. Nobody gave her blind orders. She worked for *Sprite* because she was Hawkins, no other reason. Mischa was captain now, yes, because he'd trained for it, but primarily because the two seniors in the way had died—she was cargo chief not because she was senior, but because she was better at the job than Robert A. who'd been doing it, and better than four other uncles and aunts and cousins who'd moved out of the way when her decisions proved right and theirs proved expensively wrong. No face-saving, calling her assistant-anything: she was *damned* good, she didn't take interference, and the seniors just moved over, one willingly, four not. The deposed seniors had formed themselves an in-ship corporation and traded, not too unprofitably, on their ship-shares, lining their apartments with creature-comforts and buying more space from juniors who wanted the credits more than they minded double-decking in their personal two-meter wide privacy. So they were gainfully occupied, vindicated at least in their comforts.

She, on the other hand, didn't give a running damn for the luxuries she could have had. She'd had room enough in a senior officer's quarters the couple of times she'd brought Tommy in (about as long as she could stand the juvenile train of logic), so she'd never asked for more space or more perks, and whether or not Mischa knew who really called the tune when it came to trade and choices, *Sprite* went where Marie Hawkins decided it was wise to go, *Sprite* traded where and what Marie Kirgov Hawkins decided to trade, took the contracts she arranged.

Mischa wouldn't exactly see it that way, but then, Mischa hadn't an inkling for the ten years he'd been senior captain exactly which were his ideas and which were hers. As cargo chief she laid two sets of numbers on his desk, one looking good and one looking less good, and of course he made his own choice.

Now Mischa was going to explain about Marie's Problem to poor innocent Thomas, and enlist his help to keep Marie in line? Good luck. Poor Thomas might punch Mischa through the bulkhead if Mischa pushed him. Thomas had his genetic father's temper and Thomas wasn't subtle. Earnest. Incredibly earnest. And not a damn bad head on his shoulders, in the small interludes when testosterone wasn't in the ascendant.

Predict that Mischa would want to deal with Tom, now, man to man, oh, right, when Mischa had ignored Tom's existence when he was a kid, when Mischa had resisted tracking him into mainday crew until Saja pointed out they'd better put a kid with his talent and his brains under closer, expert supervision. Every time Mischa looked at Tom, Mischa saw Marie's Problem; Mischa had a guilty conscience about younger sister's Problem, and Mischa was patronizing as hell, Thomas hated being patronized, and Mischa hated sudden, violent reactions.

Gold-plated disaster.

Best legacy she'd given Bowe's kid—awareness when he was being put upon. That, and life itself. End of her debt of conscience, end of her personal responsibility and damned generous, at that. So Tom was getting to be a human being. End report. Tom was on his own. Twenty plus years of tracking Austin Bowe, and she was here, free, owing nobody but that ship—a little before she'd wanted to be, but one couldn't plan everything in life.

It didn't particularly need to involve Tom. She'd acquired that small scruple. Leave Tom to annoy his uncle Mischa, if for some reason she wasn't around to do the job.

Nice to have a clear sense about what one wanted in life. Nice to have an absolute and attainable goal.

Mischa could never claim as much. But, then, Mischa forgave and forgot. Rapidly. Conveniently—if Mischa got what he wanted, and you could spell that out in money and comfort and an easy course, in about that order.

Not her style. Thank you, brother. Thank you, Hawkinses, every one.

Sprite might have come and gone peaceably at Viking for three, maybe four long rounds of its ports, exchanging loops with *Bolivar,* without chancing into *Corinthian's* path. That wouldn't have kept the data out of her hands—recent data, of *Corinthian's* current activities. *Sprite* and *Corinthian* never even needed to have met face to face in order for her to have what she wanted.

Watching Austin Bowe sweat? That was a bonus.

Her chief anxiety now was the surprise of the encounter— before she had enough of that most current data. The last thing she wanted was for that ship to spook out suddenly and change patterns on her. She wanted to be a far greater problem to *Corinthian* than that.

Still, she improvised very well.

Loosen up, Austin Bowe had told her, on a certain sleepover night. Adapt. Go with what happens. You're too tense.

Best advice anybody had ever given her, she thought. He'd meant sex, of course. But he'd meant power, too, which— she'd known it that night—was what that encounter had been all about, a teen-aged kid's conviction that she ran her own life, up against a thorough-going son of a bitch, not much older, used to his own satisfaction. *That* was the mistake in scale Austin Bowe had made. Her motives and ambitions hadn't been that important to him . . . then. She'd played and replayed that forty-eight hours in her head, and after the first few weeks, the rape itself wasn't as bad as having had to walk out that door, the physical act hadn't been as ultimately humiliating as *her* damned relatives, dripping pity and so, so embarrassed she'd been a fool going off by herself, relatives so upset—it was clearer and clearer to her—that she'd damaged the reputation of the ship, humiliated her relatives, gotten them all ordered out of port—and they were all so, so disappointed when she didn't shatter and come crawling to their damned condescending concern.

Hell, she got along *fine* after that, except their hovering over her and waiting for Marie to blow up. After mama died, Mischa took over the hovering, and Mischa had said to her and everybody who was interested that she'd be just fine if she ever found herself the right man.

That was funny. That was downright pathetically funny. Mischa thought if she just once got good sex she wouldn't want to kill Austin Bowe.

Or Mischa Hawkins.

Sex good or bad hadn't put Austin Bowe in charge of *Corinthian*. It might be gender, genes, family seniority, even, God help them, talent; but it sure as hell couldn't be his performance in bed, and damned if hers that night had measured Marie Hawkins' capacities, any more than Mischa's self-reported staying power in a sleepover meant he was fit to captain *Sprite*.

— *iv* —

Damn com beeped. Insistently. If it wasn't a screaming emergency, the perpetrator was dead.

Austin Bowe reached out an arm from under the covers, in a highly expensive station-side room, seeking toward the red light in the dark.

Which disturbed . . . whatever her name was. Who moaned and shifted and jabbed an elbow into his ribs as he punched the button.

"Austin. —What in *hell* do you want?"

"*Sprite*'s inbound."

He blinked into the dark. Thoughts weren't doing too well. Too much vodka. The fool woman sat up and started nuzzling his neck. He shoved her off. Hard.

"Captain?"

"Yeah, yeah, I copy." The brain wouldn't work. The body felt like hell. "Have we had any word from them?"

"No. They're in approach."

"What the hell are you doing on watch? Is this Bianco?"

"Yes, sir."

"They're in approach."

"I'm sorry, sir. No excuse. About two hours from mate-up."

"That's just fucking wonderful. Can we not discuss it here, possibly? Where's Christian?"

"I—hate to tell you this, captain."

"All right, all right, *find* him. Dammit!"

"What are we to—?"

"Make it up, Bianco, damn your lazy hide, we've got a problem. Use your ingenuity!"

What's-her-name put an arm around his neck. Said something he wasn't listening to. Beatrice was on the dock somewhere. Their son was likewise somewhere on the docks, supposedly seeing cargo moved, but *Corinthian* didn't know where Christian was at the moment?

"Aus-tin," the woman said. "Is something wrong?"

"Damn dim-brain," he muttered, and got up and looked for his clothes.

"That's not nice."

He found the light-switch. Glared at the fool, who looked scared and shut up.

Stationer, he remembered that. He had a headache to end all. He didn't know how he'd ended up with a total fool. Crewwoman off a station-sweeper would have better sense than hang onto a ship's officer with a trouble-call.

He dressed.

"Are you coming back?"

"If I do, you'd better have your ass out of here." He pulled on his sweater. If he got any rest, he'd want *rest*, not present company, a bar-crawler with a libido too active for her bank-employed husband.

Hawkins. Worst damned mess he'd ever gotten into. Sending him death threats for more than twenty years. Psych case, as best he figured it, if not then, definitely now.

Woman with a problem. Cargo chief, market and commodities expert, as he got the make on the Marie Hawkins—looking for a way to get him, which might not be with a gun or a knife, give the woman credit for brains and professional expertise, which he hadn't, the night he'd made one of the prime mistakes of his life.

And gotten a son who was reputedly *on* that inbound ship, as Marie Hawkins had continually been solicitous to let him know.

Damn. Damn and damn.

Station probably didn't remember the incident. Stationers had a lot of trouble figuring ship-time, and hell if any ship actively helped them do it. Mariner's records were blown to cold space, nothing he knew of had transferred, and *Corinthian* was clean at Viking.

So far.

"Aus-tin?"

"Damn you, you pay the tab, I'm fucking bored!"

He keyed the exit, he left at a fast clip, he didn't know why he'd ever thought the stationer fool worth the price of the room, except Beatrice had her agreement, and they kept it, and that meant Beatrice had probably found herself some young piece foolish enough to think he could handle an exotic experience.

Which, if she'd snugged in for the duration of their scheduled layover, meant that finding Beatrice wasn't a minor problem, either.

Beatrice wasn't on cargo duty. Christian was. Austin walked out the fancy doors and onto the docks and took out the pocket-com.

"This is Austin. Bianco, any information?"

"Sabrina's looking," *Corinth*-com said. "Christian's been in touch off and on. I think he's on green, right near the Transship office. He's been in and out of there."

"That's just real good. Where's our friend coming in?"

"Berth 19. Orange."

Considerably separated from them, around the rim. That was a vast relief. "They request it?"

"I don't know, captain. I didn't think—"

"Right. I copy. I'm coming back to the ship. General recall, all staff who aren't on a job."

"I'm on it," Bianco said.

As well say Red Alert. He didn't want to talk cargo where station could pick it up, although he didn't expect Viking to have any suspicion of trouble. Marie's brother was captain on *Sprite* now, he'd heard that. Possibly *Sprite* had had no idea *Corinthian* was here, but it wasn't *Sprite*'s ordinary route. Possibly they'd come in on the new station status.

Or possibly Hawkins had gotten information that made this no chance meeting at all.

And Hawkins, with her particular skills, was extremely bad news.

He started walking, looking for a ped-transport. *Corinthian* being on alterday schedule, meant dealing with second-tier station authorities, who didn't always ask close questions, as well as avoiding some of the traffic that clogged mainday official channels. It had its advantages. But on the docks mainday and alterday were meaningless; the bars and shops were always open and there was always night, always darkness above the floodlights that lit the girders, up where the lights and the cold of the pipes made their own weather.

Warehouses. Processing areas. Factories. Food production. Fabrication. The place dwarfed everything but the ship-accesses and the machines that served them.

And a crew scattered on a two-week liberty with all of Viking Station to lose themselves in—was no easy matter to locate, individual by individual, in every tiny sleepover and bar on the strip. Christian had a com. The duty staff all had coms. Certain people weren't answering.

One of Marie Hawkins' most logical targets wasn't damned well answering.

—— *v* ——

"So what do you want?"

You didn't expect a happy hello from Marie. You interrupted her at work and you took your chances. But Tom thought he should at least try, after the burn. The market figures were up on the screens. Marie, two senior cousins and four juniors were sorting through the usual welter of incoming stock market and commodities data off station feed.

But not the usual. He'd lay odds *Corinthian*'s arrival date and market dealings were somewhere in the figures on Marie's monitors. She keyed the displays, in rapid sequence, to Privacy.

He leaned against the desk, arms folded: "I just thought I'd check on you."

"I haven't turned blue. What did Mischa say?"

"Mostly that he trusts you to do your job. Right or wrong?"

"Son of a bitch."

"Which one of us?"

Marie slid him an oblique, grey-eyed look, and lifted a brow. Easy to understand how a man twenty years ago had made a move on Marie Hawkins.

"Outside of *Corinthian,*" he said, "how does it look?"

She caught that implication. He saw the second quirk of her brow, the tightening at the corner of her mouth.

"You're bothering me," Marie said, leaning back in her chair, folding her hands on her stomach. "Go somewhere."

"Mischa said you'd be fine. He *trusts* you, Marie."

"Right. Sure. I heard echoes of that, topside." Marie shoved her chair back. "What did he say?"

He'd tried to compose it. The threads threatened to scatter under Marie's sniping attacks. "Just—that you've got him scared for your safety, that he's not real certain *Corinthian* isn't going to lay for us out in the dark when we leave. He said, on the other hand, he agrees with you about doing our business and sticking to our area—"

"Where are we coming in?"

"I don't know. I haven't heard." He *hadn't*, but he didn't like the question or the direction of thinking it indicated. He didn't know whether to break the news that he was her assigned tag or not. He didn't think, on second thought, that he wanted that information to come out in the present context. "Just checking. Glad you're fine. Talk to you later."

Marie rocked forward, stood up, hauled him by the arm to the corridor. The off-shift was coming on, crawling out of bunks and stirring about preparatory to shift change. Cousins passed. Marie backed him against the wall, with, "Spill it."

"He told me a lot of stuff. Nothing that changes anything." That was, he guessed, what Marie most wanted to believe. And he took a deliberate, not quite lying, chance. "I'd like to break that bastard's neck."

"Mischa's?"

"Bowe's." He'd stepped over the edge. On Mischa's side. He didn't know if Marie was going to swallow it. But it took no acting. He was upset. Scared of her, scared of Mischa, scared of that ship out there. "Marie, I swear to you, I wish I could get him, but there's not a way in hell—"

"Is Mischa talking about restricting me?"

He shook his head, thinking, God, she's not intending just the markets. "He says not. He says you've got to do this on your own, you've got to walk out there and back and show you can face him, he's says that's enough, that does as much as you need to do."

"And tagging me?"

"He didn't say that."

Marie took a breath, ducked her head, arms folded, looked

up at him. "I've got the trade stats. I know when *Corinthian* came into port, I know what went on the sales boards, I know what's moved off green dock. It's a sluggish market, and *Corinthian*'s off-loading with nobody's buy showing on the reports, not even an offer on the boards."

"Warehousing stuff here?"

"Or hauling *for* somebody, or hauling a pre-sold cargo. Something's irregular."

"Are you going to take it to authorities?"

"Possibly nothing's illegal. Nothing wrong with hauling *for*, or pre-selling. Nothing wrong with warehousing. *Corinthian*'s been *legal* for decades. It was *legal* all through the War."

"But not totally legal."

"Not if you could get at all the picture. *Corinthian* is a small ship. It paid for a refit five years ago. If it's in debt I haven't found it."

I have my sources, Mischa had said, regarding *Corinthian* and its movements. Depend on it that the cargo officer had sources, too. And Marie *had* been tracking *Corinthian,* that part was true.

"Could you?"

"Say I've been careful not to trigger alarms. Say I wrote the transactions-search program twenty years ago. I'm no fool, kid. Not this woman. It'll smell any out-of-parameter market situation in any time frame I ask it. Plus availability of loaders, dockers, all those little details station doesn't mind giving out, while it keeps ship-records sacrosanct. I know who's been off-loading, who's bought, all that sort of thing they say they don't tell us—at least, I can make a good guess, knowing what fallible human minds come knowing."

It wasn't the picture Mischa had painted, of an out-of-control crazy, hell-bent on murder. Marie had a case. She was building it piece by piece, *with* the trade records, through the trade records, the way Marie had told him outside the lift, and, damn it, she confused him. Marie was lying or Mischa didn't give her credit for what she could do with her computers and her sense of what was normal and not—Marie was a walking encyclopaedia of trade and market statistics, imports, exports, norm and parameters, and if Marie thought she had a sense of something in the pattern when *Corinthian* hit the market boards . . . there might well be.

Unless Marie was deluding herself, too desperate to make a case, now, while they had *Corinthian* in reach of station authority.

"Can you nail him?" he asked.

"I need to get to the trade office. Myself. Do a little personal diplomacy."

An alarm went off. Late. Marie had his back to the wall in more senses than one. Suddenly it was Marie's agenda, Marie's conspiracy, not Mischa's. He made a try to save his autonomy in it. "I'll go with you. If Mischa says you shouldn't go, I'll say I'll keep track of you."

Marie looked up at him—half a head shorter than he was. Fragile-looking. But the expression in her eyes wasn't. She was steady as a high-*v* rock, while he lied to her, and while he remembered what Mischa had said: that Marie had to walk across the dock and back again, call it settled—an exit with honor.

And where was Marie's vindication in her twenty-year fight if her son and her brother tricked her and did everything? People on the dock might not find out. But the family would. The more people who were in on it, beyond one, that much harder it was to have it accepted that Marie had carried it off herself.

The more people . . . like Mischa . . . who knew that Marie was chasing *Corinthian* through the financial records, and, maybe, as Marie said, that she was finessing her way into things she wasn't supposed to access . . . the more likely Mischa was to intervene and screw things up royally.

He took a step on the slippery slope, then, knowing he was in danger, knowing Marie and the whole ship were, if things blew up.

So far as he knew, Marie *couldn't* jack the station computers from outside the station system. The access numbers that any merchanter cargo chief or ship's chief tech knew were never going to get anybody into station files: merchanter ships carried techs who well knew how to get where they weren't supposed to be in any system, but stations had learned from the War years to take precautions: even Saja couldn't get into station central banks or into a ship's recorder, and Saja was good.

"You figure out everything we need," he said to Marie. "And when we dock, you go out like always. I'll go with you. I swear, Marie. I want to."

They never much looked at each other straight on—not the way he did and she did now. His heart was pounding, his brain was telling him he was a fool, but for about twenty seconds then, Marie was ma'am, and mama, and home, and all the ship-words a man had to attach to, in the ancient way of merchanter matriarchy.

"He put you up to this?" Marie asked him hoarsely.

"Yes." If one of them could twist truth inside out and confuse a man, so could he. She'd taught him. So had Mischa. "But he doesn't know I mean it."

"You son of a bitch." Not angry, not cruel. Marie could make it into a love-note.

"You're all I've got," he said, and really felt it, for the moment, fool that he was.

"Get out of here," she said, and laughed, the grim way that Marie could when, rarely, he scored a point in their endless fencing. But she caught his arm before he could leave. "Tom. Bitch-son. Only chance. If *Corinthian* spooks, he's gone. Understand?"

In a lifetime, maybe her only chance at this ship. Only chance to win. Only chance to risk everything. He knew how much that meant. "Read you," he said, already a traitor to Mischa. "No question." Betraying Mischa was easy. But he *wanted* Marie to get the bastard—just not . . . not the way he still feared she might try.

She let him go. He walked away, to escape her closer questions about Mischa and his intentions, and decided on rec and the commissary, he didn't really care.

But once he thought about it, he knew he ought to eat: jump took too much out of a body. He decided he'd better, hungry or not, and wondered if Marie had—but Marie had probably ordered in, probably had one of the junior techs bring something to her: you could do that if you were sitting Station. He should have asked her. But he wouldn't, now, didn't want back in Marie's reach.

Cousins were thick, going and coming around the commissary area, which was no more than a district in lower-deck. He hadn't, himself, checked the boards. He didn't expect assignment different than Mischa had given him. Saja had to know that he was spoken for. He hoped to God no one else had the idea what Mischa had set him to do, but rumors about *Corinthian's* presence were running the corridors—he caught whispers, furtive stares.

And had cousin Roberta R. ask him, brilliantly, as he eased his way through the gathering around the stack of sandwiches, "You hear about *Corinthian* in port?"

Then cousin remotest-thank-God-removed Yuri Curtis Hawkins added in a not discreet undertone that he'd heard they'd had thirty in hospital at Mariner the last time the ships met, and maybe they should snatch themselves some *Corinthian* crew and "show them a thing or two."

"Yeah, right," another cousin said, "from the station brig, big show."

He shouldered his way past the comments, got his sandwich, ignoring the lot, but Yuri C. said, "Hey, *Bowe*-Hawkins, what's your idea?" and somebody else, Rodman, drawled, "Bowe-Hawkins, I hear they inbreed on *Corinthian*, what d' you think? You got all those crossed-up genes?"

"I think that ship's armed, it's not a regular merchanter, and we're not in a damn good situation if it gets pissed, cousin, thanks for the personal concern."

Hoots and catcalls for the exchange. He wasn't popular with

Yuri or with Rodman, whose eye he'd blacked, in their snot-nosed youth. He didn't care what Rodman did or said. He cared only marginally about Yuri C. or Yuri's two half-sibs, and Roberta was no hyperspace engineer. He took his sandwich, got his drink and took his lunch to the quiet of his own quarters.

It was peace, there. He settled sideways and cross-legged on his bunk, sore from the temper fit in the gym, and ate his sandwich—he couldn't even identify the flavor. Jump did that to you, too, left you with a metallic taste that was mineral deficiency.

But he was thinking—if Marie *could* tag *Corinthian* with illicit trading, smuggling, whatever—there was everything Marie wanted, on a platter.

Damned right he wasn't going to take on Rodman Hawkins. He wasn't crazy, the same way Marie wasn't. You could put up with a hell of a lot to get something you wanted as badly as he wanted the question settled, wanted Marie straightened out, or something finally resolved.

So she'd wanted to keep Austin Bowe's kid, Marie had, back when the choice had been possible. She hadn't aborted him.

And a while ago she'd requested the only companionship she'd ever asked of him. —Well, not asked, but at least not rejected when he offered. That was something. That was entirely unlike Marie.

And, damn Mischa's holier-than-thou-ism, he so wanted Marie to be right this time, he so wanted Marie to have the vindication that would let Marie score her point, win her case, prove whatever Marie had needed all these years to prove.

Damn, if Marie could get her life straightened out, if Marie could stop the pain that made her do the things she did . . .

If he could just once in his life help her . . .

He sat there eating the sandwich and drinking his soft drink while *Sprite* glided toward rendezvous. He told himself he was a mortal fool for believing Marie. But telling himself, too, that he didn't owe Mischa a damned thing.

Least of all . . . loyalty.

Take-hold sounded. *Sprite* was approaching the slow-zone.

Coming into the region of controlled approach. Insystem velocities.

After this they were well within Viking's time-packet—real-time with station com.

—— *vi* ——

MILLER TRANSSHIP SAID AN HOUR. They'd said it an hour ago, when the voltage regulator on their only 20k can transport went fritz and died the death.

Get a part from supply, Miller said, as if it was that easy. No big delay.

Hell.

Christian Bowe slammed the receiver down on the hook and went back to the table in *Fancy's,* while Fancy Leeman himself was strolling among the tables. Big guy, Fancy was, and you didn't ask about the name—Fancy caught his eye and Christian made the fist and thumb, signaling one more refill.

"So?" Capella, chin in hands, looked up, a flash of dark eyes in pale blue glitz-paint. Tattooed snake up one arm, tattooed skull and rose on her right buttock—but that wasn't on display.

Christian sighed and subsided into the chair. "Hour."

"Hour! It's been an hour! Let's just screw it. Come on, Chrissy-sweet."

"A round's coming. We give it that long."

Capella sighed. Traced a circle in the condensation on the table. The hand had a fortune in rings. The wrist had a band of stars in tattoo, and below it, Bok's Equation, in ornate letters. Navigator's mark, in certain quarters.

The hand captured his, amid the circles of two prior rounds and one double ice water.

"Chrissy."

"Christian."

Lavender lips quirked. "Chris-tian, they're not going to get that sum-bitch moving till alterday. You know that, I know that, they're going to crawl clear into next shift, they'll be Beatrice's problem, anyway. Why sit? Music is happening. *Dancing* is going on."

Beatrice was sleeping. Or whatever. Austin was definitely barricaded for the night. The drinks came. They went down too fast for prudence.

"You can call them from the next bar," Capella said, nudging his leg with her foot.

They had a fair amount of the cargo taken care of. Capella was right, the transport was probably screwed for the next few hours. Late mainday was a bad time to have a mechanical; mainday techs already had their work schedule full, they'd bitten off about what would send them off duty on schedule. If something more came in they'd just pile it up and let it wait for alterday, no matter how they told you they were 'going to get to it.' It never happened. It was unions. And they weren't going to budge on their hours requirements, not if they held their breath and turned blue.

Damn and damn. Austin could go kick ass and maybe get something accomplished. But Miller Transship's mainday management and Austin's mid-rank kid weren't heavy enough push to get things accelerated another hour or so. Capella might. That tattooed bracelet carried cachet with some techs, but it made other people nervous, and at Viking you didn't know, you just didn't know what loyalties or what agency you might be dealing with.

Besides, Capella was in a mood, Capella was ready to go off-shift, and the third drink had fuzzed things a little—hazed the blinking neon, brought a little less imminency to the situation, hell, Austin had said don't bother him with cargo problems, handle it, and wasn't it dealing with it, when you knew damned well they weren't getting anywhere? They had fifty cans yet to move. Then they could onload and use *any* transport. What came *out* of Miller's was no problem. Hire anything. Anybody. They were well within schedule as was.

"One more call," he said, and went across the room to the phone.

Station line. It was clearer than the com with the music going full bore. He shielded one ear and listened to Miller's chief tell him one more time that they were doing what they could, they'd gotten the part, well, yes, but with the union rules, they just couldn't get a crew on.

"Yeah, I know that dance," he said. "Look. I'm going to be traveling the next while. I'll keep calling. You get somebody's ass in there. Call in debts. You like dealing with us. You call in debts."

"Look," the answer came back, "there's a limit to what we can do—"

"Look, *sir.*"

"Yes, sir, Mr. Bowe, I understand that. I'm sorry, but—"

"Senior captain's going to be in there, if this doesn't get moving."

"Yes, sir. I know. We're working."

He hung up, walked back to the bar and signed the tab. Capella showed up at his elbow and they left for the next bar, Capella doing this odd little step down the deck-plate joints.

Crazy as they came, but hyperspace operators of Capella's ilk were, if possible, crazier than pilots, stayed high the whole ride and did as they damned well pleased—danced to a beat they claimed to hear in space, claimed to hear the stars, the echoes of the planets. Mean as hell, Capella was, but that was the high she gave when she tripped, the way she was tripping now —she'd take him, she'd take anything if he funked out, and watching over their junior apprentice hyper-jock and keeping her out of jail was Assignment Two. Austin wouldn't like him if he let that happen, either . . . Capella wouldn't be wrong, the hyper-jocks were never quite wrong, for the very reason the senior, book-following navigators and engineers never quite listened to them.

"Slow down, you."

Capella danced back and grabbed him, whisked him into the next bar and onto the dance floor.

Capella was hell and away more fun than Miller Transship. Capella was a drug, a natural high—glitz flickered in the strobing lights, found patterns on her skin. The snake on her arm came alive and its eye on her wrist glowed metal red, leaving trails of fire. The bracelet of stars and Bok's Equation glowed green—they could do that in the tattoo shops on Pell.

It drew attention. One drunk sod with a *Knight* patch on his sleeve wanted to dance with Capella, wanted to get up close, and there was damn all for her companion to do but object to that if Capella minded, but Capella grabbed the drunk and skipped away, contrived to maneuver him right off the dance zone and right into a tableful of *Lodestar*'s finest, who didn't like their drinks spilled.

"Come on," Capella laughed, grabbed his hand and ducked for the door before the riot spread beyond *Lodestar*'s vicinity.

Sunfire was the next bar, all gold and neon reds, big glowing sun holo in the middle of the bar, and mirrors everywhere, sending the images up and down at angles to the original. The bar served up a specialty about the same colors, with a kick like a retro, and the dance floor was up a step, where if you weren't sober you'd slide right down the edge. They were doing this number that involved back to back and turn, and then front to front and up close—

Which between the dizziness of the mirrored suns and the warmth of bodies and the shortness of breath, made the slanting edge a precarious thing.

Out onto the dock, then, carrying a couple of drinks— he'd remembered to sign the tab, that sober, at least, but they *knew* deep-haulers on leave, and they'd have tagged *Corinthian,* seeing the patch on him and on Capella—there had to be a hundred Corinthians on the dock at the moment, and somebody'd have signed the tab, if they'd have blown it, or they'd have gone to Austin, which you *didn't* want to happen. . . .

Meanwhile he'd gotten crazy enough he was linked arm in arm with Capella and trying to do her skip-step and pattern down the deck-plates.

"Chris!" someone female yelled from behind him.

Which confused his navigation, since the female he was with was beside him.

Which let him know he wasn't thinking clearly, and *that* reminded him . . .

"Hell. I haven't called Millers."

"Christian!"

Familiar voice. Crew. Cousin.

"Oh, screw it," Capella said, as he veered about. "She's no fun."

He blinked, sweating in the cold chill of dockside. A drop of condensation came down, *splat!* off some pipe overhead. That was Sabrina, ten years senior, and dead, dead serious, he saw that on her face.

"Christian, where in *hell's* your com?"

He felt of his pocket. Pulled it out, and disengaged his arm from Capella.

The red light was on. God knew how long. Must have been beeping from time to time—somewhere under the music in the bar.

"You *and* Capella," Saby said. "Deaf as rocks, both of you. *Sprite's* inbound."

Took him a couple of heartbeats. He was at a low ebb.

"Shit all," Capella said, in the same second he placed the name and realized this was a definite emergency.

"Austin know?"

"Austin's on it. What's this about Miller? What's this about a transport down?"

"They're next-shifting it, I've been trying to move them." His navigational sense was shot to hell. He was on green dock, he could figure that. He ran a hand through his hair, blinked at Saby's righteous sobriety. "Electrical problem, they tagged it, they know what it is. It's the damn Viking unions, Miller could do the job themselves, except nobody can touch it."

"We may be pulling out of here," Saby said. "Austin's furious, nobody can find Beatrice. I'd just get your rear down to Miller and tell them get the next shift up early, put it on our tab. We're on recall, everybody with no business out. I'll call in, say I've found you."

"We've got cargo on dock," he said, in the beginning of a cold, sober sweat. Austin *was* going to kill him. If worse didn't come down. "We got cans on the dock."

"Beatrice—" Saby began, but that was nonsense.

"*Find* Beatrice, if you can, and good luck—Capella, you get down to Miller and tell him his trade is on the line, don't tell him why, tell him it's major trouble, and if we get screwed we'll take him with us."

"Where are you going?"

Visions of cans in the warehouse, half of them re-labeled and half not. Visions of a broken transport stalled God knew where between *Corinthian* and Miller Transship's warehouse with God knew what aboard, and he didn't want to guess.

Sprite.

Hawkinses.

He had a *brother* on that ship. Half-brother, at least.

He was, on one level, curious. On another, he wasn't. Not until they got those cans labeled.

"Tell Austin," he said to Saby, "I'll be in the warehouse, I've got the com on, I'm listening. Just let me straighten this out."

"Christian,—"

"I'm fine, I'll fix it."

"Hell," Capella said. "Listen to the woman."

"Christian,—"

"We are exposed as *hell*," he said to Saby, walking backward, a feat proving his sobriety, he decided, considering his recent alcohol intake. Austin didn't want excuses. It was his watch.

He couldn't screw this. "I'll fix it. Tell Austin I'll fix it, there's no problem."

"Answer your damn com after this!" Saby yelled at him. A loader was working somewhere. Human voices were very small, on the dockside, easily overwhelmed by the clash and bang of metal.

Capella caught his arm and spun him about.

"Better bribe the mechanics," Capella said, with her curious faculty for realism, drunk or sober. "Cheaper than station brig, Chrissy-lad. Which we could all be in if we screw this. You got to sober up, spaceman. We got to get a watch on that ship when it comes in. Anybody comes around the dock, we just arrange a distraction."

"We get the cargo moving," he said. That was the absolute priority. Couldn't just leave those cans on the dock. Austin was applying personal diplomacy to the mechanics, he was willing to bet that—*Corinthian* was as good as down-timed herself while Millers' transport was stalled, stupid half-ass company owned theirs, which was why they dealt with them, but they were creaking antiques—

Didn't want just any transport drivers *in* that warehouse anyway.

Emergency had him sweating in the cold air. A ship showed up that he'd never expected to meet—one they'd taken care for years not to meet. The karmic feeling, things happening that shouldn't be.

And would Austin run, from Marie Hawkins? From a crazy woman? Hell. That wasn't the Austin he knew.

He used the next public phone. He called into ship-com. He hoped not to deal with Austin.

"*Where the hell is your com?*" Austin's voice came back to him.

"Sorry, I was in a noisy environment."

"*I have a damned good idea where the hell you were, Christian. Save it. Did you get the message?*"

"Yes, sir. —But we've got a transport down. They're trying to fix it. I didn't think you wanted to be—"

"I'm awake. I'm bothered. I'm mad as hell and I'm calling Miller. We've moved the count up, we've got a serious problem, and I suggest you get your ass down there and get that cargo moved. Yesterday! I'm reassessing your file, mister, the same as any crew member who can't do his job! You doubt me? You want to tell me how I owe you a living?"

"No, sir. I will—I'm doing that. No, sir, I know you don't." The nerves twitched. They remembered. Austin meant exactly what he said, and it wasn't necessary he have liberty again for the next three years if he pissed Austin any further. End report.

Capella had gotten sober, too. Entirely.

Chapter Two

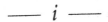

— *i* —

APPROACHING INNER SYSTEM WAS a matter of hours, at a high fraction of *c*.

Dumping that velocity while they could still graze the interface was a relatively easy matter.

Working at station-proximity speeds to get a high-mass freighter into a rotating station, on the other hand, was a tedious, nerve-wracking operation. Always be aware of the nearest take-hold point. Stay out of the lift except on business. Stay out of fore-aft corridors. Keep belted when seated or asleep.

Meaning that trim-ups might be rare when a long-hauler was following the computer-directed approach—no pilot flew docking by the seat of the pants—but stations were debris-generators, thick with maintenance and service traffic and escaped nuts, bolts and construction tiles, and, while in the zone of greatest risk a freighter pilot was no-stop, come hell or the Last Judgment, or absent anything but damage to the docking apparatus (meaning any pusher-jock in a freighter's approach path was a bump and a noise and a gentle course-correction), the possibility of evasive maneuver did exist. That meant the children battened down in the cushioned Tube in the loft, in which they could take most any vector-shift; and crew off and on duty found themselves a definite place to Be for the duration.

Which in Marie's case was her office; and in a junior computer tech's, it was the bridge. Load the file, wait for the check, load another file, wait for the check.

It left too much time for said junior tech to think, between button punches, in his lowly station sandwiched in with seven other cousins at the tail of the bridge.

It left too much time to rehearse the session with Mischa, and the one with Marie, comparing *those* mental files for discrepancies, too, but you never caught them out that easily. They didn't outright lie in nine tenths of what they told you. They were brother and sister. They had grown up conning each other. They'd learned it from each other if nowhere else. And they were good at it. He wasn't.

Heredity, maybe. Like the temper Mischa said did him no favors. He was, if he thought about it, scared as hell, figuring Marie wasn't done with double-crosses. Marie didn't trust him.

And, when it came down to the bottom line, Marie would use him, he knew that in the cold sane moments when he was away from the temptation she posed to think of her as mama and to think he could change her. Get that approval (she always dangled) in front of him, always a little out of possible reach.

But nothing mattered more to Marie than dealing with that ship. And if Marie was right and she smelled something in the records that wasn't right with *Corinthian*—you could depend on it that she'd been tracking them through every market and every trade she could access long-distance—she might have files down there in cargo that even Saja didn't know about. Files she could have been building for years and years and never telling anyone.

Load and check, load and check. He could push a few keys and start wandering around Marie's data storage—possibly without getting caught, but there were a lot of things a junior tech didn't know. The people who'd taught him undoubtedly hadn't taught him how to crack their own security: the last arcane items were for senior crew to know and mere juniors to guess. So it was load and check, load and check, while his mind painted disaster scenarios and wondered what Marie was up to.

Supper arrived on watch. The galley sent sandwiches, so a tech had one hand free to punch buttons with. Liquids were all in sealed containers.

On the boards forward in the bridge, the schemata showed they were coming in, the numbers bleeding away rapidly now they were on local scale.

A message popped up on the corner of his screen. *At dock. See me. Marie.*

— *ii* —

MARIE LEANED BACK FROM THE CONSOLE, seeing the *Received* flash at the corner of her screen. So the kid was at work. The message had nabbed him.

He'd arrive.

The numbers meanwhile added themselves to a pattern built, gathered, compared, over twenty-four years. How shouldn't they? *Corinthian* was what it was, and no ship and no agency that hadn't had direct and willing information from *Corinthian* itself could know as much about that ship as she did.

She knew where it traded, when it traded, but not always *what* it traded.

She knew at least seven individuals of the Perrault clan had moved in from dead *Pacer,* long, long ago. *Pacer* had had no good reputation itself, a lurker about the edges, a small short-hauler that, on one estimation, had simply been in the wrong place at the wrong time . . . and on another, had entirely deserved being at Mariner when it blew.

She knew that *Corinthian* took hired-crew, but it didn't take them often or every voyage, or in great number. Hired-crew skuzzed around every station, most of them with egregious faults—tossed out of some Family, the worst of hire-ons, as a rule, or stationers with ambitions to travel, in which case ask what skills they really had, or the best of them, the remnant of war-killed ships. Sure, there were hired-crew types that weren't out to cut throats, pick pockets, or mutiny and take a ship. But those were rarer, as the War generation sorted itself out.

Mutiny had never taken *Corinthian*. Which argued for a wary captain, a good eye for picking, or cosmic good luck.

Except that *Corinthian* rejects never turned up on dockside. And her crew spent like fools when they were in port—certainly hired-crew had reason to want to stay with *Corinthian*, and could count themselves well paid.

But nobody ever got off. Not that she'd found. Not, at least, in any crew record she'd found . . . and she'd searched—nothing to prevent any ship in any port from drinking down the hired-crew solicitations, and reviewing the backgrounds they'd admit to: had a program for that, too. And at Viking, where *Corinthian* had called frequently (since the second closing of the Hinder Stars, strange to say)—there were no *Corinthian* ex-crew. There might have been hires. But no one let off.

You couldn't be so lucky as to get all saints, all competent, all devoted crewmen.

So what became of the rejects? There was still a commerce in human lives—rumor said; the same commerce as during the War, when the Mazianni had stopped merchanters and impressed crew. Rumor said . . . some ships that dealt with the Mazianni still traded surplus crew for a fair profit in goods, and therefore hired-crew had better watch what they hired-*to*.

The lurkers in the dark were certainly still out there. Accidents took ships—rarely, but accidents still happened, and ships still disappeared somewhere in the dark. Couldn't prove that *Corinthian* in specific had anything to do with those rumored tragedies . . . but it had to get your attention. You had to realize . . . if you were in port with the likes of *Corinthian*, and if they knew you were on their trail . . . that your odds of accident had just gone higher, too.

You had to realize, if you were the only one aboard who

wanted that son of a bitch's hide, that certain members of the Family, less motivated and habitually more timid, would sabotage you, out of concern for their own lives.

So Tom was on her side. And Tom had talked to Mischa.

So Mischa had his spy.

Well, at least that meant walking out of the ship was easier.

— *iii* —

THE CENTRAL QUESTION, IN TOM'S mind, was how the clearance through customs was going to work—or, at least, how it was going to look.

If Mischa believed he was leaving the ship with Marie on *his* business, he'd get the permission fairly easily; but Mischa wasn't supposed to know that he'd told Marie that Mischa had put him up to it, or he wasn't supposed to know that Marie already knew all about it and they'd agreed to go diving in station records.

It was all too damned tangled, and he'd had word from Marie, which might or might not mean Marie accepted him at face value . . . or that Marie had been in contact with Mischa. He didn't know—couldn't know without asking questions that might bring Mischa and Marie head to head.

So he didn't wait for official clearance to come to him from Mischa's office. He excused himself off duty with Saja, telling Saja that Mischa had said see to Marie, and got Saja's leave to go downside the minute *Sprite* locked into dock. He shut down his station, left his seat and rode the lift downside, leaving the cousins to wonder—and Saja to ask Mischa was it true, and Mischa to give the permission, granting Mischa hadn't yet figured out that he'd gone over to Marie's camp, and wouldn't be reporting in.

He went to Marie's office, found Marie talking with customs on com, a routine call he'd heard her make since he'd first sat in on her duty station—at six or seven, close to when Marie'd first taken him home. He'd thought all this exchange of numbers and origins and cargo data mysterious and impressive, then; he'd rated it tedious since—but now he listened to it in suspense, hoping for some clue to Marie's intentions and dreading intervention from Mischa at any moment.

But nothing in the conversation sounded unusual, just Marie's easy, crisp way with station officials, all the i's dotted and the t's crossed. Station, at least, showed no indication to them that Viking was in any way nervous about their presence. He didn't hear any word of special security arrangements from station officials, didn't hear any advisement from Marie whatsoever that there was a history between *Sprite* and a ship already in dock—just a welcome in from station, a little chatter of a friendly nature, a little exchange of names and procedures.

A free port meant no customs to speak of, the way he'd understood the briefing, at least not the usual meticulous accounting of goods carried in. There were rules, mostly about firearms and drug trading, and an advisement that long-haulers would be advised to stay clear of white sector.

Meaning out of the Viking local haunts, he supposed, the territory of Viking miners, dockers, construction personnel, and the occasional citizens who preferred the free and easy atmosphere of dockside to the pricier, fancier establishments above.

In that arrangement, Viking was no different than Fargone, where you *didn't* go into insystemer bars and sleepovers unless you were truly spoiling for a fight.

"We copy that," Marie said. "We're a quiet lot. Thank you. Glad to be here, hope we can be a regular. We need to do some on-site consultation with the Trade Bureau. Can you tell me who to talk to?"

His ears pricked up. A name. Ramon French, Trade Bureau, Union Affairs. Marie made another call, said they'd been called in on short notice, hadn't any Alliance figures, wanted access to the local Trade resource library, in the Bureau, which they'd had word at Mariner that they would be able to access under the new rules. They had to establish an account, had to take care of certain legalities. General crew would exit in about an hour after shut-down, but certain officers would as soon be through customs early so they could get the credit accounts established, could Viking arrange that?

There was a good deal of back and forth after that, on screen, Marie looking for something, the program, he supposed it was, searching at high speed through the records for the patterns it wanted, while Marie talked on the station line with m'ser French, secretary in the Viking Trade Bureau, about accounts, and arranging the data search.

"Good, good," Marie said, signed off, and spun her chair about. "I take it you're coming, Tommy-lad."

"I guess I am," he said, wondering if it was really going to be that simple to get off the ship. But Marie just closed down her boards, led the way down the corridor, and keyed them through the airlock.

He was appalled. You didn't just . . . *open* the lock without the captain's order. But nobody had the lock codes alarmed, evidently. Mischa had to know what Marie was likely to do, and Mischa hadn't ordered any special security.

Which was one vote, he guessed, for Mischa having told him at least a quarter of the truth.

Which might bear on who was telling the rest of the truth . . . and whether he ought in fact to report back to Mischa. Scary proposition, to be first out of the ship . . . down the winding access, breath frosting, and out the station lock on the downward ramp.

He'd never gone through customs with Marie before. Maybe the easy attitude he saw in the officers was because Viking had just become a free port, whatever that exactly encompassed. Maybe it was just that senior crew on reputable ships didn't get the once-over and question and warning juniors got in places like Mariner and Fargone. Marie got a wave-through from a uniformed officer, the only one visible, without even a kiosk set up, or a single glance at her papers. She said, "He's with me," and the customs official waved him past with her.

Amazing. He thought he could like being senior crew, if that was what it meant. And Viking might be a grim, utilitarian place, as grim and browned-steel as his childhood memory of this station, but if it meant wave-throughs from customs, and no standing in long lines of exiting crew, he thought he could like Viking port's attitude.

Except for the other clientele.

—— *iv* ——

BERTH 19 ORANGE SECTOR WAS moderately convenient to Viking's blue section, where the Trade Bureau maintained its offices, a long walk or a relatively comfortable ride on one of the slow-moving public transports. There was, uncommon on stations Tom was familiar with, plenty of sitting room on the transport benches. You stepped aboard—if you weren't able-bodied you could flag it to a complete stop—and it also would do a full stop at any regular Section Center, but otherwise you just intercepted it when it made one of its scheduled rolling stops, stepped up as you grabbed the boarding rail, and stepped off the same way.

One of those full stops was, of course, the station offices in blue sector. Marie got up, as the stop came up. He waited beside her, hanging onto the rail until the transport slowed down. A crowd was waiting to board, confronting a good number getting off. You could always figure that blue would be the highest traffic area on the station, give or take the insystemer bars at maindark or alterdark shift-change, or the occasional concert or public event: blue held all the station business offices, the administrative offices, the main branches of all the banks, the embassies and trade offices, the big corporate offices, and the station media centers. You saw people in business suits, people in coveralls—half the crowd carried computers or wire-ins, pocket-coms, you could take your pick of accountants and security officers, official types—those usually in single cab-cars that wove in and out of foot traffic, and hazardously close to the ped-transports: step off without looking and you could get flattened.

Heart-stopping close call, that, just then, cab and pedestrians, human noise of a sort you only heard in places this dense with people. It gave him the willies . . . just too many people, all at once, going in chaotic directions, not caring if they hit each other. Marie stepped off in the middle of it. He stepped off beside her, his eyes tracking oncoming traffic.

"Straight on," Marie said, as if she'd had an inborn sense where things were—or maybe she'd checked the charts. He hadn't. He really didn't like the jostling and the racket—he'd looked all along the dockside they passed for *Corinthian* patches, or for any reaction at all from Marie, as if she'd seen something or might be looking for something other than what she said, but Marie was cold and calm, all business, Marie tolerated people shoving into them, which was steadier nerves than he had, and fell back as the crowd surged toward the stopped transport. He caught his balance as a man shoved him, looked around for Marie as the transport started to roll, with people still trying to grab the rails and board.

Marie was back on the transport.

People shoved past him in a last-moment rush for available deck-space. He elbowed back and tried to catch the boarding rail, but others were in front of him and the transport was gathering speed, faster and faster.

"Marie!" he yelled, knocked into a man in a suit, and into a rougher type, who elbowed him hard. He wasn't interested in argument. He ran, chasing the transport in the wake it made in the crowd, knocked into a woman as they both made a frantic grab for the standing pole on the rear of the transport flatbed. He caught it, and clung to it.

The woman had gone down. Others were helping her up,

he saw them diminishing as, having gained the platform, he spared the glance back. He hoped the woman wasn't hurt. He didn't know what else he could have done, and he'd made it.

Wobbly-kneed and out of breath, he excused himself past several pole-hangers on the standing-room-only transport, worked his way up to where Marie was standing, likewise holding to the pole.

She awarded him a cold glance.

"Dirty damned trick," he panted. "I knocked a woman down, Marie! Where in hell do you think you're going? Where's this about appointments with Records?"

"Did I bring you up to be naïve?"

"Dammit, you brought me up to tell the truth!"

"That's to me. Don't expect any favors from the rest of the universe. Why don't you jump off at the next stop?"

"Because I didn't lie to you! I want to help you! Can't you take loyalty when you get it?"

"I take it. For what it's worth."

"God, Marie!" He couldn't get his breath. He hung on to the pole as the transport swerved. "This is crazy!"

"*I'm* crazy. Hasn't Mischa told you? Poor Marie's just not that stable."

"You're acting like it!" There were people all around them, giving them room, determinedly avoiding their vicinity even standing shoulder to shoulder with them. He couldn't get breath enough to argue. He felt crushed by the crowds. He clung to the pole with one hand, people sitting behind them, the dock business frontage passing in a blur. Green sector was coming after blue, where, according to what they'd seen coming in, *Corinthian* was docked. "Where are we going? The obvious?"

"Not quite," Marie said, leaving him to wonder, because they couldn't discuss murder on a crowded transport.

He didn't want Marie arrested. Marie wasn't going to give him an answer here anyway, and he wasn't entirely sure, by

that last answer and by Marie's sarcasm about poor Marie and
Mischa, that Marie wasn't still on to something that didn't
involve attacking *Corinthian* bare-handed, or doing something
that could get both of them . . . he recalled Mischa's warning
all too vividly, and had a sickly and immediate fear in the pit
of his stomach . . . caught by station police and ground up fine
in station law.

Held on station while the ship went on without them. Psych-
adjusted, however far that went, until they didn't threaten anyone.

Stationers wouldn't kill you, no, they didn't believe in the
death penalty. When the psychs were through with you, you
couldn't even wish you had that option. That was what Marie
was risking, and he shut up, because he didn't *know* what the
local law was; he didn't know whether just suspicion of intent
to commit a crime could get you arrested—it could, on Cyteen
Outer Station, and he didn't want to talk about specifics or
name names with witnesses all around them. He just clung to
the pole on the overcrowded transport, watched Marie for
some evidence of an intent to bolt, and watched the numbers
pass as they trundled along from blue dock, where the government and the military ships came in—a government contracted
cargo didn't entitle them—toward green dock, ordinary merchanter territory, closer and closer to *Corinthian*.

The transport stopped just before the green section doors.
Three passengers got on, maybe ten or fifteen people got off.
A transport passed going the other direction, and stopped near
them. He stood ready to move in case Marie should try to lose
him again, and go the other way around the station rim. But
she stayed still, refused when he pointed out to her that there
was a seat free. Someone else took it. Marie held to the pole, not
saying anything, but sharp and eager and not at all distraught—
happy, he kept thinking, uneasily, happy and alive to her sur-
roundings in a way he'd never seen in his life.

They passed the section doors and rolled into green. He

didn't know *Corinthian*'s exact berth, but he had it pegged from the visual display as somewhere a third of the way into green out of blue.

He wasn't ready for Marie's hop off the transport as it slowed for a flag-down. He jumped, and tagged her quick pace along the frontage of bars and sleepovers, overtook her as she stopped and waited for him.

"What are you doing?" he hissed. "Marie, what are you doing? *Tell* me when you're getting off!"

"The berth's right down there," Marie said, gazing down-ring, deeper into green. "They're showing as offloading."

He could see the orange light, but only a single transport was sitting, loaded, at the berth. "Not moving."

"Taking their own time, for certain. I want a look at the warehouse and the company where that's going. The transport logo says Miller."

It sounded better than shooting at *Corinthian* crew. "What are we looking for, specifically?"

"What we can find. What they're dealing in." She grabbed his sleeve and drew him back against the frontage of a trinket shop as a man walked past them. He was confused for a moment, looking for obvious threat on the man, but Marie didn't let up.

"That's a *Corinthian* patch. *Corinthian* officer."

Sleeve-patch on the light green coveralls showed a black circle, an object he understood was some kind of ancient helmet. Crossed missiles. Spears. He'd learned that word from Marie. The patch had never looked half as much merchanter as military.

But, then, that described *Corinthian* to a tee.

And that might even be a cousin, striding along as if he owned the dock. Or a cousin's shipmate, he amended the thought, considering that the slurs about hire-ons and sex as a pre-req for employment that he'd heard all his life from his cousins were probably entirely true. He found himself nervous, unaccountably afraid, even in this degree of proximity to the ship and a side of his life he didn't want to meet.

"Come on," Marie said, and tugged at his arm, urging him closer to that berth.

"No!" He disengaged, grabbed her arm and drew her back. "You said you'd settle with them in the market. You said you were looking for something in the data."

"Scared?"

"You can't go down there, I won't let you go down there."

"Won't let me?"

"I won't. If they spot a *Sprite* patch, they're going to be all over us. It's crazy, Marie! If you can fix him through the market, do it, I'm with you, I'll help you, but I'm not going to see you go down there and do something stupid!"

"I'm fine. What's to worry about? Afraid to say hello to your father? I'm sure he'd be interested."

The cousins who gave him trouble had nothing on Marie. "I doubt he knows I exist. Unless you know a reason for him to."

"Interesting question."

"Marie,—for God's sake—"

"It's not a problem, Tom, I don't know why you're making it a problem. We just go a little closer, have a look around . . . "

"You lied to me."

"I didn't lie."

"Marie, what do you care now? After twenty years, for God's sake, what could you possibly *care* about that man? I don't. I don't give a damn where he is, what he does, I don't want to meet him, I don't want to know anything about him."

"Are you afraid?"

"No, I'm not afraid, but—"

"Liar yourself."

"Do you want him to rule your life, Marie? Is what happened twenty years ago going to govern your whole damned career?"

Marie's hand was in motion, and he'd gotten faster over the years. He blocked it. It stung, even so.

"Don't you lecture me!" Marie hissed. "Don't you lecture me, Thomas!"

" 'Bygones be bygones.' Hell!"

He wasn't looking for the second try. He didn't intend the force of the hand that blocked it.

"Cut it out, Marie!"

"Don't you lift a hand to me, don't you ever lift a hand, you hear me? *Damn* you!"

"I said cut it out!" He intercepted the third try, realized he was holding too tight and let go. "I'm not *him,* dammit, Marie, I'm not *him,* God, stop—*stop* it, Marie!"

She got a breath. She was absolutely paper white, staring at him with white-edged eyes, mouth open—he was shaking. She could still do that to him, he didn't know why, except that she could make him mad and that when he was mad he didn't think. He could hit her in his temper and maybe hurt her, maybe *want* to hurt her, that was the fear that paralyzed him.

She got her breath. She stared at him. "Whose side are you on?"

"I didn't know there was a side!"

"You damned well believe there's a side! Don't you talk to Mischa behind my back! I didn't have to have you. I didn't have to keep you. And what's fair—what's fair, Tom, your talking to Mischa, when Mischa never did one damned thing to help me, my own ship never did a damned thing to help me—like it was all *my* fault—"

"I know what you feel, Marie, I don't blame you, but you don't know—"

"You don't know what I feel! You don't know any part of what I feel. Don't give me that!"

"I don't want this ship to leave you in some station psych unit!"

"I'm not *stupid,* boy! Does Mischa think I'm stupid?"

"Mischa doesn't have a damned thing to do with my being here, I'm here for *you,* Marie, for God's sake, don't act like this! Listen to me!"

"Get away from me!" She shoved him off, ran along the frontages, and he ran after her, caught her, but she started hitting him.

"Marie, —"

"Hey!" somebody said, a voice he didn't know. Someone grabbed him hard from behind and shoved him, Marie broke and ran, and he was staring at an angry spacer a head taller and a good deal wider, yelling, "What's your problem?"

"That's my *mother,* dammit!"

The man grabbed him by the collar. "You treat your mama like that?"

"She's in trouble! Let me go!"

"What trouble?"

"Let go!" He broke the hold and ducked, ran toward *Corinthian*'s berth, and stopped, having lost all sight of Marie. Someone came running behind him, and he swung around, held up both hands in token of peace, ducked the man's attempt to grab him again.

"I'm telling you that's my mother, it's crew business, I'm not after a fight—just leave me the hell alone, she's breaking regs, I got to find her!"

He shoved the man off, ran down the dock closer to *Corinthian,* hoping he'd find some hidey-hole Marie might have found—there were bars and he skidded into one, hoping for a service door—saw one, but it was behind the bar. He kited back along the wall as the damnfool spacer came in looking for him. He slipped out the door behind the man's back, then ran down the row to the second bar over, and into the far dim back of the room, in case the man should give it another try. He was out of breath, hoped the man hadn't called the cops. He saw a public phone and went to it—it was too far around the station rim to rely on the pocket-com. He punched in the universal number for ship-lines, *Sprite*'s berth at orange 19, then the internal number for bridge-com.

"This is Tom Hawkins. Put me through to the captain, this is an extreme emergency."

Mischa came on, immediately, with, "Where did she lose you?"

"Green 10," he said, shamefaced. God, not even a What happened?

"Kid, stay *put*, do you copy? Where are you right now?"

He had to look up at the bar name on the back wall. "The *Andromeda.*"

"You don't budge from there. Do you copy? Don't budge. Saja's on the dock. He's had you in sight. He's been trying to catch up to you since you left, damn your hide."

Chasing us, he thought. Why? They had the com. Why didn't they just call us?

"Yes, sir," he said. "I'll be here." Imagination painted what Marie might be up to, trying to get on board *Corinthian,* lying in ambush for their crew on dockside—getting caught at it, and arrested, because *Corinthian* had probably gathered all sorts of evidence on Marie's intentions over the years, if Mischa was right about the messages she'd sent.

He hung up. He followed the edge of the room, around the tables, not to leave the bar, but because he wanted not to be visible from the door. Traffic was moderate in the establishment. A group of spacers came in and went to the bar. He spotted a darkness about the patch. It could be *Corinthian*. He couldn't tell from his vantage; and the man that was following him hadn't shown. He thought he might just sit down in the corner and order a drink, but it wasn't a table-service kind of place, you had to go up to the bar, and he wasn't eager to go up there with the newcomers.

He took a look outside, a careful look-see, anxious whether there was any sight of *Sprite* personnel, or whether the man who'd followed him into one bar was still searching.

No sign of either. But he saw Marie, down the row, just standing in front of some shop, looking across the wide dock to *Corinthian*'s operations zone.

He could go back and call Mischa. He could lose her, that

way. He stayed where he was, thinking Saja and his group could spot him that way, and thinking to keep Marie in sight.

But Marie started to walk along the frontage, still in the direction she'd been going, with consistent looks toward *Corinthian*'s area.

Stalking them. He stood watching, looked frantically for Saja to show up, and saw Marie getting further and further away.

Screw it, he thought. Mischa knew where he was better than he was going to know where Marie was if he didn't move. He started walking as fast as he could—he figured running would draw attention he didn't want. He just tried to look like someone on business, without making the noise that would alarm Marie or drive her to cover down some service access that on some docksides you found unlocked.

She stopped and took something from her pocket, he was scared to death it was a gun; but it was an optic of some sort, maybe a camera, he wasn't sure. She was looking toward *Corinthian* and he took the chance to run, as lightly and quietly as he could, in her direction.

She saw him at the last moment, spun about in alarm and then scowled at him.

"Dammit," he panted. "What are you looking at?"

"Damn yourself. The answer's Miller Transship, 23 green, no long distance from 10. They're onloading. But that's a Miller company transport. You'd know that son of a bitch was going to deal all inside."

"What do you mean?"

"I mean he's not hiring outside help. No freight handling by any outside party. He sells to Miller, he buys from Miller, Miller's his transport, his commissioned supplier . . . "

"That's not illegal, is it?"

"No, it's not illegal. It does mean there's minimal contact with people who might ask questions. God, I wish we'd been here just five days ago."

"When he was offloading."

"Damn right when he was offloading. The market's just so smooth right now. Can you imagine a ship arriving and the market not showing a single change on the boards?"

He couldn't. The market always reacted. "I don't think so."

"Bravo. You don't think so."

"So what do you think?"

"Oh, just coincidence. *Corinthian* just carries such a mix of average goods you just don't get a tick at all. Goods Miller warehoused the instant that ship hit system. And you still don't get a tick."

"Why doesn't station spot it?"

"Station may have spotted it. But it's not illegal for Miller to hold a shipment off the boards, either. *They're* a transshipper. They don't have to declare in a free or a dutied port, not since the War. Transshipped goods are technically still in transit until they deliver them elsewhere."

"With the cargo broken up and dribbled out in patterns that don't make patterns."

"Brilliant. You must have gotten deviousness from his side."

"The hell I did. What are you going to do about it?"

"Just take a few pictures." Marie lifted the camera that probably, he thought, had a close-up function that meant business.

And a couple of *Corinthian* crewmen were looking their direction, maybe out of frame from what Marie saw.

"Marie. Marie, they're looking at us. Let's just walk."

"Nerves. All right." Marie put the camera back in her pocket and they started away, but the men started across the dock, four of them.

"Damn," Tom said. "Marie,—"

"Just keep walking."

"We could go into a bar. It's safer."

"I don't like to be *in* places."

God. Marie was sane ninety-nine point nine percent of the time. And then you got the schitzy tenth percent.

"I don't care, we should get off the dock . . . get where we've got protection. . . ."

Marie threw a look over her shoulder. Started running. He did, casting a fast look back, and they had, and he caught up to Marie, grabbed her arm as they were running and tried to drag her into the nearest bar, but Marie started fighting him and he let go and put on double speed as the *Corinthian* crewmen came pounding up the deck behind them.

They knocked into a woman coming out of a bar, knocked her flat, and kept going. People were shouting.

Then he saw people start to run toward them from down the dock in the other direction, and realized it was Saja in the lead.

Marie started to change direction. "It's Saja!" he yelled at her, and grabbed her and ran for oncoming reinforcements.

But *Corinthian* personnel weren't giving up the chase. They reached Saja and three of the cousins, and Saja had pulled a length of light chain from his pocket, the cousins had come up with other contraband, and there wasn't time to think about anything but getting Marie out of there.

Except Marie wouldn't go, Marie had a piece of chain, too, and it whipped about and caught a *Corinthian* crewman across the neck. There was a pile-up of bodies as the man went down, Marie went down, and the nearest bar emptied out more Corinthians.

"Security!" somebody yelled, on their side or *Corinthian*'s or the bystanders, he wasn't sure, only a number of people had mixed into it that weren't *Corinthian* or *Sprite,* people yelling that the cops were coming, about the time a fist came out of nowhere and hit him in the temple.

He couldn't see. He stumbled over somebody's leg or arm and went down, trying to fend off the attack with his uplifted arm, hearing chains flying and people yelling—he heard somebody yell cops, and look out, and he couldn't find Marie, couldn't find anything but the deck-plates. He scrambled for what he thought was a clear zone, and met what might be the frontage wall, he wasn't sure. Hands helped him up, held onto him as the dark gave way to hazy sight and an orbiting couple of red spots.

Flashing blue, then. The cops were coming in, breaking it up with stun-sticks and bare hands. He didn't see Marie. He didn't know what to do. They were hauling people out of the tangle on the deck and arresting them and he found space to retreat at his back, people just pushing past him to shout information, who'd swung, who'd done what, the cops were shouting to calm down, they wanted officers, and they wanted them now.

He heard Saja saying he was an officer, dammit, and Corinthians started it, and somebody else shouting it was *Sprite* and there was a crazy woman trying to kill their captain, but Marie wasn't anywhere in sight, Marie was loose somewhere and she was liable to do anything . . . or some *Corinthian* could have dragged her off, he didn't know and he didn't take station police as going to listen to a spacer quarrel.

He had the chance. He just backed away, just turned and kept walking, dizzy, his head hurting. He wasn't aware of where he was walking, only it turned out to be toward *Corinthian,* and where they'd come from, and then he knew where Marie would go if she was loose. If she wasn't crazy, she'd want the evidence to prove to the universe *Corinthian* was guilty and they'd had the motive to attack her, she'd fry Austin Bowe if it was the last and only thing she could do, and the evidence, if she couldn't get at *Corinthian*'s own data, was at an address.

His head hurt. He couldn't think of it. It was in the twenties on the same dock, and that was a long hike down from *Corinthian*'s berth at 10, but nobody was offering to stop him, he was just any spacer walking on the dock, staggering a little, but spacers did, on the Strip, that was why safe, moral stationers didn't come walking here, it was spacer territory, spacer logic, even with the cops . . . couldn't say they'd actually arrest anybody if nobody landed in hospital, just fine hell out of both ships, you didn't know, you couldn't predict. . . .

Support column came up in his face. He grabbed it, leaned against it, head hurting, vision doing tricks again.

Couldn't blame Marie for running. She'd conned him. She'd used him. Made Mischa think everything was under control. She'd probably scammed Saja, too, with that trick of stepping back onto the transport, Saja'd had to wait for the next one.

But what did you expect of Marie? She was what she was. She didn't deserve to be in any psych ward, please God.

She'd pulled the same thing on Mischa twenty years ago. He wasn't any brighter.

She'd said she had trade information, she said she was working on *Corinthian* doing something illegal, at least something borderline—she said if she could get some information out of the trade office,—and she had an appointment . . . everything looked good . . . but that wasn't where she'd gone. She'd come here . . .

Wandering the ever-night of the docks, the clash and crash of loaders, the echoing of distant voices. He was walking again. He didn't remember since when.

Abundant places to hide. Abundant places to lose oneself in, if one were determined, and Marie was that. Spacers passed him. He saw patches on sleeves but he didn't know the ships. Strange to him. And he'd never been a place in his life where that was true.

Past the frontage of a sleepover. He felt his hands sweating despite the cold, his heart pumping and not keeping up with the oxygen demand. Opposite berth 18, it was. Looking for the twenties, he said to himself, and saw a transport go past.

Saw a sign, not a big one. Hercules Shipping. Commercial district. And warehouses. The character of the zone changed that quickly. Suddenly it was all warehouses, some with open doors, cans standing inside in the light, most with doors shut.

Transshippers, Marie had said. Couldn't remember the name or the number, until he saw the sign.

Miller.

Miller Transshipping.

The doors weren't open. Looked closed, except shippers didn't ever close. No neon about the sign, easy to miss, on the frontage like that, with no lights. But Miller was the name, he was sure of it.

He tried the personnel entry, heavy door with no window. It was supposed to work on hydraulics, but it didn't, you had to shove it after the electric motor took it halfway, and it wasn't illegal to walk into an office and ask directions to some place: he could pretend he didn't know where Hercules Shipping was, he had his story all ready.

But nobody was in the office. The side door wasn't locked, either, and that led into the lighted warehouse.

Going there was a little chancier, but he could still say he was lost and looking for somebody . . . please God the vacancy in the office wasn't because Marie had done something, like killing somebody.

He was lost, he'd tell them, if he ran into workers inside. He'd gotten separated from his crewmates in the transport crush, he didn't know where he was.

He walked among tall shipping canisters, cold-hauler stuff, up in racks, like a ship's hold, only more brightly lit. The cans drank up heat from the air, made the whole warehouse bitter cold. They were covered in frost.

The rack-loader had stopped with a can aboard. It was frosted as the rest. He unclipped his ID, used the edge to scrape the plate to find out what was listed in it. . . . Marie wanted to know, and he wanted to be able to tell her. Prove he was on her side.

It said the origin was Pell. It said . . . he couldn't make out the contents, the label was faint and the plate kept frosting over again while he scraped thick greyed peels of ice off it, but it said it was cold-hold stuff, it said it was biologic, that was a check-box. It said food-stuffs. He was freezing where he stood, hadn't realized it was cold-hold goods filling the warehouse. He needed more than the insulated coveralls you used on the docks. Needed gloves, because his fingers were burning just peeling the frost off, and the can drank the heat out of his exposed skin, out of his eyes, so he didn't dare go on looking at it. Deep cold was treacherous: if you felt it do that and you didn't have a face-mask, you needed to get out.

A door opened behind him. His heart thumped. He heard voices, decided he'd better go ahead with his charade. So he clipped his ID back to his pocket and walked out to see who'd come in, to give his story about being lost.

Personnel came in wearing heavy coats, in gloves; then a handful of spacers in no more protection than he stood in—in the same green he'd seen on *Corinthian* crew.

He decided to bluff it through, giddy and shivering as he was. "There you are," he declared. "I was wondering if there was someone in charge."

"What in hell are you doing in here?"

"Door was open," he said, walking toward them, scared as hell and trying not to show it. "Sorry. I thought there'd be somebody in the warehouse, if nothing else." He didn't want *Corinthian* crew to see the patch on his sleeve, please God, he just wanted to deal with the warehouse owners. "Lost my mates, got off at the wrong stop . . . I was supposed to go down to Hercules Shipping, I forgot the damn number. . . ."

"He was with her," one of the spacers said.

Shit, he thought, desperate, and made a throwaway gesture, measuring the distance to the door. "I was with my crew, except I got off too soon. Sorry if I've inconvenienced anybody, I was just looking for a number. . . ."

His legs were stiff from the cold. He wasn't sure he could run with any speed. The spacers came closer, the warehouse workers saying things about the dangers of cold cans, about not wanting any trouble on their premises.

Fine, he thought, he'd go through *them,* not the spacers. And he bolted for the door.

But the warehousers grabbed him, all the same, and swung him around to face the spacers. Six of them.

"*Sprite* crew," one of them said, and the young man who

looked like an officer of some sort said, "Looking for an address, are you?" The young man walked up and unclipped the ID from his pocket. Looked at it.

Clean-cut young officer. Stripes on his sleeve. Didn't look like as much trouble as the crew might be. Looked at the ID. Looked at him.

"Thomas Bowe-Hawkins."

Bowe, the pocket tab on the officer said. C. Bowe. Cousin of his, he thought, and didn't welcome the acquaintance.

"Well, well, well," the young man said. "Marie Hawkins' darling offspring. Search the place."

"She's not here."

The *Corinthian* clipped the tab back to his pocket, one-handed. Straightened his collar, a familiarity he didn't like.

"Thomas. Or Tom?"

"Suit yourself," he muttered. He was scared. He'd been in cousin-traps a hundred times. But there were a dozen ways to get killed in this one.

"Tommy Hawkins. I'm *Christian* Bowe. Papa's *other* son." *Other* son.

More than possible. He hadn't known, he hadn't guessed, and he looked at this Christian Bowe, wondering whether kinship was going to get him out of this or see him dead.

"Where's your mama?" Christian Bowe asked him. "Hmmn?"

"I don't know. She's not here."

"So you just went walking in the warehouses, did you? Looking for something in particular?"

"I know Miller's handling your stuff. I thought she might have come here. But she didn't."

"Come here for what?"

He didn't answer. One of the men came back from a circuit of the area. "He was scraping at the labels," that man said. "Or somebody was."

"Marie Hawkins?" Christian shouted at the empty air. The

voice echoed around the vast, cold warehouse, up among the racks. "You want your kid back?"

Marie didn't, Tom thought. Not that much.

Or maybe not at all. Echoes died into silence. He stood there, with two men holding on to his arms, and hands and face numb with the cold. Eyes were frosting around the edges, the stiffness of ice.

"He knows too much," somebody said, at his back.

"Don't know a thing," he said.

"The hell," Christian said, and turned his shoulder, hand rubbing the back of his neck, while he thought over what to do, Tom supposed, while all of them froze, but he was getting there faster.

"Put him out," Christian said then. He thought he meant out of the warehouse, and hoped, when the man holding his right arm quit twisting it.

But that man's hand came around and under his jaw, then. He knew the hold, tried to break it before it cut the blood to his brain, but he didn't have the leverage, they did, and the white suns in the overhead dimmed and faded out, quite painlessly.

—— _v_ ——

DIDN'T KNOW WHERE HE WAS, then, except face down on the icy deck with a knee in his back, pressing his forehead against the burning cold of the decking. They taped his hands and ankles together. He yelled for help, and somebody ripped off some more tape and taped his mouth with it—after which, they threw some kind of cold blanket over him and rolled him in it, until he was a cocoon. He tried to kick and tried to yell out, figuring their beating him unconscious was no worse than smothering to death or freezing to death in the warehouse, if there was anybody to know.

But they picked him up, then, head and feet, and carried him a distance, through a doorway, he thought, before they dumped him on the deck. It was the office, he gradually decided, because he could feel the warmth in the air that got through the blanket, which was a source of cold, now, instead of warmth.

He heard them walking around him, talking about the transport rolling, how it had been down; he heard them cursing somebody named Jeff and wishing he'd hurry, but he hoped for maybe one of the company owners or a customer to come in, who'd be willing to call the cops and canny enough to get out the door. Now and again he gathered his forces to try to make noise in case somebody was in earshot, and they'd kick him half-heartedly, not with any force through the blanket, and once they told him they'd beat hell out of him if he didn't lie still.

Somebody did come in, just after that; he heard the door open and close; but it was the guy named Jeff, who said he'd got the stuff, that was all. He didn't know what they were talking about; but abruptly they grabbed him, unwrapped the blanket, unfastened his collar and shot him with a hypo in the back of the shoulder.

Damn you all, he wanted to say. He didn't know where he'd wake up—or if he'd wake.

He'd met a brother he didn't know he had. That wasn't a dream.

He'd lost Marie. He hoped they hadn't caught her. He didn't know if she could survive if they took her aboard *Corinthian*, if Bowe wanted a personal revenge.

He didn't know but what they were going to dump him in a can and put the lid on and ship him to Fargone or somewhere, where they'd find an unexplained frozen corpse. He stared up at the circle of interested faces. He was very, very scared, but he was losing it again. . . .

The room dimmed. He could hear his own pulse, proving he was alive.

That was all.

Chapter Three

A BROTHER HE'D RATHER NOT HAVE met lying like a heap of laundry on the bunk in the brig, and, Christian said to himself, Austin was very possibly going to kill him, when Austin finished sorting out the fines and the penalties . . . none of which was his fault; but that didn't mean whoever approached Austin with a minor problem wasn't going to catch hell.

"I wouldn't go in there," Beatrice said, in the vicinity of Austin's office. As a mother, Beatrice wasn't the historic model . . . she'd dropped her kid between jumps, left him to cousin Saby's ten-year-old mercy, and nowadays abdicated him to Capella's, God help him. Right now Beatrice showed the ravages of a night on the docks, red eyes, hair trailing out of its usual tight twist—the glitz-paint was worn on one bare shoulder, saying Beatrice had been in bed when the search team found her or the beeper on the pocket-com finally blasted her out of whatever lair she'd intended for the next several days.

So they'd all had cancelled plans. Capella was in a funk. Beatrice looked mildly sedated, just a little strange about the edges when she grabbed him and hugged him in the corridor, not Beatrice's maternal habit. Then she got a fistful of his hair and looked him closely in the eyes with,

"You've given us a problem. You've given Austin one."

"What was I to do? He'd been looking at the cans. And *pardonnez-moi, maman*, I didn't pick this particular problem. He's Austin's."

"He won't thank you."

"Pity."

He started to leave. Beatrice didn't let go her fistful of hair. "Christian. Keep your mouth *shut*. It will die down. We can leave this fool at Pell . . . send him to Earth, for that matter, and he *won't* find his way back."

"It won't die down. There's too broad a trail, and there's that woman. . ."

"Shit on that woman!"

"Shit on the whole situation, I—"

The door of Austin's office whisked aside. Austin loomed in the doorway. "Get in here!"

"Who, me?" He honestly wasn't sure, and mimed it. Austin grabbed him by the arm, jerked him through the door, and backhanded him hard into the wall, which left him nursing a sore ear and a personal indignation.

"It's not my damn fault!"

"Why could somebody just walk into the warehouse? Where in hell was the guard?"

"Millers' had people on duty, but they had to have somebody sign the damn repair order, I didn't know they were going to leave the office unlocked. . . ."

Austin took a glancing swipe at him, total disgust. "All you had to do was have a guard on that door."

"I know that."

"You know that, *sir*, damn your impudence! You look to inherit *Corinthian*? You're a long way from it, at the rate you're going! We'll be lucky not to lose this port, *and* Miller, and all they do for us, you understand that? Does that remotely affect your social interests?"

"I was busting my ass, *sir,* getting Miller moving. I got us turned around, we just can't use any damn dockhand that comes along. We're loading, we're going as fast as the loader can roll, I've sent out the board-call. The only thing I didn't predict was Miller's man deciding to take a walk and leave the damn door unlocked—"

"Try predicting what we're going to do when the cops show up wanting Thomas Hawkins! Does that fit in your crystal ball? *Sprite* crew is all over the damn dock out there!"

"Looking for Marie, by my sources. Not interested in calling the cops, no more than we are. They're asking up and down the row, every bar, showing her picture. They probably think he's with her."

"Damn lucky they didn't arrest half the crew."

"I hear luck had nothing to do with it."

"Expensive luck. I'm not in a damned good mood, boy. Nobody's coming through those access doors or near our lock. Damned elusive woman. Damned persistent—and you snatch her kid? Thanks. Thanks a whole lot. It's just the luck we needed."

"Dump him in space. It's no different than leaving him lie in a warehouse full of cold cans. He was taking a tour of Miller's premises, for God's sake, it wasn't my doing, I don't know what more I could do than I did . . . if I'd left a body behind, you wouldn't be happy with me either, especially seeing he's your own offspring,—sir. I wouldn't want you to get the idea I wanted him dead."

"You're real close to annoying me, Christian."

"I did what seemed to me to be less liability."

"After you finally deigned to return a com call. After you gave that ship that much extra time to let Marie Hawkins loose on the dock."

"It's not my fault the transport broke down. It's not my fault everything on this God-forsaken station depends on some separate labor union—*I* could have fixed that damn transport with a screwdriver, *Miller* could have fixed the transport, we didn't know we had an emergency, and I wasn't that hard to track down, sir, I'd told Miller where I was and what general direction I was going. You could have called Miller."

"Miller isn't an officer on this ship. Damned right I called Miller, once Bianco saw fit to tell me the offloading was stalled."

"You tell Bianco what you thought about it?"

"Bianco'd told you. *You* were the officer of the watch, boy, and if you have any desire to stay an officer on this ship, I suggest you establish clear understandings with the duty officer of each watch, that you take threats against this ship damned seriously, that you don't screw with the guard I've put on our accesses, because I don't take for granted that woman won't try to slip us a bomb in one of the cans or walk onto this ship armed, do you hear me?"

"Yes, sir, but—"

"As long as they're searching for her . . . she hasn't gone to the cops or reported in. Just keep those cans moving. And let me tell you something—" Austin went to the door and opened it again. "Beatrice? Beatrice, I want you to hear this, too."

Beatrice came in . . . subdued, for Beatrice. She folded her arms and stood there glumly.

"I don't know how seriously you take the threat Marie Hawkins poses," Austin said. "But twenty years of threats and her skulking around out there don't add up empty in my book. She's got this kid—by her own letters, she's primed this kid of hers to get us, meaning the crew, *and* particularly anybody attached to me. That kid stays in the brig. Nobody takes chances with him. I'm damned serious, Beatrice."

"What do you intend to do with him?"

"Take him as far away from *Sprite* schedules as we can."

"No paternal interest."

"Filed right behind your maternal instincts, Beatrice, don't push me. Tell your offspring use his head. I am tired. I am hung over . . . Beatrice, this wasn't the best wake-up I've had in a year."

Beatrice moved in for aid and comfort. It seemed a good moment to excuse oneself out the door. Christian slid in that direction, opened the door—Austin had it set on fast, and auto-close—and walked—

"Boy. Don't screw up."

—out. The door whisked shut in his face, leaving him blank surface instead of the pair that were ultimately responsible— leaving words in his mouth, and nowhere to spit them.

He didn't hit the door. Or open it. He dropped the fist and walked the curving deck, headed for the lift.

He'd ordered the dockside crew to keep an eye out, see if they could spot this Hawkins woman—keep her off Austin's neck. No damn thanks from Austin, Austin never asked, Austin never looked to see who did what, it was just your fault if something went wrong.

Never Austin's fault. Never Austin's damned fault. Austin never made mistakes.

— *ii* —

CANS WERE OFFLOADING. You could hear the hydraulics working, distant, a comfortable, all's-well sort of sound.

Couldn't figure. What station? When had he gotten back to the ship? One spectacular blow-out in a bar, maybe, drunk till he couldn't figure. . .

Except he was face down on a bed that didn't feel like his own, and it didn't have sheets, and his mouth felt like fuzz inside while the outside felt skinned.

A moment of fright came back to him, shadows around him while he lay on a freezing deck trying to fight them off. He grabbed the edge of the bed and sat up in a hurry, legs off the edge, and a cold plastic line dragging from his wrist.

Hell, he thought, scared. Blurred eyes made out an unfamiliar room, green, not white, an unfamiliar blur of metal grid in front of him, and a spinning of his head and a queasiness in his stomach said it hadn't been a good experience that put him in this unfamiliar place. The station brig, maybe. Maybe the cops had come and arrested everybody, and Marie. . .

Marie was still out there. Maybe she'd gotten away, but he hadn't, and he couldn't remember everything about how he'd come here, just the warehouse and the cold, and people around him.

People. *Corinthian* crew.

And there was a cold metal bracelet around his right wrist, and a plastic-sheeted cable going up to where the wall met the ceiling, which he couldn't make out the sense of, except the metal grid where the front wall ought to be, and the rest was any crewman's ordinary accommodation, without sheets, without personal items, without anything on the walls, or any internal com unit—just a patch on the wall where one might have been taken out, and nobody'd cared to paint it, or anything else people had scratched up . . . skuzzy walls, skuzzy panels, where previous occupants had scratched initials and obscenities.

He didn't remember any station cops.

It wasn't Viking's brig. It wasn't the legal system that ran this graffiti-scarred cell. It was *Corinthian*. He'd become a hostage for something, or a prisoner *Corinthian* had some reason to keep, or God knew what else.

He staggered up, shaky in the knees and immediately aware the cell wasn't precisely on the main axis of the ship. He grabbed the cable that trailed from his wrist and gave it a jerk that burned his palms—but it didn't give. It went out a little aperture at the join of wall and ceiling, and it was securely anchored somewhere the other side of the wall.

His breath came short. It might be the anesthetic they'd shot him with. It might be the exertion. It might be the beginnings of panic, but he couldn't get enough air to keep the room from going around as he stumbled to the metal grid and tried to slide it one way and the other.

It didn't give, either, not even so much as to show what way it *could* move when it opened.

There was, at the other end of the narrow space, the ribbed panel that, aboard *Sprite*, rolled back to give access to the bathroom, and there was a trigger-plate. He leaned against the wall there and pressed it, and the panel rolled back, making itself the side wall of the bath.

There was a sink, a toilet, a vapor closet for a shower, same facilities his own cabin had. He punched the cold water. It gave a meager amount and shut itself off. He punched the hot, and it wasn't, but it shut itself off.

Not the ritz, he thought distractedly. He felt better that the bath worked. At least it wasn't deliberately *bad* treatment—they hadn't left him to freeze, they hadn't beaten him unconscious: they must have sent to the ship for what they'd dosed him with; and, aside from a slight nausea and a frost-burn on his fingers and the side of his face, he wasn't exactly hurt . . . but the cable crossed his legs every time he took a step or reached for anything, telling him he wasn't free, he wasn't all right, they didn't intend him to get loose, and they weren't doing what they'd done for his convenience.

More . . . he didn't know what might be going on outside, or whether they'd also caught Marie, or what his crew might be doing.

Not much, he thought, trying to be pragmatic. A, Mischa didn't give the proverbial damn, B, if Mischa did give a damn, Marie would still be *Sprite*'s first worry for very practical reasons, and, C, if Mischa did decide to do something about it, *Sprite* didn't hold an outstandingly high hand.

Unless Marie had come up with the evidence Marie had said she was looking for.

Marie lied without a conscience.

But Marie had brought a camera, Marie had committed every subterfuge she'd committed with the simple, predictable notion of getting to *Corinthian*'s dock—but whether the camera was an excuse to do it or the reason for doing it, he didn't know. She'd said there were things she wanted to ask the station trade office, and maybe she'd wanted to gather evidence enough to be allowed to get at station records, or to make someone else take a look. . . .

He didn't know. He couldn't know from here. But if Marie was in fact on to something, he knew what motive *Corinthian* could have for taking him and holding on to him, at least until they were ready to leave port, or until it was clear Marie couldn't prove anything.

Only hope they hadn't caught Marie. Only hope Marie hadn't done something to lose whatever leverage she had with Mischa or with Viking station authorities, or whoever could get him out of here.

He found himself walking the length and width of the cell, staggering as he was, telling himself he was all right, Marie wouldn't let him stay here, Marie would move whatever she had to move to get him out—telling himself they couldn't have caught her, Marie was slippery as hell, that was how he'd gotten into this in the first place, and something was going to get him out, *Corinthian* couldn't just kidnap somebody and get away with it, and they couldn't have the motives with him they'd had with Marie. Surely not. Please God, that wasn't even a reasonable thought.

He heard someone walking in the corridor, heard someone come near the cell. He went to the bars of the grid, leaned against them to try to see.

A young man. Blond hair, sullen expression, a face and a body language that jolted into recognition . . . the warehouse. *Corinthian.*

Christian.

Brother.

"Alive, after all," Christian said. "So happy to be here. I can tell."

"Happier to be out of here. What're my chances?"

"Hey. You're already lucky. Pump drugs into a body, you don't know, you woke up. I don't know what's your bitch."

He didn't think he liked Christian Bowe. But there was some

cause, he could see that, for *Corinthian* not to like the situation. Christian Bowe said it—he *was* alive: point on *Corinthian*'s side.

He looked his half-brother up and down. *Pretty* boy, he thought. Papa had good genes.

"So why'd you bring me here?"

"Hell if I know."

It was more and less answer than he expected. A disconcerting answer. "So what do you want for me to get out of here?"

"Idea of the moment, bringing you here. Don't ask me. I don't do long-range planning."

"Am I the only one?"

"The only what?"

Temper flared. "The only one, the only one you brought aboard, you know damned well what I mean."

Pretty-boy made a motion of his fingers. "No. I don't know. What do you mean?"

"Screw you." It wasn't getting anywhere. This wasn't a friend. He walked back to his bed and sat down.

"You mean your mama?" Christian asked from the other side of the bars.

He meant Marie. He was scared. And mad. He tucked his foot up into the circle of his arms and the cable dragged across his shins. He didn't look at Christian Bowe. He didn't expect any help, or any honest answer.

But if they'd caught Marie, he thought Christian would be happy to tell him so.

Machinery whined, sharply, suddenly. The cable jerked tight, jerked him off the bed and up against the wall, his arm drawn up and up.

The whine stopped. His arm did, the bracelet cutting into his wrist, his feet all but off the deck. It hurt, from his chest to his wrist. It scared him, what they could do, what his half-brother could do.

"Want down?"

"Son of a—"

The cable yanked him half his height up the wall. It made him think, at that point of rest, what the winch could do to his wrist once it hit the exit point.

"Want down?" Christian asked.

He had a choice. He knew he had a choice. He'd never backed down in his life. He couldn't manage to say I give. Couldn't find it.

The winch took up another spurt. There wasn't another inch left.

"Want down?"

He couldn't get the wit to talk. He couldn't frame an appeal to reason. Or kinship.

"Good day," Christian said, "good luck, good bye."

"Christian!"

"Please?"

"Damn you!"

Christian walked off. He hung there, against the spin of the whole of Viking station, telling himself he'd been a fool, he had nothing to win, he'd nothing to lose, he just wanted down before his arm broke or his hand went dead, which could happen, and he didn't know how long it could take.

"Christian, damn you!"

He'd been a fool. But he wasn't sorry. Hell, he wasn't sorry. He'd seen more of *Corinthian* already than he hoped to see in his lifetime, he didn't like it, he hoped for papa's curiosity, if nothing else, to draw him down to wherever his prison was, and he hoped to hell they hadn't caught Marie.

God, he couldn't breathe, he couldn't think of anything but that his wrist or his shoulder was going to give.

He heard Christian's footsteps going away.

"Help!" he yelled, "help! dammit!" and couldn't get the breath to call out, after.

Christian didn't come back. Not right away.

Eventually—he measured the time in the clunk and thump

of the loader hydraulics—Christian's shadow darkened the bars again, and Christian hung a casual forearm through the grid.

"Want down?"

Damn you, was what he wanted to say. He'd said it to his cousins. But his cousins wouldn't kill him, and something said Christian might, given the right moment.

"Yes," he said through his teeth.

"Pity," Christian said. And left him.

"Son of a *bitch!*" he yelled, and ran out of breath.

"H'*lo,* Chrissy," came from the corridor. Someone female met Christian. He kicked the wall and tried to grab the cable with his left hand, the bracelet was pressing bone in his right one. "Mmm," female-person said, "and aren't we cheerful. Told Austin yet?"

He couldn't hear what Christian said. He got the second hand on the cable. He kicked the wall, trying to get a better grip, and slammed back into the panel.

Female-person came to stand at the grid, forearms through the bars, staring at him . . . an apparition of glitz-paint, exposed skin in shimmer cloth, and a shock of pale, shave-sided hair. Bar-bunny, he thought. Traveling entertainment.

"Pretty, pretty, pretty," she said. "Austin does good work."

"You stay the hell away from him, Capella, you hear me?"

"Aww."

The cable was cutting into his fingers. Breath was short. He shut his eyes, to time out, but Capella said, "Let him down, Chrissy. He's going to turn blue."

"Don't call me Chrissy."

"Christian. Chrétien Perrault-Bowe. Be nice."

He didn't know what happened or who did what. But the cable spun loose of a sudden and dumped him onto his feet, hard. His arm swung down and life tingled back into a hand with the mark of the bracelet blazoned white.

Capella stuck her hand through the bars. "H'lo. I'm Capella. You're Thomas Hawkins. How-do."

"Capella." Christian wasn't pleased.

"Jealous?"

The hand stayed. He'd thought space-brain. But he didn't now. He saw the bracelet of stars tattooed around the woman's wrist, and felt his blood run a little colder. He'd heard about that mark. Never seen one. Navigator's mark, but one no merchanter needed—navigator off a damned Mazianni pirate, near as made no difference. The sort that raided shipping during the War, the sort that the Trade still ducked in mortal terror.

Surely, even time-lagged as hell, she was too young to wear that mark.

He walked up and reached out to the offered handshake.

Whine of a motor. The cable took up, jerked him backward and, off balance, down to one knee.

"Chris-sy," Capella said.

"Damn you!" It hurt his pride, his wrist and his knee; and it was Christian's doing, his *Corinthian* half-brother.

"Hands off," Christian told Capella. "Don't screw with him, you hear me?"

"Sounds like fun," Capella said, leaning on the bars, flashed him a feral grin. "How *are* you in bed, Christian's older brother?"

He got up from where the cable had jerked him, dusted himself with the hand that wasn't pulled in the direction of the wall. He didn't think Capella was any prospect of help. But he swallowed the Screw Yourself that leapt up first in his mind, and shot Capella a not-hostile look. "Is he always this tense?"

It tickled Capella. It didn't amuse Christian.

"Just leave him alone," Christian said. "Haven't you got a duty assignment?"

"Not in your c-oh-c, darlin'. But probably. *Don't* break his wrist. It just annoys Medical."

Christian still wasn't amused. Capella sauntered off. He expected another jerk of the cable, except Christian's hands were both in sight. Control that temper of yours, Mischa had said, and much as he wanted to get his hands on Christian's neck, he was in a bad situation. He didn't like what he'd seen, he didn't like the company, but, painful as the wrist was, and mad and scared as he was, he was in no position to carry on an argument.

"Look," he said. "Christian. I don't want any fight with you. All I want is to get my mother off the docks . . . she lied to us, she got away from us. That's all. I just want to find her and get her back to the ship."

"Expected to find her in a shipping can, huh?"

No answer for that one. The whole line of Marie's thinking was evident in where they'd caught him, scraping ice off a can label. He was no help to Marie, tipping them to more than he had.

"What's going on outside?"

"We're loading."

It wasn't the answer he wanted and Christian knew it. Pretty-boy had a tilt of the head and a smug expression that made him want to pound pretty-boy to pulp, but he couldn't come closer to the bars than he was. He couldn't do anything. He had only to hope they'd let him go and by where they'd caught him . . . he didn't think they would.

He just couldn't figure where Marie was, or what might be happening out there.

Mischa talking sense to Austin Bowe, if he had his choice. Maybe offering a pledge not to get either of them involved in station law. No ship wanted that kind of entanglement. We get our lunatic off the docks, you give her her boy back, and neither of us files station charges. . . .

"Have fun," Christian said, evidently deciding the amusement value was nil here, and shoved away from the bars.

"You want to release that cable?"

"Please?"

"Please. Politely."

Christian flipped some sort of switch beside the door. He tugged at the cable and it ran free, take-up gear disengaged. He went as far as the grid and tried to see where Christian went, but it was around the corner of the block where the cell was—tried to see the control panel for the cable, and it was out of reach, and no damn good, since the only thing you could do with it was free the gear or take the cable up, and he didn't want to turn the winch on.

Nothing like this on *Sprite*.

Nothing like this on any honest ship. It wasn't lower-main corridor, at least: off the axis but not much off, you could feel the slant in the deck. It was for keeping someone locked up *while* the ship was docked: half the heated, pressurized deck space a ship owned became vertical while the ring was de-spun and locked to some station's orientation. You didn't give up a centimeter of downside deck space to a facility that wasn't manned during dock, and that meant this was one important facility to *Corinthian,* and prisoners weren't unusual—or let off to station jurisdiction, where you'd think a hired-crew ship would be glad to dump its problems for good and all.

You did get the skuz of the spacer trade among hire-ons, they had that universal reputation. A Family ship very rarely took one or accepted a passenger, and that only after careful background checks and an oath from God that the individual was trustworthy. But this . . . this place, occupying valuable dock-positive space, was built to contain people the ship didn't intend to turn over to station authorities, people who could try to break out and take over the ship. The cable arrangement meant you couldn't get further across the cell than they wanted you to go. The bracelet had a kind of lock he'd never seen before, a lever that shut, that had no wobble in it, no hint of how it opened.

He went back and sat down on the bunk, and worked and worked at the lock in frightened silence.

There wasn't anything else to do. Wasn't any other hope. He didn't know if they'd caught Marie or if they were still looking for her. If he was held hostage—that was a joke.

He wasn't sure at this point that Marie wanted him back. Justifiably.

— *iii* —

THE LOADING OPERATION WAS A steady flow of data on Austin's office monitor, a steady stream of canisters thumping through the cargo access port, contiguous at the moment with the passenger ring, so it sounded through *Corinthian*'s ring structure like some monstrous heartbeat.

Machine parts was the principal load they were taking; also radioactives, medical and industrial, transshipped; chemicals, organic and otherwise; minicans of rejuv, lately legal, tapes, transshipped; minicans of personal goods and small commercial freight, transshipped and some originated at Viking—no mail: they hadn't a bond for that, and he didn't want the background check. But this was the payout cargo, this was the one where Miller bought on spec and they rebought, and sold at their destination; this was the one that paid the bills and kept them running. It was an eclectic load, and a few minicans went up the lift and into the ring, where they'd jury-rigged passenger accommodations into warm-cargo space.

The further you got from Earth the pricier Earth goods got, simple proposition, but the further you got from civilization, the pricier, too, the sweet taste of the motherworld. And pay they would, in credit and in various ways.

If—

Com beeped. *"Excuse me, sir,"* the voice said, from the bridge. *"Marie Hawkins. On the com. For you. Do you want to take the call?"*

Damn the woman!

Tell her go to hell? Let *her* have the frustration?

Better hear the threats, he thought. Better give the woman the satisfaction. Five got ten she *wasn't* calling with Mischa Hawkins' blessing and go-ahead. The woman was still on the docks somewhere. *Corinthian* had gone on the boards as Departure: 1400h. And if she was out there—and he'd bet she was—she knew.

"Quillan?"

"Sir?"

"She's at a phone. Probably within sight of our dockside. Get a team looking."

Not a damned word from Mischa Hawkins. The cops hadn't arrested anybody after the set-to, just tagged the ships involved and a judge had slapped both *Corinthian* and *Sprite* with thousand credit fines, with a warning.

Damned right a warning. "You keep your people clear," he'd phoned *Sprite* to say. "And we will."

"Aye," Quillan said. *"Put her through, sir?"*

"Put her through," he said, and heard the click. "Marie Hawkins?"

"You son of a bitch," Marie Hawkins said. *"How are you, Austin?"*

"Oh, getting along. How have you been?"

"Just fine. Alive. Saner than you'd like. I just wanted to call and thank you."

"That's nice." You wondered where she'd planted the bomb. Or if she knew they had her kid. "Did you have something more in mind? It's been a few years, Marie. Things got a little out of hand. I apologize for that."

"You're senior captain now. Congratulations. And a—is she your wife?"

"Nothing official. It's just not our style."

"Beatrice Perrault."

What in *hell* was the woman after?

Beatrice at least was safe, on duty. Christian was below, inside the ship.

"Beatrice, yes. I hear you've moved up to cargo officer. Congratulations. How do you like the work?"

"Love it. I owe you so much. My start in life. My son."

Did she know? He had no idea.

"Would you like to come aboard, Hawkins? Have a drink, discuss mutual interests?" He didn't think so. Possibly she was taping the call, for playback to authorities. He didn't expect an acceptance. "There's time before undock. You've noticed we *are* pulling out."

"I've noticed," Marie Hawkins said.

"So what about the drink? Apologies?"

"I don't think so."

She hung up. He shouldn't have pushed.

"Captain, we—"

"—didn't have time. Damn it, watch the frontage! If she's calling from one of the bars, we can still catch her. Haul her in, if you can do it without a fuss. Relay that."

"We're looking."

Damned crazy woman. Mischa Hawkins probably didn't know where she was, or they'd cheerfully reel her in. *Sprite* was on warning with station authorities, and Hawkins had sent one terse message: *Call us if you have any contact with any* Sprite *crew. Neither of us can afford this.*

Nobody'd raised hell with station offices yet about the missing son—so they hadn't figured where *Thomas* Hawkins was, yet. Probably they thought he was keeping company with Marie.

Which meant if they didn't find Marie, they couldn't know to the contrary; Marie probably thought her kid was with the group the cops had turned back to *Sprite* and told stay off the docks—Marie wasn't interested in being found, and so long as Marie stayed out of *Sprite's* reach, nobody was going to know Thomas was missing.

If they couldn't catch her—she was still doing *Corinthian* a favor, just staying out there. Best hope they had of getting out of here.

—— *iv* ——

"CHRISTIAN."

Christian cut his eyes toward the overhead and leaned his

back against the wall. Where it figuratively was, already, with Austin.

"Sir."

"You stay inside the ship. That's an order, boy."

"I was just going. . ."

"Maxie's seeing to it. I want a double-check on the warm-hold count. Get on it."

"That's Maxie's job!"

"See to it, damn you! I'm full up with your excuses!"

"Yes, sir," he said, and when he heard the com click out, pounded the paneling with his fist.

Saby put her head out of ops and stared.

"What?"

"What, what, Austin's what, he's on my case, is what." He stalked to the office, shoved past Saby and sat down at the console.

Punched keys. *Not* his favorite job. Maxie's job, and, thanks to brother Thomas and his crazy mother, no last tour on dockside, no chance to slip back to the shop for the earrings Capella had lusted after, no chance to go back to the vid shop for the tapes he'd eyed . . . you didn't load up on stuff while you were on liberty, you waited till the last minute, if you didn't want to pay delivery.

Cheap cost, on this occasion.

Saby shot him a feed from her terminal. Lots and lots of boring serial numbers and clearances.

"So is anybody asking about this kid?" Saby asked.

"How would I know? Austin's not talking. Beatrice is hung over as hell and on station. Damned Family-ship prig."

"I'd be scared," Saby said. "In his place, I'd be damned scared."

"He's a Family Boy. Ship-share, all the best, don't you know. I wish I'd left him. Say he must've hid out after the fight, we wouldn't have this problem." He set the computer to scan for WH's and location, the sole intellectual function the job needed for the pass. "His mother's out there looking for

Austin, Austin's hiding aboard, hauls the whole damn crew in, it's damned ridiculous. Now my half-brother's gone poking about in Miller's and we've got ourselves a problem."

"What was he doing in Miller's?"

"Looking for his mama, what else?"

"I'd like to know what mama was looking for. It wasn't Austin."

Cousin Sabrina had a brain. Cousin Sabrina was using it. He shoved back from the console, turned the chair and looked at her, rethinking, absent temper, *what* Thomas Bowe-Hawkins had been doing scraping labels.

"What's her source?" he asked Saby. "Since you know so much."

"I don't know what her source is. He might."

Saby'd wiped his nose when he was a brat—till he got older and Saby had justly told him go to hell. Now he ran with Capella, Saby supered the computer techs, handled Hires, trouble-shot cargo functions at need, and took her lovers on dockside. With all the dockside willies to choose from, she hadn't hired or slept with a psych-case yet.

Better than Austin could claim. Austin listened, when *Saby* said who was crazy and who wasn't.

So where did she always see that far ahead of him, damn her?

The computer came up with a Warm-Hold headed for the wrong hold, and beeped.

Damn, damn, and damn. "Who in hell checked that through? Can anybody in our crew read, or just maybe use the laser, God! I don't believe this." He punched through to the dock chief. "—Connie, Connie, do you hear? I want a number pulled off the list, fast, 987-7. Get that mother upside into warm 2 before they load it in, that's not for deep cold."

Connie took his time writing it down. Connie said they'd look for the number. Christian ran his hand through his hair and wondered how long it had been since he'd slept.

Half-brother. With a mother out there looking for Austin's hide. And a real interest in the cans.

Yeah.

Tom Hawkins knew.

"If the program finds another mis-route, handle it, will you?"

"Where are you going? —You better not go out there."

"I'm not going any damned where. It's a good question." He put in a call for Austin's office, the direct link. "Austin?"

"What's the problem?" came back, not patiently.

"Austin? My half-brother down here? Saby's got a real interesting idea. Marie Hawkins being onto something . . . half-brother knows how, and who, and if there's cops mixed up in it."

Silence from the office.

"So we should ask him," he said, since Austin didn't draw the conclusion.

"Are you finally figuring that out?"

"I'm not fucking stupid, *sir!*"

Which wasn't the brightest thing to do with Austin when Austin was looking for a fault. He heard the com cut out. He tried the re-call.

Ignored. Ignored, ignored and ignored.

"Son of a *bitch!*" he yelled, at no one accessible, and slammed his fist onto the console.

Connie came back on with, *"I think it already went in, Chris. We got to reverse the loader to get it back."*

"Get it out," he said. And when Connie came back on with, Can we wait till we're finished loading? he checked the contents, only about 50,000 credits worth of fancy liquor that didn't like freezing, and said, kindly, nicely, "No, you get the sod that passed this list, have him find two volunteers, and you have him hand-carry that mother topside through the lift."

"That's against union—"

"You carry it, Connie, or you get it carried! Those are your choices! Hear me?"

"Yessir."

He cut the connection. He sat glaring at the computer screen, and felt Saby staring at him, a rational, too-damned-superior presence prickling at his shoulder-blades.

So he wasn't reasonable. So was Austin? So was Beatrice? So was anybody in the upper end c-oh-c, reasonable? It wasn't a job requirement.

—— *v* ——

ANESTHETIC AFTEREFFECTS DIDN'T make a body feel at all good, Tom decided. He'd never had anesthetic before, assuming it was something medical and not outright illicit—but once he'd decided that he couldn't get the bracelet off, that he couldn't reach any useful switch panel and he couldn't do anything, in general, except wait, sweat, and nurse his headache, he figured he could just as well do that flat on his back on the bunk. There was a white-diamond patch on a let-down on the wall over the bunk—universal symbol for deep-space emergency supplies. He flipped it in idle curiosity and it was stocked with trank and nutri-paks. He was tempted, about the trank— just time-out and let the hours pass. But you didn't abuse the stuff. And the packs were for emergency—you left them for that. You toughed it out, that was all, though, please God, he wasn't going to need them, they'd get him out of here.

His stomach was upset, his head hurt more than the wrist did—that he was outright scared might account for a good part of the upset, but he kept trying to keep a reasonable attitude. *Corinthian,* in his best theory, was hanging on to him as insurance for Marie's good behavior. *Corinthian* didn't want him. It was going to be all right. Somehow the captains would sort it out and get Marie back and him back and *Corinthian* would leave Viking port before anybody got hurt.

Or Marie would figure the game, notify the cops, call the lawyers and get him out of this herself. Beat out Austin Bowe for good and all, and maybe after that, please God, get her life turned around.

Make her peace with him, and Mischa, and the universe in general.

Yeah. And Viking would reverse its spin and the sun would burn black. He couldn't even recognize the Marie that scenario would ask to exist.

Meanwhile the thump in the guts of *Corinthian* kept up, regular as a heartbeat. Nobody interrupted the loading, no contingent of police came looking. Wherever Marie was, she couldn't or wouldn't stop the flow of goods into *Corinthian*.

A man passed the cell and stopped. Tom lifted his head, stared at the man between his feet, the man looked at him as if he was a museum exhibit, and walked on. Skuzzy-looking bastard, Tom thought with a prickling of defensive instincts. Wouldn't like to meet that one on dockside, and that was walking the corridors out there.

That was the first.

Then others, not much better—older guys, a few in green coveralls: the rest in the skintights that were getting to be popular, earrings, glitz-stripes on the skin, jewelry . . . not a real tidy lot, he said to himself, a few of them worse than others—and with no front wall and no privacy in the cell he was sitting there for all of them to stare at.

Most did. Some laughed, as if it was funny he was there. He didn't get the point. "Well, well, well, who's this pretty thing?" a guy asked—a guy with his hair in braids, a tattoo around his neck, and so many tattoos on his bare arms he was green and purple, all snakes.

Tom stared. He would have stared on dockside. He'd not *seen* that many tattoos. "You want a chocolate?" the tattooed man said. He was drunk. Extremely. Others grabbed him away.

He didn't know what to think. He got to his feet and went to the bars to look after the group and see what was going on in the corridor, wondering whether that was an authorized entry or were dock-crawlers taking a drunken tour of the ship while the cargo ports were open. He heard shouts in the corridors, the usual noises of meetings and comparisons of stories, after a liberty.

Crew, he decided.

Suddenly the noises weren't friendly. He heard angry shouts, guessed from chance words he could pick up that two of the crew had had a prior set-to on dockside, and heard other voices trying to break it up, some woman yelling there were going to be officers.

"He's got a knife!" somebody yelled. Somebody hit the paneled walls, he heard the thump. And someone yelled, "Get him, get him, *get him!*"

Another thump, a lot of shouting. He couldn't see anything. Then:

"Damn, it's Michaels," he heard, and by everything he heard, some officer had come in on it, was asking questions, who'd started it, who'd flashed a weapon. A man got hauled off to infirmary on this Michaels' orders, and then. . .

Then a deal of cursing, a thump again against the paneling, and a measured, meaty thud, of something meeting flesh, not just the once or twice he thought might be justified, but it went on, and on, and on, until the screaming stopped, and something heavy hit the deck.

"Get him out of here," somebody said. The voices after that were all quiet.

He found himself with a death-grip on the bars, shivering in a cold more inside than out, and more than ever wanting out of this cell.

Not a Family ship. He'd just had a demonstration what the penalties were, and how they were dealt out. No word with the captain, nothing of the sort.

He'd thought he'd had a hard life. Now *Sprite* seemed a sheltered, protected existence, where Mischa's frown was a reprimand, where crew didn't carry knives against their shipmates. He'd never heard the sounds he'd just heard, out of any human being, sounds that had gone straight to his nerves, and brought a quiet over the whole ship.

He heard other traffic in the corridor and retreated from the gridwork, went back to his bunk and sat down with his back to the face of the cell, so he wouldn't have to deal with anybody. Wherever he went the cable trailed, and reminded him that even if the door opened he hadn't a chance at escaping . . . or putting up damn much of a fight against anybody with a key and access to the cable switch.

Ransom wouldn't work. He'd been in a place he shouldn't have been and they knew he knew, and if the station cops came asking, he didn't know what *Corinthian* might do, but he didn't think they were going to turn him loose to tell the police or the merchant trade at large what he'd been doing or what he'd seen and not seen.

Not if gossip was right about *Corinthian*'s business.

Traffic came and went outside.

And it had to be board-call, *Corinthian* calling in its crew, even while the loading was still going on. You didn't ordinarily crowd up the ship with crew underfoot until they had something to do—unless they'd for some reason had to get off the docks.

Unless they were shortening their dock time and planning to pull out.

In which case he didn't see a thing Mischa or Marie could do about it. Station police could say Stop, and demand to search the ship, but only if they could come up with plausible evidence: a merchanter deck was the same as foreign territory, merchanters didn't allow boarders as a matter of principle, while stations depended so much on ship traffic they just wouldn't push that point unless they had very clear evidence of a customs crime.

That left him nothing to do but sit and worry at the lock. He searched the bath for anything he could use for a pick, but he couldn't find anything—there weren't any drawers, and he tried bashing it with the butt of the wall-mounted razor.

But it didn't do any good.

Just after that spate of noise-making, the loading stopped.

The whole ship sat in silence, except the rush of air in the vents.

He went to the bars again, trying to see something, anything to tell him what was going on.

Then came the unmistakable thump as the hatch sealed. A moment later the louder thump as the lines closed down and detached, and a siren sounded throughout the ship, no word from the captain, just that lonely, warning sound that said hazard, hazard, take stations, the ship is moving.

It was a nightmare. The misjudgment. The mistakes he'd made, that led this direction, step by step. Thinking that he'd win Marie's . . . acceptance, if no more than that. He'd gambled his safety. Thought he might win Marie's acceptance—and her sanity. And he'd lost.

He hoped Marie was free, and safe. He hoped nobody had gotten hurt on his account.

But it was decidedly time to sit down and take hold. Which he did, with a lump gathering in his throat. He located the safety restraints on the bunk and sat down, cross-legged, not expecting but a short zero *g,* and a gentle shove, not worth belting in for.

It was far more than a gentle shove. He grabbed the frame of the bunk and the safety hold on the wall, and braced his feet, one on the deck and one on the mattress—thinking he'd just made a serious mistake.

He didn't know how long the acceleration was going to last. He dared not let go the handholds he had to get the safety restraints fastened. His heart was going doubletime.

He didn't *like* the ship putting out like that. He didn't *like* a pilot who skirted the regs and a bridge that didn't warn people when they were moving.

It struck him then that there couldn't be kids or seniors aboard. It just wasn't, wasn't, wasn't a Family ship, never mistake it again, and if he didn't lose his grip and break his neck during launch, he'd be luckier than he deserved for trusting anything about it.

They went inertial then, a moment of float, and he snatched the restraints across and jammed the first and the second clip shut with shaking hands.

After that he lay flat on his back and felt the stomach-jolting *g*-shifts of maneuver of a ship that didn't care about crew comfort, and didn't engage the ring for crew safety, or warn anyone beyond sounding the siren.

In a hurry to leave and doing a show-off bit of maneuvering, he could read it—screw you all, the pilot was saying to *Sprite,* and to Viking, and maybe to all civilized places, maybe just because Austin Bowe was pissed, who knew?

Chapter Four

— i —

"Marie."

Depend on it. Saja found her. Turned up at her elbow in the Trade Bureau offices, all concern, all indignation.

Marie keyed up another file in the Financial Access section, downloaded it . . . they said a ship at Viking Free Port had open access to the trade records. Translation: they let you look. If you understood the software and knew what files might be significant, good luck, you had a chance, but the too-damned-helpful system wanted to pre-digest the reports for you if you got into the market area, not give you access to the raw data, and *that* was a piece of computer cheek.

So *Corinthian* had pulled out. Spooked out, left, maybe to change its whole pattern, her worst fear, and she was not in a mood to be lectured to by Family.

Maybe, with luck, and substantial evidence, she could get the cops into Miller's warehouse.

"Marie."

"I'm not deaf." The station files were in database and wouldn't be accessed from *Sprite*'s ops boards, the Rules were against it. Unfortunately so was the barrier system. So one trekked in and asked questions, and even load-splicing couldn't fit the total DB onto any data storage medium that the casual questioner might carry into the Trade Bureau.

"Mischa's been worried."

"I don't know why." Another splice. Another capture. Hours to reconstruct the bastard when she got it home.

"He's not happy about the fines, Marie."

"I imagine not. Sorry about that. We'll make it up."

"You're due back to handle offloading."

"Charles can do it. He's perfectly competent."

"What are you doing?"

"Trade information. Data. What else is the Trade Bureau for?"

"Fine. Fine. I'll tell him. —Tell Tom get his rear back on duty. You don't need him here."

Saja was Tom's officer, on the bridge. Saja had reason to ask.

Saja had actual need-to-know where Tom was. And should, by now. She turned away from the monitor and looked at him straight-on, with the least disturbed inkling of things not quite in order.

"He's not with me," she said. "Have the cops got him?"

"The cops didn't arrest anybody, either side. He's not with you. He's not on the ship. I called them five minutes ago, max."

Wandering around the docks looking for her. "The damned fool," she said.

"That ship's out of dock, Marie. It's outbound."

She knew where the ship was. She looked at the clock on the wall of the Trade Bureau. Hours out. Computers ate up human time—you lost track between keystrokes and during processing.

And Saja was saying Tom could be *with* that ship?

She didn't think so. "He's not that stupid. He's searching the bars, is where he is."

"We've got people all over the bars. We're looking. For you. And for Tom. You're accounted for. Where's Tom?"

"Wherever he thinks I'd go. Bars. Sleepovers. —Miller Transship." She didn't want to suggest that last name. She didn't want them forewarned. But—"*Corinthian*'s broker. Miller Transship. Warehouses. Phone *Sprite*-com, get them to inquire at Miller's, just down the row from *Corinthian*'s berth."

"Miller's," Saja said, and went, she supposed, for a phone.

They just weren't searching right. Tom was going to duck them. The kid was no fool.

But the more they stamped around searching for the damn kid, disturbing evidence. . .

Most urgently, they needed to find the damn kid and quit stirring things up, before he or they did do something stupid.

She was uneasy. Couldn't really remember where she was in the data problem. Damn the brat, he'd always had a knack for disturbing her concentration.

And Tom probably *was* staying out of reach and deliberately out of touch with *Sprite* simply because he thought *she* was staying out of touch (true, until now) and he was looking for her. It could take a while to reel him in.

Though you'd think once *Corinthian* had gone on the board for Departure, the kid would catch a notion that the game was up at that point, retreat, call *Sprite* and report in . . . since *she,* at that point, had no more reason to stay under-surface.

Damn.

He *would* show up. He *had* to show up. She didn't want to leave her search looking for an erratic, jump-at-shadows brat who was old enough to take care of himself.

She jabbed a key, dumped the current operation, pocketed her data-cards on the way to the door, and swore to kill the kid when she found him.

—— *ii* ——

TOM STARED AT THE CEILING, feeling the push on the ship and thinking how if he'd had the presence of mind to have counted when the shove started he could have told something about the actual v, based on the undock pattern.

But what did it matter? *Corinthian* was going and he was going with it,

No way *Sprite* could throw over that government contract to chase after him. Not even Marie could talk them into it.

Only hope to God that Mischa's fears were exaggerated and *Corinthian* wasn't going to lay for *Sprite* out in the dark.

Out in the same dark, a body could go out the airlock and never be reported, if his own biological father wanted to get rid of him. And what paternal interest had Austin Bowe ever needed in the offspring he'd probably . . . spacer-fashion . . . scattered on God-knew-what ships? Men didn't generally keep up with their own. They had their own ship-board nieces and nephews, if they had sisters. And always they had cousins. Men didn't have to give a damn. And Bowe hadn't a reputation for fatherly concern. The Bowe he'd heard about *could* throw a man out the airlock.

Better than some ways to go, he thought in morbid self-persuasion, while the ship ripped along toward that deep cold. The absolute zero was supposed to get you before you felt much. You froze solid before you could get a breath of vacuum. You frosted your lungs. Your eyes froze and your blood froze and you'd be floating with the dust, exactly the way your outbound breath had left you—until some star near enough went nova and you got shoved along on the wavefront and included in the infall of a next-generation star.

Or none might be near enough and you'd just drift there till entropy slowed down the stars for good.

A permanent sort of half-life, as it were.

Permanent as the galaxy. No damn *fathers* to deal with.

Father, hell! There had to be a word for a guy with as little invested as Austin Bowe.

Rapist talked about his relations with the mother in question. Society hadn't made a word for his relations with the kid that resulted.

Hadn't made a word for the situation between them or given him a word he wanted to say to Austin Bowe.

Thanks for screwing my mother? Thanks for not showing up till now. Screw *you,* sir, for a damned self-centered son of a bitch.

Acceleration was steady at +2 or thereabouts. The straps would hold against five and six times that. He'd no fear of them giving way. But *Corinthian* spent energy like it was handed out free, and he measured his breaths, feeling the anger of a ship forced out of port, maybe out of civilization altogether.

Or—remotely possible, if Marie had found her evidence— and his heart picked up a beat—they could have the military on their tail.

Which wasn't good news, to think of it. Go up in a fireball, they would, then, and good-bye Tom Hawkins.

It was a nightmare. He didn't know where it had started, whether he'd been in it all his life and this turn of things was someone else's doing, or whether he was that abysmally stupid he'd let himself in for it, going into that warehouse and caring about Marie.

He didn't want to think about reasons. He'd never got it straight about caring for people. His aunt Lydia who'd studied psych had told him when he was five he was emotionally deprived and he never would be normal. So he figured he had to copy, because he was different enough, and he figured he'd better pick good people to copy, like his nursery-mates, some-times, like Marie sometimes, when he was living with her. Like Saja, again, when he got to know Saja. Mischa. . .

Definitely not Mischa.

Saja was all right. People liked Saja. But Saja wasn't stupid.

Saja wouldn't have gotten into it. Even if he cared what happened to Marie. And he didn't think it was Marie's fault, him being in the warehouse, he couldn't blame that on her.

He couldn't tell why things happened, most of the time. He certainly couldn't figure this one. He didn't know as much as most people. He'd always figured in the scales of the universe he'd somehow come a little short of what ordinary people got, and not known a lot of things ordinary people knew. It wasn't not knowing his father. A lot of people didn't know that. It was not knowing other things. It was like so damn many contrary signals from Marie and from aunt Lydia and Mischa and them changing their stories all the time, and the fact nobody else liked him much, of his agemates. There was just something wrong, there was something he'd missed, and getting snatched away from *Sprite* like that, and never seeing anybody again, it was just one more ripping away of information he couldn't get now. He wasn't going back, nobody could get back to their ship unless they were on the same route . . . he'd accumulate station-debt waiting, even if Bowe let him go finally back at Viking; and he wasn't honestly sure Mischa would spend the ship-account to get him out of hock.

Marie would. Marie was rich in ship-account.

But maybe Marie wouldn't want him at all, then, except to get information about Bowe. Maybe she'd call him a fool and say she didn't know why she'd bought him back . . . he could hear her tone of voice, as if she were talking to him right now.

But when he imagined Marie yelling at him about being a fool, about going in the warehouse, it sort of put things in perspective, as if now he knew what he'd done, and where he'd been stupid, trying to intervene in Marie's business. The law of the universe was, Marie knew what she was doing, and you didn't put your hands into it or you risked your fingers. *That* was the mistake he'd made.

So he did understand. And the universe had a little more solid shape around him.

But he decided then, calmly, that he did want to meet Austin

Bowe after all—at least to see the man and know whether they looked alike, or what Marie had seen staring back at her all these years. That would tell him something, too, about the way of things. And that information was on this ship. That was something he could learn about himself. He could listen to Bowe. He could find out the man's habits and figure out if there was anything genetic that just somehow he'd gotten, in the way of temperament, or whatever else could get through the sieve of genetic code.

Marie said . . . your father's temper. Marie said . . . your father's manners. Your father's behavior . . . And he *tried* to cure it in himself, he tried not to lose his temper and he tried not to be rude, and all the other things Marie attributed to his genes.

Aunt Lydia said most people could pattern themselves off positives. He learned to avoid negatives. Aunt Lydia said he had to define himself, by himself.

And most of all . . . not do things that pushed Marie's buttons.

But maybe—it was a dangerous, undermining thought, and he worked all around it for a moment—maybe, even remotely possibly . . . there might even be another side to Austin Bowe. Maybe Marie'd pushed *his* buttons, the way she had other people's, and things had just blown up.

Not to excuse what happened. Nothing could do that.

But maybe what she'd told Mischa and what Mischa had told her might have confused the facts.

And he didn't know why Marie should have gotten the entire truth from Mischa. *He* never had.

And . . . more and more dangerous a thought . . . if there was another side, considering the position he was in, it did make sense to ask Bowe's side of things. And even if it was bad . . . and even if he couldn't accept it . . . considering he was stuck here, considering he had somehow to get along with this crew. . .

Such as they were.

. . . he'd learned what happened when you (Lydia's saying) poisoned the water you had to drink from.

He didn't know where this ship went. The rumor-mongering They who ran rampant on *Sprite* said it didn't stay on the charts, that it found Mazianni ports somewhere in the great dark Forever.

He could handle that, he supposed. If all *Corinthian* did was trade with them, he could justify that . . . after all, nobody had a guarantee the goods that *Sprite* brought to port didn't end up being cheated over and run through illegal channels. They weren't responsible. It wasn't immoral. Illegal, highly, but it wasn't like they were doing anything that cost any lives. . . .

He began to sink slowly into the mattress surface. That was the passenger ring engaging as *Corinthian* went inertial at its outbound velocity.

A *v* far more than most merchanters handled. Light-mass cargo, he thought, staring bleakly at the sound-baffling overhead. Had to be light mass, relative to the engine cap. You wondered what they were hauling.

Luxuries was the commonest low-mass article. Food-stuffs that wouldn't compress. But generally, Viking exported high-mass items, so you hauled heavy, and took the light stuff for—

A siren blew three short bursts. Disaster? he wondered, taking a grip. His heart had skipped a beat. His thoughts went skittering over every horizon, leaving nothing but the wide dark, and the cosmic chance of a high-energy rock in their path.

Then over com, a woman's voice, accented with a ship-speak he didn't recognize.

"We are inertial for the duration, in count for departure. Count now is . . . sixty seconds, mark."

His heart found the missed beat, thudded along in heavy anticipation. It was real. They were going. He reached for the panel with the white diamond, got the drug out, the needle-pack—shivering-scared, until he had that in his fist. If you didn't have that you didn't come out of jump whole, you left pieces of yourself . . . that was what the universal They also said, and if you were curious on that topic . . . they had wards on certain stations where they sent the kids that experimented with hyperspace, and the unlucky working spacers that for some emergency or another hadn't had a pack in reach.

" . . . *count is twenty and running.*"

He had it. He had it. He was all right, as all right ran, on this ship.

" . . . *fifteen.*"

He thought about Marie. He thought he loved her.

(He didn't, really, but Lydia said he wasn't going to be capable of it, yet. Like the prince in the fairy story, he was going to be crazy until somebody loved him . . .)

But if he had loved anybody it was Marie, and he hadn't loved anybody, if not her, and right now the place where Marie ought to fit—felt like a twisty hollow spot, filled up with anger and hurt where she'd lied to him and ducked out on him, and absolute terror that he'd never see her again and never know what had happened to her.

Because Marie was the edges of the universe. Marie was right and wrong. Marie was the place to go to for the answers and he didn't have a map without her.

Lydia'd say that wasn't normal either. But it was all he had. And nobody else was going to get him out of this. Nobody else gave a damn.

Lydia didn't. Lydia said he was a misfit and a time bomb on the ship. Lydia'd said he'd go off the edge someday, and they ought to find him a nice safe berth on a station, where he could get adopted.

He had nightmares about Lydia finding ways to leave him. Like Lydia convincing Mischa, who didn't like him anyway. And when Marie would send him back to the nursery because she was sick of him, and when the nursery would complain that he was too old, he hurt the younger kids and he wouldn't take their sleep cycle, because all the other kids and all the mothers except Marie were on mainday. . . .

And the nursery workers all wanted to watch vids while the

kids were asleep, but they wouldn't let him watch the ones they did, they said go to bed, go to sleep, if he just behaved himself Marie might take him back. . . .

The siren sounded again. Warning of jump imminent.

"Count is five . . . four. . . ."

He squeezed the pack. Felt the sting of the needle.

" . . . three . . . two . . ."

Marie wasn't coming, wasn't ever coming to get him, where he was going.

— *iii* —

THE WAVEFRONT OF *CORINTHIAN*'s passage was still coming at them when the clock on *Sprite*'s bridge said to anybody who knew anything that *Corinthian* had just left the system.

That information hit Marie in the gut—for God knew what reason, because, dammit, she didn't owe the kid. It was the other way around. Highly, the other way around. She'd searched up and down the frontage where she'd left him, she'd gone back to *Sprite* to pursue matters as far as she dared with the police, almost to the point of getting swept up and detained herself. It hadn't been a good experience, and meanwhile *Sprite* crew wholesale was still out searching every nook in every bar and shop they could think of for a damned elusive twenty-three-year-old offspring who ought occasionally to read the schedule boards.

Miller Transship claimed to know nothing. The station police called station Central, and Central called the stationmaster, who called *Corinthian* long-distance, himself, big deal, while *Corinthian* was outbound.

Surprise: *Corinthian* denied all knowledge of Hawkins personnel aboard.

Then *Corinthian* said, which they needn't have said . . . that if they should turn out to have a stowaway, they'd drop him at their next port.

The stationmaster said, all mealy-mouthed, Do that, and signed off.

In justice . . . there wasn't a choice about it. There wasn't a ship in hell or Viking system that could chase that bastard down once they'd finally roused the stationmaster with word something could be wrong . . . even *Sprite*, mostly empty. Couldn't, with the head start he'd have had, and their tanks still drawing . . . and for a station to call an outbound ship to dump *v* and limp back the long slow days it would take to reach station from where they were, plus buck the outbound traffic, against all regulation . . . meant big lawsuits if station couldn't prove their case; and catch-me-if-you-can if the merchanter in question wanted to claim they were in progress for jump and missed the transmission. By the time they got back again, witnesses had scattered and it was, again, better have good evidence and a good reason.

So they had to watch the son of a bitch become a blip on station scopes.

And that last, that unnecessary bit of information about stowaways, was a clear message from Bowe, damn his smug face—*she* knew. They could just as well pull in the search teams, Tom *was* on that ship, Bowe had taken away the only thing she had of his, and the remark about dropping Tom 'at their next port' was a threat, not a reassurance. God knew what their 'next port' was, if it wasn't some Mazianni carrier in want of personnel.

If there'd just been proof to give the police, if there'd been any concrete evidence of a kidnapping. . .

But what could they have done? If she got the evidence now, the station administration could bar *Corinthian* from coming back—supposing the evidence was iron-clad. But it wouldn't be. It was all circumstantial. If the station needed their commerce more than they needed justice done. . .

But Viking was just newly a free port. Viking didn't want any dirty, unfathomable merchanter quarrel on its shiny new trade treaty. *Sprite* was from one side of the Line. *Corinthian* was from another. The next time *Corinthian* docked, was Viking going to search *Corinthian* for personnel *Corinthian* had plainly just told the stationmaster wasn't going to be aboard next time?

"It's gone," Mischa said with a shrug of his shoulders. "Nothing we can do."

Nothing we can do.

Nothing we can bloody do.

A sanctimonious shrug from Mischa, who'd been watching the clock—and was damned well satisfied to wash his hands of Tom Bowe-Hawkins.

"Nothing we can do," she echoed him. "You son of a bitch, you mealy-mouthed, self-serving son of a bitch, you *know* he's on that ship!"

"That's far from certain, Marie."

"Oh, nothing's ever absolute with you, nothing's ever just quite clear, is it?"

"Marie. This is the bridge. You're on the bridge. Control it, can we?"

" 'Control it, can we?' 'Control it?' 'Just shut up, Marie? We know you're not quite stable, Marie? Too bad about your *kid*, Marie, you can get another one? Why don't you go get *laid*, Marie, and cure your Problem while you're at it, Marie!' "

"Reel it in, Marie, you never gave a damn about that boy!"

"I never gave a damn? Oh, let's talk about giving a *damn*, Mischa, excuse me, *captain* Hawkins. They could sell him to the Fleet for all we know—they're always short of personnel, he's a good-looking kid, and we know what happens to good-looking kids they get their hands on, don't we, captain Hawkins?"

"We don't even know he's not on dockside. Let's talk about ducking orders, let's talk about kiting off on your own, why don't we? The kid had orders to keep up with you and keep in touch. He violated those orders or we wouldn't be asking where he is right now."

"Oh, now it's *his* fault! Everything's someone else's fault."

"Fault never lands in your lap, does it? You ditched your tag, Marie. I'd have thought you'd have learned your lesson twenty years ago."

"Damn your interference! If I hadn't had to dodge you, I'd have the evidence on that son of a bitch, we'd have him screwed with the port authority and Tom wouldn't be in Bowe's ship right now!"

"There is nothing we can do, Marie."

"There was nothing you could do on Mariner, either, was there? I know what it feels like, Mischa, *I know,* and I don't take 'nothing we can do.' That son of a bitch is laughing at us, he's *laughing* at us, do you hear? Or do you give a damn?"

"Marie,—"

"Marie, Marie, Marie! We know his vector, I know that ship, I know what his elapsed-time is like, he's going for Tripoint, and on to Pell, and we can catch him there. He won't be expecting it."

"Out of the question."

"Hell with you!"

"Marie, let's talk sanity. He may not be going on to Pell. You may not know his schedule as well as you think you do. We're not going off in the dark with that ship. We're not equipped for that. No way in hell, Marie. No way in hell!"

She looked at the clock, jaw clenched, arms folded, as the minutes kept going. Let Mischa think he'd won. Let Mischa think he'd made his point.

"I can make the credit at Pell, Mischa. You load us for Pell and I can turn a profit." She lifted her hand. "Swear to God."

"Out of the bloody question."

"No, it isn't."

"For God's sake, that's across the Line, they'd charge us through the nose for a berth, we've no account there, and if you're right about Bowe, the kid will never see Pell. . . ."

"The kid, the kid, the boy's got a name."

"Thomas *Bowe*-Hawkins."

Tried to make her blow her composure. But she knew what

she was going to do, now. She knew. And when she knew, she smiled at him, cold and immovable as a law of physics.

"Pell," she said, "and we make a profit on the run. Or get yourself a new cargo chief."

"It's no bet."

"I'm not betting. I'm telling you. If it's not Pell—get yourself another cargo chief. I quit. I'll find a way to Pell."

"You're out of your mind, Marie."

"So you've said. To everyone in the Family. But you know how this ship was doing before, and how it's doing now. Cold, hard numbers, captain, *sir*. I know what I'm worth. I've got the numbers for Pell. No question I can make our dock charges *and* come up in the black. Swear to God I can. Or I kiss you all good-bye, right here."

"Marie, this isn't even worth talking about. Go cool down."

"Cold as deep space, darling brother, and dead serious."

"That ship could be meeting some Mazianni carrier right out there at Tripoint in two weeks. We could run right into it."

"For *what?* Bowe told them he'd have a kid to trade them? They do those deals in the deep dark. Mazian's ships don't come in this far."

"We have rendezvous with our regulars, we have people's lives you're proposing to disrupt, appointments—"

"We'll get back on schedule. We'll all survive a little sexual deprivation."

"Try a sex life! It'll improve your mental health!"

"Mon-ey, Mischa. Mon-ey. Or poverty. Skimping to make ends meet, the way we did when dear Robert was running the cargo section. Because he *will* be, again. Make your choice."

"You don't sit on this ship and not work."

"You weren't listening, Mischa, dear, I said I was leaving the ship. I'll find a way. I'm damned good. And *good* ships anywhere it wants to."

"As hired crew. You *think* you'd like your shipmates on a hired-crew ship. Earn your way in bed, why don't you?"

"Because I don't have to. I can have passage on a Pell-bound ship in four hours, captain Hawkins, you watch me, because the numbers are in my *head,* and I'll use 'em, you'd better bet I will. I'm crazy Marie, aren't I?"

"You're talking like it."

"Fine! I'll put it to a vote in the Family, *captain,* sir, which of us this ship wants to have making the decisions. I'll tell you even Robert A. will vote to keep me, because *he* doesn't want the job back, he doesn't want to lose his creature comforts. Neither do any of the seniors, and the juniors can't touch me! Let all the Hawkinses decide. I'll challenge you for the captaincy if I have to. And I have the right to call a vote."

"And make a fool of yourself! Everybody knows—"

"I'm sure you've told them often enough. Poor Marie. Poor crazy Marie. Poor crazy Marie who's the reason this ship runs in the black—"

"Poor crazy Marie who's the reason we lost Mariner for fifteen years! Poor crazy Marie who lost her nerve the only time she ever snagged a man, and started a riot that damn near ruined us! Anything you make for us is payback, sister, for what you cost us in the first place."

"Any trouble you had is because you sat on your ass for forty-eight hours. If you'd had the balls to do something before they got stupid drunk, I could have gotten out of there. But physicality just isn't your job, is it?"

"Maybe if you'd had a sex drive you could have handled what you asked for, damn you—duck out on us, ignore every piece of advice, no, you had to have your own pick, didn't you, and now he's got your kid? It's not my problem."

"Ask a *vote,* Mischa. Or I will."

Mischa didn't want it. That was clear. He stood there. And finally walked off across the bridge and stood staring at nothing in particular.

There were advantages to owning nothing, having nothing, wanting nothing in your life, except one man's hide.

And he couldn't have her kid.

Couldn't dispose of her kid. Or keep him.

That added something to the equation. She wasn't sure what, hadn't expected that reaction in herself, was still trying to understand why she gave a damn.

Because, she decided, if she'd had to hand one individual aboard *Sprite* over to Bowe for a hostage, it wouldn't be poor, people-stupid Tom, who was the first Hawkins to try to take her side in twenty some years.

Even if he had screwed it beyond all imagination.

Damn him.

—— *iv* ——

DREAM OF THE DARK AND NOWHERE, a lonely and terrifying no-thing, abhorring the fabric of the ship, and the ship almost . . . almost violating the interface.

The ship lived a day or so while the universe ran on for weeks, while the ship's phase envelope was the only barrier between you and that different space. You rode it tranked down, ever so vaguely aware of your own essence. When you were a kid the grownups admitted that the monsters you dreamed in transit were real, but (they said) the captain could scare the monsters off, because a kid believed in his imaginings, and a kid believed in adults just as devoutly.

But kid or adult, the mind painted its own images on the chaos—

Marie had told him pointedly there wasn't anything to meet out there but a body's own guilty conscience: if he minded what he was told he'd be fine and if he didn't he'd go crazy and be all alone with his misdeeds forever. He'd told that to the other kids and scared them. Aunt Lydia had said he was too smart for his own good. Aunt Lydia had said captain Mischa should have a talk with him, but Mischa had just said don't carry tales and don't talk about the dreams and don't make trouble, boy.

He dreamed about Marie sometimes. He'd dreamed about Mariner and the bar and the drunken men before he was twelve, then—it was between Fargone and Paradise, and he'd felt different things about Marie, sometimes scary, sometimes erotic, weaving back and forth in unpredictable ways, about all the things he'd heard happened, and about the things he'd read in tapes he wasn't supposed to have.

But he stole them, all the kids did, and they'd all tangled up. . .

That was only normal, aunt Lydia had said, when she'd found out. It was the first time she'd ever used that word about anything he'd done, and in spite of that, he didn't *feel* normal. You didn't have dreams like that about your mother and feel normal.

But Marie had said, with rare (for Marie) calm, that he was growing up and he was confusing things, which was, for once, a better explanation than aunt Lydia gave. Marie gave him tapes, too, deep-tape, the same quality you used for school.

Only the tape gave him dreams and for a long time he dreamed about a robot, a wire-diagram woman who wasn't anybody in particular. She had a metal face, and he used to want her to sit on the end of his bunk and talk to him, not about sex, finally, just about stuff and about things he liked to do and where they traveled. She was a friendly sort of craziness, that lived in Marie's apartment and in his own quarters. Sometimes she had sex with him. And sometimes she just talked, sleeping by him, about ports they might go to someday.

But the metal-faced dream had died when he'd slept with his *Polly* crewwoman. Or she'd gotten Sheila's face and become Sheila Barr, because the metal girl didn't ever come back again. He could just see her sort of standing forlornly behind Sheila's shoulder, looking a little curious and a little like the expression he saw in mirrors. . . .

So maybe his wire-woman had become him, in some strange way.

But he'd damned sure never told Sheila who he dreamed she was, and never admitted it to aunt Lydia, who was so firmly, devoutly, desperately attached to other people's sanity.

Marie might have said, on the other hand, Hell, at least she won't get pregnant, and probably wished his wire-woman good morning at the breakfast table and asked did she want tea.

That was the way Marie had dealt with his childish fancies, made fun of them and sometimes fallen in with them. She said they were all right, she'd introduce them to hers sometime, and that had scared him, because he didn't think he wanted to meet Marie's dreams, in this space or any other.

But sometimes—often—you felt a sexual dream coming when you were falling into jump. Psychs like aunt Lydia always said, Don't do it,—particularly if you aimed at being operational crew, because if you ever got into that habit, it happened too easily and you might not come back in time to handle operations . . . addictive, they said.

Nothing about the experiences was real, of course, except your own side of the experience, and that felt very real—when you were coming out of hyperspace, every representation the senses made, the brain had to find some symbol for, so things would always appear chaotic.

And it could be sex. It could be very good sex. Or, for no reason at all, it could become a very disturbing nightmare, out of symbols a brain started calling up from some closet of the half-awake mind. Though sex was the most common.

So of course if you were a stupid kid who'd heard from his peers about fantastic trips, you tried flying that way a couple times, getting yourself off by the time-tested methods until you scared hell out of yourself at least once, ended up on deep trank for maybe the next two trips, and learned to do math problems instead while you went null.

Didn't want to go into jump seeing the brig around him.

Didn't want to think about piracy and ships getting blown.

Didn't want to wonder about Marie. That was a deep, deep

mental pit he didn't want to excavate on this trip. He tried equations, tried programming problems, and he kept losing them, kept finding fantastical bits of nonsense running through his head . . . childhood rhymes and Rodman's poetry, Tommy's a *Corinthian*, Tommy's a *Corinthian*, lock him up with iron bars, iron bars, iron bars, then throw away the keys. . . .

London's bridge is falling down, so leave them alone and they'll come home, pretty maids, pretty maids all in a row. . . .

Pack of holo sex cards turned up in his study cubicle. Aunt Pat found them. Marie said, So? What's new? But nobody believed he hadn't put them there.

He wasn't stupid. If he had them, he wouldn't have left them there, in the study cubicle, for Roberta R. to find, next session. Roberta cried and said he was a pervert.

Pervert, pervert, pervert, Roberta said to him when they met in the corridors, and somebody wrote it in ink on the cubicle desk, where he'd find it. . . .

Incest, aunt Lydia informed him severely, isn't a nice word, Tommy. Do you understand incest?

He hadn't. He didn't. Aunt Lydia explained it.

Sex isn't a thing we think about on-ship, ever, ever, ever, Tommy, we don't tease our cousins that way. We don't think thoughts like that, now do we understand, Tommy?

He understood, all right: he went and bloodied Rodman's nose for what he understood, which settled one bit of business, and got him tagged as a bully, this time, but he still hadn't got it. He understood some of the pictures, when aunt Pat showed them to him and accused him of putting them there, but he'd been so stunned by the images that his guilty curiosity couldn't muster a defense . . . he couldn't quite identify some of the images as body parts until he was older, but he could still play back that memory like a tape in his head, and after that, just to figure it out, he told himself, he kept sneaking looks at books he wasn't supposed to have and tapes he wasn't supposed to see, trying to resolve what he'd only half-guessed, and getting feelings aunt Lydia said he wasn't supposed to have. It was what That Man had done with Marie. It was his beginnings. And the feelings became his, not That Man's, and he couldn't leave it alone, and couldn't stop thinking about it, until he *was* doing it in jump, and the nightmares and Marie's stories all tangled together.

He came out screaming and aunt Lydia said he'd better have deep trank next time. Marie said somebody'd better watch him and he couldn't come home like she'd planned, she had to be on duty. Kids went through that sometimes, Lydia said, meaning nightmares in jump. They got over it or you had to leave them on some station—he wasn't supposed to hear that part, and Marie got mad and said if he had a few less of Lydia's theories he'd be saner.

So he resolved to keep his mouth shut and not to have the nightmares again, because being left on station was the worst one . . . he only had Marie, and Marie wouldn't leave him, Marie had told aunt Lydia go to hell and keep her advice to herself. He'd been terribly proud of Marie, then, and told himself Marie did really want him, she just wasn't good at showing it. So he did calculations the way the seniors told him to, next time.

It didn't work, quite, but he kept his mouth shut about it.

He lived. You didn't die from dreams.

Ship was going *up*. . . . You could feel it, a strange feeling, like everything was spreading wider and standing still when there wasn't any referent for still. . . .

Think about Sheila, *she* was his safety-valve when his mind started free-wheeling and the ship went strange, think about meeting Sheila . . . he could see her down the dockside at Mariner, silver-flash coveralls, small figure in the distance, near the huge gantries, the way he'd first seen her, his *Polly* spacer, who never talked about him, never listened if he did, sometimes, slip. She told jokes, she made fun, she said she liked him, never would love him, forget that crap, that was too serious, and most of all she taught him to calm down, laugh a little, and let her do some of the instigating, that was what she said.

She was older, Sheila Barr was, and she'd told him once how she occasionally thought about having a kid, and kept changing her mind. She didn't want that commitment, but she wanted the immortality. He'd never thought about either. He'd been busy surviving his own childhood when he took up with Sheila Barr, hadn't been ready in the least for immortality, just desperately—a little vindication with the guys. . .

She won't look at you, Rodman had said.

But she did. She had. She waltzed him into a sleepover for fourteen straight days and darks and showed him things he'd never gotten out of tapes or holocards—he came back knowing things the cousins didn't, he quickly found that out, and set Rodman's nose mightily out of joint when the youngers listened to him as one who Knew.

So he got a reputation, such as it was. And proved he could still beat hell out of Rodman, one on one. But he still froze up, getting dates when *Polly* wasn't in port, which, God, he didn't want Rodman or anybody else to find out . . . he managed. Looks helped, he had that over Rodman, by some, and brains, but it didn't cover everything, and on some liberties he just hung out, disappeared a night or so, claiming he was missing Sheila, which was true, for different reasons.

Silver figure turned dark in his dream. Wasn't Sheila he was meeting, then, on that dock. For a moment he was scared it was Rodman. The whole image started coming apart on him, and Sheila's dark-haired, lanky self went strange, indefinite, separated from him by a gridwork of steel bars. . . .

Pale, then. Capella's blonde, brazen flash and try-me attitude, Capella standing there with her bare arms resting through bars he recalled he wasn't dreaming, with the bracelet of stars evident on her wrist. It wasn't the freedom of the docks he was in, he was in a box he couldn't get out of, and an exposure that let the whole ship come and stare at him if they liked.

Capella gave him an I-don't-give-a-damn rake of the eyes,

leaned there, enigma like the fatal holocards. Her hands were death and life together, the serpent and the equation that cracked the light barrier, the bracelet no honest spacer wore. . . .

"Get up," she said, this apparition. "You can do it. Take a walk."

Nobody could. Not really. But in his dream he unbuckled the restraints and got up, and walked part of the way.

The bars weren't there.

"Well, well," she said, "Christian's older brother. How are you?"

Colors washed to right and left of him, red and blue and into infrareds and ultraviolets, a tunnel at the black peripheries of his vision. He daren't come any further. Christian wasn't his friend. This woman wasn't. This dream was destructive. He could make it go away.

But Capella came to him, a series of advances without movement, Capella's arms came around his neck, and Capella's mouth was on his. They weren't standing. They were on the bed. A voice spoke faintly, or he remembered it, about waves being everywhere, or particles being the same, all the while he was feeling waves of another kind and carried along a wavefront of mindless, endless sensation.

(Don't do it in jump, the senior cousins said, or you'll go crazy.)

He was shivering again. Was living it again, a physical spasm that climaxed and quit, leaving him cold. Didn't want it. Did. He was paralyzed in the between of choices. Wasn't sure he could get that high again, it was like a drug, that was what they said, wasn't it? You'd never be able to do it realtime, you'd freeze up?

Everything spun, a whirlpool of primal urges, a coming and going of sound so deep it hit the base of the brain and the base of the spine.

"It's all right," Capella said, out of that sound. "You can't fall."

Liar, he thought, gasping for breath, feeling the abyss behind his head, as if he could just, if he shut his eyes, pour himself through the bottom of his own brain and fall forever. He felt himself sliding, sensations flowing one after the other across his skin . . . colors that crawled across the room, splashes of color that whipped away into the dark and withered and slipped away, in laughter, in a crashing great energy that broke in waves of grating, murmurous sounds.

Hard, slim body against his, riding the waves of compressing subspace, then spiraling violently, over and around and down, voices echoing in his ears, louder and louder, bodies involved with his, multiplying with the voices that were the music, the erotic and the horrific tangled and snarled into each other. He gained a moment of escape and it wasn't Capella, it was Marie clawing at him, it was a band of drunken spacers, it was the spacer with the snakes, half purple and green, hands he couldn't escape, violence and need twisting through him and around him until the waves of force flooded up into his brain, twice a hundred hands and twice again the arms and legs that closed about him, one layer onto another in a mathematical, sequential blur.

Until he was inside the living universe, endless interlace of rhythmic filaments that were living flesh and human minds, thunderous sound, violence over with now, —until he realized the waves were his own heartbeat and space became one screaming edge inside him, that fall through the back of his head. . . .

It was his body in the dark, or all the ship hurtling into an annihilating spin, tearing his hands from grips and tearing the ship apart, bolt groaning away from plate, and everything rushing away from center. . . .

—— *v* ——

RED DREAM, COASTING THE INTERFACE, dream of red violence and dark, anger that had no destination until now. Until now it had always just been, and carried its own energies, destruction and creation, tearing apart a life and making a new one.

But this time it had a place to go and something to reach for.

Sprite was running fifteen days behind him, with a full hold, headed for a sink of dark matter, three points that danced a complex pass around a common center, a pit in space-time into which all realspace matter that passed this way was damned to fall.

System of failed stars, potential unachieved, radiating masses forever tagging each other, like *Sprite* with *Corinthian.* But the numbers added right this time. Cosmic rendezvous. Union.

Consummation.

He was there in the space where all space touched. Marie dreamed his ship brushed hyperspace at this very instant, occupying the same space-time. He was that close. He had to feel her breathing, had to feel her anger and the high and the power it gave her . . . the energy of the ship became one hollow, drunken roar, I am, I am, I am, against a universe otherwise void. She reached orgasm with it, multiple times, with the thought that he didn't consent to her being there, he didn't consent to her knowing about him what he'd thought was secret . . . he didn't consent to her tracking him and making herself an inseparable, inescapable part of his life every day, every hour since their meeting. . . .

Dear Austin. I love you the way you loved me.

Look over your shoulder *now,* you son of a bitch.

—— *vi* ——

THEY WERE ALIVE. THEY EXISTED again. That was always the first assessment when the ship dropped into Einsteinian space and linear time.

But it wasn't right. He shouldn't be lying on his side, face against the wall.

On the deck. The tiles were cold under his arm and his hip and his knee. Cold air traveled over bare skin. He was half out of his clothes. His skin stung, raw with scratches.

He moved, panicked at the queasy sensation of coming out of jump, and knew he shouldn't be loose like this . . . a ship exiting jump might have to take emergency action, he wasn't belted, he could break his neck . . . he didn't know where he was, room was a meter too wide as he rolled over, but he scrambled on his knees, saw the bunk and the restraints and scrambled in, breath hissing between his teeth as he struggled to get the first belts fastened, instinct in a spacer-brat as sure as the fear of falling.

Snap. Lock fastened, upper legs, *snap*, the one across his chest, snap. He was all right then, hard-breathing, at least telling himself he'd beaten disaster if it came.

Except it wasn't *Sprite*. Except it wasn't his quarters he was in.

Bars beyond his feet. Walls he remembered, now, in dismay. *Corinthian*.

Heart started a dull, leaden panic, telling him that his danger wasn't past. And he didn't know what could have happened to put him where he waked, against the wall, except maybe they'd exited subspace before this and he'd unbelted too soon . . . he still felt the last racketing of sex through his blood and brain, last echoes of a bad trip and a nightmare to end all. His skin felt raw, coveralls mostly unzipped, he didn't know how he'd done that, either, but he'd gotten up, maybe started to go to the shower and fallen.

Hell of a dream. He lifted his head to look at himself and saw red scratches all over his chest, his pale blue coveralls had bloody specks, from a subspace hallucination.

Healed and half-healed scratches, and lately-made ones? Not all recent.

Scratched himself, was what he'd done. He felt embarrassed as hell, and hoped to God there wasn't an optic spy somewhere, or a tape record.

He couldn't face it, if there were. He let his head fall back, just to let his blood flow back to his brain and let the walls stop rippling in his vision. He'd exerted too much just now in getting back to his bunk. He'd broken into a clammy sweat, and the air circulation felt cold, stinging salt in the scratches.

Worse, he felt a wave of nausea and told himself he'd been a double fool, first exerting himself to get back in his bunk and then not getting to the nutri-packs on priority, because sneaking up his veins right now was the grandfather of all sick headaches.

He triggered the e-panel one-handed. He clawed the packs out of the wall-storage onto the mattress and ripped one open, hands shaking, fumbled out the sipping tube, valved so you didn't have to raise your head to use it, thank God. By the small time it took to do that much, the pain that wasn't quite pain yet was building up as pressure in his temples and behind his eyes, an old, old acquaintance. And to keep it company, his stomach was behaving under its own precarious rhythm, as if some bone-deep jolt out of hyperspace hadn't left his consciousness, or quit running over his skin in waves of fever heat and clammy sweat.

Sweat had soaked his clothes. Sometimes you got the brain stem confused, pushing too much, too fast. Sometimes the confusion could go into arrhythmia, breathing disorders, serious business if you were by yourself and you didn't get medicals, which he was, and wouldn't get, and nobody was going to be walking down the corridor out there looking to take care of anybody until the ship had dumped down to system speed— wholly unlike a Hawkins fool he could name who'd unbelted, thinking he was in his own cabin, got up and fallen on his ass. Thing to do until help was available was calm down, breathe deep, drink the fluids and keep it down. Ship wasn't his friend. But they didn't want him dead.

Three swallows. Long period of deep breathing. Three more swallows. Somebody would eventually check on him. Just hold on.

The ship skimmed the interface again. Major pulse, momentary grey-out.

Then red, red, red, and red, dammit! then green flashes . . . splashes of sound and vibration. . . .

The stomach tried to turn itself inside out. Terror . . . did that to you.

Capella. Guy with the snakes. Green and purple snakes. Crawling all over him. Capella *and* the snakes, climbing up his legs, holding him down, the bars weren't there anymore.

Sensation that wasn't part of any subspace dream he'd ever had. . . .

Sexual high, and raw terror.

Then down again. Skuzzy, scarred walls. Mattress under his back. Nice, safe bars, between him and the nightmares.

Breathe. Drink the fluids. Don't throw up.

Please, God. He didn't want their medics. Didn't want their crew in here, didn't want that grid opened. . . .

Next sip. Didn't see any snakes, didn't feel them slithering around him.

Couldn't remember what it felt like now. It had been vivid, before.

He was coming out of it. Winning against the pulses that sent him back to illusions, and physiological. . . .

Shit. *Shit* . . .

God. God, God, God . . .

Calm. Quiet. Breathe.

Easier if you had the output of instruments in front of you. Lying here scared stiff and with the sweat chilling in the current from the air ducts . . . you didn't know where the ship was . . . you didn't have any information what was going on, they didn't even signal you. . . .

He wasn't used to that kind of sloppiness. Wasn't the way *Sprite* did business. Made him mad.

Wasn't used to the signals when they did give them. Damn sirens. No human word out of anybody. Wasn't a way to run a ship.

His biological father was in charge up on this bridge. Marie wasn't down in cargo. The condition of the universe had done a total reverse. He wasn't going back. Ever. He didn't know where he was going. His head was starting to ache, right between the eyes.

Second . . . or was it third . . . ? skip at the interface.

Long, long skip. Erotic feelings ran up and down his body, found center . . . God, he couldn't stand it. Couldn't stop it.

Scratches healed and otherwise . . . both? How did you *do* that to yourself?

He shut his eyes, pressed fingers against the sinuses. Kept feeling the scrapes on his skin, stinging with the sweat, aftermath of pure stupidity. He tried to be mad. Mad was the way to get through things. Marie said.

Stupid thing to do. Stupid, stupid, stupid. Hell of a nightmare. Jerk off in jump-space and you were lucky you didn't do worse . . . deserved everything he got, absolutely, he'd learned better, if he could just stop the physiological reactions. . . .

Maybe the trank was a brand he hadn't used, and he was having a drug reaction, he didn't know. He damned sure meant to ask, if he could find anybody on this ship disposed to care about details like that.

Long quiet, then. But you couldn't trust they weren't going to dump down again, you couldn't trust anything. Just try to make the feelings go away.

The siren blew two blasts, then. God, how was he supposed to know what it was? Impending evasive action? Impending impact with a rock? Considering the headache, he wasn't sure he gave an effective damn.

But after the echoes died, he heard that indefinable stirring of life in the ship's guts that meant definitive all-clear, distant, ordinary sounds, confirming the ship was about its routines, safe, and crew was moving about.

Safe as this ship ever was. Safe as the crew could make this ship. Not for him, maybe. But at least they were alive together. At least it was down to human motives and human reasons.

His father's ship.

His *father's* say-so and his *father's* set of laws, amen.

He lay there and drank the nutri-packs, two of them, before

his stomach decided it wasn't going to heave everything up, and before his head decided it wasn't going to explode. He let the belts go when he'd come to that conclusion, lay still with one knee up and an arm under his head, finding no reason to venture more than that. The noises in the ship now were noises he understood, mostly, somebody banging around with a service panel, checking on filters or plumbing. Somebody was shouting at somebody else about schedules, except you didn't shout obscenities like that down *Sprite*'s corridors. It occurred to him he'd never heard a stream of profanity like that in his life, and Marie was no prude when she was pissed. It actually attained meter and art.

Another voice then, jolted him . . . familiar voice, voice he wasn't going to forget—along with the beating he'd heard before they left port. "Get your ass out of there!" came near and clear, and he thought he'd move, if that voice was yelling at him.

Memory of something hitting flesh and bone. Vivid as the other side of jump.

Wasn't sure the guy had lived through it. If they cycled the airlock while they were out here in the dark between stars . . . that might tell.

Body trade, he said to himself. Marie thought so. The cousins did. Live merchandise and dead spacers, you couldn't depend there'd be a great deal of care which, on certain ships, on ships that didn't mind selling out other merchanters: whole ships blown because somebody'd spilled the numbers and set somebody up, back in the War; and they said, the hunters were still picking targets, little ships that just might not make port again—ships with irregular routes, minimal crew, no great atrocities, no known Names, like a Family ship. Just the little, marginal haulers . . . easy to pick off.

A rattle sounded in the corridor, then, something metal bumped the wall just outside, where someone was walking, and in sudden fright, he remembered the cable and didn't wait to be snatched off his bunk by the wrist. He got up to one knee on the bunk as the noise-maker showed up with a hand-carrier and a stack of covered food trays.

The guy with the snakes. The drunk with the chocolates. He watched apprehensively as the guy shoved a tray through an opening in the gridwork, clearly expecting him to come into his reach and take it from his hand.

"You actually the captain's kid?" the guy asked when he did venture over to the bars.

"Tom Hawkins," he admitted, and took the tray, not willing to give the man any provocation—the tattooed arms were as thick as most men's legs, the fingers that gave up the tray were thick with muscle and callus.

"Tink," the snake-man said.

"Tink?"

"Name's Tink. Cook's mate. How-do."

"Glad to meet you." He wasn't, not even halfway. But what did you say? And the guy didn't act crazy.

"You must've pissed the captain off real bad."

"I guess." What could you say to that, either? The guy when he wasn't scowling had a rough, but downright gentle kind of face. And still scared hell out of him.

"Tell you, kid, you got to do what he says. He don't never take no. Shoot you first. I seen him do it."

"For what?"

A couple of blinks as Tink sized him up. "Guy carried a knife topside. You don't ever do that. That'll get you dead."

"I'll remember that."

"You bridge?"

"Cargo." Quick lie. He *didn't* want them to know he was computers.

"You sign on?"

"Is there any other way to get onto this ship?"

Tink thought that was funny. He had an infectious grin. One canine was a brighter white than the rest of his teeth.

"Is there?"

"Yeah. Happens."

"They do much of that?"

Tink's face went slowly sober. He looked one way and the other down the corridor as if to see whether anyone was listening. And there was people-noise from the left-hand direction. "Sometimes. But listen, however you got here, you don't skip ship. Work here's permanent. No matter how you come. Hear? You don't skip."

"What do they do if you try?"

Tink's face screwed up as if he was short of description. Then Tink looked down the corridor and straightened away from the bars.

"Food's not bad, though," Tink said, a little louder. "They give you a big allowance dockside. Can't fault the pay at all."

"Glad of that." He was standing with the tray in his hands. Tink went away and talked to somebody down the corridor, and he went back to his bunk, kicked the cable out of his way and sat down to his after-jump snack—which was a sandwich-roll and a cup of something he couldn't identify, but the sandwich-roll wasn't at all bad.

Tink wasn't so bad, either, he decided. No matter if he flashed on Tink's tattoos in bad dreams, it was a good sandwich and the drink really wasn't half bad, either, after you got the first swallows down and got used to the flavor.

That was the only good part of being here, except the ship was in one piece and he was.

Barely.

Jump space was an unsettling experience, no matter how many times you'd done it and how you'd acclimated, you were always a heartbeat away from crazy and-or dead, and, God, people could do odd things, coming out of it.

Had to have been on the down-slide, when they were making drop. Medics said you couldn't move, during jump, something about long motor nerves being just too slow to coordinate in the feedback to the brain and inner ear, or some such crap that probably made sense to the physics people and the medics, but there was still a lot the medics didn't know, according to the folklore, or couldn't make clear, even to people who didn't want to believe the fools. The science people were still arguing whether brains could remember anything happening during jump. Or whether events *could* happen in hyperspace that affected realspace matter. Consensus said if anything seemed to have had an effect on something that belonged in realspace, namely human brains, it was nothing but a sequential memory screwup, like in a witness situation, where nobody could agree on what happened first, or what colors somebody was wearing. Further you got from it, the less certain the memory was.

Meaning you only thought you'd done it, or you'd done it before or after jump and only deceived yourself how and when it was in relation to other things.

But myth regularly took over where medics left off, and probably all over human space, they told about *Grandiosa* and the night-walker, how this crewman had gone crazy during jump and *could* move, and went out and bloodily murdered his shipmates until *Grandiosa* got crazier and crazier and people wouldn't trank down and went crazier and crazier. . . .

Then the night-walker changed the jump coordinates and screwed up the navigation and ate all the rest, that he'd hung in the ship's food locker.

Bogeymen. Ghost stories. Kids' lofts were full of them. They were all stupid stories, probably told them about water-ships on old Earth, or on the old sublighters, and there was no *Grandiosa* on record anywhere, older cousins said so.

The fact was, in jump you were always naked to forces that you didn't understand and that physicists couldn't measure because physicists couldn't measure without instruments and instruments didn't work there, or at least didn't produce consistent results. You couldn't stay awake and aware through it no matter what, and it was too much like dying, crossing that boundary, which a long-hauler spacer did, six, seven, eight times a ship-year.

He didn't want to think about it. He heard Tink's voice, down the corridor, talking with several somebodys. He'd finished his snack and he was sweaty and cold, now, he wanted a shower if they'd just stay stable.

Supposing the shower worked, which he couldn't expect, considering the bars and the cable and all—nobody was interested in his comfort.

Then he looked at the cable on his wrist and realized he couldn't get his clothes off.

"Damn!" he said, and wanted to throw the tray against the bars.

In the self-same moment he was aware of a shadow against the grid.

A woman stood there, the way Capella had, in his dream.

Not Capella. Dark-haired, the same stance . . . but not the same. And not a dream.

He got off the bunk. His visitor was wearing the same green coveralls he'd seen on *Corinthian* crew dockside . . . professional woman, he thought, cool, businesslike. Had to be an officer. Maybe medical, come to check on him.

"Are you all right?" she asked, with the kind of accent he dreamed he'd heard before, somewhere, maybe the intercom, he wasn't sure.

"Yes, ma'am," he said, and her mouth quirked. A pretty mouth. He was respectful, but he wasn't dead . . . he felt this strange, sandpapered-raw sense of nerves with her, a consciousness of his own skin, scratch-scored and sensitive in intimate places, and didn't even know what about her demanded his attention. He just . . .

. . . reacted. And stood there embarrassed as hell.

"Christian's brother, huh?"

"Yes, ma'am."

She seemed amused. "I'm not ma'am."

On some ships there was only one, senior-most, matriarch. And she clearly wasn't.

"Sabrina Perrault. Sabrina Perrault-Cadiz. Saby, for short. Tink says you're Cargo."

"Yes, ma'am." It was his lie. He had to stick by it. At least it was something he knew. He was going to ask about the trank, before somebody forgot. . . .

"Thomas. Is that what you go by?"

"Tom."

"Tom Bowe-Hawkins. I'm sorry you got snatched. I really am."

"Thanks. —I take it you're Medical?"

"Not me. No. Cargo."

His lie caught up with him. Called his bluff. He knew stuff from Marie, but that was all he knew.

"It's not a bad ship," Saby Perrault said.

He didn't know what to say to that. Couldn't argue. Any ship you were born on, he guessed, wasn't an unbearably bad ship, if it was the only one you ever knew.

"I guess," he said. "You could tell the captain I'm not a fool. You could let me loose. I'm on this ship, I assure you I don't want to sabotage anything."

"Not my say," she said, with a lift of the shoulder. "But I'll pass it along."

"You ever talk to the captain direct?"

"Sure. You want me to tell him something?"

He was sorry he'd asked. He didn't want to. He didn't know why he'd opened his mouth. But Saby was the least threatening human he'd met aboard and he wanted to know where the chain of communication was. "Yeah." He tried to think. "Say hi. Love the food. Tink's a human being. The bunk's lousy."

Saby laughed.

"I'll do that. Anything you particularly need?"

"Change of clothes. Shower. Shave."

"Shower works. There's a shaver on the panel."

He held up the cable. "Key."

"Not authorized. Sorry."

"I'm stuck in these clothes. I don't have my kit. I don't have anything but what I'm in. They didn't encourage me to pack."

"Do what I can. Has to be cleared."

"You mean the captain has to clear it."

"Do what I can," she repeated, and gave a shrug, and started away.

"Sera,—"

"Ms," she said. "Ms. Perrault." She'd stopped, just in view. Looked at him. He looked at her, with the disturbed feeling . . . maybe it was the dream . . . that he desperately wanted her to come back, he wanted her to talk, and fill the silence and be reasonable . . . because she did seem humanly sympathetic. Sane. Somebody who might believe he wasn't crazy, or explain to him that his father wasn't.

She knew his father. Even sounded easy in the relationship. Friendly.

A whole several breaths she stood there, and he couldn't think what to say to keep her talking, and she didn't find anything. Then she walked off with all the promises of help he'd had since he'd come aboard this ship . . . promises that suddenly, on a friendly voice and an infectious grin, suddenly had him weak in the knees and wanting her to stay for one more look, one more assurance he wasn't alone down here, she *was* going to appeal to the captain on his behalf and get the man who'd, after all other considerations, fathered him . . . to come down here and become a face and a presence and listen to his side of things.

And pigs will go to space, he told to himself, without any knowledge what pigs were, beyond creatures that built flimsy houses. He'd no more knowledge what was the matter with him, beyond shot nerves and jangled hormones, or whatever had made him scratch himself bloody in an erotic dream that had gotten wholly out of hand. He didn't have any miraculous truth to communicate to Austin Bowe, he didn't have any just cause to trust Tink *or* Saby Perrault-Cadiz-whoever-she-was, and damned sure not his so-claimed half-brother, who clearly didn't like him on sight. He'd been set up before in his life—earliest education he'd gotten, not to pin hopes on a cousin suddenly just too damned friendly, and too unreasonably on his side.

He wobbled back to his bunk, vengefully jerked the cable out of his way, sat down in despair and punched the mattress with his hand, there being nothing else in reach.

He hated them, he hated them one and all, Tink and Saby and Christian and Capella and every other name he knew along with his father's.

And along with that hate, he was scared, scared, and messed-with, and pushed-at. The scratches stung, he was soaked with sweat at the armpits and around the waist, he wanted a shower, he wanted a shave, he wanted free of the damned cable.

At which he gave a two-handed and useless jerk, pure fit of temper.

"Mmm-mm," someone said from the grid in front, and there, straight out of his dream, *was* Capella, sleeveless, bare arms on the bars, star-bracelet in plain evidence. "Just doesn't do any good, Christian's-brother."

"Go to hell!"

"Been." The star-tattooed hand made a casual loop. "Bored with hell. *Corinthian's* more fun. How's the stomach?"

He was suddenly, erotically, acutely, conscious of the scratches his clothes concealed, before he figured she didn't mean that.

"Jump's no novelty."

"Yeah. You and me, merchanter-son. Jump's still a bitch. I'm sincerely regretful of the circumstances, and I do hope you stay here where's much safer, if you get my drift."

The stars on her wrist meant Fleet. Meant a special fraternity of the breed, the ones that smelled their way through hyperspace, and *felt* the presence of ships they preyed on. That was the folklore, at least.

"Where's the next port?"

"Pell, right now. If you're real nice, who knows, they could let you off there. But—there's else, pretty lad. And you don't truly want to go there."

"Mazian."

"Did I say that name? That *is* a son of a bitch, Christian's-brother, and I'd never say that name to a stranger, myself. I'd not say a thing more, where you are."

He felt cold and colder. "That's the trade this ship keeps."

"There's trade and there's trade, Christian's elder brother." Someone was coming, and Capella straightened up, throwing a glance in that direction. "Be smarter."

Christian walked up, took a stance, arms folded. "New tourist attraction?"

"Hey. He's decorative. Scenery, Chrissy. Do you mind?"

They argued. He sat where he was, on his bunk, wanting to stay out of it entirely. Christian grabbed Capella by the arm, lost it when Capella jerked away, and the two of them ended up withdrawing down the corridor, not out of earshot.

His mind was on one word. Mazian. He'd wanted to believe . . . he didn't know logically why he'd even care about his biological father's honesty as a merchanter, when he'd had information to the contrary all his life. He didn't know what he had possibly invested in the question that Austin Bowe might *not* be the villain Marie portrayed him to be. . . .

Except his personal survival hung on that point. Except he didn't know what was going to happen to him, or where he might end up. Mazian's Fleet, as a destination . . . he didn't even want to contemplate.

As for Capella's bracelet. It was, just lately, a fashion, in some wild quarters, just a fad . . . like the star and dagger of the elite marines—some rimrunners had supposedly taken to wearing it, the ones still legal, the ones the cops couldn't necessarily arrest on specific charges, but this woman hadn't a glove over it or any shame. Far too young to have fought in the War . . . but you couldn't rely on that, among spacers. Sometimes young meant . . . experienced. Sometimes young meant a deal more jumps, a deal more time in hyperspace, and you couldn't tell, except, somehow, the myth said, the look in the eyes.

That, the bracelet and the fact Bok's equation went with it, which wouldn't be the case with some fad-following bar-bunny or a fringe-spacer wannabee. Navigator, engineer . . . rumors weren't certain *what* the wearer was, except a Fleet that couldn't use the stations any more still survived, still turned up to give merchanters' nightmares and nobody knew how, unless they'd found jump-points the regular military couldn't find or couldn't reach.

And the wearers of that bracelet had, legendarily, something to do with that ability. All sorts of stories had come out, since the War. He'd grown up on them. *That* was the discrepancy in their ages.

Closest thing to a night-walker you'd ever meet in real life.

And regularly in bed with his half-brother, was what he was hearing in the argument in progress. In bed, more than one sense. Obligated, by what Christian said.

"Screw you," Capella said, a little down the corridor, but clear as clear. "I don't *owe* you, Chrissy, don't try to pull that string. You won't like what comes up with it."

He held his breath. He didn't know why. There was violence in the air.

Christian said, then, "You let him *alone,* Pella. That's the bottom line. You keep your hands to yourself."

"Sure," Capella said. "Sure."

That left him chilled, that did. He didn't want to be the focus of a feud—let alone on this ship, with his half-brother, and that woman.

We were just talking, he wanted to yell, the age-old protestation. But he didn't think the pair down there gave a damn for his opinion.

—— *vii* ——

NO MECHANICALS. NO PROBLEMS since they'd dropped into Tripoint. They had to take the *v* down all the way to system-inertial, with the load they had, which was a shame, because there was a real reason, in Austin's opinion, to make a little

haste through the jump-point, in this dark navigation sink between the stars; reason, but not reason enough that they
shouldn't take time to run the checks and catch their breaths.

A good few days, he figured, before *Sprite* could get itself
tanked and loaded—which was some respite before they had
to worry about *Sprite* being on their tail.

But they well might be, by now. He didn't put it past Marie
Hawkins. And he didn't bet the cargo officer couldn't move
Sprite in her own directions.

Knock on his office door. He was on a costing calculation,
on various options. Inputting. He didn't want interruption.

But the knocker also had the private key-code; the door
opened without him keying it from the desk.

" 'Scuse," Saby said, easing in against the wall. "Minute?"

He held up two fingers. Generosity.

"Thomas Hawkins?" Saby began.

One finger. Well-chosen.

"Talked to him," Saby said. "You said."

"Minute and a half," he said.

"Not attitudinal. Smart. Scared. Says the bunk's lousy but
he likes the food."

"Fine. He won't starve."

"I really think you should talk to him. At least once. You'll
always wonder."

"Damn your dockside psych. No, I won't always wonder."

"He's not what you think."

"That's twice. Fifteen seconds."

"Scared of him?"

"Five."

"Ignorance killed the cat, sir, curiosity was framed."

"Time's up."

"Yes, sir," Saby said. And slid out the door and shut it.

Kid had an uncanny knack: she said a hire was trouble, and
trouble was what happened. She said an unlikely guy was all
right and got them the best cargo pusher they'd had. She said

take this woman, and he hadn't listened, and the guy that they had taken instead, they'd been especially sorry of, down to finding him a permanent situation.

Now Saby went and stuck her young nose in a damned sensitive problem. Who set Saby to evaluating *that* personnel acquisition? Who assigned her downside, anyway? Saby wasn't even on-shift.

Spare time occupation. And he could live without seeing Marie Hawkins' kid. He could sleep at night without it.

He could sleep at night seeing the kid to the same permanent occupation the last machinist's mate had found. The universe had nooks to put things in. Slam the door shut and the hell with the problem. Marie Hawkins had contributed genes to the kid. Maybe arranged for him to get aboard, put him up to it, who knew? One determined fool could do a lot of damage to a ship before they caught him at it.

Com beeped. "Austin," he said.

"You're not afraid of him," Saby's voice said.

"You're on double watch, damn you!"

"Yes, sir," Saby said. And cut the com connection.

Chapter Five

— *i* —

"Chrissy-sweet," the argument in the corridor wound up, "if I want to go I go. If I want to stay I stay. You want me to go is not the question here. It is never the question. Not here. Not dockside. Capish?"

"I understand. I understand damned well. Go to hell!"

Things had gotten very far from reason. Tom sat still on his bunk and let the firefight go on without his input.

But Capella lingered, strayed to the brig frontage to lean on the cross-bars and smile sweetly.

"Tommy-person, don't piss off your brother. I suspect he's jealous."

He didn't answer. Didn't say a thing as Christian turned up in his barred view of the ship. Didn't say a thing as he watched Capella pass out-of-field and on down the corridor.

"You're a pain in the ass," Christian said, he thought to him. "You know that?"

"Not by choice," he said.

Suddenly the cable took up and snaked around his leg, dumping him first on the deck and then past the end of the bunk, slamming him against the wall.

"Dammit!" he yelled.

"Son of a bitch," Christian said. "You keep yourself out of *Corinthian* business, you keep yourself away from *Corinthian* crew, you don't ask questions, and you don't listen to the answers if somebody hands them to you, you fuckin' stay out of our business, you hear me?"

He got up. In the meantime somebody else had turned up in the area outside, with a wave of a shirted arm and a: "What in hell is this? I think you've got duties, mister. If you don't, *find* some."

"Sir," Christian said, scowling, and got out of the way as the gridwork shot open and the new arrival walked into the cell—

Blond like Christian, tall—officer, you hadn't any doubt about it, and that wasn't by a longshot by reason of the black skintights, or the shirt, an off tone of shimmer red-purple. "Hawkins, are you?" the newcomer asked, hands on hips, occupying the way out, and he hadn't any doubt who he was dealing with. He stood his ground and glared, tight-jawed, seeing no need whatever to answer.

"So are you Marie Hawkins' little present," Bowe asked, "or what?"

"I don't know what you think I saw. I don't know what there was to see. I don't care about your business."

"Stupid must be her genes. Not mine."

"Yeah, real damn bright, the stuff at Mariner, you son of a bitch! You left a hell of a reputation on *my* ship!"

Bowe came closer, between him and an exit that wouldn't help him, with the cable on his wrist. He understood the game. He stood and glared, and Bowe glared back. Taller than he was. As big. And with the home advantage.

Bowe stared at him. Finally: "This isn't *Sprite*, boy. And there's a wide universe out there that doesn't give a damn what you want or whose mistake you are. You keep out of my way. You don't cause any trouble. And I might let you out on some civilized dockside. . . ."

"Yeah. And otherwise?"

"You watch that mouth, son."

"Go to hell. I'm not your son."

A hand exploded against his head. He hit the wall, rebounded and hit Bowe with all the force he had.

Or tried to. The cable snagged. Bowe cuffed the other ear, he hit the wall again and slid down it onto a tucked and trapped leg, half deaf. He went for Bowe's knees and hit the wall a third time.

Freed the knee. He came up yelling, "You son of a bitch, I'll kill you!"

Bowe got him in an arm lock and shoved him at the wall, face-first.

"Will you, now?"

"Damn you!" He had one hand linked to the cable. He twisted half about, got the other fist wound in Bowe's shirt, and Bowe rammed a fistful of coveralls up against his throat and shoved him at the wall again, hard head, yielding panel. . . .

"I don't think so," Bowe said. "Call it quits, boy?"

"*No!*"

Another bounce of his skull against the panel. Blood wasn't getting to his brain. He was going out. He brought a knee up, tried for Bowe's throat, and his skull met the panel again.

"You're being stupid, boy."

"You don't win," he said. Everything was grey. "You don't win."

Bowe dropped him. Legs buckled every which way, and the boot soles resisted on the tiles, pinning him against the wall and the bunk as he fell. He tried to grab the bunk with his free hand, and couldn't get purchase to get up. Bowe walked out.

Gave orders to someone. He had a pounding headache and a shortness of breath, and he got an elbow onto the bunk, enough to lever himself out of the angle he'd wedged himself into. He rested there getting his breath, trying his hardest not to throw up.

Shadow loomed over him. He rolled over to protect himself, saw Tink and another guy about the same size.

"Tried to tell you," Tink said with a sorrowful shake of his head.

By which he figured Tink wasn't there to kick him while he was down.

The opposite. "You need Medical, kid?" Tink asked, patting his shoulder.

He didn't think so. His ears were ringing, his head hurt and the legs still wouldn't work predictably, but he shook his head to the question and tried to get all the way up.

Legs buckled. Tink caught him.

"Get a cold towel," Tink said, and, "No, they ain't got 'em in here, down in the galley."

"I'm all right," he insisted, but Tink looked at his eyes one after the other, said he should get flat and wait for the towel.

Didn't want to. Wanted to be let the hell alone. But Tink didn't give him that option.

Bowe's orders. Son of a bitch, he kept thinking, son of a bitch who'd hurt Marie—Marie'd told him, told him details he didn't want to know—before he knew what sex was, he'd known all about rape, and after that, sex and Marie and Bowe were all crosswired, the way it wasn't in normal people, he understood that. And now this huge guy with the snakes, and Capella, and Christian, and the damned holocards and subspace and the scratches, and Bowe . . . it felt as if something had exploded in the middle of him, right in the gut, pain Bowe had handed out, or Marie had, or whatever in himself had deserved to be in the mess he was in. He sat there half on the floor and started shaking, and the big guy, Tink, just gathered him up and hauled him onto the bunk and covered him up.

"Shock," Tink called it. "You'll be all right, just breathe deep."

Might be. Might well be, an accumulation of images, an overdose of reality. But deep breaths didn't cure it. No matter where he looked, he was still where he was, he was still who he was, nothing cured that.

— *ii* —

YOU COULD FIGURE, YOU COULD damned well figure, Christian thought, with the echo of Austin's steps still recent past his vantage point. He folded his hands tightly under his armpits—he'd learned, at fourteen, the pain of bashing one's fist at *Corinthian*'s walls, or his personal preferences against Austin's whim of the moment. He'd gotten the orders, the same as Tink had: Thomas Bowe-Hawkins was going on galley duty, *Austin* wasn't talking, Austin had just had every button he owned danced over and hopped on by Thomas Hawkins, and it didn't take a gold-plated genius to know Austin wasn't in a mood to discuss the Hawkins case, Austin wouldn't be in a mood to discuss the Hawkins case in a thousand years, with him, ever, end report. Austin was headed back to his lordly office, Capella was on bridge duty, running calc, Saby was on report *and* on duty—everybody who'd taken a hand in the brother-napping fiasco was on report or on duty.

"*Christian,*" came the call over his pocket-com.

Correction. Everybody but Beatrice. Maman wanted to talk to him, bless her conniving soul, maman had just heard the news, and he'd right now as gladly have taken a bare-ass swim in the cold of the jump-point as go discuss half-brother with Beatrice.

"*Christian, immediament, au cabinet.*"

Now, Beatrice wanted to see him, in her sanctum sanctorum, her office, down the corridor and around the rim from Austin's precincts. Beatrice was evidently turning *Corinthian*'s helm and Capella's course-plotting over to Travis an hour and a half early for the purpose—one supposed they weren't running blind and autoed at the moment.

So he took the lift topside, to the inner ring, soft-footed it past Austin's shut door, to Beatrice's office. He took a deep breath, raked his hair into order, and presented himself, perforce, to maman, —who got up and poured two drinks.

Stiff.

He took his. He sat down. Beatrice sat down. He took a drink. Beatrice took a drink and stared at him. Life had left few marks on Beatrice, except about the eyes, and right now they were sleep deprived and furious.

"This Hawkins," Beatrice said as if it was a bad taste, "this Hawkins. What do you know about it?"

"What should I know about it? I brought him aboard because I hadn't any choice. . . ."

"You could see this coming, with that ship inbound. You had to take every action to make this Hawkins a problem—"

"I hadn't any instructions that said leave a man to freeze!"

"We're not talking about that. You're in a position to make judgments, you're in a position to observe—I'm telling you use your head. That boy is a threat to you, do you understand? Austin won't see him, no, of course Austin won't so much as look at him—does this say to you he's not interested? This boy's had nothing but Hate Austin poured into his veins. And does this deter him? No. Altogether the opposite. Does a man tell Austin no? Does he?"

"Not damned often."

"And this boy?"

"This *boy* is older than I am."

"Bravo. You notice the point. This woman. This boy. — Austin does not take kindly to 'no.' It's a major weakness in him."

"So what do you want me to do?"

"Use your wits. This is not our friend. And there are degrees of rebellion that won't amuse, do you see? Find them. Make them. Deprive this Hawkins of any reasonable attraction in this business. We have too much at stake here for self-indulgence, of his fancies or of yours."

He didn't ask how he was to do this. Beatrice wasn't long on details. Beatrice wasn't long on sleep right now, clearly, and about time Travis took over out there. Bad jump. He saw the signs of it. He took down half his drink. Beatrice took all of hers. He set his glass down and got up and went for the door.

"Damn Saby," Beatrice said, having, apparently belatedly, remembered another offender on her agenda.

He stopped, his hand on the switch. *"She's* involved?"

"Saby's character judgments. *Oui. Certainement.* What else but my sister's child? Saby the judge of character. *Chut!*" Beatrice took up his glass, lifted it, silently wished him out the door and out of her thoughts.

The air was clearer outside. Ideas weren't. Maman's perfume was still in his nostrils, along with the scent of brandy. It clung to a man that dealt with her.

Corinthian's alterday pilot. Perrault and not Bowe.

And tenacious of her position.

Maman never wanted a kid, that was sure. Probably Austin hadn't been thrilled, in so many words. But maman when she came aboard and knew Austin in the carnal and the ambitious senses, had made the professional sacrifice. . . .

Beatrice always did know Austin better than Austin knew himself.

Gave Austin a new experience, laid out of sex maybe imminently before birth, shoved him off on ten-year-old Saby and put a fresh coat of gloss on her nails.

So Beatrice was worried. Never ask whose ass was threatened. With Beatrice it wasn't a question. Beatrice was worried and Beatrice was pissed at him for not freezing his Hawkins half-brother into a police puzzle.

And *he* didn't know why he hadn't, except the whole business had caught him off guard, and he'd made a fast decision, a decision he'd stuck by when it got complicated, and when, in *Corinthian*'s predeparture hours, it had looked less than sensible.

But nobody'd told him to kill anybody. Nobody'd told him ·
it was a requirement. And, dammit, Austin had shot a couple of fools, but not on dockside—he'd seen Austin be scarily patient with guys who'd crossed him in bars and on the docks,

when he'd thought Austin wouldn't take it . . . that was the example he'd had, and where did everybody get so damned know-everything when he'd played it by the rules he'd been handed?

It was the way with every damn piece of hell he caught, he was supposed to have read it in the air, in flaming letters, different than anybody else on the ship.

Don't get involved with the cops or with customs. Don't do anything to get hauled into legal messes.

Wasn't murder?

Wasn't killing Austin's own bastard kid just a little nuisance to the ship?

Wasn't giving Marie Hawkins grounds to call the cops and name names just a little slight possibility of trouble, if her own kid turned up as an icicle in the warehouse *Corinthian* was using?

Nobody ever considered that. They didn't have to consider it, now. He'd handled that part. He'd removed that possibility and kept their record clean. And now Beatrice as much as called him a fool.

While Hawkins did the only damned thing that would have stopped Austin from dumping him on some Sol-bound ship at Pell. Hawkins had said no. Hawkins had all but spat in Austin's eye doing it, and now Austin wouldn't dispose of him anywhere until he'd won. Count on it, the way you counted on a star keeping its course, or a mass-point being in the space you launched for.

Austin would win. Austin would win, on whatever terms the contest took.

Seeing to it what those terms were. . .

Hawkins wanted off the ship. Well and good. He wanted Hawkins off.

Fair exchange.

—— *iii* ——

IT WAS GALLEY SCUT. NOTHING IN the least technical, just a lot of scrubbing to get the galley's contribution to the electrostatic filters down as close to zero as possible, which meant scrubbing the floors and cabinets after every meal on every shift, polishing the surfaces, sorting the recyclables, including the slop that went to the bio-tanks to feed the cultures, of which you didn't want closer knowledge—but the product was salable. And you cleaned the water outflow filters, more crud for the tanks to digest, and if you didn't have a cable attached between your wrist and the wall, you went down the corridor and did all the recycling filters, too, but Tink did those.

Except the cable, he was glad to have the duty, anything but lie in a cell with nothing to do but think about his problems, and Tink said, joking, Be careful, if Cook found out how clean things could be, he could get stuck on permanent scrub.

He decided Tink probably looked like he'd cut your throat because really he'd rather not have to. Tink turned out to be a nice guy, a genuinely nice and overall kind individual—he didn't recall anybody he'd ever run into who just gave things away like Tink . . . the chocolates-offer when Tink was drunk he decided hadn't been a come-on, at all. He'd been stuck in a cell, Tink had a bag of rare imported extravagance, and Tink would have probably given him three or four just because he looked sad, that was the way Tink seemed to operate. No systems engineer, for sure, but if Tink had thought he'd screwed up something in installing the filters, Tink would have fixed it himself and never told the cook.

So he took Tink's advice and didn't scrub so hard, for fear Cook would demand the same out of Tink . . . and it couldn't be Tink's favorite job.

Tink's favorite, in fact, seemed to be doing the pastry stuff, making ripples and curls and sugar-flowers that probably no-body in this crew was going to appreciate. But Tink made them anyway. He said it made the food look good and if the food looked good the ship got along better. He said if you hired on crew it was important they felt like they got quality food and quality off-shift entertainment and quality perks on dockside. That way you got them back aboard with no trouble.

"This ship treat you all right?" he asked Tink. The cable that linked him to a safety-line bolt didn't inspire belief in the system.

"Real good," Tink said, making another sugar-flower. "Big allowance dockside. I tell you, there's guys didn't appreciate the captain when they started, but they know where that allowance comes from. You stay on his right side and you don't hear from him; and I tell you, he give a few guys a chance or two, that's not bad. Never cut their allowance. Just put a tag on 'em. That's pretty good, anywhere you look for work."

Didn't say what happened if they got altogether on his bad side. Or if you were his unwanted son. "They beat this guy. I heard it."

"Yeah, well, Michaels."

"He's the officer."

"He's the round-up man. Gets the crew in. Guy pulled a knife, he knew better."

"He live?"

"Oh, yeah. Busted ribs, busted hand, guy name of Tolliver. I tell you if he don't come about and do right after this, crew'll kill him."

"Seriously kill him?"

"Out the lock," Tink said, and a flower happened, and a curlicue. "This crew got no need for a guy who don't appreciate what we got here." Tink pursed his lips and concentrated on embellishments for the moment, so he was scared Tink didn't take to the question. Tink added, frowning, "Suppose a Family ship's got better. Some of us ain't got that option, you know?"

"I don't know. If *Sprite* got a look at that cake, they'd steal you fast."

Tink grinned and laughed. "Ain't so sure."

"So it really is pretty good here."

"Best deal us hard–ass hired–crew's going to get." Tink shot him an under–the–brows look. "Captain's your papa. You should make officer real easy."

"Looks like it, doesn't it?" He gave the cable a shake. But he didn't want to turn bitter with Tink, who clearly didn't know. "Maybe." He laughed, to throw Tink off the track. "Maybe out the lock next, who knows?"

Tink was quiet a bit, starting another frosted pastry, thoughtful-looking, his lip caught in his teeth. "Didn't know my father or my mother. Don't know what ship I was. Ship was blew to hell, there was pockets, you know, and they got some of us out. That ship passed me on, I don't remember the name." Tink's brow knit. "Don't remember either name. I remember standing in the airlock. I remember the crossover when we come aboard. But I can't remember the names. And then there was another ship, and then Mariner, till she blew. Some things I remember. I remember Mariner all right. But not the ships. Don't know why that is."

He could guess. Thousands of people blown to cold space, a handful of survivors, most of them kids . . . even stationers put the kids inmost and protected from hull breach.

"I hear," he said cautiously, because he wasn't sure Tink had ever been through school in the sense a Family kid had, "I hear a lot of the Mariner kids don't remember."

"Yeah. Funny thing, I remember that part, remember the sirens and the smoke and all." Tink filled a pastry cone with blue, and made a part of a design. "Remember 'em coming through in suits, with lights, looking for survivors." The design became a star. And another, smaller. "Bounced around a bit, couldn't do any damn thing, but I didn't want to sit on any station after that." Star after star, little and big. "So I started out with galley scut, same's any kid. Graduated to advanced scut and general maintenance. Studied di-e-tary science, and got a couple good posts. . . ." A series more of stars and a whimsical sprinkle of silver beads. "The guy who taught me to do this, he was real old, hospitaled off at Pell, he used to let me do a lot of stuff, illegal, you know, no station permit, but he didn't pay me. I watched him do it, I spent my whole leave learning the basics. Next time I got a leave there, the old guy'd died, so I taught myself the rest."

"That's beautiful."

"Huh." Tink looked at him as if to see was he kidding. Grinned. "Most guys say, hell, that's stupid. Then they argue over who got what piece."

"You could get a job anywhere. Station chef'd hire you."

"No station. I ain't getting blowed to hell, not Tink."

"Can't blame you for that."

"No damn way."

"How long have you been with *Corinthian*?"

"Fifteen years. Fifteen years." He looked at the pastry. "That do it?"

"That's real pretty."

"I seen roses on Pell," Tink said then. "That's what the flowers are, is roses. They got this big greenhouse, you can take a guided tour. Cost you five c. It's worth it."

"Pell's where we're going?"

"Yeah. If you get dock time, if you want to go, you can come with me. It's an hour tour."

"I don't think they're going to let me."

"More 'n you just backtalked the captain, isn't it?"

Tink wasn't so slow. "Yeah," he said. "Don't think he's ever wanted me alive, let alone on his ship."

"Huh," Tink said. That was all. And his estimate of Tink's common sense went way up.

— *iv* —

THE LIGHTS DID THAT BRIEF DIMMING and rebrightening that was maindawn and alterdark, that ancient re-set of biological clocks for the two main shifts together, that odd time that two entire crews who shared the same ship should meet and cross and exchange duties. One shift's first team was eating breakfast, one shift's first team was eating supper, while the seconds of one shift were making ready for switchover and the seconds of the other were at supper if they liked, or rec, or sims or whatever . . . it was a great deal the same as on *Sprite,* a great deal, Tom supposed, the same on every ship in space, a lot the same on stations, so it must say something about what Earth did or had done . . . he'd never figured, but he supposed so.

Officers' mess was elsewhere. . . . Tink put pans on a cart, no different at all went into it than the general crew got, by his observation. One pastry went to the officers, one to the crew, set out on the sideboard, on display, and on the breakfast-dinner line you could have whatever appealed to you, Cook said, just dish up what they wanted, no quotas, no fuss. Meanwhile they had their own meal, himself and cook, whose proper name was Jamal. Cook was all right, seemed to like him. Jamal had what looked like knife scars on his arms and down the right side of his face, and he'd never seen anybody carry scars like that. But he guessed Jamal hadn't been where he could get to meds, or didn't want to, or some reason he'd never met in his life.

Jamal wasn't the only one. The crew that drifted in . . . just wasn't *like* the people he associated with, which meant like Hawkinses, and the safe bars and the high-class sleepovers of Fargone and places *Sprite* went. Men and women had missing fingers, marks of burns here and there, what he took for old cuts, stuff, God, a surgeon could still fix, along with guys clearly over-mass, and one woman blind in one eye. He saw tattoos, and shaved heads or long hair—he looked at the first arrivals with the panic feeling he'd walked into the wrong bar. But he stood his ground, behind the fortification of the hot line.

"Well, well, well," the comments ran, from female *and* male, "look at you, pretty."

Or: "Reluctant sign-up, looks like."

Or: "Hey, cook, something *new* on the menu?"

"Name's Tom *Bowe*-Hawkins," Jamal said.

"Bowe," the murmur went around.

He just dished up the meatloaf and gave a tight-lipped smile at the offender.

After that it was quieter, with him dishing out main items while cook handled the pastry-cutting—Tink was right, the boundaries among the flowers and vines were as disputatious as trade negotiations.

He could relax after that. The crew looked like dockside hustlers, but the humor wasn't anywhere totally out of line. He snatched a bite himself, the meatloaf, having counted what drew the most second helpings. It was good. He managed to have a mostly uninterrupted supper, give or take the late arrivals who came trailing in. Pastry was as good as it looked, real cake, which meant flour, which wasn't easy come by or cheap—you usually got it on special occasions or in stations' fancier restaurants, at ferocious prices.

Lot of money. Or—he revised the thought—just nearness to the source—and Pell, where they were bound, was a source. You couldn't prove anything against *Corinthian* by the sweets and the cake. He didn't have to think it was stolen.

It wasn't, overall, too damn bad a situation. The crew ragged him, but he'd had that everywhere. He just kept his head down, kept his panic reaction in check, and did his work and didn't bother anybody . . . didn't look for another run-in with Austin Bowe down here in crew territory, and that made him easier with the company he did have.

He finished the cleanup and helped set up mid-shift snacks, the sort that got delivered out. And it was scrub down the galley and the filters again . . . not a big job, because Jamal wanted it done every meal, and a rinse with detergent would do it.

The galley's standards didn't speak of a sloppy ship, at all.

"Guys don't look real regulation," he remarked to Tink, when he and Tink were working side by side; and he'd gotten so used to Tink's appearance he forgot he was saying that to a guy whose arms were solid tattoos of snakes and dragons.

"Hey. You stick with me, I know a good artist on Pell. Glow in the dark."

He couldn't imagine. Couldn't imagine going back to *Sprite* with a tattoo.

And then he recalled where they were, traversing the dark of Tripoint, on their way to places *Sprite* wouldn't find them, didn't care to find them, and he got a lump in his throat and asked himself what he was going to do—except Tink had had things a hell of a lot worse, and he told himself somehow he *could* survive, and there *was* a future.

"You worried about the crew?" Tink asked him.

"No," he said. "Not really."

"A lot of these guys, like me," Tink said, and shoved a filter into its slot, "you knock around a lot, you know. Play hob getting work. You get a real solid berth, you damn sure appreciate it. Some's dockers, however. You may have detected."

"Its own dockers, this ship?" That wasn't usual. You *hired* your off-ship workers. You had to, far as he'd ever heard Marie deal with cargo. But maybe if a ship really didn't want outsiders handling its cargo . . .

Tink didn't answer right off. Maybe it was something Tink wasn't supposed to say. Maybe it was a question he wasn't supposed to ask. "Hey, the unions want to insist, all right, our guys handle it to the gateway, they take it after. And most of these guys are all right. Just ever' now and again you figure they got a little stash they're hitting . . . the long, deep dark's the place they get spooky. They don't got enough to do. They start hitting the stash, you know, four, five days . . . that don't improve their personality a bit."

"I wouldn't think." Maybe he really shouldn't have asked. It dawned on him—if there were trades in the deep, and that was *Corinthian's* business—even there, somebody had to handle cargo, and umbilicals, and all the mate-ups, in an exchange of cargo, or whatever. Dockers . . . were what you needed in that operation, dockers and cargo monkeys, not your tech crew.

Tink got up and dusted his hands. "I got to get a new overhead filter. This indicator's turned."

Definitely shouldn't have asked, he thought to himself. "Yeah," he said, "all right." As if his approval meant anything. Tink terminated the conversation, went off to storage to look for the right filter—Tink wasn't lying about that, he was sure.

Tink stayed gone a bit. Possibly, he thought, there wasn't a filter in stock where it ought to be . . . if that happened, you had to check other lists, because usually you could sub something, but you also chewed out Supply, and asked why the computer hadn't reported it.

If it hadn't, *he* could fix it, instead of scrubbing tables—if he wanted to admit he knew enough to be a danger to the ship. Which he didn't intend to do, not without knowing more than he did, not without some sort of peace between him and *Corinthian,* that maybe seemed a little nearer since he'd dealt with Tink, but far from certain, since there were clearly right questions and wrong questions and things Tink didn't want to discuss on his own.

A good thing, was it, for hired crew? Maybe the best berth any of them could ever hope for? The ship paid . . . damned well, evidently. Evidently the ship could afford it without a blink. In either case one had to ask—

Latecomers arrived, a noisy six, seven crewmen who'd missed the serving hour, who saw the food line taken down and weren't happy. "Jamal?" one called out, and got no answer.

Guys who thought they might not get supper weren't a happy lot, and he was uneasy being out front instead of behind the counter, in the galley-proper, where only galley personnel belonged, according to the sign. He went over to the gap in the counter, eased past a guy standing in his way.

"Tink's here," he said, "he just stepped out. He'll be back—"

The man behind him stepped on the cable, jerked his arm.

"Who are you?"

"Tom Hawkins. Tom Bowe-Hawkins." That name had never been an asset in his life, but it seemed that way now. "Excuse me." He closed his hand on the cable to pull it free, looking at the man dead on. The trouble warning was flashing through his nervous system. It doubled when the guy didn't move his foot. "I pay favors," he said.

"Well, what *about* some favors?" the clown said. "You handing it out, boy?"

"You want meals off-schedule, you ask and say please, or you talk to Cook about—"

The guy jerked the cable. He was ready for it, but the guy outweighed him. He had the counter corner between them. He used that for a brake, but the pull put his arm in hostile territory and hurt a wrist getting sorer by every pull on it—hurt it considerably, and the guy grabbed his arm to jerk him around the counter and into the galley.

Another jerked on him and he got him—threw all the weight he owned at the target he found clear—the guy's throat, that being what he exposed, and grabbed the guy's sleeve as he slid across the counter and the others closed in. He had one hand free, the other was tangled with the cable, and he couldn't swing, but he tried to grab the cable and get it around a neck, any neck, he wasn't particular. He got part-way up when he landed, got hits in anywhere he saw open, between efforts to keep them from doing a complete take-down, the way they were trying, not just the one, all of them. "Get him, get him, get him," someone yelled, and as the sheer weight shoved him down, his head hit the cabinet handle, boomed off the doors, his shoulders hit the floor and five or six guys were piling on him, weighing his legs down, hanging onto his arms. A blow caught his temple and knocked him blind, a knee landed in his gut, and he kept trying to swing, but he couldn't get the one hand clear, couldn't get out of the vee they'd jammed him into, and couldn't fend the next blow or the next or the next. . . .

"What in hell are you doing?" somebody yelled, and he kept

trying to swing—caught one with his elbow. "Break it up. Now, damn it! Break it up!"

Somebody waded in and pulled the guys off him, told them to get the hell out—didn't sound like Jamal, didn't sound like Tink . . . he still hadn't gotten his sight back, but whoever had gotten them off ordered them out, said he wouldn't put them on report, just get the hell out. "This is my brother," somebody yelled next his ear, the same somebody holding him on his feet. "You lay a hand on him again and I'll kill you."

Christian? He didn't believe it—but somebody who called him brother was holding him up, arm around his bruised ribs. His knees weren't working at all well, he couldn't get his breath. One of them had hit him in the gut, and he couldn't keep his feet when his rescuer let him down to the deck against the cabinet and lifted his eyelids one after another.

" 'm all right," he said, trying to get his wind back. "Can't see—they caught me one in the head."

"Goes away," Christian said, and it was, to the extent he could make out lights and darks, the white of the floor, the dark of Christian's knee. He was preoccupied getting his breath and still didn't comprehend why Christian who'd given him hell till now was holding him from falling on his face—his *Polly* girl'd hold him like that, defend him like that, but, different, he thought dimly, different, never had anybody pull him out of a fight who hadn't likewise lit into him, and him being close to falling on his face, and the rescue being somebody he didn't otherwise trust . . . he didn't know what he thought or felt . . . whether he resented it or didn't when Christian shouldered his weight, ran a hand through his hair and called him a damned ass in a tone gentler than Marie ever used with the same endearment.

Stupid to trust the guy who'd jerked him up a wall on a cable.

But Christian dug a key-card out of his pocket, and used it on the cable lock, just took it off, and rubbed his wrist and pulled at him. "I'll give your regrets to Cook. Come on. Up. Up."

He didn't know what he thought. Didn't understand the game, but he hurt, he couldn't see, and up on his feet was where he wanted to be, except the whole room was tilted. Christian kept him upright—kept him from falling on his face—he was seeing blurry tables in a vacant galley, now.

And Tink came back.

"What's going on?" Tink asked. "I just stepped out to storage, sir, I was with him all the time—"

"Six, seven fools," Christian said. "I got him, Tink. He's all right. I'll fix him up."

He wasn't sure about that proposal. He wasn't sure he wanted Christian taking him anywhere, and he wanted Tink to stick with him, but Tink didn't raise any objection as Christian steered him past the tables and out the door—what could Tink do anyway? Christian was an officer on this ship.

It was up to him, then. He made a try at walking on his own, but he still couldn't see anything but shapes, and he wasn't, it turned out, walking straight. Christian threw an arm around him, hauled him away from impact with the wall.

"Don't be an ass," Christian said, "difficult as that may be for you."

"Go to hell."

Christian jerked him hard enough his head snapped. "I can beat up on you. They can't. That's the rules."

Seemed perfectly clear. He got a breath as they walked. "Where're we going?"

"My cabin."

He planted his feet. Tried to. He wasn't at all stable, even standing, and Christian dragged him along anyway. By now his vision was clearing, but a headache arrived with it, and he thought a bone in his forearm might be cracked, where Christian was pulling on it.

Another jerk. "Don't give me trouble."

Hurt, being hauled on like that. Didn't have the brain operative enough to argue otherwise, and he thought for a moment he was going to throw up, right there in the corridor. He didn't want to do that. Wanted a bathroom, wanted to sit down, and if Christian had a place closer than he could otherwise get to, fighting wasn't worth it yet, wait-see . . . hope the rescue was a rescue and not an ambush in itself.

Christian steered him for a blurry door, opened it, on a wide cabin with real carpet. Chairs. Bunk. Lot of pillows.

"Don't bleed on the bed." Christian dropped him onto it. "You hear me?"

He wasn't trying to. He was looking for somewhere to lean his hand, but it was bleeding or bloody, his nose was bubbling, and Christian went back to the bath and ran water while he considered whether he was or wasn't going to heave his gut up.

Not, he decided after several breaths and a wait-see. He propped himself with his hand on his knee, mildly tilted, on the edge of the bed, while Christian brought him a wet towel and insisted on going at his face with it, mopping his nose and his mouth, his eye. He was shaky. The cold towel obscured his vision and he wasn't sure where up was. The tilt warned him.

Christian shoved him backward, flat, and said catch his breath.

Good idea, he thought. But it rode his thoughts consistently that Christian wasn't his friend, the captain of the ship had ordered him to be in the galley, and if there was a set-up for blame possible, Christian wasn't necessarily the one going to catch hell—he just couldn't think through the haze and the headache to figure out what the game was.

"Listen," Christian said, settling, a weight on the mattress edge beside him. "The guys made a mistake. I don't want it blown up into an incident that can sour this trip, you read me clear? Mad crew can make a lot of trouble."

It sounded like an actual honest reason. A serious reason. He wasn't brought up a total fool—a ship in space was wholly vulnerable. This ship in particular was vulnerable to its hire-ons or any total crazy they happened to get aboard. Was Christian saying they were already running scared of the crew, or what, for God's sake? And was Christian in some kind of personal bind about what had happened?

His head hurt too much to figure it out. Christian meanwhile got up and rummaged through his clothes locker, after something, he didn't figure what, or want to know. He just wanted back in the galley or back in the brig without being used or manipulated into something that could bring their mutual father to bounce his already aching body off the bulkhead again, that was his chief concern. He'd just had it fairly good where he was, today, and he *didn't* want a set-to with anybody right now.

Except—

Christian came back, threw some clothes onto the end of the bed. "You concussed? Anything broken?"

He ran his tongue around his mouth as he lay there. Stared at Christian down his nose. There were cuts. Teeth ached. Everything ached. "Ribs, arm, maybe cracked. I don't know." He couldn't help it, *couldn't* keep his mouth shut and give up a fight with a guy who had one due. "What's it to you?"

"All right, all right." Christian waved his arms. "Cancel, stop, go back. Bad start, all right? Bad start. My damn temper. —But I caught hell for bringing you aboard. Austin calls me a fool. Everybody calls me a fool. But it was a judgment call. Don't ask me what I was supposed to do! You're the one went poking into what didn't involve you, and now everything's my fault. When I'm wrong I catch hell for it. When I'm right I catch hell. When I'm right and they're wrong I catch double hell, but I didn't plan this, I did the best I could, all right? I got you out of there. Probably Austin would've, if he was there, just the same, but it's my fault since I did it and he didn't have to, you understand me?"

Most guys wouldn't. Not half. But he'd lived with Marie. "Yeah," he said, and struggled to sit up, with a hand pressed against his forehead, because his brain hurt.

"So I'm sorry," Christian said. "Bad start. Austin pounded *me* against a wall. And he didn't pass the warning to all the guys. The ones that pounded you, they won't, twice. They'll walk wide of you, and me. I have it over them in spades right now. They'll do me favor points, you, too, if you don't make a case. Rough guys, but they know they're on notice."

"I won't be anybody's target. Not anybody's. Not theirs. Not yours."

"I said I was sorry. I'd had my own run-in with Austin, all right? —There's a shower. Clean clothes. Couple of days yet before jump and then you can lie still and let it heal. You'll be fine. Won't even scar."

Christian could say that. But a shower was attractive. *Real* attractive. Clean clothes . . . it felt as if the coveralls had grown to his skin. He'd sweated in them. He'd bled over them. He loathed the feel of them. And the loan of a shower and clean clothes . . . was a bribe worth a peace treaty, far as he was concerned. He started to get up.

"You make it on your own?" Christian asked.

"Yeah," he said, and hauled himself up, one hand on the wall.

A little dizziness then. But his sight was mostly back. He got up in the unaccustomed great space of the biggest junior officer's cabin he'd seen, and wobbled back to the shower.

Forgot the clean clothes. He turned around to trek back again, but Christian brought them to the bath and left him alone, afterward, to knock around the small mirrored space, getting undressed.

After that was warm water vapor, luxury detergent, the kind-to-abused-skin sort, and he could have sunk to the bottom of the shower and stayed there a year, but it had an auto-cycle he hadn't set right and it went to blow dry long before he wanted it.

He opened the door a crack and snaked an arm out for the

clothes, such as they were. He'd never tried skintights. Never had the budget and never wanted the cousins laughing at him.

Black. Shimmer-stuff. Damned little left to the imagination, one size fit all, or you definitely shouldn't think about it.

He hadn't a mirror inside the shower and he wasn't at all sure, except they were clean, dry, more comfortable than they looked, and the shirt—blue—at least was tunic-style. Tabs at the side that made the waist fit—another one-size, and the loose sleeves, anybody could wear who didn't have arms to their knees. He wasn't sure. He felt like a fool coming out of the shower, and stopped in the doorway for a mistrustful glance at the mirror.

"Better," Christian said, "A little *style*, Hawkins, couldn't hurt."

Heat from the shower hadn't made him steadier. He wobbled. He glared at this implied deficiency in Hawkins taste. He stuck his foot in his boot in the doorway, and leaned on it, working the heel on while he braced a hand against the wall.

"So you want off this ship," Christian said.

Escape? A deal with Christian? No way in hell did he trust it. He balanced and shoved the other foot in the other boot.

"This is a true or false. Possible even for a Hawkins. Fifty percent chance of being right. Do you want off this ship?"

Christian might want rid of him. That part he could believe, the way he couldn't readily believe Christian's stepping into a brawl only to save him. He didn't know how obvious his suspicions were, or what it could cost him to challenge Christian with the truth. But he decided on confrontation, for good or for ill. "Not to any Mazianni carrier, if that's the trade you're in."

"Yeah, yeah, we just load up the fools and Mazian pays top price, loves to buy those fools. Use your damn head. Where are we going?"

"Pell's what I've heard."

"Not a bad place to ship from. Civilized port. Lot of ships. Go where you like. Can't beat that."

Christian left a silence in which he might be expected to say something. He didn't. He didn't trust anything about the offer, didn't trust Christian's motives—

"Look," Christian said. "Sit down." Christian indicated the end of the bed, and reluctantly, because his knees weren't that steady, he went back to the bed and sat. "You may have noticed," Christian said, leaning against the wall near him, one booted ankle over the other, working the heel back and forth, "that Austin is a difficult sod. I said we hadn't an auspicious beginning. Much less so with maman, Beatrice, who *doesn't* like your presence. We are the victims of two ferocious women, one of whom wants to kill us and the other of whom wants to kill you before you kill us."

"I've no desire whatever—"

"I'm perfectly certain you're an independent and difficult spirit, yourself, but maman, understand, Beatrice . . . will absolutely not tolerate you on this deck, not as Marie Hawkins' offspring, certainly not as Austin's, competing, shall I say it, with me? Shall I say plainly that Beatrice wants you out of here, you most certainly want to go . . . and it seems to me that you have no evidence against us, nothing but a merchanter quarrel, —and we all know how quickly stations wash their hands of our untidy affairs. I would never tie myself up with station police and lawyers, on the Alliance side of the Line, lawyers and court dates and station law—you don't like station lawyers, do you, Hawkins? You're not that crazy."

"No."

"Not going to be that crazy."

"No."

"Pell has customs. But you've got your passport. . ."

God. They *would* have it. *With* his papers, that said he worked computers.

"—Found it on you. No problem. Just get you out the airlock all legitimate and you take a walk."

"And end up dead."

"Hawkins. Hawkins. I had my chance in the warehouse. But the fact that you're, realtime, my slightly *older* brother, suggests to certain members of this crew that you might find a niche aboard, that you might pose some threat to interests that have worked a long time to secure the positions they have, do you see? Not that I'm immune. I could rather like you, as a human being. You have certain engaging qualities, occasional flashes of actual intellect, you don't know the depth of dimness I have to deal with in the crew, God! you'd be such a relief! But I'm not about to see you become a focus of dissension, or find partisans. This is a rough crew. We manage very borderline individuals. We simply can't afford anyone challenging an officer's authority, do you see? So for various reasons, and peace with maman, who is our chief pilot, far more essential than either of us, and a perfect *bitch* when she's taken a position, I'm perfectly willing to have you disappear at Pell."

"And if something goes wrong?"

"If something goes wrong you end up back aboard. Or with the Pell cops. Choose aboard, is my advice. You wouldn't like the cops."

No spacer liked the cops.

This spacer didn't like the idea of being shanghaied into another crew, either.

And it scared him that Christian's logic halfway persuaded him.

"So?" Christian said. "Deal?"

He shrugged. He'd had a lifetime of Mischa ducking questions, apologizing his way past personnel decisions. He didn't like the taste it left in his mouth. Didn't like what this maneuver implied about Christian's style of command. 'We can't afford anybody challenging an officer's authority.' Hell.

So Christian helped him escape?

"Yeah," he said, not daring, not wanting to say anything that could change Christian's mind. It wasn't for him to critique whatever got him back to *Sprite*.

Christian got up.

"Better get you back," Christian said. So the deal seemed done.

—— *v* ——

OLDER BROTHER WAS THINKING ON the way back to the brig. Older brother was limping, too—the guys had exceeded suggestions, and that was a problem. "Tell anybody that asks," Christian said, "that it was me that gave you the black eye."

"Is it black?"

"It will be."

Damned odd, Christian thought, everything was so placid of a sudden. They came to the brig, and he figured then that all the rules still applied, in Austin's book, and therefore in his, no matter that older brother wasn't in fighting form. "Cable," Christian said, and Hawkins went inside, picked it up off the floor and locked the bracelet on his own wrist. "Let me see it."

He shut the grid. Hawkins came to the bars and let him inspect the bracelet. The wrist and hand were bruised dark, ugly and painful looking. And the lock was solid.

"Yeah," he said, thought about offering to change hands with the lock, but, hell, they weren't a charity. He started off down the corridor, to leave older brother to his own amusement, or to get to sleep, or whatever, but it occurred to him then that there were reasons security might lock down tight after the rumors got topside, lock down in ways that would screw everything. Besides, older brother might do something entirely stupid if Austin came down in Austin's morning to check on the rumors that were bound to get started—he didn't trust Jamal's discretion or Tink's to hold them off five minutes longer than it took a casual mention to get up to the bridge. ✒

So he went back to the bars, leaned there. Hawkins had sat down on his bunk.

"Hawkins. A warning. If our mutual papa says you're scum, say yes, sir, thank you, sir. That's all. No matter what."

Hawkins' jaw set. You could see the muscle clench. "Man's an ass."

"Hawkins. A small touch of sanity. You're already on scrub. You want to find yourself working four shifts on scrub? No sleep? That's your choice. You keep your mouth under control."

A moment of surly silence.

"Son of a fool bitch," he said, "I'm trying to get you out of here. I'm trying to save your ass. Can we have a yes out of the savee? Can we have a thank you, just a trial run?"

Hawkins kept glaring at him. Didn't trust him, and properly so. But then Hawkins said, "Yeah. Thanks."

"Mouth, Hawkins-brother?"

"Yeah." Hawkins dropped his stare, at least. Tucked a foot up under the other leg and winced. "I hear. I understand you."

"Easy to pronounce, please and yessir. Get you out of a lot of situations."

Hawkins didn't say a thing.

"Damned fool," Christian said with a shake of his head, but he knew the look, he saw it on Austin, he saw it in mirrors when he'd had a run-in with authority. He withdrew his arms from the bars and went on down the corridor with his own blood pressure up, and with an intense urge to do bodily harm to Hawkins before he got off this ship.

So it didn't make sense that the bloody mess the guys had left Hawkins in should turn his stomach queasy, or make sense that the bruises he'd left had touched the same nerves. He'd seen worse. He'd probably done worse, he didn't keep count.

Didn't know why, when he got up to the bridge and went through his initial shift-change checks—an hour late—he kept flashing on that parting argument and Hawkins' bruises—his fault—and how, just quite strangely, in a ship full of hire-ons you couldn't trust and a handful you knew you could rely on to guard your back, he had an instant expectation of Tom Hawkins' behavior, the body language, the way he worked, an expectation what he was thinking and what it took to get him off a point he wanted to hold. . . .

But, dammit, he had no choice.

He walked the aisles, monitored their course. They'd been lazing along for a full run of the clock in the dark of Tripoint, eating, sleeping, checking and fixing and maintaining. Midway through his watch they'd do a long burn, no traffic problems here, get up to speed on their outbound vector toward Pell.

After which it was Austin's watch, and Beatrice would take them through. He managed the shift, when the number one crew was off . . . he set up the numbers and the number one crew ran them. Routine, this place, this nearest mass that was nothing but a radiating black lump in the starry dark. The techs were hewing to a long-established procedures list, for this precise place.

"Got it. Thanks." He signed a check-sheet, meaning the bridge hadn't blown up an hour-thirty into the watch.

The techs around him were in danger of falling asleep of boredom—a contagious condition. Mainday shift on an alter-day ship only punched buttons and checked readout. And stayed ready for the instant of absolute terror that could be an inbound rock. It did happen. Or an inbound and oncoming ship. With Marie Hawkins possibly on their tail—who knew what was a possibility?

The further he got from the moment the more it seemed crazy to have taken Hawkins into his own quarters, behind locked doors. Hell if he'd have done that with hired crew. Austin would skin him if the guy didn't stick a knife in him for his trouble. Stupid, what he'd done. Gave him cold chills just thinking about it.

But he *had* read Hawkins. He'd been absolutely confident. He'd known and he'd guessed right—the way he'd gone from gut-level irritation to body-sense understanding what Hawkins was doing. Next was guessing what the son of a bitch was going to—

Hands touched his back.

He yelled and spun around with an elbow for the offender.

Capella was faster than that, and a centimeter out of range. "Don't walk up on me! This is the bridge, not a—"

"Not what?"

Capella had logical business on the bridge, the mainday chief having every right to be where she was.

Meanwhile, among the techs, Bowe, Perrault, and eclectic, not a head had turned. Everybody on the bridge knew the situation between the captain's-son-mainday-chief-officer and the lend-lease navigator. He grabbed Capella's wrist and got her started in the officeward direction—and let go once she was launched. Hold onto Capella when you weren't joking and you were asking for a broken arm.

Which he wasn't. He led the way off to the central corridor, back to his office, and near enough to Austin's quarters and Beatrice's that he signaled quiet until he'd triggered the door.

"Need a favor," he said. "You know where they put older brother's effects, in downside Ops."

"Yeah. The safe."

"You know the combination."

"You want his stuff?"

"Yeah. But I can't get down there as easily."

Capella gave him a suspicious stare. "Yeah?"

"Dockside's on me this trip. And older brother's taking a walk while we just can't be responsible."

"Wait, wait, brake it, mister."

"Passport. Papers. ID. I want it."

"Christian-person. Walk like . . . cold, or walk like . . . off?"

"I mean I'm letting him go, shoving him off at Pell."

Capella's brows went together. Bang. "Straight to the cops. If *Sprite*'s on our tail . . . if that ship comes in while we're there—"

"They had their full offload and load yet to do and we're wasting no time here. We'll be offloaded, loaded and out before they make a ripple at Pell."

"You're betting the ship. You're betting the whole fucking ship."

"I'm *protecting* our asses. He's trouble. He's major trouble on board."

"You're jealous."

"I'm not jealous."

"Hell you aren't."

"Crew's complicated enough."

Family was complicated enough. That was the truth. Austin never listened. Zeroed in on this Hawkins. Never once saw he'd done the best he could, bringing Hawkins aboard, never wanted to talk about the solution—oh, no, *that* wasn't Christian's business.

"You know," Capella said, "there are places Hawkins could be besides Pell."

He glumly shook his head, to all Capella's . . . associations. And to all the other places Hawkins could end up.

Including the deep-cold dark, stabbed in some crew fight. He didn't know why he couldn't have arranged that option—he could have put it off on some sumbitch like Edgar Hogan, or Tolliver, who could probably be arranged to do it, and to pay for it—except there was suddenly a line between him and Capella there hadn't been a moment ago, and a caution there'd never needed be before. If he'd crossed that line himself, somewhere, he'd not known it had happened—in that warehouse, maybe, or down in the galley just now.

Because Capella would kill—and he discovered he wouldn't. Couldn't. He didn't know whether that was a fault or a virtue, when their collective lives depended on it; or whether it was strength or weakness, when he knew the universe *he* lived in wasn't neat, or clean, or inclined to give anything for free the way it was in those damn books Capella read.

He did everything Austin wanted. He worked his butt off to

get one well done out of Austin all his fucking life. But, oh, Hawkins got Austin's attention—got Austin's complete attention, che*a*p, on the going market.

And the guy was everything . . . intelligent, reasonable, easy to like . . . that he fucking *wasn't*.

"Chrissy, Christian-sweet. You want advice? Don't—don't do this. It's too risky to let him out. The cops, that's one. And Austin, if he finds out you had anything to do with it—"

"You give me advice," he said, "on something you know about. I'm telling you. We want him off this ship, we want him the hell invisible, to us and to the cops. For the ship's sake."

"Marie Hawkins is not to ignore. If she comes spreading tales—and a witness climbs out of some drainpipe—"

"Not a shred of evidence. None. Nothing they can use. *She'll* look the fool. What will *Sprite* have? One of their own crewmen? Back where he belongs, with his maman? What a crime! What a disaster! His mother claims kidnapping. But with what evidence? His word? No, I want the stuff, Pella, dear. You've got the access. Use it on my behalf and I won't tell about the brandy."

"You son of a bitch."

"*Fils de Beatrice, absolument.*" He caught Capella's arms as they came about him, as Capella's teeth came very near the sensitive spots of his neck. "Does it occur to you that Austin's preferences run in a pattern?"

"Absolutely." Capella's hands, freed, wandered to his lower back, arms pulled him close. Hips moved. Teeth grazed his ear. "Like father like son. Take ten, Chris-tian, duty can spare it. A whole boring month in hyperspace. . ."

Austin would skin him, the higher brain said. Lower brain was taking over rapidly, now was now and the couch in his office was a convenient immediate destination.

Himself on the bottom this time, Capella taking over—while he was thinking, distractedly, of older brother stuck in that cell, older, easy-to-like brother—and he came back to here and now with Capella shoving his hands out of play above his head and trailing kisses progressively below his neck. The risk of running toward jump without him on duty, the risk of violating orders, saying screw-you to Austin and knowing his own judgment about *Corinthian* was as valid—not that Austin would consult him. That was what sent him toward a dark, suicidal high, half-wishing physical harm was a real risk at Capella's hands.

Never fucking listened to him. . . .

— *vi* —

At about maindark, mainday shift change on this alterday ship, the lights briefly faded, tribute to a lately hostile sun, and a voice that might be Christian's came on over the general com, saying, Take hold. They were starting acceleration toward a jump at 0448:32h, shift to alterday crew slightly before that.

A more formal warning and certainly more information than they'd gotten with Austin Bowe on watch, Tom thought, deciding that, over all, Christian seemed more reasonable than his father by a wide margin.

Immediately after that announcement, the siren sounded, and if a spacer was conscious, semiconscious, or sane, he grabbed after the belts and fastened them.

Then he tugged the blanket up against the chill that seemed a permanent part of jump, and snugged down for a secure rest. Acceleration began, with an initial slam that hit all the floating organs, and then a steady pressure—familiar as a sense of moving, getting up to speed, toward Pell, he told himself, and maybe toward freedom. He began to turn that promise of Christian's over and over in his mind, yes, it could be true, Christian might have the reasons he cited; or, no, it wasn't true, it was a set-up and he ought to tell somebody who could get word to the captain something was going on that he wouldn't approve—

But then, third side . . . he couldn't get away by staying on the ship, and, fourth, even if it turned out to be a set-up, he might still turn the tables on whoever set him up (likely Christian) and get to the police.

Except—fifth—Christian was absolutely right about going to station police, it scared him, the way Lydia, damn her screwed-up meddling, had once had him terrified of being left on station; but there was a reasonable adult fear in it, too—depending on the seriousness of what *Corinthian* was involved in, it was a way to get tangled up in Pell's Legal Affairs office, in a cross-border incident, called in at least as a witness in some God-only-knew court case that could drag on and involve drugs he didn't want to take, when all he remotely wanted to do was get a ship to Viking and have a reasonable chance of meeting *Sprite* on a port call, give or take a year. Viking was an immediate port for Pell, there had to be numbers of ships going and coming, all the time. If everything Christian said was true and he had his papers, he could be out of there maybe in hours from the time he hit Pell docks, and have all of it behind him.

But—six—he could talk his way into free passage, maybe; but a year's wait, on Viking, even eating out of vending machines, was, God, he didn't know, 15000c, at sleepover rates, if he starved himself and stayed in the cheapest places he could find. That was the next worry. Either Christian would keep his word and bid him farewell on Pell's dock, scenario a, and he was on his own, to get transport . . . or, scenario b, back to the set-up . . . Christian might have something in mind else. Like double-cross. Like . . .

Like setting him up to be killed, so nobody would ask questions.

Could Christian do a thing like that? It was the most logical thing for Christian to do, if he didn't come with a conscience, if Austin didn't intend to let him go, ever, if . . .

God, he'd lost count. But scenario three, or eight, or whatever—if Christian was right, and Austin might try to work him into crew, beat hell out of him until he learned to say yessir to Austin the way Christian did—

But after that, Austin wouldn't let him go, either, he'd just be on better terms with Austin. Which he by no means wanted. Christian and Christian's mother damn sure didn't.

So they agreed on something. The question was what they actually intended for a solution to the tangle.

He just wanted to go to sleep. God, he desperately wanted not to think.

But then he had a colder, more awful thought, and pulled open the panel beside the bunk.

No trank to keep him sane. No packets. He'd used them all. Nobody'd resupplied the locker. On *Sprite,* they checked and rechecked them, made sure every one was refilled.

Christian was in charge, on mainday. Christian was running things and Austin wasn't on duty.

Now he really couldn't sleep. Accel was hell enough and most times you could sleep through it, if you didn't mind feeling *g* in two directions at once, but right now the knowledge of that empty panel and the lack of a com in the brig combined to upset his stomach. He kept rolling Christian's motives over and over, told himself, one, it was a long time until 0448h, and the minute someone started stirring about he could get attention to the problem. And, two, maybe if Christian was trying to scare him, he could get other attention at shift change. . .

Maybe the dark-haired girl would come back. Even Capella. It was no good lying and sweating, there'd be a chance to talk to someone, surely, they weren't going to go without a final check.

This, in the ship that didn't sound but cursory warnings when it moved.

It was an hour before they went inertial. He got up then, risking his neck, God, stiff and sore, every movement he made—maybe the ribs were cracked from the fight, maybe not, but that was minor compared to the chance of being left with no supplies down here. He yelled. He banged the walls, he yelled again at every remote sound he heard, hoping someone would hear.

Eventually he heard someone walking in the corridor, and screamed to anyone out there that he hadn't any trank, dammit, he needed help, he needed somebody to tell the captain. . .

Tink came walking up, with a tray—with trank and the nutri-packs on it, along with breakfast, or supper, or something, and one of Tink's decorated pastries.

Relief flooded through him and left a flutter like electric shock.

"We weren't going to forget you," Tink said. "We weren't going to forget you, no time we ever forgot the brig."

"I didn't know you were in charge. God, I'm glad to see you."

"Yeah, yeah. Galley always sees to stations. Always a snack first—first class stuff, here."

"It's wonderful." He tried to make light of it, feeling foolish. "Thanks, Tink." But he was shaking so when he took the tray through the opening in the bars that the liquid shook in the cup. "Sugar-flowers. That's real pretty."

"Made it special. I'm real sorry I left you alone yesterday. I am. Wouldn't've happened if I hadn't left."

"Not your fault. It's all right, Tink."

Tink looked troubled . . . beyond 'it's all right.' "Scuttlebutt was . . . there was an order."

"On what?"

Tink evaded his eyes. Found an interesting spot on the floor to the far side of the bars. "Like, it was just an order."

An order. And Tink just happened to need to change a filter?

"Tink?"

Tink still didn't look at him, quite.

He felt a twinge of regret. Of disappointment. Of anger, for Tink's sake . . . and his own.

"Yeah," he said, "I copy. Thanks. Thanks, Tink. Really, thanks."

"I didn't know they was going to do that!"

"You didn't know my brother was going to do that. I should've figured it."

"He ain't a bad officer," Tink said. "He's a layoff, but things get done.—And he's fair, most times. The captain's got him bothered."

"About what? What's enough, to go to that trouble? Tink, Tink, he's saying . . . he's saying he'll get me off at Pell. That I can go free. Is he lying?"

Tink looked at him then. A long, troubled look.

"What's the truth, Tink? I swear . . . I swear I won't say where I heard it, just tell me, and I'll believe you."

"The junior's a nice guy," Tink said. "He really is. Tries to take the crew's side. Stood between the hire-ons and the senior. Michaels. Michaels is who you don't cross. But the junior'll always hear you, if there's a side you got, you understand me? I don't figure what he did, it ain't like him to set somebody up like that, except he's got some notion you're a problem—on account of your mama. I hear she's got a grudge with the captain."

"You could say."

"So maybe that's it." Tink cast a nervous glance down the corridor. "Tom, I got other places to get to, I got to hurry. We got jump at Oh Five, just short. Can't collect the tray, just kind of dump it in the shower when you're through, all right? And latch the door? I got a lot of stations to get to, before. But I come here first."

"Yeah," he said, "yeah, thanks, Tink. Sincerely, thanks."

He took the tray back to his bunk, sat down, dug in to the synth eggs-'n-ham, which wasn't bad, but peculiar. It had leafy stuff in it, that wasn't algae. Strong-flavored stuff. Maybe it was another thing they got off a living world, like a real spice. He'd had a few—just a few.

But he figured it had to be all right—Jamal kept the galley so clean, if green stuff turned up it was legit, and safe, and probably expensive. And once you thought that, it began to taste fairly good.

Not surprising, he told himself, what Tink had said. He'd

had a halfway instinct about it, that he couldn't trust Christian's motives.

So Christian had him beaten to hell so he could get him to believe what he was going to say.

So he'd been a fool when, for about a dozen heartbeats, he'd leaned on Christian Bowe, believed he'd found someone in the universe who gave a damn slightly more than Marie gave.

Stupid, he said, to himself. He was ashamed, outright angry that he'd given serious credence to Christian's persuasions.

But hell if he'd let on. He'd be far more foolish to let on to Christian that he knew what he did know—and he had confidence in what Tink had told him. Tink didn't have any motive to lie to him. Christian did. Tink hadn't looked at all comfortable telling him what he'd told him—Christian had been so, so smooth, not a flicker of conscience in his delivery.

All of which argued that he had an ally in Tink, if he wanted to put it on Tink's shoulders, but he could get Tink in a helluva lot of trouble on that account, too, and he didn't damn want to, for Tink's sake.

He ate the pastry, thinking about that. It was as good as it looked, dark, with a rough, smoky flavor different than any chocolate he'd ever had. He thought it might just be real, and he wasn't sure if everybody got it, or just people Tink wanted to do it for.

Whatever—it was good. Whatever—Tink didn't need to apologize for being absent. Whatever—Tink had no reason to tell him what he'd told him, except some sense of fairness, except maybe everything he thought he read in the man was true—because Tink didn't read out to him as vengeful, or a habitual or purposeful liar. He'd do a lot for Tink. He hadn't *met* anybody like Tink, on *Sprite* or on the docks, and Tink had a piece of his priorities, if Tink ever somehow needed something he could do.

But he could think of a thousand reasons for Christian to lie, and to want him off the ship—if only for the reasons that Christian had plainly admitted to him as his reasons.

It made . . . not quite a lump in his throat, but at least a welling up of feeling he hadn't expected to apply, on this ship. Didn't know why he should be surprised. Even Marie'd double-crossed him, in her way—played him for a fool, ditching him on the docks the way she had.

The truly embarrassing thing was, he couldn't learn. Cousins had caught him in sucker-games, and you'd think he'd get cleverer—he had, give him credit, grown more reserved with them. But the harder Marie had shoved him away the more desperate he was to get close to her—

Kid mentality. Panic instinct. Once, in a corridor downside, she'd told him she wasn't speaking to him, and walked off—he'd followed, gotten slapped in the face, and kept it up, and gotten slapped . . . he'd been, maybe, five, six, he wasn't sure, but it came back to him sometimes with particular clarity, the smothered feeling, the feeling he had to hold on to Marie, and he'd known he was making her madder, he'd known she was going to hit him every time he caught her, but he kept doing it, and grabbing at her clothes and screaming his head off—she kept hitting him, until Marie got a better grip on her panic than he had on his—it *was* panic, he'd figured that out somewhere years later, panic on her side, panic on his.

God knew. They did it to each other, simply existing. He'd gone to that warehouse in some confused sense of responsibility for Marie he would have thought he'd learned not to have.

She'd kept him, Mischa had said, for reasons that had scared him—that ought to scare anybody with a conscience and a responsibility—but had Mischa done anything to protect him?

Not one solitary thing.

A half-brother who wanted rid of him. A father who wished he'd never existed.

He wasn't anybody *Sprite* expected anything from, either, —hadn't Mischa said so? He'd screwed up. Everybody expected it. Why in hell shouldn't he deliver? Only major time he'd ever helped Marie, he'd screwed up.

And why spare Christian, or his father? Why cooperate with

anyone at all, except to spite the powers that created him? Try helping them, maybe. Worst thing he could think of to do to anybody.

Didn't want to hurt Tink, though, really didn't want to hurt Tink, or get him arrested, or lose his license—he didn't even know the guy but a couple of days, but Tink didn't deserve it. Wasn't fair that he couldn't think about *Corinthian* anymore without remembering specific faces, guys like Tink, guys like those sons of bitches he'd like to find when he didn't have a cable on his wrist, but he didn't want to kill them, just . . .

Wasn't damned fair. *Corinthian* hadn't been faces to him. Hadn't been people like Tink, at all.

Which meant he should disappear fast when he got to Pell, just out the lock and out of port, no note to the cops, nothing that could screw his father the way he deserved.

Chapter Six

— *i* —

Numbers were spieling out toward jump, arbitrary destination at this point, but crew of both shifts on last-minute errands needed the time to reach secure places. The bridge was all shift-changed. The last, the pilot switchover, was quick, exchange of a couple of words of report, and Beatrice settled into her post, still mildly pissed, you could tell it in the set of her jaw.

Mildly pissed was more worrisome than raging hell in Beatrice's case, and Austin kept an eye on the aristocratic, pale-skinned arrogance that was one damned fine pilot smiling with perfect friendliness at her outgoing shift-mate.

Mildly pissed meant that some event had made *la belle Beatrice* a little happier about the cause célèbre Beatrice *wasn't* talking about, namely Hawkinses. She wasn't giving him advice, he had *had* all the advice he wanted, and he strongly suspected the meeting between Beatrice and Christian, that he was sure he wasn't supposed to know about, had had something to do with a handful of dockers trying the new boy on board, *something* to do with Christian's pulling said new boy aside—for a talk, presumably.

From which, exit Tom Hawkins with new clothes—expensive clothes. Christian's. They were about the same size.

"On target," Beatrice said, without looking at anyone. "Five minutes, mark."

Beatrice was, face it, jealous—jealous of her position, which never was threatened *except* by her damnable moods. So her personal effort had produced a shipboard Bowe offspring. It hadn't been *his* idea. Ten years of immature brat whose whereabouts had to be assured before the ship moved, thank God for Saby or the Offspring would have gone smack against the bulkhead for sure. Ten more years of juvie phobias, psychoses, and damn-his-ass attitudes before the brat was supposed to turn into an adult with basic common sense.

Which meant knowing when to take a wide decision and when to realize he didn't have all the information and he should ask before he did something irrevocable.

But, oh, no, Christian wouldn't ask. Christian knew everything.

Christian was full of bullshit.

Christian had been tormenting Hawkins, probably from the time he came aboard, right down to the instant he caught him at it, and now Christian was a sudden source of wardrobe and brotherly sympathy?

Don't mind papa, he beats up on all of us?

Double bullshit.

Christian had gotten Hawkins' temper up in the encounter they'd just had . . . and he'd gone on to try that temper, quite deliberately—only prudent, considering Hawkins had had that particular mother for a moral and mental guide, Marie Hawkins whispering her own sweet obsession into young Hawkins' ear, guiding his steps, maybe right onto *Corinthian*'s deck, who but Hawkins could possibly know?

Hawkins' back had hit the wall and he'd come up yelling *I'll kill you*. Which was the truth. Maybe only for that moment, and maybe only in extremity, it was the unequivocated truth—but extremities occurred, moments did happen, desired or not, and Hawkins was a bomb waiting all his life to find such a moment.

It made him unaccountably angry, that Marie Hawkins had done that to the boy. He couldn't be sure, of course, that he could write the whole of Hawkins' reactions down to Marie Hawkins' account, but when Hawkins had come away from the wall shouting what he had, his own nerves had reacted off the scale, just . . . bang. Kill him. Grab him and beat his head against the wall until he yells quit.

And afterward, reverberations in himself far out of proportion to the quarrel, shaky-kneed reaction that hadn't let up for half a damned hour after he'd walked out of that cell and back to the territory where the captain ruled as lord and master of *Corinthian.*

He didn't know why. He wasn't accustomed to react like that to a confrontation, not with crew, not with Beatrice, not with Christian.

So he didn't know why he felt a personal hurt for Hawkins' reaction. Maybe that Marie Hawkins had done something off the scale of his personal (if more rational) morality, doing that to the flesh of her own flesh—couldn't say he was surprised. Marie Hawkins hadn't become a lunatic *after* they'd spent forty-eight hours barricaded . . . she'd been crazy before they'd ever shared a bed, and it might be, to his observation, a genetically transmitted imbalance.

So why did Marie Hawkins' unfair action get him in the gut? What did he fucking care about Marie Hawkins or her kid?

Most spacer-men never met their offspring. And vice-versa.

Which seemed, from where he sat, now, an eminently sensible idea. He hadn't had a sister. Not even a female cousin. He'd have been spared shipboard offspring in the lateral *or* the vertical sense—if Beatrice hadn't double-crossed him and tossed her contraceptive.

Damn the woman. She'd had no right, no bloody right, to do that in the first place, and none at all, now, to play the jealous fool with him over a woman he cared absolutely nothing

about and the offspring he'd never remotely planned to deal
with.

"Mark. Three to jump," came from Beatrice.

Go on dockside separately, they did, he and Beatrice, that
was the agreement. They didn't account to each other for their
bedmates, they trusted each other for basic good taste—and
suddenly Beatrice went green-eyed jealous over a cold-natured
Family bitch whose primary interest the first and only night
they'd slept together was in seeing him fried?

He had an uncomfortable idea precisely on what inspiration
Beatrice's birth control had failed, now that he thought of it.
And why *Corinthian*'s chief pilot had inconvenienced herself at
least long enough to deliver that statistically rare failure into
the universe, Beatrice talking, like a fool, about personal curiosity, and biological investment, and primal urges. . . .

Bull*shit* if Beatrice had primal urges that didn't involve Beatrice's immediate and personal convenience.

He'd been disinterested, then intrigued by the birth process,
and subsequently bemazed by the unique life they'd gener-
ated—which he didn't think of then as a power game.

But that life unfortunately didn't spring to full-blown intelligence, rather languished in fetal helplessness, doddering incon-
venience, juvenile silliness, juvenile rebellion, and finally
juvenile half-assed confidence in its own damned ability.

Hawkins was a shade older than Christian. A shade more
deliberate (Christian planned by the second), a shade more
reluctant to open his mouth (Christian had no brake on his), a
damned sight more apt to studied ambush (Christian was subtle
as an oncoming rock), and, to an unanswered degree, capable
of deceit.

Get the truth out of Hawkins. That was essential. The boy'd
lied about his license, knew a comp tech was persona non grata
on a hostile ship. He'd thought that through, at least.

Get Hawkins to figure out the rules of the real universe, and
that included the basic folly of bucking a ship's captain. The
kid needed an understanding of practicalities.

"Mark one," came from Beatrice.

Kid. Hell. Christian was a kid. Hawkins . . . wasn't.

By what degree not a kid and with what intention currently in his mind remained to be seen, but it wasn't a juvie temper fit that had sent Hawkins away from that wall headed for his throat, it was a man pushed to the limit he was willing to be pushed, and he knew to a fair degree, now, where the flash point was with Hawkins.

Hawkins himself didn't know. But Hawkins would discover it. Hawkins would learn, in the process, what his options were—because—he himself had realized it at an instinctive level in the moment when he'd sent Hawkins to the galley—you couldn't turn Hawkins loose and expect him not to come back at you. You learned, running hired-crew, who would and who wouldn't be safe under what conditions. You bet your life on your decisions in that department, your life, your livelihood, and the ship and everyone in it on your understanding of human nature. You learned to assess who had brains and who was just fucking mean, and *how* they'd move when they moved—you knew it even if the man himself didn't know.

And this Hawkins could maybe forget an ongoing personal grievance for maybe a day, a week, however long it took things to sort out around him. But this Hawkins, when he'd made you a serious case, *didn't* forget, didn't give up, once he had his feet under him. Never give Tom Hawkins room to lay plans. Never give Tom Hawkins the idea you were going to do harm where he had an allegiance.

"Mark ten seconds to jump. Eight . . . seven . . ."

Son of *a* bitch. Hawkins was.

". . . six . . . five . . . four . . . three . . . two . . . one . . ."

Gone.

Bad luck to you, Marie Hawkins.

— *ii* —

SPRITE DROPPED IN . . . electronic impulses probed the dark.

Found no echoes, no substance but the nearest radiating mass.

Which didn't surprise Marie.

Didn't have a hope Bowe was here. She knew his habits. Knew the way he thought. He wouldn't take the chance. Hadn't tracked the man for twenty years without understanding *how* he worked and what his tactics were.

So he was out of Tripoint, maybe spending a day or two he knew he could afford, but he wouldn't cut the margin fine enough to compromise the gap between them. He wanted all the loading time at Pell he could get. He'd run through Tripoint fast enough to make him comfortable, not fast enough, of course, that it could possibly seem to his crew that he was running from a confrontation with little, unarmed *Sprite*, and with Marie Hawkins.

But he'd struck at her—personally. Spitefully. She was supposed to lose her composure—possibly make bad decisions. Push the Family into a dry run?

Lose money, maybe fatally for *Sprite* and its operations? The Family wasn't crazy and *Sprite*'s cargo officer *knew* the Pell market, though she'd never been there. She knew it because it was part of the web, she knew it the way she'd known the specific figures of adjacent markets for twenty years, always holding herself ready to divert *Sprite* on short notice if she found Bowe in reach.

Planned ahead, damned right.

Sorry, Austin. I'm not a fool.

And I've *got* the votes in *Sprite* crew. Mischa didn't want an election called.

"He's not here," Mischa called down to say.

Bravo, Mischa, late again. I know that.

"Marie?"

"I hear that." She bit her tongue short of the acid remark she wanted to make. She left Mischa nothing, nothing to take hold of. It drove him crazy.

"We're transiting the point as fast as we can. Exit as soon as we run the checks."

That was the prior agreement. Mischa needed to call her, early on in their arrival at Tripoint? Mischa surely had a point to make.

"Maybe Tom's worked right in, do you think?"

Oh, Mischa *was* bitter. Rubbed salt into it.

"You always said," Mischa purred into the silence of the ship, insidious as the systems-sounds, *"like father, like son."*

"Did I? Maybe he will. Maybe he'll use the figures I taught him."

"What figures?"

"Mischa, Mischa, what do I deal with? In and out of my office all the time . . . why do you *think* Saja put Tom on main crew?"

Electronic pop. The com had been bridge-wide until then. She'd bet on it.

"I've had about enough, Marie."

"Yeah," she said. "Only this time we're doing something."

"Don't push me, Marie."

"Don't put me on broadcast again."

Click.

Straight out of jump and into a personal argument. Marie sipped the nutri-pack and shut her eyes, alone in the cargo office. Jump-point entry didn't need cargo officers but one, in case something went egregiously wrong and they had to blow the holds and shed mass. But now entry was a fact, the rest of Cargo main shift came straying in, to start checking readout from the warm-cans, and the other specific-conditions cans in the hold, checking the computer records, making sure nothing had changed in data and nothing had screwed in programs . . . big excitement. She was trying to recover a train of thought from before jump, she always insisted to do that.

She'd been thinking about Tom, on that ship. Asking herself

if Bowe would go so far as harming Tom. Asking herself if she cared, except in so far as she hated like hell Bowe getting any point against her.

Didn't know if that was a normal way to feel. Damned sure not the way the ballads and the books had it. Not the soppy way the child-besotted declared they felt it. If there was mother-love then there was a shadow-side of that instinct, a dark side the ballads and the books also had: the imperative to give birth and the imperative to destroy the life, in the wrong season, the ill season, the winter, the drought, the feud, the war—she'd studied the question, read prehistory and psych and civ. And understood what she'd done when she'd kept Bowe's offering inside herself, and sometime rejected it and sometime tried to deal with it until it became a him, then Tom, and lastly, God help her *and* him, poor, damned, disaster-bound fool.

She'd mistrusted instinct. Mistrusted it and alternately ridden it in violent reverses of personal direction throughout her life. This time she was following it, from moment to moment scared to death, and from moment to moment wildly willing to take the risk, life or death, win or lose.

Getting Tom back . . . she wasn't so sure. She wasn't so sure she wanted back anyone who'd had to do with Bowe.

Unless Tom took up her cause and settled accounts himself, which, on the one hand, she'd wanted once, and then felt differently—because it wouldn't be her doing. Because Tom wasn't, as she'd thought once, simply her doing. Tom belonged to Tom, and you couldn't ever quite predict what he'd do.

What he'd do would probably be stupid.

No, *foolish.* Tom wasn't stupid. *Ignorant.* And ignorant people trusted people, or assumed they knew. She knew how to see through the illusions of human behavior, but Tom didn't. He'd proved that, persisting in a kind of loyalty to her, blind, gut-level, helpless. She'd tried to reason with it, kill it, drive it out of his head, but he could never see she didn't have what he was looking for. He couldn't understand the impulse she had when he screamed his baby screams to fling him out of her arms and against the wall, he couldn't understand the violence she felt when he looked at her and said, Marie, why? or Marie, why not? and he wouldn't take the answers when she gave them. She'd taken him home and stood the questions and the demands as long as she could and she always took him back to the kids' loft when she started wanting to hurt him, when she started to dream at night and fantasize by day about doing terrible, cruel things to him. The Family couldn't stop her. If she chopped him in small pieces, the Family wouldn't do anything: she was too important to the ship. The Family wouldn't do anything but keep the other kids out of her path, and that suited her fine, she hated kids, hated their noise and disorder.

Most of all she despised Tom, when he looked at her in stupid, hateful need, expecting her to give him what she'd gone out on Mariner dock looking for in her own blind juvenile instinct, the expectation of affection Bowe had betrayed and Mischa had, because nobody cared.

So now the kid wanted her to validate the worst lie she'd ever learned the truth of? The kid wanted to run the cycle all over again, and she wanted to kill him or detach him or beat the expectation out of his eyes—the way she wanted to kill him now for being where he was, and for changing the equation that was her and Bowe. . . . Tom couldn't stay out of her life, one thought ran, couldn't stop screwing things up, and making what should be simple into a muddled, fucked-up mess; and meanwhile another thought ran, He didn't deserve having happen to him what had happened to her, *didn't* deserve where Bowe could send him, onto some damned Fleet dark-runner— the initiation stupid kids got into the Fleet was what she'd gotten at Mariner, what she'd learned too late to save herself. *She'd* known then what Bowe was and understood the fuck-you gesture he'd made at *Sprite* even when he'd turned her back to them, all full of violence, full of hate . . . she was a bottle full of demons, the sort of demons that existed in everyone, but Bowe had let her meet his, and she'd waked her own, that was the way she imaged it. The whole universe went ignorant of their own demons and denied they had them. But she knew. And Bowe knew. They'd been intimate with them for forty-eight hours.

And sometimes, sometimes when she dreamed in the deep between points of realspace, she made love with Bowe, real, sharp-edged, bitter love, not rape, except as *she* made things happen in her dream, and he didn't have any say about it. It was love, and it wasn't. It was sex, and it wasn't. It was a power-trip, and it wasn't. It was screw-you and damn-you. It was the only place she could feel the sensations she'd looked to him to make her feel, and she only felt that when she let go her grip on the solid universe. Bowe was the only human she knew who understood the absolutes of the demons. The only one who could understand. Certainly not safe, clutch-on-reality Mischa. Not Saja. Not any Hawkins. The whole Family was delusional. The whole premise of their existence was desperately tied to a morality that earned them comforts they wanted. They lived in the grip of their demons without ever seeing the raw, real dark that drove them.

But she had.

Mischa talked about morality and necessity and respectability.

But she saw how all that worked, and how they kept a careful shield up and how they didn't look too long into mirrors, too deeply into their own eyes.

She did.

And maybe, she thought, in that deep dark behind her eyelids, maybe Bowe had been equally desperate. Maybe Bowe'd gone looking, too, that day on the docks, and maybe he'd let loose his demons and loosed hers and they'd always be bound . . . maybe it tied him and her in such a way they went on screwing each other in a non-biological sense, creative only when they were joined, locked in a reality that nobody else could see.

Sometimes she desperately needed to know Bowe was out

there. Sometimes she wondered if he needed her in the same way.

And he took Tom to himself.

Why?

What did he want? What did he need? Of all his demons, which one was in the ascendant at that moment?

Or had Tom sought him out?

Don't hurt the kid, she wished Bowe, in the way she sometimes talked to him in absentia . . . he was a far better conversationalist than the Family offered. He's mine to kill, and I didn't. Don't you presume, you bastard. You haven't paid for him. I did.

Hurt him and I'll have your balls, you son of a bitch.

Until then, we can go on having these little talks. We can go on meeting in the dark.

Or I can turn up on your dockside. I can meet you at Pell, *with* my ship.

Or I can track you across the universe, solo. You're my obsession. My life. My reason for living.

Thank God you exist. Otherwise I'd be stuck with Mischa, fighting on his scale. And I'd strangle for want of oxygen.

—— *iii* ——

DREAM OF A SPIRAL TO NOWHERE. Sometimes it had colors and sometimes not. Sometimes it had sound, like a humming machine, deep and powerful.

Sometimes it was the brig, but the walls and the bars came and went, tilted into polyhedrons and dimensional oddity.

Sometimes shadows passed very fast. He thought of nursery rhymes and the man that wasn't there. He'd been that man, that boy, not there. Cousins had taught him that rhyme and now it wouldn't leave his head. He'd gone to sleep with it, and with the shadows, that twisted and turned one into a shadow, a presence he felt more than saw, a breath of change in the air about him.

He wasn't afraid, in this visitation—aroused, more than anything, but not acutely so, more a languid half-aware state, in which something brushed against him, made a dizzying slow incline in the surface under him, shadowed the air above him.

He dreamed a textureless voice, for a subjective long while. It told him in an idle, distracted way, about the War, about the hazards and the solitude of the fringes of the fighting, about space deeper and more silent than any merchanter would know—and qualities in hyperspace that proved it had events linked to Einsteinian space by the deformations of spacetime a star made. One could trade temporality for position and vector for event potential.

Meaning, the voice said out of empty air, and with a touch of wicked mirth, you do damn well hope you potentiate toward the next star. But there are places you don't do that. You can feel them in the numbers, in the interface. That's how we found them.

He'd the strangest notion someone had come to visit him, just to pass the tedious no-time, and sat pouring this strange conversation into his ear. He hadn't the least notion who'd found 'them' or what 'they' were. He'd missed that part. But he found himself oddly safe and comfortable lying still and listening, feeling or dreaming, he wasn't sure, but he wasn't in danger.

Wasn't in danger when the shadow leaned down and kissed him on the mouth, saying, Sweet boy, I've traveled more lightyears than you. I'm ever so old, if we should compare notes. Can you open your eyes? Can you look the dark in the face?

He didn't see things clearly. He wasn't sure what he saw.

"You have to get used to it," the voice said, in its no-time, distorted way—like it was playing back a second or so out of synch with his heartbeat, but that didn't make sense, it was just the way the brain heard it, or that was what the voice told him he was hearing, simultaneously, or first, he just couldn't get hold of when things were happening to him, or how he'd ended up skin to skin with his visitor. Sequential memory was nowhere. It was a mental end-over-end tumble, out of control. Physical sensations cascaded out of order. He was out of breath and not getting air, then spinning faster and faster as his heart speeded up and the sensual and sensory traded places in rapid succession.

Was it sensuality traded for spatiality, vector for potential? He couldn't remember the answer to his question, or why he'd asked it. He hadn't any breath. He couldn't get another. Then he found a way through the interface, came spinning through the dark into white space, and the sickening conviction of falling that came at system-drop.

Was out for a moment or two. Came back, gasping for a single breath, like a newborn.

"Don't believe Christian," someone said. "Nothing's free."

He was alone, then, couldn't put reality with where he was or where he'd been, until the next pulse at the interface dropped his stomach through infinity and sent his heart and lungs struggling after the demands of his body.

Lying naked on his bunk, beneath the blankets. Clothes neatly folded on his feet. . . .

Shit, he thought, in language he reserved for jump-drop. Marie's language.

That's a stupid thing to do. That's just abysmally stupid. Why did I do that?

Must have done it. Tranked to the eyeballs and on autopilot. Way to break your neck.

Damn fishtank, this place . . . get up, get dressed, before the crew starts stirring, can't trust this crew won't go for any skin they can get, please and thank you or not. . . .

Jump-dreams like he'd never had in his life. Sex the way it couldn't be in real life. He'd real memories. He'd the jump-dream still more vivid, still felt the heat and the arousal of a second body, real as realspace, real as Einstein's laws and Bok's famous loophole.

Where had a comp-tech junior crewman gotten to dreaming about physics he'd never had make sense to him even in deep-tape?

Where had he come out of jump with understandings he hadn't gotten, with numbers and Greek letters floating in the dark inside his brain?

The wobbles hit his stomach. Hard. He made a grab at the panel beside him, where he'd disposed the nutri-packs. They fell out onto the mattress. He took one in a shaking hand, seeing at the same time that the bruises around his wrist had healed, feeling the damn cable as it dragged across his body, underneath the blanket.

But he hadn't a stitch on.

He stopped with the pull-tab in his fingers, lifted his head to see the rest of the cell, his heart pounding, helpless to feed the oxygen fast enough.

Couldn't get his shirt off without the bracelet being off. But his clothes, including the shirt, were neatly folded, lying on the blanket on his feet.

Christian's face, Christian holding him up . . . down the hall. Christian's clothes . . . skintights, and a sensual feeling in clothes he wasn't used to. . . .

Christian being so damned nice. . . .

God!

It was too damn much. He couldn't hold his head up, he was getting sick, and breaking into a sweat, thinking back into that pit of dark he'd come through, and past it, to the Tripoint jump, and the scratches he'd waked with there.

He felt a rising nausea. He could scarcely coordinate his fingers to pull the tab on the nutri-pack. He tried to calm down and think about that, only that, just getting his stomach settled.

Wholly absorbing problem for the moment. He sipped, counted his breaths, told himself somebody'd messed with his trank, and he'd hallucinated.

But hallucinations didn't get that shirt off without the bracelet.

Hallucinations hadn't left him lying on the floor last jump with scratches all over his body.

Something had happened. Someone had been walking about. When the brain and the body were in some kind of profound slowdown, tranked-out. You didn't dare skip trank . . . doing that was stuff for the vids, for people who paid money to get scared out of their wits. It was for fools who believed the stories, that Mazian's navigators and engineers could think through jump. . . .

But, God, they did, they had a night-walker aboard. Somebody who didn't trank was wandering the corridors for a God-forsaken month of no-time, coming in and out of locked doors, whispering in your ear, fingering whatever and whoever she pleased, while everybody was lying helpless as pieces of meat.

And that bracelet of stars. . .

He didn't want to think about it. He lay still and, finding the one packet would stay on his stomach, ventured another, ghastly lemon-synth. He had to talk to Tink about lemon. Didn't want lemon in the next batch. Please God. Not another one.

Another *v*-dump, pulse against the interface. He came to with the mingled taste of lemon and copper in his mouth, and seemed to have bitten his tongue.

Then the all-clear sounded. At least he surmised that was the reason of the siren blast, this time, and a woman's voice said, velvet soft and razor steel, "This is Perrault. Free to move about. We have Pell's signal."

He undid the safety restraints, flung his legs out of bed, sat the edge, wobbly and aiming for the shower in his next effort.

Not a damn stitch on. The scratches . . . had healed. Like the bruises.

He braced an arm against the other wall and staggered along it to the bath and the shower, hell with any voyeur passing in the corridor . . . he got the door seal mostly made in spite of the trailing cable, enough that the lock would engage and the vapor jets would work. He shaved, with the razor connected to the console—and scrubbed and scrubbed, while the detergent vapor blasted out at him and made clouds he breathed with the air.

Spooked, he decided. He felt . . . as if the craziness about this ship had crept into his bed while he slept, as if, if he scrubbed hard enough, he could stop smelling a musky, spicy scent he dreamed he'd smelled in jump, and stop feeling as if something had done things with him, to him, he didn't remember.

Paranoia and a streak of kink he'd never figured, he kept telling himself. Whatever brand of trank it was, it wasn't the dosage he was used to, it wasn't working right, he was hallucinating, and he had to talk to the meds about it and get the dosage adjusted before he *did* come out in mid-jump. . . .

But underdosing couldn't explain the cable on his arm and the clothes folded on his bunk, no more than it explained the equations running around the edges of his brain. Maybe, he thought desperately, maybe he'd understood the deep-tape better than he thought. Maybe information he'd picked up had clicked in and it all surfaced in his subconscious and made him think about tape he hadn't had for ten years.

Bok's equation . . . and snakes . . . and Christian . . .

Hell if it had.

It hit him then . . . a fit of shaking he couldn't control. He wasn't even sure it was fear—or exhaustion, or sickness, or just the overwhelming heat of the drier cycle. He sank down where it was private and safe and let the hot air blast around him, hair on end, knees and elbows knocking together, teeth clicking in sporadic shivers the air didn't warm.

So why give a damn if somebody got off for a month at his expense? He wasn't hurt. Didn't matter what somebody had done to him that he didn't half know about. Didn't matter what he'd done, asleep. . . .

He jerked, swung his hands back to catch the walls beside

him, half-twisted a knee . . . it was that violent, that vivid an illusion of falling. Sexual arousal. Pain. Terror. He was back in jump-space.

Held his eyes open, even from blinking, while the surfaces dried in the vortex of warm air. He couldn't see the shower wall. He knew it was white. He couldn't remember white. He tried, desperately, and got something like UV. Glaring. Burning into his open eyes.

White, then, finally, white. Ordinary, cheap, gold-flecked paneling. The roar of the fans.

He had to get out of *Corinthian*. Christian had promised to let him go, he remembered Christian's quarters, the clothes, the talk . . . and he knew he couldn't trust the offer . . . nothing's for free, echoed in the back of his skull. Nothing's free.

He shivered, quick spasm of physical revulsion, not sure what he remembered.

Couldn't be safe on this ship. *Someone* was wandering the corridors playing grotesque pranks, God knew what. A voice patiently telling him how hyperspace was configured, the equations running through his head like a nuisance piece of music, along with lying half-awake in a chaos of sequence, everything out of order, every sensation piling up with the last one—she'd said . . . she'd said . . . only the numbers were true.

His body reacted—quick, physical arousal.

Another spasm of shivering hit, then. And anger, this time—overriding everything but the common sense that said that if there was such a creature as a night-walker and if it was Capella, as he suspected . . .

He rested his forehead on his arms, he stared at the shower floor between his feet, and the snaking trail of the cable, the governing reality of his situation on *Corinthian*. He'd not *liked* the people he was with on *Sprite,* . . . but he'd never been other than part of *Sprite*. He'd never had this sense of being stalked, never had to feel he hadn't any resource whatsoever to protect himself. He was, point of fact, terrified—not so much of the night-walker whoever it was: that grotesque, strange episode wasn't so bad as the notion he couldn't do anything about what these people decided to do to him, no matter *what* they decided to do to him. . . .

And somebody was telling him don't believe Christian? Don't believe in a way off this ship?

He had to. He fucking had to. He didn't know what the next joke might be. And the captain knew—the captain had to know what was going on, knew there was such a thing as a walker, he knew who it was, and he sat smug while Christian and Capella played their dominance games, one against the other, and both of them with him—so, so damned funny, it had to be, to them. . .

Another shiver hit him, diminished in force. He felt sick at his stomach.

"Mr. Hawkins," he heard, from outside. Male voice, stranger. Harsh. It sent him scrambling for his feet, and he heard the motor move the grid on its track. The next might yank the cable and him through the shower door and across the brig. He caught his balance on the wall, scraped his back on the water-vents doing it, and flipped the shower door latch.

Buck naked, confronted an officer he didn't know, who gave him a stare as if he was a sale item in the bargain bin.

The pocket tab said *Michaels.*

He remembered the thump of blows falling, in the corridor, the man Tink called trouble. The presence turned out middle-aged, greying hair down to his shoulders and face set in an inbuilt scowl.

"Sir," he said.

"Galley, mister. You're on duty."

"Yes, sir, thank you, sir. Two seconds. Getting my clothes."

He flinched past Michaels in haste, grabbed his clothes off his bunk, pulled on underwear, skintights, —he couldn't put on the shirt, and Michaels came and keyed open the bracelet, indicated he should get the boots on and get moving.

Which he did, pulling his shirt on as they left, no questions, no uninvited word of conversation or question with this man—

Michaels might find some excuse to use that spring baton he carried clipped to his belt; and he was vastly glad that they went straight down to the galley, with no detours and not a word exchanged.

Except Michaels said, when he delivered him to Jamal, at the galley section counter—"Kid's shaky. Light duty."

Shook him as badly as a curse. The dreaded Michaels personally braceleted his left wrist to the cable coiled up on the counter and walked out, all the while the cold traveled a meandering course to the nerve centers and started a tremor in the gut, in the knees, in the chest. Oh, God, he thought in disgust, but he couldn't stop it, he couldn't walk away and pretend it wasn't going on—it went to all-over shakes. Reality was coming apart on him, in red and blue flashes, right over the white galley walls.

"Hey." Jamal pried him loose from the counter and about that time Tink arrived in the galley—"Kid sick?" Tink asked, grabbed his other arm, and between his shaking and his attempts to walk on his own, the two of them got him into a chair at a mess table. They hovered over him, debated calling somebody—"No!" he said, and somehow they materialized a cup of real fruit juice, a cup of the nutri-pack stuff, an offer of coffee or tea . . . he just sat there like a fool and shook, trying to drink the fruit juice . . . it was real, and rare, and he wasn't about to waste it . . . with Tink patting him on the shoulder and saying how he should just sit there until he felt like moving, it was all right.

Damned near shook the cup out of his hand when Tink said that. He tried to figure why it made the shakes worse, and couldn't, but somewhere in the back of his mind was the lonely feeling he not only couldn't leave Tink, he didn't want to leave Tink . . . don't trust Christian, kept ringing in his head, but he didn't know if that was any truer than Christian's offer.

Crazy, he told himself finally, when he could set the cup down without slopping it, when he could glance up at the mundane white and blues and chrome of the galley and realized he'd been seeing something darker and less organized, some place with black patches and some place that was *Sprite*'s corridors, and cousins, and Marie's office, and the muted beiges of Marie's apartment. He was suddenly close to tears. He didn't know why. He didn't understand himself.

He didn't need to understand. He needed out of this ship. On any terms. Any at all.

He got up, tossed the cups, got a sponge and set to work on the counters with a vengeance. Didn't know, didn't know, didn't know, there was a lump in his chest where certainties had used to be. Pell system was where they were now, but its docks were a foreign place, and the rules were foreign—he didn't know what Christian was going to do.

A voice in his head still kept saying, Don't trust him.

Had to be Capella.

Why, for God's sake, did Capella get off on tormenting him? Because he was there? Because she sensed he'd crack? Because he was the new guy and the rest of the crew knew her tricks?

It was as crazy-patchwork as all the rest of his thinking. Nothing made sense.

Capella's little joke, maybe . . . but he wasn't to play games with. His *father* took him seriously. Christian at least seemed to consider him a threat. He didn't know why Capella shouldn't.

Point of vanity, maybe. But he deserved more precaution than that. He deserved more respect than that.

Dammit!

—— *iv* ——

LONG APPROACH, THREE WHOLE days to dock—Pell was a huge, busy system: outlying shipyards, auxiliary stations for heavy industry, and refining—local traffic, but in the ecliptic, which an inbound long-hauler scorned. In at solar zenith, a quick slow-down and a lazy plowing along through the solar wind toward the inner system. You figured on an easy on-board schedule if nothing had gone fritz—did your routines, pursued your hobbies, if any.

And made reservations for liberty dockside, where needed.

Inner system, nearest Pell's Star, was primarily cloudy Downbelow, sole habited planet, first alien life and first alien sapience humanity had found. Those were the facts every kid learned in primer tapes.

Which hadn't done either the Downers or humanity a whole lot of good, for what anybody could tell. The discovery of the Downers had spooked Earth's earthbound religions and helped start the War, that was so—no great achievement for humanity, except the whole of space-faring humanity wasn't under Earth's thumb any longer.

Wasn't Christian's generation, personally. *He* didn't see any particular value in the War. Or in Earth. Or in planets in general, except as places to anchor stations, from which one could do nice safe dives into hazard and get back to civilization. He didn't personally plan to take a dive like that, but it was nice some could, and bring up refined flour and condensed fruit juice.

And as for the famous eetees, Downers and humans didn't breathe the same oxy-ratio, humans didn't tolerate the high CO_2 on Downbelow and most of all didn't tolerate the molds and fungi rife on the planet. Downers needed the CO_2, one supposed, and had to wear breathing assists in human atmosphere. So Downers carved their large-eyed statues to watch the heavens no different than they ever had, as if they were looking for some other, better answer.

Downers worked on Pell Station, for reasons no one evidently understood, but most of all, one supposed, because Downers *liked* the idea of space. Downers worshipped their sun, they served a time on the station and went back again to their mating and their birthing and burrowing and whatever else they did—he'd been fascinated by them when he was a kid, knew every Downer stat there was, useless hobby, right up there with Earth's dinosaurs and Cyteen's platytheres. Humans lived on Pell Station, the sole Alliance Station, poised between the Beyond and Earth's native space. Regularly, the science people descend to their carefully insulated environments, to pursue their carefully monitored projects, and, irregularly, and depending on the season, ordinary tourists could do a tour onplanet—which he'd been hot to do when he was a kid, but there was a waiting list longer than a ship's docktime, and now he'd grown out of his interest in eetees, human or otherwise. You saw Downers on the station, skulking along near the maintenance area . . . little furred creatures with—one had to take it on faith—big dark eyes and pleasant faces behind the breathing masks.

Even so, you weren't supposed to talk to them, trade with them, touch them or impede them 'in any way whatsoever, under penalty of law and a substantial fine. . . .' Which was probably for everybody's protection, humans as well as the eetees.

One wondered if, things being otherwise, he could trade the furry bastards a slightly used brother.

On off-shift, he paged through the current offerings in the *Pell Station Guide*, the vids, the books, the imports . . . rich list, from local produce to Earth imports.

Embassies: Earth and Union.

Financial Institutions . . . a long list.

Government offices . . . another list.

Institute for Foreign Studies, Pell Branch.

John Adams Pell University. Oxford University Special Extension: Earth Studies.

Angelo Konstantin Research Institute, tours available.

New Alexandrine Library, reproduction paper texts available.

Museums. Cultural exhibits. Local artifacts. Botanical gardens.

Religious Institutions . . . the list was a page long.

Restaurants, from fast food to cultural, ethnic, and scenic, entertainment live and otherwise.

Stores, Ship Suppliers, General, Special Listings.
Sleepovers, various classes.
Technical centers. Special training. Recreational courses.
Trade Organizations.

And so on, and so on, pages of ads for suppliers, outfitters, services, importers, exporters, manufacturers, associations, lawyers, specialist medical services, reproductive services . . . a trading ship was self-contained for almost any necessity: but the choices on a major station were legion.

Two hundred eighty-five restaurants. Name your ethnicity.

Sleepovers that made you think you were camping on Down-below surface. With virtual rainstorms.

Walk-through theater.

Venus Hotel. Adults-only tape links. Experience your partner. Luxury accommodations. Restaurant class A pass. 200c and up. On-premises security. Ship registration and age ID required.

He Captured that address.

It wouldn't look as if he didn't want to be found. And if—or when—Austin did come asking . . .

He pushed another button, got the ship list back.

He'd hoped for somebody like *Emilia.* No such luck. *Christophe Martin* and *Mississip,* both Earth-bound, were the best of a chancy lot. He put his bet on *Martin,* with a departure listed for 36 hours; and on the fifteen thousand hard-won credits he had in Alliance Bank. Five thousand might tempt *Martin's* recruitment officer. But 'might' was too chancy a word. Ten. It hurt, it really hurt, but ten was a sure thing.

The closer he got to the decision, the closer *Corinthian* drew to Pell and dock, the scarier it got. Not that elder brother had a shred of evidence against them, not even ID, if he didn't give it back, and he didn't intend to.

In point of fact he was scared stiff. Austin might not have figured out yet that Hawkins was a threat. But he had. Too damned clean. Give brother priss a year or two to get an eyeful and an earful of *Corinthian's* business. Family Boy that he was, he'd start to pull back, just too, too clean for *Corinthian,* just too by-the-book. He'd leave them, sooner or later he'd leave them or he'd slip the evidence to somebody about the trade *Corinthian* ran.

He saw the problem coming. Think ahead, Austin kept saying. So he did.

Sometimes, dammit, you did things you knew you'd pay for—because you could see far enough to know where doing nothing was going to leave you. Sometimes you did what was good for the ship.

Wasn't that what Austin used to say to him?

Didn't mean Austin wouldn't have him in the brig when they left port.

But he could get out of that. He could survive that. He couldn't survive Austin finding out older brother was ever so much more spit 'n polish and ever so much more yessir, johnny on the spot, sir, than Christian. Older brother might even have trade figures in his head that Austin might very much like to know. Older brother could get himself worked into *Corinthian* if they didn't watch out, worked in so deep that younger brother Christian just didn't know anything anymore—point in fact, he'd seemed to know less and less the harder he worked to get Austin to admit he knew anything at all.

Point in fact, *Corinthian* couldn't survive Hawkins' attack of law-abiding conscience when it came. He saw it. He even half-way *liked* Hawkins, for the same straight-up mentality that attracted and infuriated Austin, he saw that, too. But *Austin* had illusions he *was* righteous, Beatrice had that pegged.

Trouble was, Austin wasn't damned righteous with the authorities in Hawkins' case. It was the righteous sons of bitches who didn't have any doubts when they did you in, and Hawkins was so straight you could feel honesty dripping off him—feel it in the way Austin went slightly crazy dealing with him. Hawkins being more right than Austin . . . got Austin dead center, and to prove he was God, Austin was just going to suck older brother deeper and deeper into *Corinthian*, never understanding what stupid younger brother understood as a fact of life: that wars between two righteous asses ended up in double-crosses and a wide devastation.

Righteous had never described *him,* at least. On *Corinthian* there could only be one, clearly Austin, and the rest of them slunk around the edges of Austin's principles and Austin's absolute yesses and absolute noes—and kept the ship out of hock.

—— *v* ——

"THAT'S WELCOME, *CORINTHIAN*, you're in queue as you bear. Pretty entry, compliments to your pilot and your navigators. Market quotes packet will accompany, trade band. Mark one minute."

"Flattery, flattery, Pell Control. Can it get us a berth near green 12? Acknowledge receipt nav pack. Stand by for *Corinthian* information packet, band 3. Transmitting in thirty seconds. Please signify receipt and action on signal."

Light-lag still bound conversation. Compressed com was an artform. You jumped from topic to topic and had to remember several threads of conversation at once, with your answer and more of their conversation coming a large number of minutes later.

As well as trusting the com techs to snatch the hard compression data when it came, a squeal the computers read. Beatrice was preening, most likely. Austin propped one heel on the other ankle and sighed, hoping for that berth.

They could always breathe easier at Pell. Wholly different rules . . . a completely independent station with a bias toward instead of against ship-law, ship-speak, and captain's rights. Run by a council only part of which station elected, at least two of which were always merchanters or merchanters' legal representatives . . . nothing got done, in fact, that merchanters didn't want done.

Corinthian wasn't an Alliance merchanter—couldn't get that clearance and didn't try. There were too many hard feelings, and there were records *Corinthian* didn't want to produce. But they didn't need the certification to trade here. They did get the protections of ships' rights that the merchanters' Alliance had written into their contract with Pell. They got the benefits of Pell banking, which kept ships' accounts at a very favorable interest, and backed them with a guarantee of services to the ship out of an emergency fund: *Corinthian* was signatory to it and *Corinthian* paid into it—if you ever got into trouble that let you limp anywhere, you made for Pell and its shipyards in preference to Viking or Fargone if you could possibly make it.

Which *Corinthian* had done on one notable occasion.

But mostly . . . the law Unionside (and never mind Viking's new status, he personally counted Viking as Union law) couldn't run inquiries here. Pell didn't cooperate. Matter of principle.

Sovereign government—mostly consisting of ships. Matter of principle indeed. You could get trade figures, the same as everywhere. But the internal records couldn't be probed.

Damned nice port to be registered to.

And if you were Pell registry, you got a priority on the berths you wanted, the docking services, all sorts of amenities. So *Corinthian* wasn't Alliance, but she *was* Pell-registered, and that made it home, much as *Corinthian* owned one.

"Number twelve is free, *Corinthian*," Pell Central said. "How long will you require dock? You have personal messages accumulated. That transmission will follow, in one minute. Mark."

"Thank you, thank you, Pell-com, for the accommodation. Request you schedule us for a ten-day. I'll turn you back to *Corinth*-com, now, Pell, thank you. Helm's in charge."

Beatrice shot him a look. He smiled, unbelted, *Corinthian* running stable as she was, and went over to Helm. Squeezed Beatrice's shoulder.

"Shift change. Twenty minutes. See you."

"Yeah," Beatrice said, not cheerfully.

Berth 12, opposite the warehouse, easy transport. If it

weren't for Hawkins, he'd call it a picture-perfect run, ahead of any trouble that could possibly catch up with them.

There was, however, Hawkins.

He'd a few places he personally liked to go at Pell, and he was ready to go mind-numb and forget his problems. There were times he and Beatrice worked admirably well together, and there were times not. This run was one of the times not. He was anxious to have breathing room.

But there was Hawkins.

Still might be smarter to ship Hawkins out from here. He didn't want to. He didn't know why. Curiosity, maybe, what Hawkins was. Maybe the thought that Hawkins was a bargaining piece if Marie Hawkins did at some point show.

Maybe, deep down, the thought that the boy wasn't all Hawkins. That he had some investment in the boy, and *that* might make the boy worth something, if he could get past twenty years of Marie Hawkins' brainwashing.

Had to deal with the kid. Had to do something, he supposed. If he packed him off to Earth or parts elsewhere, he'd ask himself what he'd given up, what the kid had become . . . he didn't know why in hell he should care.

But he'd worry, among other things, that the kid's path might cross his again, in the way of ships coming and going, and he might have an older, cannier enemy by then.

That was the reasoning that had been nagging his subconscious. He usually discovered good, sane reasons for what seemed instinct in himself. He'd stayed alive and kept his ship alive. He'd made his mistakes before he took over the ship. Since, he'd been far more careful.

Sober responsibility, mature judgment and all that.

In that light, he probably ought to have the kid up to his office and find out if scrub duty and another jump had mellowed him.

But probably it wasn't a good idea to do it now, when he had a mild headache and the kid might have the same. He'd satisfied his curiosity back at Tripoint. He was going off-duty, he needed to stretch out and let the kinks out of his back . . .

hell, after dock was soon enough. Let the kid see all the crew get liberty, while he was stuck aboard, let him ferment a while in absolute boredom.

But Hawkins was going to mean keeping extra security aboard. And somebody wasn't going to be happy to be in charge of that.

Do a split watch, bonus pay, give a couple of the guys an extra five hundred apiece and let them spend it on reduced dock time. He could find volunteers.

Hawkins was already going to cost the ship a thousand c, not even figuring the early undock at Viking. Not even figuring the future security costs, when they made Viking port again.

It wasn't like having a second son. It was like having something stuck to your boot, that, try as you might, you couldn't shake off.

Chapter Seven

— *i* —

THE GALLEY DIDN'T SHUT DOWN on approach to dock, no, it was up to its elbows in business. Tink was doing special pastries for the security detail that had to remain aboard . . . because of him, Tom thought glumly, neither Tink nor Austin being privy to Christian's plans.

And the pans of food for two hundred plus crewmen during their outbound hours . . . all had to be ready. They went into the freezer.

Meanwhile the mess-hall vid screens had come on, with what might be a canned view of Downbelow, with its perpetual clouds, greenhoused, he understood, so you could rarely see the continents or the oceans. The indigenes below that cloud cover looked heavenward in hopes of a glimpse of their lord Sun. Made amazing large-eyed statues to do the job for them in the case someone lapsed in duty, he supposed—divine stand-ins.

When he'd been a kid he'd dreamed of Downbelow. Never looked to see it, seeing how the War brought a border between them. He never . . .

"H'*lo,* there," a voice said, out of other dreams, the deep,

echoing dark of hyperspace. Blond, in an officer's fatigues—
Capella arrived, drew a cup of coffee.

And said hello, for God's sake. Hello didn't mean an assault.
No reason for his gut to go to jelly or uncertainty to rise right
through his knees.

"Feeling better, are we, Tommy-person?" She came and
leaned elbows on the counter to sip her coffee. "H'lo, Jamal,
hi, Tink. Smells good in here. Pasta stuff?"

"Pasta," Jamal said. "No samples."

"Spoilsport. —Tommy-person." She reached across the
counter and touched the back of Tom's hand with her little
finger. "Tommy-person. You can come scrub *my* quarters any-
time. Some of us appreciate quality."

They were about to dock. He was about to leave the ship.
And Capella came to harass him a last time. Parting gesture.
He hadn't seen her since system-drop. He was seeing black
from second to second, was acutely aware of his own skin, and
the touch of ghostly fingers in his sleep.

"Eh?" Capella asked. "What do you think, Tommy-person?"

"I don't think the captain would approve."

"Do you do everything he says?"

"Right now I do. Yes, ma'am."

"Ma'am," Capella laughed, and he remembered Saby hadn't
liked it either. "Oh, come on, Tommy-pretty. You can call me
chief, on duty, and I'll call you Hawkins. On my own time,
and we are on my own time, here, Capella's just fine." Her
finger traced down the bone above his index finger. "I bet they
could spare you for a cup of coffee and a small sit. Especially
if I pull rank. How about?"

"I can't."

"Jamal?"

"I don't—"

Christian . . . arrived in the door and paused there, just the
single beat it took to say Christian hadn't expected Capella to
be there, and he didn't like what he was seeing. He had an

instant guilty feeling, and he didn't immediately know for what; a fear Christian might take jealous offense, and screw the escape, if he ever intended it—a fear Capella's purpose *was* to screw it. It was quiet in the galley. Jamal and Tink had stopped work, and didn't say a thing.

"Time for older brother to go back in his box," Christian said cheerfully, walking up to the counter. "Put the toys away, Cappy."

"Aww," Capella said, and shoved away from the counter—tossed the cup into the disposal. She looked at him—she had a wicked look, a naturally predatory look. He didn't even think she intended it. Or it was supposed to tell him something he didn't know how to read. She gave him a theatrical sulk, and a lift of the chin, flashed a dazzling grin at Christian Bowe. "I'll take him back."

"Not a chance." Christian had a key. Tom let him unlock the bracelet, endured Christian's proprietary hand on his shoulder, asking himself what he should believe. "I'll handle it. See you. The promise stands."

"Going to cost you," Capella said.

And didn't say a thing more as Christian nudged him into motion.

But he couldn't go without a look at Tink and Jamal. Couldn't say a good-bye that wasn't supposed to happen—that from second to second he wasn't sure was going to happen, or that he wanted to happen. He only looked to fix their faces in his mind, and chanced to see a very different Capella standing by the counter, a Capella all business and grim as hell's gates.

Christian swung him around abruptly, took him the familiar route back to the brig. A quiet route. The lowerdecks crew were doing their last minute scurrying about, and half the passenger ring would be securing for dock, crew and stations that belonged there gathering thick in docking stations, corridors crowding up along the take-holds.

There were lewd comments, offers to take 'the new boy' onto the docks. Christian didn't spare a glance, just hurried him around the turn to the brig, a corridor full of its own offers and comments . . . worrisome comments from dockers at take-holds up and down, waiting for the grapple-to and the lock to open. Rough crowd. Rude crowd. They held it down when Christian said stow it, but Christian didn't have to wait out the docking in an open-fronted cell, and it wasn't aimed at him.

Besides which, Capella had made Christian mad, and Christian wasn't talking to him, until Christian took him inside the brig and to the far rear by the bath, face to face with him.

"What did Capella say?"

"Didn't. I don't know what she wanted. She hadn't gotten that far." His back was against the wall. It wasn't a position he wanted in a fight. At least the cable wasn't on, this time.

But Christian didn't shove him further. Instead, he reached inside his jacket and pulled out a dozen passports, Union red and Alliance blue. Thumbed open the topmost, red.

To his picture, his name. His passport, his papers, all the freedom to pass customs and take hire, even to prove his identity and origin. Everything was in that red folder. He reached for it—but Christian snapped it shut and held it with the others.

Christian's terms. Everything was, and Christian was smug and smooth.

"After," Christian said. "After we walk out. Duty officer carries the papers on all the dockers, that's the way we work. They go out first. It's going to look like you slipped through . . . I was taking you to Medical, right?"

"I guess."

"You hit your head during dock. Only on the way to Medical, you broke and ran for it, and mixed in with outbound crew. Probably you faked the bump. Got it? Only that's just the story I tell about how you got out, am I doing this in small enough words, slower brother? I do things like always, take these guys out and you just come along with me through customs . . . these guys have zero percentage in calling me a liar. They have to deal with me tomorrow, and they won't notice a thing when papa asks, how's that?"

"I need my papers."

"What I've got here," Christian said, pocketed the passports, and reached in a side pocket for a short stack of notes, Alliance cash. "That's two hundred, immediate save-your-ass cash. I can give you a name, a ship that'll take hire. Name's *Christophe Martin*. I'll walk you down there, myself. Get you hired, get you papers, Martin's going out tomorrow."

"Where?"

"Viking. Meet your approval?"

Breath came short. "Yeah." He suddenly had to revise everything. The two hundred, he hadn't imagined—and the recommendation to another, outbound ship, immediately, without having to hang around Pell. It was everything he could hope to get on his own, heaped up and running over, if he could get his hands on those papers.

It only didn't add on Christian's side, on *this* ship—the passport missing, on a guy who also turned up missing from Christian's escort . . . Christian was going to catch hell for it, was what it looked like.

Maybe that was why Capella had wanted to talk to him, maybe that was why the voice in his dreams kept saying Don't trust Christian . . . and maybe *because* the warning had come in hyperspace it threaded its way into his waking mind without any denying it . . . that voice was Capella, too, he was sure it was, and he couldn't help doubting, and couldn't figure what Christian was doing.

An expensive favor. Clearly. He might have to revise his opinion on Christian. Maybe Christian was paying a price for what he did, and *had* to shove him out the door hard and fast and for his own selfish reasons, but Christian hadn't had to give him the money.

Christian left, without putting the cable on—left him to the catcalls and promises of the crew outside. He'd heard the door lock. For the first time he was glad it was locked, and he hoped opening it wasn't just a button push.

"Hey, pretty-boy," someone yelled.

He went to his bunk and sat down. In a moment more, the take-hold sounded, and he took a firm grip on the inset hand-hold, next to the e-panel.

Interminable minutes, then, to dock. He sat and tried not to chase those circular paths of thought again, why, or how, or what the choices were. His were all made.

Maybe there was a chance of seeing Marie again. Of his own quarters, on *Sprite*.

Hell, they'd have bumped somebody into his space. There was always a waiting list, and his cousins wouldn't have waited till the sheets were washed.

Didn't bloody miss them. That was the unhappy truth. Marie . . . Marie wasn't an affection, she was a bleeding wound. But she was his bleeding wound. He couldn't but ask himself where she was and what was happening to her. He *liked* Tink. He was glad he'd met Tink. He couldn't say that about a lot of people. But he had to get back. Something about bad pennies always turning up.

Mischa was going to be so glad to see him. Rodman was going to die. It was a kind of revenge. Let them think they were rid of him. He didn't know what Rodman would say. He was almost homesick to hear it. Didn't even want to beat hell out of him. They were getting old for that solution. In a couple of weeks subjective time, he'd suddenly arrived at that point of maturity.

Give him a couple of weeks with Rodman, he'd recover his edge.

Bump and touch. It wasn't easy to claim a head injury with *that* dock. No fault to find in the station's computers, the ship's engineers, or the pilot at the helm.

Butterflies hit his stomach. As soon as that touch came, the crew outside the bars left their take-hold points and started for the airlock, while the echo of the grapples locking was still ringing through the hull. The corridor emptied. Fast.

Then he thought . . . maybe Christian won't come. Maybe it's all a joke.

Maybe Austin caught him with the documents. Maybe Capella spilled the whole business.

Inner lock opened, then the outer, *crash-crash-thump*, with the slight rush of air you almost always got. It smelled . . . of something he'd never in his life smelled. Exotic and *fresh*, and wonderful. It was Pell. Downbelow.

He wanted to go. He truly wanted to.

The grid started retracting. Christian showed up, outside. "Hurry up," Christian snarked at him, and he hurried, out and along with Christian, overtaking the crew in the airlock. Christian yelled for quiet, ordered a line-up along the wall, started calling out names and sorting through the passports and papers.

"Anybody I didn't call, stay the hell aboard, go find the chief and tell her you need documents."

There was one, who swore and complained he'd turned in his fuckin' papers, he hadn't had them, it was a *Corinthian* screw-up.

"It's a clerical, all right. Just get back there," Christian said, and strode along the ragged line, holding him by the elbow, the fistful of passports in the other. "Come on. Stay a damn line, for God's sake! Look like business, and don't mouth off to Pell customs, they got a nasty habit of dropping you out of computers, screw your accounts, you don't need that kind of trouble, so *shut up!*"

There were hoots and catcalls that died fast as Christian led the way down the access, the crew and Christian in coats, himself in his shirt sleeves, which he hoped to God nobody in customs was going to question. He might be hyperventilating—the cold made his breaths too short, and made his chest hurt. Frost whitened every surface but the heated floor. Heated plates, too, as they came down the ramp and into the vast echoing shadow of the dock, under white lights that, like stars, glared from far aloft in the girders, lighting nothing until the light reached the metal decking and the waiting customs agents, at the check-through at the bottom of their ramp. Neon from the bar frontages pierced through the dark and the spots, faint traceries of bar and shop signs, freedom, just that close ahead.

If breath was short before, it was all but choked now. Don't look nervous, he said to himself, every spacer kid learned it, never look nervous with customs, don't look like you're carrying anything, don't get too friendly, please God there's no glitch with the papers . . .

God, I didn't get an entry stamp at Viking, do you get an exit stamp at a free port? Last I got was Mariner, four months, maybe, four months realtime . . .

Agents didn't even look at the stamps. If you strongly looked like your passport picture, if you were approximately the right gender, that was fine, they didn't even run the microchecks or fingerprints or anything . . . just go on, keep the line moving, and you were through. He couldn't believe it was that easy.

Christian grabbed his elbow. "Not far," Christian said. "Everything's set."

"I need my passport." It was always the sticking-point in the plan. Christian *needed* it aboard ship to support his story. He needed it far worse. His actual license was in *Sprite*'s records. His files were the other side of the Line. He'd never felt his identity, his whole claim on existence, so tenuous as it was with that red folder in Christian's hands.

"Just keep walking. Let's do this fast, for God's sake, I've got to get back. You'll get your damn passport."

"What berth?"

"We're at 12. *Martin* is 22."

Ten berths wasn't a pleasant hike at the tempo Christian took it. The air felt heavy to him, giving him more than he wanted, but laden with scents that made it seem thick to him. Breaths didn't steam on this dockside, but, maybe it was the chill he'd gotten in the tube, maybe it was the raw fear of something going wrong, that fast walking couldn't break a sweat—he was keeping up with Christian, a step behind at times, thinking maybe it would have made sense to hop a ped-transport, it surely would have made better sense . . .

But the display boards were saying Berth 20, and 21, and that was 22 ahead.

A group of four men was standing in their path. "You just go with them," Christian said. "Everything's set. It's all right. Here's your passport, there's your escort aboard, you don't need papers, they'll fix you up whatever papers you need. You've got the two hundred."

"Yes." He took the red passport folder, tucked it into his pocket as they walked toward the four men meeting them. Couldn't see any departure boards from here . . . he wanted to see was the ship on schedule and he lagged a step to turn and get a look back over his shoulder, at the section/berth display for 20 through 25. He picked out the 22 under Berth, and right beside the reassuring digital *Christophe Martin, Pell Registry,* was, in smaller letters: *Sol Station One, +30:23h.*

Christian grabbed his arm, jerked him around.

He didn't think. He broke the grip and bolted for the dockside wall, into the thickest traffic he could find.

"Hawkins!" Christian yelled after him. And: "Get him, dammit!"

He dodged pedestrians, a taxi, a can transport. He ran as far and as fast as he could. A stitch came in his side. His knees began to go, tendons aching. Obstacles blurred. He kept missing them, as long as he could keep going, finally jogged down to a walk, sweat burning off in the icy dry air, throat raw, legs and arms going increasingly to rubber. He didn't bend over to get rid of the stitch, nothing to make him obvious in the traffic. Shirt and black skintights weren't unusual in the crowd near the heated frontage, just too recognizable. He expected *Corinthian* crew at any moment to overtake him and ship him off to Sol, where he'd never get back again, never, ever match up with *Sprite*'s course, too many variables, too far from everything he knew. Besides that, Earthers were weird, with weird, irrational laws, and he didn't want to go where, for all he knew, *Martin* might be under agreement to dump him.

Legs wobbled under him. Spacer-boys didn't run distances.

Do anything you like in null-*g*, maybe sprint the length of lower main, but no races on dockside. Only thing in his favor, Christian and the guys from *Martin* didn't have station-legs, either. And terror was on his side.

Nobody overtook him. If they'd lost track of him somewhere, they'd have had to factor in the chance he'd dived into a shop or a bar, or taken a lift up to the station's upper levels, and once they did that, Pell was a huge station, not easy to search with any degree of quiet. He ought to go to the cops, he ought to, but no way in hell was that an option. Best was the lifts, while he was still ahead of the search and they hadn't a chance to post watch by the doors.

He had the credit chits Christian had given him—a gift to salve Christian's conscience or just property *Martin* would have taken from him to pay his bills aboard, he didn't intend to find out. He had the passport Christian had given him—maybe that was conscience-salving, too, because Christian could have stranded him for good and all if he had just handed that over to *Martin* crew.

He took it out of his pocket. It was the right official cover. But it didn't have the thumb-dent on the edge his had. He opened it and it was just color repro inside, a good, professional forgery.

The wind went out of him, then. He wasn't sure where he was walking. He flipped through the pages, dodged pedestrians, told himself he was a fool, he'd seen the folder, he'd believed it—but no customs agent was going to pass it at close inspection. Christian had switched it on him, maybe had the real one and the fake in his pocket, and he was on Pell without a legitimate passport to let him go to the station offices, or apply for work. His license was there, all repro, nothing he could legitimately take to any ship's master.

He bumped into a man—excused himself. He was light-headed and close to panic, and, with that near-incident, he shoved the passport into his pocket and kept walking, half-blind, heart beating in great, heavy thumps.

Stupid, he kept saying. Stupid, stupid.

The only worse thing that he'd escaped . . . . was being on *Christophe Martin.*

—— *ii* ——

NOT GOOD, WAS ALL CHRISTIAN could say to himself as he reached *Corinthian's* dockside. Not good, in the way an oncoming rock wasn't good.

Michaels had seen to the details—had the cargo crew taking care of business, setting up with Pell transport. A glance around told him at what stage routine was at the moment and Austin couldn't fault him for that—Michaels was on his job and it wasn't as if he'd kited off with things undone.

What he *had* done was a trouble he couldn't even graph. It wasn't supposed to have happened that way. Things weren't supposed to have skewed off like that, they had no right not to have gone the way they should.

"Chris-tian."

Capella's voice. He waited. Capella overtook him at the edge of the ramp.

"Well?" Capella said.

"Son of a bitch," he said.

Capella didn't even start with: What happened? She dived straight to: "Where is he?"

"I don't know! How should I know? The damn fool bolted, kited off, I don't know where he is!"

"Fine. Fine. *With* the passport?"

"He thinks." He patted the pocket where he had the real one. "He's not going anywhere without this. He'd be a fool to go to the cops. He knows it."

"Yeah," Capella said, implying, to his ears, that people had been fools before. That she was looking at one.

"He wasn't in any danger, *Martin's* a fair ship—he just—

took off when he saw the guys waiting, I don't know what got into his head. We've got to find him."

"We've got to find him," Capella echoed. "Yeah."

He wanted to hit her. He knew better. That bracelet *wasn't* a forgery. "Pella, we've got a problem. We've got a major problem out there. Yeah, it's mine, but it's the ship's problem if we don't get him before the cops do. We can't go out of here and leave him loose—God knows what he'd do. We've got to use this port."

"Well, maybe we should stand here, I mean, if he wants Corinthians, he can just walk right up to the ramp and ask."

"Don't be an ass!"

"I'm not the ass, Chris-baby."

"Chris-tian."

That was Austin. He'd left the pocket-com on.

"You told him!"

"Not this spacer," Capella said. "Was your trail that immaculate?"

"Chris-tian."

He thumbed the com up. "Yessir, I hear you."

"Do you want to come aboard, Christian?"

No shouting. No cursing. Panic hit him. He wanted Austin to yell at him, swear at him, just simply bash him against a bulkhead and beat hell out of him. He'd never heard Austin so calm about something he'd done.

No, he didn't want to come aboard. He wanted to take a bare-ass walk in deep space rather than come aboard.

"Yessir," he said past the obstruction in his throat. He threw a condemned man's look at Capella, an appeal to the living. "Organize a search. Find him. Get him back."

"With what promises?" Capella hissed. "A pay raise? Promotion to tech chief?"

He couldn't stay to argue. Capella was his only hope. He mounted the long ramp, got his wave-through from customs, and walked the tube to the airlock.

Austin didn't meet him there. The inner lock was shut—optional, and *Corinthian* generally opted, not relying wholly on station security. He coded through into lower main. Austin was standing down by ops, waiting with arms folded.

"Sir," Christian said when they were face to face. He still expected Austin to hit him.

"Where's your brother?" Austin asked him.

"I don't have a—" The answer fell out, faster than he wanted. He shut up. Austin waited.

And waited.

"He was trouble," he said to Austin's steady stare. "He'd be trouble. He's too scrubbed-*clean,* he'd find out we're not and he'd go straight to the cops, some time we'd never know it."

"So?" Austin said. And waited.

"I set it up with *Martin,* down the row. Trip to Sol. They'd leave him there. He'd stay gone."

Another silence, the longest of his life. "I have a question," Austin said finally.

"Sir?"

"Who appointed you captain?"

"Nobody. Sir."

"Who told you your judgment was more important than mine?"

"Nobody, sir."

Another silence. He'd never dealt with Austin in this mode. He'd never seen it in his life. He didn't want to see it again.

"This ship doesn't agree with your judgment, then."

"Nossir." He saw himself busted to galley scrub. For years. He saw Austin selling him to the Fleet. Beatrice wouldn't like it. But Beatrice herself might be on the slippery slope with Austin right now.

"I have a suggestion," Austin said.

"Sir." He asked what Austin wanted, he did what Austin wanted. He only hoped to stay alive. Hitting him would have blown off Austin's temper. He prayed for Austin to hit him and call it quits. This . . . didn't promise forgiveness. Ever. No confidence in him. Ever again.

"I want you to go out and find him," Austin said softly. "I want you to get him back here without tripping any alarm. What are we agreed to with *Martin?*"

"Ten thousand c."

"You paid it?"

"Yes, sir." It was the only defense he could claim. "My money."

Austin only nodded. "You'd better get out there."

"Yessir," he said, paralyzed.

"So why are you standing there?"

"Yessir," he said, and backed off a pace before he dared turn and make for the lock, feeling Austin's stare on his back all the way.

Chapter Eight

— *i* —

AUSTIN WAS ASKING HIMSELF BY NOW whether he needed a son. Asking himself maybe what Beatrice had had to do with the older brother affair. Or what Capella had done.

Guilt was a contagion. That was what Christian discovered. No one of his associates was going to thank him for what he'd involved them in. He couldn't even find most of them.

He walked the docks with no notion in this star system or the next where it made sense to look, or where a fool with a forged passport was going to run. He hadn't caught up with Capella, who, for all he knew, was lodged in some sleepover with a stranger she'd yanked off the docks, the hell with him, Tom Hawkins, and the mess he'd made . . . she'd raided the safe for him, she'd told him he was out of his mind, and if Capella caught hell from Austin, she knew how to pass it along. No Capella. No Michaels. Nobody answered his pages. He'd thought at least he could rely on *Martin*'s crew to join the search. *Martin*'s captain having ten thousand of his money, it ought to buy something.

But *Martin* was pulling out of dock on schedule. The same reason he'd picked *Martin* was taking that resource out of reach.

He couldn't go to the police. He thought of excuses . . . he could say he'd forgotten to give his brother his passport and if the fool would just go along with it . . . but you couldn't rely on Hawkins taking the cue and keeping his mouth shut. Hawkins wouldn't benefit from ending up in the hands of the police, but *Corinthian* would benefit far less, and Austin would skin him alive. With salt and alcohol. He didn't want the cops. God, he didn't want the cops—or the customs authorities.

He'd searched every bar in running distance. He'd checked public records. He'd checked sleepover registers. He'd put a page on the message system: *Tom, call home to* Corinthian. *We have a deal.*

But the son of a Hawkins bitch wasn't buying.

He didn't want to call a general alarm with *Corinthian* crew, over what was bound to be scuttlebutted as his fault. The rumor had to be going around. There hadn't been any witnesses to that scene in lower main, but something was going to get out, and the whispers were going to run behind him for years, he knew they were. Bad enough as it was, if he somehow could retrieve the situation—and Hawkins.

But it looked grimmer and grimmer.

Then he did spot a familiar backside. A shock of blond, spiked hair. A familiar swing to the walk.

"Capella!"

Said swinging walk never interrupted at all. He sprinted, overtook, grabbed an elbow. Gingerly.

"Not a sign," Capella said darkly. "Not a perishing *sign*. And I've called in favors."

Favors where Capella knew them might involve cages they didn't want to rattle. Very dark places indeed.

"I've been out for two fucking *days,* Pella, I've been top to bottom of the station, I've been through records, I've been in the bars, I've been through computer services, I've put messages on the station system. I've looked in station employment and the spacer exchange. I'm out of places to look."

"You look like hell."

He rubbed an unshaven face with a hand that felt like ice. Tried to imagine what he was going to do or say if he didn't find Tom Hawkins at all. Or if he couldn't claim to be in command of the crew that did.

"When'd you eat last?" Capella asked.

He didn't know. He shook his head. Remembered bar chips. A drink. God knew when. He hadn't slept. Hadn't showered. Hadn't shaved. Hadn't stopped walking in hours.

"Come on," Capella said, and steered him for the frontages.

"We haven't time. Pella, if we don't find him . . ."

"Yeah, your ass is had. You just did us all such a favor. Come on."

"Austin's going to kill me."

"Chrissy-sweet, I'm going to kill you, if captain-sir tosses us both off the ship, damned right I am." Capella didn't give up his arm. She steered him into the dark of one of Pell's 'round the clock bars, into a vibrational wall of beat and light and music. He all but turned and walked out, confused by the input, except for Capella's governing hand on his arm. Capella walked him up to the bar, tapped the counter in front of the barkeep with a black fingernail. The bracelet of stars glowed green. And the barkeep looked up with a stark, hard stare.

"Man wants something edible," Capella said, "before he falls over. Can do?"

"Done," the barman said, and shoved crackers at them. "Stew coming. What are you drinking?"

"Vodka and juice for him," Capella said. "Rum for me. Scanlon's."

"You got it," the barkeep said.

His knees made it to the table next the bar. He sat down. Good thing there was a chair under him.

Capella settled opposite. Folded her arms. Stared at him dead-on.

"We have got to find that son," Capella said. "Think, dammit! Where would he go? Is he religious? Has he got a kink? A vice? Has he got friends here?"

"No. —Hell, I don't know. How would I know?"

"*Sprite* ever trade here?"

"No. I'm sure of that."

"No business contacts. No companies with offices in places they do trade. Banks. Outfitters. Insurance companies. Religious organizations."

"I don't know! How could I know?"

"You could have asked him. You might have been curious. You might have wondered before you chucked him off to *Martin.*"

"Don't accuse me!"

The barman brought the drinks. Capella handed over her crew-card. "Put standard on it. I do math. Thanks."

"He's got two hundred," Christian said.

"Two hundred what?" Capella asked.

"Two hundred in chits! I wasn't going to turn him out broke! He's got two hundred in hand. A fake passport." He got a breath. The air was cold, sullen cold, all the way to the center of his bones. He could admit, at least, the rest of his disgrace. "*Martin*'s got ten thousand."

Capella hadn't expected that. Clearly. She sat for a moment, then shook her head and gave a whispered whistle. "Shit-all. What've you got left here?"

"Five. Five to my *name,* Pella. I didn't want to kill him!"

You never knew, with Capella, how anything played, or whether she thought you were sane or crazy. She sat staring for a moment and finally shook her head, looking away from him as if that much insanity was too much for her.

In her universe. In his. In Beatrice's. In Austin's. He didn't know. He just never understood the rules. He never had. He got one set from implication and another set from Austin's expectations, and Beatrice's, and another still from Capella's, and he just never understood the way to fit them together.

"Christian," Capella said, then, and took his hand in hers, on which the bracelet of stars glowed as independent objects. "We'll look. All we can do. We'll look, and I'll call in a couple more favors. I don't know what more we can do."

"Austin's going to kill me."

"Yeah. I do wish you'd thought about that. But in realspace we play with real numbers, don't we?"

Chapter Nine

— *i* —

People came and went, tens and twenties the hour, and there wasn't a place to sleep, except the public restroom, as long as nobody came in. He had the 200c . . . but he didn't dare go outside the area or use up his cash. He didn't know the station, didn't know the rules, didn't know the laws or what he could get into or where the record might be reporting. When you ran computers for a livelihood you thought of things like that sure as instinct, and Tom personally didn't trust anything he had to sign for. You didn't, if you wanted to avoid station computers, use anything but cash.

At least Christian's money wasn't counterfeit. At least *Corinthian* hadn't reported him to the cops. And he'd gone for the one place on Pell he knew he might find a friend . . . straight to the botanical gardens Tink said was on his must-do list every time he got to Pell.

The gardens, moreover, were a twenty-four hour operation . . . tours ran every two hours, with the lights on high or on the actinic night cycle, even in the dark, by hand-held glow-lights. Hour into hour into shift-change and shift again, he watched the tour groups form up and go through the glass doors. He watched people go through the garden shop, and come away with small potted plants. He shopped, himself, without buying. He knew what ferns were. There were violets and geraniums aboard *Sprite*, people traded them about for a bit of green; and *Sprite*'s cook raised mushrooms and tomatoes and peppers in a special dedicated small cabin, so he understood plants and fungi and spices.

He had more than enough time to sneak a read of sample slide-sets and even paper picture books on the shop stands and to listen to the public information vids. He learned about oaks and elms, and woolwood; and how buds made flowers and how trees lifted water to their tops. It kept him from thinking about the police, and the ache in his feet.

But every time new people arrived through the outer doors, he dropped whatever he was doing and went furtively to look over the new group, dreading searchers from *Corinthian* and hoping anew for Tink, scared to death that during some five minutes he had his eye off that doorway he was going to miss Tink entirely.

So supper was a bag of chips from a vending machine and breakfast the next day was a sandwich roll from the garden shop cafeteria, because by then he was starved, and he'd held out as long as he could.

He skipped lunch. He figured he'd better budget his two hundred, as far as he could, against the hour the director's office or the ticket-sellers or gardeners or somebody noticed him hanging around and began to suspect he was up to no good.

Meanwhile he tried to look ordinary. He didn't spend more than an hour at a time in the shop. He walked from place to place, browsing the displays, the shop, the free vid show. He lingered over morning tea in the cafeteria, where he could watch the outside door through its glass walls, and drank enough sugared tea, while he could get it, that the restroom was no arbitrary choice afterward. He constantly changed his pattern in sitting or standing. He didn't approach people. If they spoke to him he was willing to talk, only he had to say he was waiting for a group, and claim the truth, that he hadn't had the tour, but, yes, he'd heard it was worth it. Once a ticketer did ask him could he help him, with the implied suggestion that he might move along, now, the anticipated crack of doom—but his mind jolted into inventive function, then, and he said he'd made a date and forgotten when and he didn't want to admit it to the girl. So he meant to stand there until she showed. He was desperate. He was in love. The ticketer decided, evidently, that he was another kind of crazy, not a pickpocket or a psych case, and shot him tolerant looks when he'd look toward newcomers through the doors. He'd mime disappointment, then, and dejection and walk away, playing the part he'd assigned himself without much need for pretense.

That bought him off for a while, he figured. But he also took it for a warning, that if it went on too long the ticketer was going to ask him again, and maybe put somebody official onto him.

So he embroidered the story while he waited. He was desperately in love. He'd had a spat with the girl—her name was Mary. He couldn't call her ship. She was the chief navigator's daughter and her mother didn't like him, and now he couldn't find her. But he thought she might be sorry, too, about the fight. He thought she might show up here, to make up. He borrowed shamelessly from books he'd read and vids he'd seen. She had two brothers who didn't like him either. He thought they'd told her something that wasn't true, that started the fight . . . well, he *had* missed their date, but that was because he'd gotten a call-back to his ship and he couldn't help it, and he'd tried to call her, but he thought her mother hadn't passed on the message.

"No word yet?" the ticketer would ask him.

And once, "Son, you ever think of sleep?"

He looked woebegone and shook his head. It didn't take acting. He was so tired. He was so hungry. He watched the tour groups gathering and going in, he watched the young lovers and the parents with kids and the spacers on holiday and the old couples who came to do the evening tour. He saw the amazing green and felt the moist coolness from the gardens when the doors would open, cool air that wafted in with strange and wonderful scents. You could do a little of it by computer. You could walk in a place like that. You could even get cues for the smells and hear the steps you made, on tape. But the brochure—he'd read every one, now, in his waiting, from the selection they had in the rack—said that it was unique, every time, that it changed with seasons, that it could put you in touch with the rhythms of Earth's moon and seas.

He stood outside the vast clear doors, and turned back again when they shut, and went back to his waiting, figuring maybe Tink had business to do first, and wouldn't come here until maybe tomorrow.

He didn't know. He was hungry and he was desperate. He thought (thinking back into his made-up alibi) that he might pretend to be some total chance-met stranger calling in after Tink, and maybe get a call through *Corinthian*'s boards and out to him through the com system, but maybe they'd suspect, maybe they had a voice-type on him and they'd figure he might try to contact Tink and they'd come up here and haul him away with no chance of making a deal.

Hunger, on the other hand, he still had the funds to do something about. He splurged a whole 5c on a soup and salad, which was astonishingly cheap on Pell, especially here, where green salad was a specialty of the restaurant.

It looked good when they set it in front of him. He didn't get it often enough. The soup smelled wonderful.

He'd only just had a spoonful of the soup when he saw, the other side of the glass, coming in the doors, a dark-haired woman in *Corinthian* coveralls.

He let the spoon down. He ducked his head. His elbow hit the knife and knocked it off the table. On instinct he dived after it, as a place of invisibility.

He straightened up and didn't see her. Presumably she'd gone to the gathering area, just past the corner. He turned around to get up.

Stared straight at *Corinthian* coveralls. At dark hair. At a face he knew.

"Ma'am," he said, compounding the earliest mistake he'd made with Saby.

"Mind if I join you?"

He was rattled. He stumbled out of his chair, on his way to outright running, and ended up making a sit-down-please gesture. He fell back into his seat, thinking she was surely stalling. She'd probably phoned *Corinthian.*

"Have you called them?" he asked.

Saby didn't look like a fool. He could be desperate enough to do anything, she couldn't know. He saw calculations go through her eyes, then come up negative, she wouldn't panic, she knew he might be dangerous.

"Not yet," she said. It had to be the truth. It left him room to run. "I hear you didn't like Christian's arrangements."

"I don't trust him," he said. "Less, now."

"The captain wasn't in on it."

"I never thought so," he said.

"Christian's in deep trouble," Saby said. "Have your soup."

"I'm not hungry."

"Listen. The captain wants you to come back. The passport's a fake. There's just all kinds of trouble. There's some real nice people who could get hurt."

The waiter came over, offered a menu.

"Just coffee," Saby said. "Black."

The waiter left. Tom stirred his tea with no purpose, thinking desperately what kind of bargain he could make, and thinking how it was a ploy, of course it was. But a captain had a ship at risk because of him, a ship, his trade, his license, all sorts of things.

Which meant once Saby made that phone call, all hell was going to break loose, and they'd take him back, they'd *take* him back, come hell or station authorities. Couldn't blame anyone for that. Any spacer would.

"He'd really like it if you'd come back," Saby said.

"Yeah," he said. "I guess he would."

"I don't think he'd have you on scrub anymore."

"I like scrub fine. It's good company."

"We don't want trouble."

"I know you don't. I don't. Just give me my passport and you won't hear a thing from me."

Saby looked at the table. The waiter brought the coffee. She sipped it, evidently satisfied. "So why did you come here?" she asked him, then.

"I heard about the gardens. It was a place I knew to go."

"I didn't plan to find you. I just happened here. —But if I called the ship, you know, if I told them you were coming back, I think it would make them rethink everything. I don't think you'd end up in the brig again. I really don't."

"I get to be junior pilot, right?"

"I don't think that."

"It's not a damned good offer."

"What do you want?"

He didn't know. He didn't think any of it was true. He shook his head. Took a spoonful of cooling soup.

"Well," Tink said out of nowhere. Tom looked up. "They're looking for you," Tink said.

Last hope. A ball of fire and smoke.

"Did you tell her?"

"Tell her what?" Tink asked.

"That I'd be here."

"I didn't know you'd be here," Tink said, sounding honestly puzzled.

It was too much. He shook his head. He had a lump in his throat that almost prevented the soup going down.

"Tink was going to the gardens," Saby said. "He always does. I said I'd meet him here."

"Not like a date or anything," Tink said, sounding embarrassed. "She's an officer."

"Tink's a nice date," Saby said. "Knows everything there is about flowers."

"I don't," Tink said.

He'd been caught by an accident. By the unlikeliest pair on *Corinthian*. Nothing dramatic. Tink and Saby liked flowers. What was his life or what were his plans against something so absolutely unintended?

"Call the ship," he said. Tink clinched it. He didn't want the cops. He didn't want station law. "Tell them . . . hell, tell them you found me. Say it was clever work. Collect points if you can get 'em."

"You seen the gardens?" Saby asked.

He shook his head.

"You like to?" Saby asked.

Of course he would. He just didn't think she was serious.

"You got to," Tink said. And to Saby: "He's got to."

"You want to?" Saby asked.

"Yeah," he said.

"You through?" Saby asked, and waved a hand. "Finish the salad. We've got time."

"Good stuff here," Tink said. "We're taking on a load of fresh greens. Tomatoes. Potatoes. Ear corn. *Good* stuff. . . ."

He'd only gotten potatoes and corn in frozens. He thought about the galley. About Jamal. Ahead of Austin Bowe, damned right, about Jamal, and Tink. A homier place than the accommodation his *father* assigned him. The pride Tink had in his work . . . he envied that. He wanted that. There were things about *Corinthian* not so bad.

If one had no choice.

"You want to go the tour, then?" he asked Saby. "I swear I won't bolt. I promise. I don't want you guys in trouble."

"No problem," Saby said. "I give everybody one chance."

He shoved the bowl back. Half a soup. Half a salad. He hated to waste good food, especially around Tink. But he didn't trust more Corinthians wouldn't just happen in, on somebody's phone call, and it had gotten important to him, finally, to see the place he'd seen beyond the doors, the path with the nodding giants he thought were trees. He'd heard about Pell all his life, some terrible things, some as strange as myth. He'd not seen a Downer yet. But he imagined he'd seen trees, in his view through the doors.

And if he'd only a little taste of Pell . . . he wanted to remember it as the storehouse of living treasures he'd heard about as a kid. He wanted the tour the kid would have wanted.

Didn't want to admit that to his *Corinthian* watch, of course. He thought Tink was honest, completely. But he wasn't sure Saby wasn't just going along with anything he wanted until reinforcements arrived.

"I got a phone call to make first," Saby said.

"Yeah," he said. "I guess you do."

He was surprised she was out in the open about it. It raised his estimation of Saby, and made him wonder if she had after all come here, like Tink, with Tink, just to see the trees.

He watched her walk away and outside the restaurant. He went to the check-out and paid the tab, in cash. He went out with Tink, toward the ticket counter, finally.

"Let me get the tickets," he said to Tink. "It's on my brother. He gave me funds."

Tink didn't seem to understand that. Tink seemed to suspect something mysterious and maybe not savory, but he agreed. Tink looked utterly reputable this mainday evening, which was Tink's crack of dawn morning—wearing *Corinthian*-green coveralls that hid the tattoos except on his hands. His short-clipped forelock was brushed with a semblance of a part. He had one discreet braid at the nape. Most men looking like that were looking for a spacer-femme who was also looking. Not Tink. And he understood that. At twenty-three, he began to see things more important than the endless search after encounters and meaning in some-one. Some-thing began to be the goal. Some-thing: some credit for one's self, some achievement of one's ambitions, some accommodation with the illusions of one's misspent childhood.

Saby came back from her phone call, all cheerful, her dark hair a-bounce, mirth tugging at the corners of her mouth. "The captain says about time you reported in. I told him you were waiting to take the tour. He said take it, behave ourselves, and we're clear."

"He said that?" He didn't believe it. But Saby didn't look to be lying. She was too pleased with herself.

"Come on. Let's get tickets."

"Got 'em," Tink said.

"Christian's compliments," he couldn't resist saying. "His money."

Saby outright grinned. And pulled him and Tink, an elbow apiece, toward the staging area.

— *ii* —

IT WAS ROSES TINK FAVORED. But trees and the concept of trees loomed in his mind and forever would, palms and oaks and elms and banyans and ironhearts, ebony and *gegypa* and *sarinat*. They whispered in the fan-driven winds, they shed a living feeling into the air, they dominated the space overhead and rained bits and pieces of their substance onto the paths.

"If a leaf's fallen," the guide told them, "you can keep it. Fruits and flowers and other edibles are harvested daily for sale in the garden market."

Leaves were at a premium. Tourists pounced on them. But one drifted into his reach, virtually into his hand, gold and green.

"You can dry it," Tink said. "I got two. And a frozen-dried rose."

"The hardwoods come from Earth," the tour guide said, and went on to explain the difference between tropics and colder climates, and how solar radiation falling on tilted planets made seasons—the latter with reference to visual aids from a tour station. First time the proposition had ever made sense to him.

Then came the flowers, in the evolution of things, the wild-flowers and finally the ones humans had had a hand in making . . . like Tink's roses, hundreds and hundreds of colors. Individual perfumes, different as the colors. The reality of the sugar flowers. The absolute, sense-overwhelming profusion of petals.

It smelled . . . unidentifiable. There was something the scent and the assault of color did that the human body needed. There was something the whole garden did that the human body couldn't ignore. He forgot for a minute or two that he was going back onto *Corinthian*, and that if things had gone differently he might have had a hope of his own ship.

But that might come around again.

There might be a chance. There might be . . .

Fool's thought, he told himself, and felt Saby's hand on his arm, and listened to Saby talk about the roses, and the jonquils and iris and the tulips and hyacinths. Figure that the cornfields and the potatoes were much more important, yielding up their secrets to the labs as well as supplying stations and spacers direct. . . .

Interesting statistics about the value they were to humankind. About human civilizations riding botanical adaptations to ascendancy.

But less inspiring than the sensory level . . . and he was glad that the tour wended its final course back to the whispering of the tall trees, back to that sweet-breathing shadow. His legs ached from walking. Felt as if they'd made the entire circuit of the station.

Maybe they had. But he took the invitation the guide offered, to linger a moment on the path. He didn't want to go out, where, he'd been thinking the last half hour, a whole contingent of *Corinthian* crew must be waiting for him.

Maybe Christian, too. Probably Christian—madder than hell.

But a ship was a place. A station wasn't, in his book. He'd had his taste of dodging the station authorities just trying to evade questions from the botanical gardens staff. He didn't want to do it dockside and in and out of hiring offices, trying to stay out of station-debt, which, if he got into that infamous System . . . no.

Which meant a return to *Corinthian* was rescue, in a way, and he was willing to go. But he didn't want to lose the souvenir leaf—the garden was a place he wanted to remember and wasn't sure he'd see again. So, fearing a little over-enthusiasm on the part of the arresting party he was sure was waiting, he asked Saby to keep the leaf safe for him. "Sure," she said, and slipped it into her sleeve-pocket.

So the tour was done, and he walked out with Tink and Saby.

Didn't find the reception party—and he was so sure it existed he stopped and stood in the doorway, looking for it.

"She's a pretty one," the ticketer at the door said—to him, he realized then, and then, in the racing of his bewildered wits, remembered the lie he'd told, about waiting for a girlfriend.

"Yeah," he said, and only wanted to get out of there before some other remark started trouble, but Saby laughed, took the cue and hooked her arm into his, steering him away and on, toward the doors.

"Tink," she said, "it's all right. You don't know where we are. Right? We'll make board call. Captain's orders."

Tink didn't look certain about that. *He* wasn't certain about this 'don't know where we are' and 'captain's orders' . . . not that Saby was likely to use physical force. But Saby clearly had the upper hand in the information division, and *he* could be in deep trouble, for all he knew, headed for one more ship like *Christophe Martin*.

Tink said, looking straight at him. "Tom, —if she says it's so, it's so. If she says do, you do it. All right? Is that all right?"

Tink meant it. Tink meant it a hundred percent, like a nervous mama turning her kid over to a stranger she almost trusted, and he had it clear who was in what role in Tink's book: if he did anything Saby could complain of, Tink was going to find him, he had no question.

"Yeah," he said, and meant it. "No problems. I *want* to go back to the ship. I'm willing to go." It finally occurred to him to say that, and he thought at least Tink would believe him.

"Come on," Saby said, tugging on the arm still linked with hers, and he had the momentary, panicked thought that if anything happened to Saby, if any remote, unpredictable accident happened to Saby Perrault, he was a dead man, not alone in Tink's book, but with the rest of *Corinthian,* the same law that had brought *Sprite's* crew to Marie's defense, however belated, the same that defended every merchanter on dockside and made stations skittish of any challenge to ship-law, if two ships decided to settle a problem, or if, however rarely, a spacer disappeared off a dockside. Saby could call down all of *Corinthian,* hire-ons the same as born-crew, he got that clear and clean from Tink.

And he was, on those grounds, as much a prisoner in Saby's light, cheerful grip as he would have been in the hands of the delegation he'd expected.

He didn't see where Tink went. Maybe to the shops, maybe to another lift. But Saby coded Blue 9/20 on the lift pad where they stopped. The car took a moment or two arriving.

"That was nice," Saby said, hugging his arm tight. "It's always different, the gardens. I try to go at least once. I don't want to be on a planet. I really don't like the thought of infalling. The gardens are really just close enough for me. They do weather sometimes. I think that's just on the morning tour. They say you can plan on getting wet."

"I'm not going to run away," he said. "You can let go."

She didn't let go. She kept it physical—meaning knock her down if he wanted to run. And you could die for that, if Tink got hold of you. "I'll take you back to the ship," she said, "if you really want."

"What's my choice?"

"The *Aldebaran.* I talked to Austin. He's just really pissed at

Christian. He said it's my call. The *Aldebaran*'s a really nice place. Good food. Class One. You tell me you won't do anything stupid and you can stay there and we can have first-class food and soak up the latest vids. No sex in the offer, understand, just a place to be for a few days."

He was relieved at the no-sex part. Wasn't a mach' thing to be relieved at. Or maybe it was. Human dignity. If you reckoned that. He didn't like being shoved, ordered, ultimatumed, or kidnapped. He'd grown very touchy about kidnapped.

"Why?" he asked.

But the car came, and they got in, with two other riders aboard. Saby smiled. He smiled. Acted easy. The other passengers did, clearly romantically inclined, hand in hand. Everybody smiled at everybody. Saby hung on to his arm and his nerves were strung tight as wire, the whole short distance out to Blue 9/20, where they got off and the other spacers stayed.

"What's the deal?" he asked, then, in the brief privacy they had as they walked.

"The offer?"

"The sleepover. The fancy food. You."

"I told you. I don't come with the room."

"Yeah, that's fine. I don't, either. But why?"

"Because you're not a fool. Because Christian's got it coming, and Austin's pissed. That's enough."

"I don't see it."

"Do you dance?"

"Do I dance?"

"I know this restaurant. They've got a view, this huge real view of the stars from the dance floor. I can teach you."

He'd never. He'd never imagined. He'd never, in his life. Saby was a tumbling infall of propositions and changes of vector he'd never, ever, expected to deal with.

Dance?

Stationers *danced.* Spacers . . . did, but not on *Sprite,* they didn't. He couldn't imagine.

"I don't know," he said. "I guess." He was thinking more

about the food. He'd lately been hungry. He'd no assurance he might not be again.

And they walked the dockside, to a frontage with the very small, gold–and–silver sign that said *Aldebaran.*

Any spacer would say, high-class, expensive, and ask, being prudent, Who's really financing this?

Saby? Austin? Or somebody else? Like another ship . . . with proprietary ideas.

Saby input an access code and showed him through the doors into a very beige, very pricey-looking reception area. Amenities were listed on the walls, with code numbers. Display cases lined the room. He saw, at one pass of the eye, directions to a gym, to a barber/stylist shop . . . to a jewelry store, restaurants, one breakfast, brunch, lunch, one dinner. He drew in a breath, shook his head, reckoning himself far out of his credit budget— you could feel the money in your pocket ebb just in looking at the case-displays.

"Anything you need urgently," Saby said. "Personals? They have those in the bath, in every room. That's all right."

"I've got a hundred eighty seven cee," he said. "Actually it's Christian's."

"Oh, good," Saby said cheerfully. "Buy whatever you like. I've a phone call to make."

"To the captain? Or to him?"

"The captain, —naturally. Be good. We'll eat here, tonight. Are you hungry?"

"Hungry. Sleepy. Tired. Mostly tired."

"Dancing when you're rested," Saby said, and went to the desk, to make her phone call . . . after which there might be God knew what. He hoped just for a chance to sit down. But he'd gotten to the slightly crazed, half-giddy stage of sleep deprivation, and he wandered around the room and looked at the displays, that was all, mentally blank. He was aware of Saby on the phone, at the desk. He was aware as she crossed the room toward him.

Entirely cheerful. "Captain says fine, it's all right, anything you need—in reason. Have you found anything you have to have?"

"Just a bed, just sleep." That was the honest answer. It was all he could think of now, now a room and a bed were that close. So Saby coded them through further doors. It was down the corridor to number 17, and inside, to a private room with two beds.

He went straightway and fell face-down on one, not eager for conversation, his legs tired from walking and standing, his eyes stinging from sleeplessness. He said to himself that if Saby wanted to call the cops or *Corinthian* or anybody, he didn't care, so long as he could get a little rest that wasn't hiding out in a restroom or sitting on a waiting-area bench.

A blanket settled over him. If Saby was the source of the blanket, he was grateful—the room was chill, and he hadn't the self-awareness left to figure out what to do about it.

Pleasant, he thought about Saby. Nice. Tink said she was all right.

But clearly reporting to his father. That wasn't a recommendation.

But it was opposite sides of the room, Saby didn't bother him, the blanket made him comfortable as he was, and the lights went out. He hadn't even the interest to open his eyes as he heard Saby settle into the other bed. Stark naked or in the sexiest gown he could imagine . . . couldn't muster a shred of interest. Face-down and going, gone.

—— *iii* ——

THE MUSIC IN *JACO'S* made the glasses shake. The walls were all screens, on which old vids played endlessly. It was a horror-show to the left, a riot scene to the right, a murder-thriller straight ahead.

In the immediate vicinity, it was impending apocalypse, one day before board-call and no brother.

Not *one* sight, sound, clue of Tom Hawkins, and no call from the station police office.

Thanks very likely to 200c of his money. 10200c, correction.

Correction again, 14750c, after he'd paid the computer time, the records searches, the bar tabs, the working-time of various crew who had to be put on duty-time to find the son of a bitch, and he couldn't ask Austin to foot the bill.

Clock on the wall said 0448m/1548a, meaning approaching suppertime on *Corinthian*'s main-crew schedule, meaning Austin was awake and *he* was having supper an hour and a half before alterday dawn. On one wall a giant spiny monster was flattening an ancestral Terran city and on the opposite, one guy was choking another while some dimbrain woman stood and watched and screamed.

"There you are." Capella pulled a chair back and dropped into the seat with a clatter of bracelets. "God, 0500?"

"Found anything?"

"Not a damned thing." She slumped back and, the waiter being instantly on them, "Sandwich. Cheese. Rum and juice. I need vitamins."

"ID."

She pulled her card from her sleeve-pocket and the waiter ran the mag-strip through his handheld, logged the charge and handed back the card.

"14756.50c," Christian said glumly, and had a sip. "My guess . . . just my remotest guess is our big chance is tomorrow. Board-call starts at 1500 and ends at 1830, and I'm betting he'll be watching from somewhere, either right at the first or right toward the end."

"What makes you think it?"

"Genes. Can Austin turn hold of a question? Older brother won't be satisfied until he *sees* the ports close and the lights go out and he sees our departure telemetry on the boards—until then it's not enough. *He* won't believe it until he sees our outbound wavefront, but that's outside our parameters. I want to be on that dock tomorrow right down to the last, I want to have your eyes and mine where we can see anybody watching us. Because he will come down to watch."

"Best hope we've got, I guess. Guy's nice-looking. My notion is he's snagged a free stay with somebody—no knowing he even knows what day it is."

"Oh, he knows," Christian said. "I'd bet anything he knows to the second when that board-call is. And if we do spot him—"

"Going to be interesting hauling him past the customs check."

"Ship-debt. We've got his papers. We've got his sign-on at Viking."

"He really sign on?"

He hadn't, of course. "The papers I've got say he did."

"Be careful how long you flash those. Pell cops aren't blind. They *know* their local artists."

"What the hell else am I going to do? This is expensive paper, Pella."

"Yeah."

"You're not making any headway."

"Christian, I have called in debts you would not want to know about. I have talked to people I never wanted to talk to, at expenses you don't reckon in any bank account. Don't talk to me about effort in this not noble cause, dear friend. These are people I *never* wanted to see, and they don't come cheap."

His heart sank. "How much?"

"Those that ask for cash—2400, at current."

"I haven't *got* it, God, Austin's going to leave *me* in station-debt."

"Cash, Chrissy-sweet, cash is the only way. My ID has *smoked* from the withdrawals. It smells of brimstone. Your account isn't dead, but it's on life-support, and we are eating sandwiches till we clear this port, that much I do know, or you don't want to see the hell we'll be in. Austin does not want me to access these people, Chrissy, Austin will have my hide for the places I've looked, which *won't* report to Austin, so there.

Just don't you tell him, and you cover that tab, Chrissy. You cover it."

"That's three quarters of everything I own but ship-share, dammit!"

"As I recall, Christian-love, this was not originally my idea. I would have predicted elder-brother wouldn't have liked the trip to Tokyo and London. I just really didn't think it was his artistic preference."

"Shut up! God! give me a little understanding! Where was your advice when it could have done some good?"

"I don't recall I was consulted. Cajoled, entreated, asked for illegal acts, but consulted. . ."

"How is he in bed?"

"Who?"

"My half-brother, dammit. How good?"

"We are suspicious, aren't we?"

"He's dangerous as hell. A Family Boy? All full of conscience? All full of principles? My father's off his head. I'm not! I've nothing against Hawkins personally. But nobody sees, nobody sees a damned thing dangerous in him!"

"And *we* can't find him," Capella said. "I don't see Austin disturbed. I see the captain quite, quite calm—considering the gravity of the circumstances. Possibly because he's not speaking to you. Or—possibly—"

That veer sideways took a second to think about. Two seconds. "The son of a bitch ran for the ship? And Austin didn't say?"

"It *is* a place we haven't searched," Capella said. The sandwich and rum arrived, which meant a brief distraction to sign the tab.

"He wouldn't," Christian said.

The waiter left. Capella took a bite of sandwich and swallowed. "I don't know. It'd be the smartest thing elder brother could do, in his situation—supposing he's noticed the passport's fake."

"No. Surely not."

"We are down to surely nots. Aren't we?"

"Point."

"Doesn't cost anything." Another bite. Then Capella's eye strayed. She swallowed, belatedly. He looked, in the chance the distraction was named Hawkins.

Negative. He saw nothing to attract Capella's attention. Bar traffic, nothing but.

But Capella took the paper napkin and wrapped the sandwich. Tossed off half the drink at two gulps.

"What *is* it?" he asked.

"Somebody I don't want to meet. Just sit still. Don't attract attention."

"*What* somebody?"

"Chrissy. Just listen. Stay calm. In a moment I'm going to get up and go, and you sit here long enough to see if anybody follows me. Then you get up at your leisure and go left outside, go left, just keep traveling. I'll watch for you and intercept."

"What in hell's going on? Pella? Is it cops?"

"Just do it, dammit. Man in a grey shirt, blue glitz, dark hair, can't miss him." Capella's eyes tracked something past his shoulder, cold as deep ice. "If he follows, don't let on, just keep walking. I'll be watching. Just wait till I'm clear plus some. If he follows me . . . still, you follow. We steer this to a venue we like. Got it?"

He didn't. Hadn't. Not the fine details of what Capella proposed to do about it.

But Capella slid out of her seat and walked, quietly, for the door, while he tried to pick out the newcomer she'd described, and did. He was giving an order at the bar, meaning he planned to stay; or asking a question, which might send him to their table: Capella wasn't exactly inconspicuous in an establishment. At least the guy didn't look in his direction.

Until the bartender pointed at his table.

Immediately the guy and two others started over. It wasn't in the instructions. Neither was this guy bringing help with him.

He sat still. Hell, he was a *Corinthian* officer, not open to hassle or harassment without involving more ante than any other ship might want. So he looked them up and down like germs and stayed his position.

"Looking for Capella," the first guy said, him in grey and blue; and leaned a knuckle on the table-surface. "Where'd she go?"

"I dunno. Back to the ship." That was a right-hand turn from here. "She was going to check something. Why?"

Blue-and-grey made a flip of the hand at the muscle behind him. One left, presumably on Capella's track. That tore it.

"Wait a minute," he said.

"Just a personal matter," blue-and-grey said.

"With my wife?"

Blue-and-grey stepped back, looking shocked, and laughed outright. It was an unpleasant face. Somebody a woman might have been interested in, maybe, but this was a man that'd knife you, this was a man who still wore open shirts when the waistline was getting a little much for skintights.

This was a man he didn't like, on instant instinct.

"You?" blue-and-grey asked, still laughing. And started to walk out.

The trouble was, he was still figuring how this fit with Capella's safety, which occupied all circuits and input a wait-count while the sumbitch with the mouth was walking to the door on him, while his gut level reaction, to grab that sumbitch by the throat, had adrenaline flooding his system and doing no good at all for the brain.

He carried a knife in his boot. So, he figured, did the two leaving, and so would their friend, the one he'd misdirected down the dock.

Meanwhile, if blue-and-grey and his friend were thinking at all, they'd guess he'd misdirected them, and head the other way out of here, on Capella's track, if they hadn't had a man outside to catch an escapee in the first place.

It went against the grain to call for help. But he took the com out—this close to the ship, he didn't need the phonelink—and punched in, on his deliberate way to the door. "*Corinth*-com, this is Christian, in *Jaco's,* we got a code six tracking one of ours spinward out of here, guy in blue and grey, extreme bad manners, relay and get me immediate help here."

Cops routinely monitored the coms as well as the ship-to-station links, and that was too damn bad. Trouble was headed at Capella's back and he was on the way—it wasn't so much what blue-and-grey might do to Capella that scared him . . . it was the ruckus bound to explode if somebody pulled a knife or a piece of macho argument on *Corinthian's* chief spook—*Corinthian* didn't want any more legal trouble, and bodies were so hard to—

Something hit his head—dropped him to one knee with stars flashing red in his brain, and he came up at the target, straight-armed somebody he couldn't even see, approximately at the throat, impacted a face with the heel of his hand, surprise to him.

But the guy went down anyway, and papa hadn't taught him to turn his back on any attacker. He saw a shadow-someone in the red flashes and grey, trying to come up off the deck, and he rammed his hands down and his knee up. Bang. Guy went backwards, flat.

Then he whirled around and ran leftward up the dockside, on what he was sure was blue-and-grey's trail. Red flashes were still floating across his watering vision, it was still grey around the edges, and balance consequently wasn't a hundred percent, but he was dead on course, with blue-and-grey and one other some distance ahead of him.

He didn't see Capella. He kept going, double-fast, figuring on giving Mr. Sumbitch another quarrel to take his mind off her, figuring on his *Corinthian* backup to be coming, and hoping some *Corinthian* would have the basic sense to drag the sod he'd left behind him into the bar. Cops might ignore bar-business until it spilled onto the docks, but bodies in doorways were a guarantee of notice.

Just, if Capella had come out, too, and run into a trap . . .

"You!" he yelled, at blue-and-grey, with a stitch coming in his side and his head going around—he was too dizzy to chase the guys at a dead run. But run was what they did, then, damn the luck, just took out, both of them.

He ran, his head pounding like hell, vision fuzzing and tearing. He knocked shoulders with somebody in a better mood than he was—caught-step, recovered, chased the two until he knew he didn't know where they'd gone—then leaned against a friendly support girder near a pharmacy frontage, sweating and aching for breath.

Pocket-com was beeping, when things got quiet. He fumbled after it and thumbed it on. "Christian. Yeah. Lost the guy. Got a fix?"

"What in hell's going on?"

God. *Corinth*-com had rousted Austin out. Wasn't what he wanted.

"Dunno, sir, I was walking out of *Jaco's*—" He gasped for air. "—and some damnfool hit me over the head."

"Thieves?"

"I—" It was better than any lie he could think of. He didn't know what Capella was into. He didn't spill Capella's confidences—and he thought in the best functioning of his battered brain that an urgent request to cover her rear was at least in the neighborhood of a confidence. "Yes, sir, maybe. I dropped a guy in *Jaco's* doorway. They find him?"

There was a delay while, one presumed, *Corinthian* asked on another channel.

"Travis says negative. Phone if you've got detail."

Get off the com, Austin meant. Travis was mainday Engineering, and he'd been that for years, no green fool.

"Yessir. Working on it. —Sir. Have you seen my brother?"

A pause. *"Negative."*

As if Austin wouldn't lie.

Damn!

Austin clicked out on him. And where Capella was . . .

"Chrissy!"

His heart did a flip. He turned around. Capella was there in the ambient noise of the docks, ghostlike, not a warning.

"Shit!" He got a breath. "Guy clipped me on the head. I was scared they'd got you . . ."

"You get him?"

"Got away. Who *were* those guys?"

"Them, I don't know. Not a ship-patch in the lot, but they're no station-slime."

"Blue-and-grey. You knew him."

"Yeah, I knew him."

He didn't like the tone or the faraway look Capella sent in that direction. Capella didn't talk about times past. Or the Fleet. That was the deal. "Pella. Need-to-know, here. Just—is it personal? Or what?"

Capella could have a real bar-crawler look, type you'd pick up for a fast one and maybe cheap, till she went all business and gave you that down-the-gun-barrel stare. "I want to know what ship he's on. I want to know who just came into port.

"Capella." He had his business track, too, when he had to. And he knew what he had a right to ask. "The one question. Personal? Or not?"

Capella didn't answer for a moment. Then: "You remember those doors I said I rattled looking for elder brother?"

"Yeah?"

"Bad stuff. Real bad stuff. This is not a friend and it has a ship, apparently, I can't think how else it got here. I'd sincerely like to lie in port until this leaves. It has to leave. Eventually."

They'd seen port-scum. They'd dealt with it. *Corinthian* had had encroachers on their territory, in port, and in space. He'd never seen Capella spooked into sobriety by any opposition. She just got crazier.

She wasn't now. Cold sober. Not laughing.

"Pella. We've got that Hawkins ship . . ."

"Screw the Hawkinses. This is Mazianni, you understand me."

Capella didn't use that word. Not about herself. Capella said Fleet. *The* Fleet, as if there wasn't any other. As if they still served something besides survival.

"No," he said. "Pella. Tell me the truth. I swear—it doesn't go past me."

Long silence. Then: "Worth your life. Mine. Yours. The ship. Yeah, I know we've got Hawkins troubles. But screw 'em. Blow 'em. Ships have got lost before now in the deep dark. But we can't *go* out with this guy on our tail, and he will be, he can *feel* us in the dark."

"We can't not!"

"If Patrick's in port, this isn't the time I'd have sent shock-waves through the informational ambient here, you know what I mean? You seriously understand?"

"Patrick-who?"

"Patrick's enough. Used to be *Europe*."

"Mazian himself?"

"Yeah."

"He's alive."

"Oh, yeah. Stuff I can't say, Christian-person."

"Christian, dammit. I have a name."

"Yeah. So did I. But names are little things. Winner. Loser. Right. Wrong. This side, that side. All that shit. On old Earth—they used to be superstitious about names. Like if you could call somebody the right one, you could catch their soul. And you don't *want* to engage on that level, you truly *don't,* Chrissy-love. You don't want that karma with me."

"Don't play me for a fool, dammit, I don't know your words."

"I like you. Like you too much."

"Is that why you're sleeping with my brother?"

"Chrissy, . . . Christian. Is that a matter? Is that sincerely a matter? We are talking about survival. We are talking about something. . ."

Capella didn't finish.

"Yeah?" he said, *not* dismissing the matter of older-brother and Capella and what he thought had been going on.

"Christian. Not all of us trade with you. Some have their own notions. I need to talk with the captain."

"Yeah," he said.

It was all *he* knew to do.

—— *iv* ——

SABY WAS RIGHT. THE RESTAURANT view was spectacular, a real viewport (fortified, the sign at the door assured the patrons: even the Battle of Pell hadn't compromised it) that reached from polished black floor to mirror-finish ceiling, a revolving view of the stars and the planet that spacers themselves rarely saw so directly. To either side, making silhouettes of the tables, dwarfing human dancers, the walls were high-rez screens, with magnified, filtered views, that spun and whirled in a camera-construct, a montage of images that a spacer's body reacted to in expectation of accel and vector shifts that didn't, of course, happen.

Meaning a spacer could get motion-sickness walking across the floor, if he was a cabin-dwelling merchanter whose well-loaded ship didn't regularly do the maneuvers those shots described, but whose stomach knew when a *g*-shift ought to happen. Tom kept his eyes on the level surface where the floor was real as the waiter captain led them to their table. A stationers' revenge on spacers, that tape was, that produced those images . . . or the stationers that produced it had no remotest idea they'd made an amusement ride for a spacer's force-trained body.

Dance, did the woman want? Damned show-off spacer-femme. He was going to fall on his ass before he reached the table. Tripped over his own feet, but the chair saved him.

Grace under pressure.

They sat. They had cocktails. The food was good, if scant by his reckoning, small vegetable things he hadn't seen on the tour, and a good sauteed fish with, they advertised, genuine herbs (not difficult) and genuine citrus sauce, an expensive and tongue-puzzling treat. But not an extravagance at Pell. He'd *seen* oranges growing. He'd got himself a leaf—well, Saby had it, but he'd caught it in mid-flight. He'd seen fish swimming in a man-made brook, almost enough to put him off eating this one. But not quite. It was good. The lights came and went and whirled about the polished floor.

And against the light, shadows came, once, that he took for children, until a handful of spacer-diners near them stopped, and stared.

He looked, too, and saw the glint of breathing-masks with a little increase of heart rate. Downers, a handful of them, and the sight richocheted off the study he'd done as a boy—off all the sense of the strange and unfathomable that a boy could romanticize. Alien intelligence, if eccentric and even childlike to human estimation.

"Look," he whispered to Saby, not to be rude, because they were quite near.

"Local sun's sacred to them," Saby said. "They can come here. It's the law."

"Law, hell. They're people. It's their world." He'd thought he almost liked Saby tonight. Not with that attitude.

"Yeah," Saby said. "But good there's a law. Damned shame we have to make a law. What I hear . . . we had to explain crime to them."

"They have deviants."

"Not criminals."

He was discussing criminality with a *Corinthian* crewwoman. "No kidnappers?"

"No reason, I guess." Saby refused the bait. "But I wouldn't be a Downer. I'd rather have our faults . . . since we can't figure theirs. Seems safer."

The waiter came. Saby ordered a drink. He did. The band

had started. He saw the Downer-shadows bobbing to the music, knees bending ever so slightly, to tunes light, classic, rather than current. Couples were walking onto the floor.

Going to fall on my ass, he thought.

They had the cocktails. His was lime and vodka, hers was import Scotch. The music was slow and soft, and the Downers had filed away to the edges of the dark. They lived in the arteries and veins of Pell Station, where their oxy-ratio was law. They maintained, they worked, they asked no pay but the sight of the Sun of Downbelow, Pell's Star. They worked a season or two and then went down again to the world, in the springtime of their main continents, when, the brochures said, Pell had to take to human resources, and make do without its small and industrious helpers. No Downer would work in springtime. Mating consumed them. Females left their burrows and took to walking, simply walking, wherever their fancy took them; and males followed them, far, as far as their resolve and their interest could drive them, until the last gave up, lost interest, resigned the Downer lass to his last rival, who had still to find a place, and dig a nest, and satisfy the far-walking adventuress of his craft and his passion and his worth. What need of nations or boundaries, or such territorial notions? The object of their desires went where she pleased.

Not likely they'd form a government. Not likely they'd fight a war.

Not likely they'd have achieved their dearest dream, to see their Sun, except as human guests.

But they traded their agriculture for human goods, they maintained complex machinery they had no innate impulse to invent themselves. Ask what they might become, or understand, or do, in centuries to come.

"Penny for your thoughts."

"Huh?"

"They say that, this side of the Line. Penny for your thoughts. What are you thinking?"

"About the Downers. About getting into things you don't

understand. About fools that go wandering in warehouses. Why haven't they hauled me back to the ship?"

Saby lifted a bare and shapely shoulder. Pretty. A distraction to clear thinking. You could get to looking in her eyes and missing the thoughts entirely.

Saby didn't answer his question. Never had. They'd sat in the room for most of three days, shopped via the vid system, used the *Aldebaran*'s restaurant, the *Aldebaran*'s gym, the *Aldebaran*'s hair salon, swum in the pool, baked in the sauna . . . had no personal conversation, just a Race you to the other side, and a, What's your favorite color? kind of dealing with each other, shallow, safe. Saby liked green, loved to dance, preferred coffee to tea, liked the skintight craze and bought him some for evening as well as day. Saby could take an hour in the bath and run a chain of figures in her head instantly. Those things he'd learned about Saby. But talk about the ship, Christian, the captain, even Tink, —no. Dead cutoff.

"What could I have seen in that warehouse?"

"I don't know. What were you looking for?"

"You could be a lawyer. Was it something I could have seen or just a chance to get at my mother's son?"

"That's then. Now's now." She sipped her whiskey. "They've a marvelous dessert. Orange creme cake."

He wasn't even tempted. "You," he said. "No thanks."

"Board-call's tomorrow. Are you going to go?"

"Have I got a choice?"

"Oh, you could raise a fuss right now. Yell for the cops, all sorts of things."

"I could end up stuck here. Legaled to death. I'd as soon be dead."

"So you'll go back without a fuss?"

"Sure." His turn to shrug. They'd been through it before. He didn't know why she'd started down this track. "No passport. No choice." He dreamed of answering that board-call, showing up and having *Corinthian* hand him to the cops, claim they never knew him. He didn't understand Saby. They'd spent a lot of money. Saby had spent it . . . on her account, Saby said. Or he'd spent Christian's cash.

But he could get to that customs gate only to discover it was *his* account she was accessing and the ship wasn't paying. In that case, he *had* that station-debt, and he had to pay it, if the ship wouldn't. No passport, no ID, no ship willing to pay for him. That was the scenario he'd slowly put together—Saby swearing to customs that he'd lied to her, they were his charges, not hers, with a whole ship to back her story and damn him to a spacer's hell.

"You're worried about something," Saby said.

"I can't imagine why."

"I don't know what. Whether you can trust me? Is that it?"

"It's an obvious question."

"You're a nice guy. You are. I told the captain that."

"Thanks. Did you tell him not to knock me into walls? I'd appreciate that."

"I really like you," Saby said.

His heart went thump. Brain cut out of the loop. *Why?* was the last logical thought.

"You want to dance?" Saby asked, and reached out her hand on the tabletop. "Come on. Slow-dancing. Nothing fancy."

He really didn't want to. A, he didn't want to make a fool of himself. B, he didn't know where the conversation had taken the turn it did or why Saby suddenly got personal. He'd a drink to finish, but the mouth wasn't working and the brain was on shut-down. He tossed off the rest of the drink to calm his stomach, hooked fingers with Saby—let Saby tug him to his feet and walk him out into the dreadful tilting visions of the walls and the reflections on the floor. The alcohol hit, and he was right in front of the big viewport, where the stars were moving and small and far, behind the silhouetted dancers. They were potentially in people's way, but others managed not to bump them, and Saby turned him toward her, holding both his hands—kept one, drew one behind her waist, at the curve of a—he wasn't dead—satin-clad hip.

"Relax," she said, and laughed, and bumped his foot with hers. "Step, step, step, turn—"

The room spun. He managed to breathe and move, step, step, step, turn, with Saby, and they hadn't knocked into anybody. They moved with the traffic, joined the movement around the swirling floor, the sweeping walls.

"Isn't that easy?"

She made him lose where he was. The dreadful face of the planet was coming into view—he got the count back, desperately, and took Saby's lead for a giddy turn, abandoned hope of equilibrium, and began to figure Saby wasn't going to steer him into collision, he just had to stay with it, feel when she moved, listen to the music . . .

"There," Saby said, "now you're getting it."

It was more commitment to Saby's guidance than he wanted, period. He'd held back. He'd maintained a stolid non-involvement and non-interest in Saby Perrault—he'd read a book, sat on his bed, they'd discussed colors and her harmless preference for coffee over tea. But he was occupied in keeping up, now, and, he guessed, by Saby's mercy, not making too much of a fool of himself—nobody was staring, and Saby seemed happy. The alcohol buzz made the images fuzz, and his heart that thumped in panic at the grand sweep of the planet, the deadly gulf of infall, found a sustainable level of adrenaline and kept time, thump, thump, thump to the music and the dizzy turns.

Silence came like a stop in the universe. He stood, hard-breathing, dizzy, with one hand where not-dancing made it too familiar, and the other sweating in Saby's grasp. Everybody applauded, the band got a second wind, and while some drifted back to the tables, Saby said it was a slow tune and she'd teach him that step, too.

It wasn't so organized as the fast step, just kind of wandering back and forth, no way for anybody to be conspicuous, the stars there beyond the shadows of other couples, Saby's body brushing his on a regular sort of movement that he . . . didn't really mind. Much. Often. He was wary. He asked himself if he was being seduced, or if she was—taking a stupid chance, if that was what was happening. But if Saby wanted to end this up with bed, he could agree with that, he'd been clever as long as he could, and stupid was taking over with a vengeance.

Wasn't his fault. Wasn't any way out of the trap he was in. Might as well enjoy anything that came before. There was, tomorrow, inevitably the day after. And Austin.

The dance ended.

"Want to sit?" Saby asked.

"What do you want?"

"Want to dance," Saby said. So they did, a fast one this time. He remembered. Saby floated in his arms, threw changes and embellishments into the steps and the turns he couldn't match—she was gorgeous. The light of magnified stars sparked on cut-away sleeves that fluttered against her and away again, her hair eclipsed the light like a swirl of shadow—he kept up with her, he took her cues, and when the music was done, she laughed, breathless, and applauded, dragged him back to the table when the music was done.

Two fresh drinks were sitting there. He didn't think that was a good idea. He sipped at his, out of breath, himself, with far less work, and she sipped at hers, the same, until they'd both caught their breaths and cured the dry mouths.

The music had settled to a saner pace. "Go again?" Saby asked.

"Sure," he said. He hadn't had all his drink. He wanted water, but the waiter was invisible, and Saby was happy . . . a yes could do that, it was easy, and it wasn't with most people in his experience—a new experience, she was, no negatives, hell, you could get too easy, you could get to *like* making Saby happy. So here he was, going out onto the floor, for one dance and then two, slow and sane dancing, just wandering back and forth. Saby leaned her head on his shoulder, and body moved against body, her instigation: he didn't want her complaining tomorrow, telling her crewmates and her captain he'd had the ideas and she hadn't.

Because maybe it wasn't a come-ahead. He couldn't figure, and all the higher brain managed was a warn-off, a wait-see. Brain-base was on slow ignite, and feedback from the lower body circuits was hitting warning, warning . . .

Music faded. Applause and sort-out was a reprieve. They stared at each other in the giddy dark and . . . he wasn't sure whose initial motion it was . . . joined the drift back to tables and drinks.

They rested, they got at least the moisture in the drinks—he wanted water, Saby said she did, and they tried to catch a waiter, but the next dance was starting. They danced some more, the drinks kept refilling every time they got back to the table, and by then they were immortal and impervious to successive rounds. They danced, they drank, they danced until the stars were blurry, until, in the ending of a slow number, while they moved in a slow, brain-buzzed drift, the speakers announced shift-change, and last call.

They got their breath. The waiter showed, with the reckoning. He didn't dare to ask.

"Tab us to *Corinthian*," Saby said, and showed her passport. "House percentage. —And bring some water, please."

They never got any water, just sips of the last refill. And the receipt and a chocolate.

—— *v* ——

So the second chief navigator wanted to board and talk. Capella had to pass on an urgent piece of news. *Capella* had to talk to him. Of course Christian wasn't in the vicinity.

Like bloody hell, Austin thought, and it didn't take a master intellect, once Capella showed at the lock, to predict it had to do with the dustup on the dock, that the dustup had a lot to do with Christian asking extra security outside, and had a damned lot to do with Christian's scouring around and making more noise on the information market than *Corinthian* habitually liked.

Which, logic argued, might just drop a small amount of fault for the situation on the captain's own plate, for not yanking Christian's authorizations and codes before they docked, but, hell, he expected at least eighteen years worth of maturity out of the twenty ship-years the kid had lived, he expected a degree of basic sense of consequences, and *he* wouldn't have sneaked Hawkins out the lock, or involved *Christophe Martin,* which was the start of the whole info-blowup. It could have racketed clear to the stationmaster's office if he hadn't put a fast brake on it. Right now he could wring the young fool's neck, Christian knew it, and damned right Capella came alone, soft-footing it into lower main, trading on her connections. You got a Fleet navigator on quasi-permanent loan, all right, but you consequently had to ask yourself what that individual could and would do if you came to cross-purposes, and you had to ask yourself a second time, when said individual immediately locked on to your admittedly attractive mainday chief officer-and-offspring, whether it was wholly as physical an attraction as Christian's young ego could assume it was. Warn him, yes. Repeated warnings. Like pouring current into a non-conductor. Of course Christian knew all that, Christian knew everything, Capella was just a good time. Capella was *intelligent,* Capella was good conversation.

Capella screwed his brains into overload and Christian had revelatory insights, oh, damned right he did.

Heredity didn't warn him at all. Paternal experience was irrelevant. The wages of sin walked down the corridor and arrived face to face.

"Sir," Capella said. "There's a spotter for somebody out there. Guy named Patrick, that's all I know."

"The hell that's all you know." Worst-case became, in a single, disastrous instant, the present case, and you didn't know how far it had proliferated: but Capella if not Christian knew why she'd asked for a hearing—*knew* she'd let a situation slip over a line past-which-not, by this unaccustomed and stark quiet of manner.

"Can we talk, sir?"

"We can talk," he said. And maybe he should run scared of her connections, but hell if he was going to. "Do I assume somebody's screwed up? Do I assume this involves your solution to the problem?"

No bluff. No flinch. An arrogant stare. "If I could have caught him, yessir, I should've done, but I couldn't account for the four with him and I didn't want the cops."

"So what's your recommendation?"

"Lie in port. It's not a sure bet *Sprite*'s coming in. It *is* a fact that that something's already here."

"Who? What?"

Forget getting all the truth out of Capella. It took her a couple of beats to censor. Or lie.

"Renegade. Scavenger. Little stuff. No threat to us. But he'll track us. He'll find the dump. He'll kill us if he can . . . to shut *me* up."

"I can understand that motivation."

Capella's chin came up, eyes a clear try-me, and he gave it back:

"You are an *arrogant* sumbitch. My son's just a good lay, is he? Good boy, a little dim, do anything you like on his watch? Or did he scare you into this?"

Long, long silence in the corridor, and Capella's nostrils flared.

"Didn't think it would go this far."

"Yeah."

"Yes, *sir,* I fucked up. I considerably fucked up."

He let the silence hang there. He'd never been sure what captain or what interests Capella served. But it was down to basics, now. When something threatened the ship you were on . . . it was suddenly damned basic; and he let that admission hang there long enough for Capella to hear it herself.

"But in some measure," he said ever so quietly, so she *would* hear it, "your friends are something we can deal with outside Pell system. In some measure, you're up to that, aren't you?" He'd never challenged *how* she handled navigation, or her other faculties. It was the closest pass he intended to make to that touchy matter. He challenged her nerve. And her skill. And waited for his answer.

"I think—" she began to equivocate. It wasn't ordinary for her.

"I know," he said, cutting her off. "I *know*. Period. If *Sprite* gets here, what action do you suggest, second chief navigator, to prevent a search of our records?"

"It's our deck, sir."

"That's fine. We can lose docking privileges pending our release of those records. This isn't the War, second chief navigator. We may be necessary to the Fleet, but our little hauling capacity isn't necessary to Pell Station, and our brother and sister merchanters aren't just apt to rally round *Corinthian* in a quarrel with other merchanters, does that occur to you, second chief navigator?"

A Fleet navigator wasn't an entity to piss off. You agreed to take on the inevitable Gift from the Fleet and you agreed not to ask questions; you agreed that was grounds for very severe action in certain quarters. In effect, you took a ticking bomb aboard, and you hoped to hell nothing ever set it off: there was nothing but Capella's personal inclinations and physical restraint to keep said navigator from walking out on that dock, finding this Patrick, and turning coat in five minutes. It was a hell of a chance to take.

But it had gotten, thanks to Capella and Christian and Marie Hawkins, down to a similar hell of an alternative.

"Yes, sir," Capella said, equally quietly, "it does occur to me. But if we don't get Hawkins back . . . we're still screwed, no matter whether *Sprite* comes in here or not, which isn't proven they will, sir, that's my thought."

"I am so glad, I am so very glad we agree on that, second

chief. But take it from me that we *are* going to board call tomorrow on schedule, that this is the course we're taking, and that, while I have thought of spacing Christian, I expect his ass in that airlock, safe, sober, and in your company. After that, I expect your professional talents to be on, period, capital letter, On. Can we agree on this, second chief?"

No blink, just analysis, like the face she wore on the bridge. "Yes, sir," she said.

"Good. That's real good. Because I appreciate the seriousness of what's happened out there. And I value officers who do. Ahead of my son, at this moment. Do you copy that?"

"Yes, sir."

"That's all, then."

Capella nodded a courtesy, turned with a touch more precision than the habit of the crew, and walked . . . you could see the military in the backbone, the way you could see her move around her station on the bridge, economy of everything.

Damn-all worst woman in the available universe for Christian to take to bed. Marie Hawkins was safer. Much.

He'd said, just now, —he was sure Capella had heard him : Choose a side. Get the hell to them, or take orders from me.

It remained to see, it did, how much she'd fill Christian in— how much she'd dare fill Christian in, if she meant to stay on *Corinthian*—because Christian wasn't going to be an automatic choice to succeed to the captaincy, not now, not since Viking, and damned well not since the stunt he'd pulled here . . . was still pulling, staying clear of him, not coming in to report, himself. There were times to revise priorities, there were times to be sure messages got through . . . you didn't hand off to a bedmate not even remotely connected to the crew, if Christian had even made the decision that brought Capella in to report what couldn't go over com.

He didn't take it for a given. Not now. Not any longer. And that touched a personal investment he hadn't thought he had in Beatrice's unasked-for offspring. It affected him. It made him personally, painfully angry.

He stood there, asking himself why he gave a damn, and since when.

—— *vi* ——

LONG TRIP THROUGH THE LIFT system, alone for some of the trip, but they didn't talk—too many drinks, probably, Tom decided, a headache coming.

And an inevitable reckoning, tomorrow, the prospect of which, now that the music had died, and Saby's manner had gone remote and still, didn't sustain the mood for bed-sharing. He wasn't up to intricate personal politics. He wished he was gone enough to skip the excuses and the assurances, just to go face-down and maybe get some sleep that might, in the face of a not very pleasant tomorrow, desert him all too easily.

They reached the *Aldebaran*'s doors. Saby screwed the access code twice, couldn't find her manual keycard, and swore, going through all her pockets.

"I'm sorry," she kept saying. "Damn."

"It's all right," he found himself saying. "Maybe we could phone *Corinthian*'s board." It could only, he told himself, mean a shorter station stay. "Central'd have to put us through."

"Oh, hell," Saby said. "No. Let me think. It's eight-six-one. . ."

"Five?" He'd watched her code it a dozen times. "It's not bottom row."

"Eight-six-one . . . You're screwing me up. Eight-six, eight-six, eight-six—"

"Five."

"It's not five."

"Eight-six-five-one—"

"*Two*-one. Eight-six-two-one-nine-nine-one." Saby leaned on the wall and coded it into the pad. The light turned green, the latch opened, they were in, and the same code worked all the way to the room.

The card, figure it, was on the table. Right by the door.

"Damn," Saby said, and took it and put it in the coveralls she probably was going to wear tomorrow. She looked tired and out of sorts, and went to the bath and ran one ice-water. And a second one.

"Cheers," she said, bringing him his.

He was sitting on his bed. She was standing. They drank the ice-water they hadn't gotten. Saby laughed, then, tired-sounding.

"What's funny?"

"Nothing," she said. "Just a thought."

"Fools that trust Corinthians?"

A frown. "No."

Sexual tension was gone, no echoes but a remote regret it hadn't, couldn't, have lasted. Maybe, he thought, that was her rueful laughter. He asked, cool and curious, "—Were you supposed to seduce me?"

"No. Not. Nada." She squatted down, peered up at his face, bleary-eyed herself, and shook at his knee, an attention-getting. "Tom, it's going to be all right. Believe me."

"Yeah. —Truth. Who really got the tab tonight?"

"The captain. Cross my heart." She did. Almost fell on her rear. She didn't look like a conspirator.

"What? Fatherly generosity?"

"Christian shouldn't have done what he did. That's all." She patted his knee and got up, turned out the light, then, before she wobbled over to her bed and threw back the covers, evidently at the limits of her sobriety. They never had gotten undressed together—just took the boots off. Shared a room. She sat down in the night-light and kicked her flimsy shoes off, one foot and the other—he shoved his own off and hauled back his sheets. Horizontal for eight hours seemed very attractive right now.

So, with regret, did the woman crawling into covers. Pretty backside, when he looked that direction. Pretty rest of her. Not highly coordinated, getting her blanket over her fully-dressed rump.

"Damn nice guy, Tom. You are. Wish you were just a little, little bit not so nice."

God, now, now, she invited him, when his skull had started to fog from the inside and the rest of him hadn't a desire for anything but face down in the pillow.

But, hell, Bed Manners, his *Polly* spacer used to say, and taught him ways at least to see she got to sleep.

So he hauled himself up off the mattress, came over to sit on her bed. She hadn't left much room at the edge and she was fading, but he'd made the trip—he took her hand in his—pretty hand, limp hand. Fingers twitched. Eyes opened.

He leaned over and kissed her mostly on the mouth. Her fingers twitched again. He figured he'd done his bit for politeness and told himself bed was waiting on the other side of the room, but . . . but she was so damn pretty, she was so damn crazy, he just sat, her hand in his, thinking how with his *Polly* girl you didn't need much to figure what she was thinking.

But with Saby . . . with Saby. . .

Hell, he thought. He was physically attracted, he was in the mood and now *she* was zeroed out.

He shifted down to the end of the bed, not too gently, hoping to rouse a little attention by quasi-accident. Didn't work. He wanted her. Still. And worse. He grabbed her ankle under the blanket. Shook her foot. Hard.

Not a twitch. He sat there a moment, thinking it was a hell of a thing to do to a guy.

But if he woke her out of this sound a sleep she was going to come out of it mad.

Which wasn't the reaction he wanted.

The bed was wide enough. It was the last night before board-call, and he didn't think he was going to sleep, now, he was just going to lie there, wide awake, and worry.

But hell, too, if he was going to turn up in somebody's bed uninvited. There was a rude word for that. So he got up and headed for the bath and a—he glanced at the clock—an 0558 hours shower.

"Tom."

Now she was awake. She sat up on an elbow. The glitz blouse sparked blue in the night-light. "You want to?"

"Want to, what?" He was in a mood to be difficult. Now she wasn't. She reached out a glitter-patterned arm, a mottling of shadow and light.

"Do it, you know."

"Were you asleep?"

"No," she said, to his surge of temper. "Curious."

"Curious, hell! I'm not interested!"

"I've got a ship to protect!"

Loose logic always threw him. He got as far as the bathroom door. And stopped. And looked back.

"From what? From *me*? I'm not the one walking the corridors in the deep dark, thanks, I've *been* screwed, or something like it, by one of your night-walking shipmates, and nobody asked *my* permission."

"Shit," Saby said, and sat upright. "You're kidding."

"It's no damn joke. I'm *not* flattered. —I prefer to be awake, thank you, the same courtesy I give anybody else."

"Shit, shit, shit." It was dismay he heard. Saby got out of bed. " 'Scuse me. It's not me that did it. I know who. Damn her. I'm sorry."

That was fine. So it wasn't Saby crawling the corridors. He never had thought so. And he didn't need the shower, now, but he wasn't inclined to sleep, now, any time soon, and the bath was an excuse not to deal with Saby.

"Tom."

"I'm not in the mood, now. Forget it."

"Tom. Wait. Talk."

"What's the difference? I'm going back. Nothing in hell else I can do. You win. You've got all the answers."

"It's not going to be like it was."

"Like what? Shanghaied off my ship? Is that going to change?"

"Other things can change. You can work into crew. The

allowances are huge, I mean, it's not just the captain picking up the tab, the hired-crew lives real well. You couldn't do better on *Sprite*."

Some things maybe you didn't want to question. Some things could be real trouble to question. But he was in it, deep, and deeper.

"What's *Corinthian* haul?"

"No different than *Sprite*."

"The hell it isn't."

"We sell, we buy, no damn difference—"

"Then where? Is that the question? Where do you haul it *to*? Can we handle that one?"

Silence, the other side of the dark. Then: "Ask Austin."

"*Austin*, is it?"

"Most of the time. To us. To regular crew. You could do what you trained to do—"

"On a damn *pirate*?"

"Just a hauler. *Nothing* we're ashamed of. We're damn proud of our ship. We've reason to be proud."

He wanted to believe that. He had no idea how many dicings of logic it might take to believe it didn't matter . . . who you traded with, or for what, or with what blood on it.

Silence again. And dark. Then: "I've already said more than I should. Aboard the ship, I'll tell you. You don't talk in sleepovers. Some stations bug rooms. Pell doesn't—that we know of. But still—"

He'd never heard that. But no station had ever had a motive to bug *Sprite* crew's rooms. And it didn't change anything.

"Yeah," he said, "so the pay's good. That says a lot."

"I'm not a criminal. Austin isn't."

"That's not the rumor."

"I sleep at night."

"Is that a testimony to your character?"

"You don't know our business, you don't know a damn thing. You're assuming."

"I'm going back because I can't go to the cops without getting stuck on this station. That's all you need. That's as much as you can buy, I don't care what else you're selling."

Another silence. A thunderous, long one before Saby returned to her bed, shadow in shadow, a rustling in the dark. She sat down. He couldn't see detail by the night-light, it was too close to her. He couldn't see her face, whether she was just mad, or hurt.

Didn't need to have said 'selling.' Wrong word. Real wrong word. He'd been on the receiving end of words too often not to feel it racket through his nervous system.

"Sorry," he said. "I can believe you. Not him."

Silence. A long time. He didn't want the solitude of the bath, now, but he didn't think he was going to sleep. Still, she didn't move.

Not for as long as he waited.

"Saby, dammit, I'm sorry."

"Sure. No problem." The voice wobbled. Unfair. "Go to bed. I said no sex. I don't need the damn favor, all right?"

"Saby. This is stupid."

"Fine."

"My father told you to get me in bed?"

"No!"

Wrong step, again. He *couldn't* sleep with Saby hating his guts. He wasn't going to sleep. *She* was going to talk to him and calm down. "I liked tonight, Saby. For God's sake, I did. I had a good time." He couldn't restrain the barb. "When papa lets me out of the brig I'd like to do it again, somewhere."

Long pause. "There's still tonight."

"I'm not in the damn mood! God!"

Another watery silence.

"Dammit," he said, "I'm worried. —I'm scared, all right? I'm making the wrong choice, I'm doing something stupid, maybe I *should* stay here and deal with the cops, maybe it's better I get stranded for the rest of my life, I don't know!"

"Tom."

"God,—fuck off, will you?"

He hadn't meant to say that. He was rattled. He was cornered. It was six in the damn morning of the day he had to go back or go nowhere for the rest of his life.

He saw the shadow lie down, heard the rustle of sheets drawn up.

"Saby."

Silence.

"Saby, dammit." He went over to the bed. He sat down on the edge, shook her foot.

Jerk of that foot, out of his vicinity. "No favors. I'm sorry. Forget it."

He sat there a moment, obdurate against the silence. He tried to think how to patch it. Found the foot again and patted it, a lump under the covers.

She didn't move.

"It was an experience," he said, unwilling to break it off in her angry silence. "It's been a good time." More silence. But no jerk away from him. "It's just over, is all. Bills come due. Don't know if I can handle this one."

Foot moved. Second one joined it. Wiggled toes against his leg, once, twice.

He patted it, too. "Get some sleep." He started to get up.

"Tom." Saby reached out an arm. "Tom, —"

"Don't play games. Go to sleep."

"It's not games, dammit. I can't talk to you, I can't make sense."

Still upset. She'd found his arm, he found her knee. He sat there, just glad he'd made some kind of peace, moved his hand, she moved hers, a clumsy, mutual peace-making that wasn't, then, only that, he wasn't sure if it was him, or her, going past that, but they were past that, her arm sliding up, his sliding down, bodies shifting—

"Tom, . . ."

He wasn't thinking, then. Lower brain took over. His hand moved, found a hip, whatever, among the sheets—mouth found mouth, hands moved at liberty, knees looked for places to be, amid a tangle of covers, and covers grew more tangled, bodies more urgent, brain going lower by the second. Knew he was in trouble. He'd never wanted sex as much as now and he hadn't even solved the damn sheet-tangle. She was doing better with his shirt. He started on hers. Yes-no was out the airlock. Decompression. He was breathing, that was all he could swear to. They were one creature, with the damn sheets somewhere involved, but clothes went, buttons, zips, whatever was in the way—went, until breathing itself was in jeopardy.

Nothing logical, no cautions, no stop-waits, Saby made him crazy and he didn't know why it was different.

He arrived, blind-deaf-red flashes in deep dark, no breath at all until he sank into a sweating, gasping tangle of sheets and skin, Saby's fingers wandered up and down his neck—she didn't say anything, wanted more, maybe, than he could do, and it was going to be awhile, for him, but not for her, so he made love to her, careful, oh, so careful, afraid he'd been too rough—didn't want to hurt anybody, never had, just everybody trapped him, everybody had their own agenda, and Saby, latest and least involved jailer he had, just wanted more—was that news?

She didn't say anything, the dark told him nothing his hands didn't find out, but she had a second and, quickly after, a third trip, holding to him, saying finally, oh, God, oh, God, over and over, didn't know if it was all right, but Saby was having a good trip out of it, that was all he picked up, and he knew Austin had hurt Marie, but he wasn't hurting Saby, she just held tighter to him and wanted until he wondered how long she could go on and whether he could do damage—but: The last night, kept racketing through his skull, and: Last chance. 'Nuf, she said once, and, oh, God, but her hands and her body were still saying something else, after which . . . after which he hit that quick, mind-numbing flashpoint. Lower brain took control again, and the night warped around him, long, long, release—

Then nowhere for a while, floating in that chaos-place where time didn't run the same, or directionally, or anything, hadn't the Voice said it to him? He went there, every which direction, he didn't think what he was doing, sensation just Was, and still echoed.

Came to with a body draped over him, that waked and stirred when he moved a leg that had fallen asleep. Body burrowed against him and held on, keeping him warm against the air . . . didn't know who it was for a moment, didn't know where he was, but he remembered, then, it was Saby, and he couldn't see the rest of his life in front of him. It was all dark, all blank, after where he was.

"You awake?" Saby asked him.

"Yeah," he said, and she moved over him, payback, he thought, sure he'd been too rough, but she wasn't—he kept expecting it and not admitting it, and she grew scary and strange to him as the night-walker—or the walker wasn't ever who he thought. Maybe nothing on the ship was what it seemed, nothing safe, not his life, not his freedom from kinship to them, not his sanity, not since he'd gone out in that warehouse and made jump with *Corinthian.* His anger wasn't there anymore, his fear wasn't, Saby'd taken it all inside, left just the no-place in front of him, the dark that wrapped him around and invited him, dared him, wanted him. . .

Saby pulled him in, Saby held on to him, Saby said she'd make everything all right: she was down to promises, like his *Polly* crewwoman, who always said she liked him, never that she loved, and he wouldn't have believed that, anyway—it wasn't in his universe, wasn't here, just . . . Saby, Saby, in the corridor, on *Sprite* . . . Saby, pushing him away . . .

"What's the matter?" Saby asked, and passed a hand over his shoulder, but he'd gone shivery and a little spaced, and asking himself where his mind was, that he made that jump, Saby to Marie. Bad navigation, crazy stuff she'd called up in him. It made him ashamed, and scared again, as if he'd crossed some strange space where identities and faces changed, floating lights, like the chaos around the night-walker.

He twitched, bad jump, quick intake of breath, couldn't help it, he was falling for a second.

But Saby had him, Saby brought him back with a pass of her hand across his forehead, down his face.

"You all right?" Saby asked. That was a trap. Serious trap. If you believed she gave a damn, . . .

If you thought Marie cared . . . if you ever thought that . . .

"Tom? Hey. Hey. Bad dream?"

He drew a breath, let it go, relieved Marie had retreated from conscious level. Didn't want to think about Marie, she got into dreams and they turned in strange directions . . . Marie held him close in the dark. He was eight, maybe nine, too old to sit on anybody's lap, the lights had cycled off, but Marie was in a mood to talk, and she held him and rocked him and told him about rape, and murder.

Other kids had fairytales for bedtime, but he got this story. He felt mama's arms hard and angry . . . and heard about sex and pain. . .

"Tom? For God's sake, —"

Air was cold. He felt chilled.

Sheets whispered and slid. The lights went on, dim though they were. She just looked, that was all. He didn't have anything to say. He didn't want to work himself in deeper than he was.

She reported to his father, no question.

She knew he was a hazard to the ship. He could do anything he wanted in bed, she didn't mind, but it didn't change him being Hawkins.

"Station's no good place," she said. "You *don't* want to be here."

Jerked him back to the real choices, she did. He was that transparent. If she saw more than that, she might be scared, herself.

He brushed her arm. "I'm not crazy." And then—being the sumbitch Marie said he was, he couldn't help it: "What's the report you give my father?"

Dark eyes—pretty eyes—didn't even flinch. "Space Christian. Keep you."

"Yeah?"

She didn't amplify. Her eyes shadowed. He'd brought the lie into the light. He moved his hand on her arm, deliberate distraction. Went further down, onto her bare leg, warm skin, warm color . . . there were no secrets he hadn't explored, no promises left, no lies.

Her hand settled on his. "Tink said you were all right."

He'd forgotten the garden. The garden and Tink and Saby on the path. It came back, with its own logic, that didn't make damn sense, that never had. Tink liked him. Tink said . . . be good to Saby. Or Tink would break his neck.

Tink knew. Tink understood he was a danger, the same as Saby did. He liked Tink. It wasn't damned fair, the two of them, against one guy, walking him down that green path, making him feel . . . welcome. Part of. With. Included.

Hurt, now. Hurt was when you got your feelings involved. Hurt was what inevitably happened, when you let yourself believe somebody wanted anything but their own agenda. Christian had conned him. Now Saby had conned him, damn her, leave Tink out of it—Tink probably trusted her, too.

She lay down with him again, leaving the lights on. She promised him it was all right, she rested her head on his shoulder. And maybe there was a guard outside. Maybe they'd bugged the room. Maybe they'd done that days ago, and he wouldn't get the chance to walk to the ship. Maybe they'd just come in after him and beat hell out of him first, —but what could he do?

— *vii* —

WASN'T THE LAST TIME they made love, all the same. They skipped breakfast, slept-in, and whichever one of them would wake, they agreed, had leave to wake the other by whatever means.

It was crazy. It was a way for Saby to keep his mind off the board-call, a way he could physically, mentally, blot it out. He knew he was using and being used, at that point, but hell, was it new? and neither of them minded.

"Did I hurt you?" he got the nerve to ask, and Saby said no, but Saby had a motive to lie, a lot of possible motives—maybe she didn't call for help because she wanted the favor points with Austin, maybe she wanted not to need help. But he was careful—his *Polly* girl had taught him a lot about what made her happy. His other lovers had never complained and never left before their board-calls or his.

He was still rattled. He couldn't understand how in very hell he'd flashed on Marie like that, or what had scared him so about it, until Saby made him flash on Marie again—she cuddled up tight with him, after, and pulled technique on him: that was how he thought of it—clear that she was no novice. Saby said, Lie still, and he drifted in such a self-destructive funk that he told himself What the hell and wondered what she could do solo.

No novice at all, Saby was, probably the one they sent out to snag guys in. She'd tell them all she loved them, and they signed on, signature that gave a ship legal rights to recover strays. But, all right, it beat a press gang. Had to admit. . .

"God!"

"Easy, easy, easy." Saby's mouth stole the rest of his breath, and their daylight-dark exploded in red and blue awhile, but as a means to wait out the board-call, it was still . . . better than sanity.

"You could share quarters with me," Saby murmured against his ear. "Just clear it with Austin—" Hands did things elsewhere that made him short of breath and truly not focussed on his father and their feud. Or even remotely on logic. "God, I *want* you, Tom, I never *wanted* anybody, I never, never found anybody—just sleepover stuff, you know, never with crew, I always said it was bad business, relationships aboard, just stupid, but I could, I would, this time, I really, really could, Tom, I want you."

"Shit-all." His language, like his morals, had gone. "You can visit me in the brig."

"I know you're computers, I'm in ops, you had any experience?"

He deliberately misunderstood. "Thought it showed."

It won him a punch on the arm. A gentle one. Saby leaned over him in the dark they'd kept, long after lights had cycled to day. Her hair brushed his face. "Don't be an ass."

"It's hard."

"Don't be one to me, anyway, I'm serious, Tom."

It had been fun, right down to 'serious.' His heart started increasing beats. Outright fear. He didn't know what to do with a statement like that. He didn't know where to take it, except to agree and keep his mouth shut and show up at *Corinthian*'s dock on time.

Or grab the perpetrator with both arms, roll her under and kiss her until she wasn't asking any more questions, because he wasn't good at lying— If Saby wanted to help him, yes, he wanted the help. Lie for it, cheat for it, all right, the coin she dealt in wasn't unpleasant at all. And he didn't know, once he thought of that, where that betrayal fit on Marie's scale of things, whether he was victim or victimizer—he just didn't want to hurt or be hurt by anybody, didn't want to believe anybody. Once you did that. . .

Once you did that, then you just walked helplessly, stupidly into what people did for fun or for profit.

The wake-up alarm went off, finally. Autoservice from the front desk said, robot-idiot that it was, Time to get up, time to get up, time to get up . . . until Saby reached out a hand and killed it.

Morning light came up, autoed, cold truth after the night they'd had. He could envision where he was going, back to the brig. Which he didn't mind.

He wanted Capella to let him alone. He wanted to go to the galley every day and deal with Tink and Jamal, he didn't want to be opted anywhere else. He just wanted a long, rational life where nobody would bother him—he didn't think that was too much to ask of the man responsible for his existence, seeing that Austin surely wanted his own life uncomplicated, too. Tink would swear to his good behavior. Tink could do that. There were people everybody instinctively seemed to like, and Tink was one of those, the same way he was one of the other kind.

"Can you find Tink?" he ventured asking, when they were dressing; and when he knew Saby was about to make the inevitable phone call. "You think Tink could walk in with us? You think Tink would mind?"

Saby looked a little surprised, maybe . . . a little perplexed. "Tom," she said, "everything's going to be all right. I promise."

Creative no, in other words. Con job.

"Yeah," he said, "all right."

Tink wouldn't tolerate him getting beaten up, wouldn't tolerate any treachery, Tink was pure as his sugar flowers, uncomplicated. *Corinthian* folk could sell him out. Produce fake papers. Say he had a contract with them, or screw him in some means—or just do the mach' business on him, show him not to run, after this. All right, lesson taken: he'd been hit before, he could survive it. They never believed you got it intellectually, the mach' types didn't.

And Austin *was* one of their kind. Maybe so was he. Genetics at work. Maybe it was why he got in trouble.

"Tom. —You don't believe me, do you?"

"Sure." But he was a rotten liar when he was rattled. And he was rattled—and short on sleep and mildly hung over. "Sure, I believe you."

"Tom, . . ." Whatever Saby was going to say, she didn't, then, just took on a hurt look. He didn't know why. Not exactly. He guessed he'd been rude, he'd burst the bubble of false trust. "Why in hell'd you . . . ?" she started to ask.

But she didn't finish that either, just looked upset with him, or the situation, or something maybe he'd led her to think.

"I'm sorry," he said. He meant it. Saby'd been all right. "We don't need Tink. It's fine."

"You think they're going to pull something, don't you?" She sounded surprised. As if it couldn't possibly occur to her. "You think this whole thing's a set-up."

"Hey." He waved a hand, Stop, enough. "No problem."

"Shit." She jammed her hands into her belt and looked at him sidelong, from under a fall of bangs, as if she was re-adding everything.

"I said I wouldn't run. You didn't have to do anything. But thanks. It was nice."

Her mouth opened, her head came up, she would have hit him with the back of her hand. Hard. Except he blocked that one with his arm. He wasn't moved to hit her. But she was mad, furious with him, and he didn't know which of several things she was mad at.

"Don't hit," he said, "I don't like it."

"For God's sake, . . ."

Another censorship. Her eyes watered. Her chin quivered. He'd made her mad, but he couldn't read it, couldn't react to what didn't make sense. He could defend himself if she hit him again, he wasn't going to take that from her, but he equally well wasn't going to get into personal arguments this close to the end—he was just scared, was all, scared of her tears, scared of him getting mad—he wanted to like her, he wanted so much to like her, and that was the most dangerous thing. . . .

"Where did you get the notion," she asked him, "that I didn't give a damn? Where did you think I *lied* to you? Tom, —"

He panicked, backed up when she reached, she'd gotten to him that badly, and she just stared at him, confused, hurt, he couldn't tell. Maybe it was even real, but he'd thought that too many times. It wasn't reasonable it could be true now, when he didn't even know her, except she liked roses and coffee and blue glitter-stuff. . . .

"I didn't lie to you," she said. "I didn't need to lie to you. Do you think I did?"

She hit right on it, and the lump wouldn't go away. He was scared of that little, little step she was asking, everything he'd tried to give away, too long, too desperately, until he'd learned strong people didn't want it and weak ones drank you dry.

But he'd hurt Saby. Dammit, it wasn't fair of her to be mad—*he* was mad, and hurt, that she was mad.

"I *like* you," Saby said. "I *want* you to bunk with me. I didn't think, I didn't think I was, like, pressuring you . . ."

"You're not."

"Why Tink? Why do you trust him?"

"I don't know," he said, and that was the truth. "I don't know."

—— *viii* ——

FIGURE THEY'D BE FIRST IN or last in. But among the first, it turned out—a mortal relief, the phone call from Saby advising *Corinthian* they were leaving the *Aldebaran*. "Can you be there at customs?" Saby asked, tacit reminder there was a customs problem.

Easy fix, in fact. "Boy called," Austin said to the agent at the kiosk out front of *Corinthian*'s ramp, and handed him the Union passport. "Lot activity of in and out the ship, he went out with the group—officer had the passports—"

The agent thumbed the passport. Ran the mag-strip for the visa, and it flashed Valid. "Checked through."

"Yeah, he was supposed to get it from my son, something came up, he ran off on that problem . . . he's twenty-three, scatter-brain, *we'd* been trying to find him to get it to him—

this morning, he panics and phones our com, and now it's a problem."

"Yeah. Kids. I got two. Twelve and sixteen. Four-room apartment."

"God."

"Kid coming in?"

"On his way."

"I'll have it here, no problem." The agent put the passport under the desk. They talked about other things, the economy, both sides of the line, the entertainments on Pell, the free-port situation . . . for a ship's captain at board-call, he was uncommonly leisured; for himself, with strangers, he was uncommonly conversational, but from where he stood, talking, he could see the whole dockside behind the customs line, a dim, utilitarian deckage, a neon-lit frontage of shops behind the two girders that were part of Pell's main structure.

They talked about kids. He tried to imagine. About wives. He censored his arrangement with Beatrice. A couple of Downers waddled past, bound for somewhere. Transports lumbered along . . . Pell government was still talking about that transport rail system, the agent said, but the transport companies and the warehouses on Pell liked the status quo, on which they made money, and detested the rail, in which they endlessly debated all the share-plans the station could draft.

A couple of crew showed up, the early ones, Michaels and Travis, with slightly startled looks to see the captain standing waiting.

"Captain," Michaels said. "Need a word." And Michaels diverted him aside from customs long enough to ask if he wanted anything. Michaels had basic good sense, in the essentials of discreet trouble-handling, and he would have left Michaels to take his watch down here, if it were slightly less explosive.

"I'll handle it," he told Michaels. "Just start the count. Develop a board glitch, we don't display until we're on last boarders."

"Done," Michaels said.

A group of eleven came in, techs, a couple of dockers . . . *Corinthian*'s monetary and liberty-time bonus for arrivals in the first hour of board-call got no few takers, but still, spacers were spacers, liberty-loves were hard to leave, and expect the real rush right down at the bottom of that first hour, and the last just right before the deadline, mostly the dockers, in that group, a few D&D's that took some dealing with, but if Sabrina didn't make it in the next quarter hour, she was going to find herself at the end of a long, long . . .

A closed taxi pulled up close, braked, and opened a door. No banker, no official got out, just, improbably—three *Corinthian* spacers, one Sabrina, in her usual fancy-business, Tink, in his bar-crawling gear, down to the bare arms and the tattoos and the earrings, and of course his threadbare duffle and the bagfuls of edibles. Last out, God, Tom Hawkins, sudden fashion queen, blue skintights, fancy black sweater, mod haircut, and a designer carry-bag, purple and orange—taste would out, evidently. Saby'd said he 'needed a few things.'

He set hands on hips and watched this apparition walk up to customs . . . got a questioning look from the agent, who surely couldn't do a confident ID on Hawkins' new side-fall haircut. He nodded, the agent pulled out the passport, delivered a sober lecture to Hawkins, probably about being sure about the passport, Hawkins nodded, seemed dutifully impressed and sober, and the agent gave the whole group a wave-through . . . you bought it *at* Pell, customs wasn't interested, unless you just radiated shady deals. And nobody could know how to rate this taxi-load.

Hawkins and Saby cleared customs, while Tink was still chattering at the agent, offering him a candy or something, Tink was a walking sugar-fix. Meanwhile the passport headed for Hawkins' pocket.

Austin held out his hand. Smiled tightly.

Hawkins stopped so abruptly, evidently just now seeing him, that Sabrina ran into him.

Austin crooked a finger. —Hawkins meekly came and, to his outheld hand, delivered the passport.

"Stow your stuff with Saby," Austin said then, as they walked, as he pocketed the passport. "Log in with ops, no word to anybody what happened, do you copy? And I'll see *you* in my office thirty minutes to undock, on the mark, Mr. Hawkins. —Saby, you get him there."

—— *ix* ——

IT WAS *HIM*, DAMMIT, WITH Saby, and Tink, Austin was waiting the other side of the barrier, and Christian had not a question in his mind.

"He *knew*, damn him! He knew all along! Damn her! *Damn her!*"

"Damnation to go around," Capella said, leaning against the store-front. "We've still other strays to watch."

Redirection. In Capella, suspect it.

"You knew. You damned well knew!" He was furious. And Capella, having talked to Austin aboard, having had a chance to ask questions . . . came back with a grim look, a, "He's keeping the schedule," and, to his, "Why?"—"Thinks Hawkinses are as serious a threat, evidently."

Capella swore she didn't, personally, think *Sprite* was on a scale with their other problem. But the taxi was gone from the customs area, Tom Hawkins was walking up the ramp with Saby, who, dammit, owed him some loyalty, being his cousin, being who'd brought him up—

And it looked to him like a problem, a *major* problem, Hawkins in his new clothes and his new haircut—he hadn't recognized him. He'd thought he was some better-class recruit than they even usually got, somebody Saby had recommended.

But, no, it was a surplus, conniving brother, whose clothes alone cost more than the 200c he'd been carrying—who *hadn't* had a passport, who'd had no way to lay his hands on his

without *Corinthian*'s complicity; who hadn't had a credit card
. . . if Family Boy had money stashed in banks the other side
of the line, he couldn't have accessed it without ID.

Somebody else's money. *Corinthian* money.

"Austin's damn clearance," he said. "Look at him!"

"Looks pretty good, actually," Capella said. "And Saby.
My, my, my."

"You *did* know!"

"I know now. Give up the quarrel, Chrissy-lad, it's over,
it's won, this is why papa Austin said what he said."

"About what?"

"Just that he'd made up his mind. That *Sprite* was more
threat than one Mr. Hawkins. Damn right. He had this one
tied up and wrapped around his high-credit finger, just yank
the string."

It didn't make sense to him, except that Austin had played
him for a fool deliberately, Austin had spent whatever it took
to make him look a fool not only to Saby and Tink, who were
in on it, but in front of Capella, who might have been under
orders, in front of the whole crew—people laughing behind his
back, enjoying the joke.

He looked at Capella, searching for any hint of that laughter
at his expense. He couldn't find any hint of it, but Capella
wasn't easy to catch, no expression at all.

A handful of dockers arrived, Gracie Greene and Metz, Dan
Blue, Tarash and Deecee, trouble, all of them, he watched them
walk up to customs, and his gut was in an upheaval, thinking
. . . they were going to hear about it, everybody who'd been
out in the search after his brother had to have known, at some
point, and here he stood, playing the fool, while his brother
went into the ship on his own terms.

"Fuck it!" he said, and grabbed Capella by the sleeve, heed-
less of safety. "It's a couple of hours till all-aboard, there's a
bar, there's a restaurant . . ."

"I thought we were economizing," Capella said.

"Hell! I've got a k or so left, what do I fucking care? Fucking smart-ass Family Boy, on Austin's fucking credit, while I spend everything I've got? Fuck it, fuck it all, let's blow it, everything—"

"Chrissy, —"

"I said everything! What do I need? A father who fucking cares what I do? A cousin with one shred of basic loyalty? A partner who doesn't go screwing my brother? What's the matter with me, Pella, what's the matter with me?"

Capella delayed to look at him. Long. "Got all your parts," Capella said. "Things work."

"Don't be a damned ass!"

"Maybe you better work with what you got," Capella said, "what you stand in when you shower, hmn? It's all anybody's got."

Philosophy wasn't Capella's long suit. She threw it at him now and again, she whispered it in his ear when the ship made jump, she confused him when he was mad, and blew it off, which *no*body else could do.

"Dance," Capella said, "is a lot nicer than looking for stray brothers. Couple drinks, a few dances—long and dark after, Chris-person. Long and deep and dark. I'd dance, myself."

"You're crazed! You're absolutely crazed!"

"It's my calling. But there's now, and thereafter's such quiet, Chris-ti-an. Hear it. Listen to it. Don't waste time. It's so scarce."

"Don't con me! You knew, you knew what my father was doing!"

"Guessed, maybe. Didn't know." She hooked his arm with hers. "Last trip of all, maybe. There's something in the dark, I don't know where."

"*Sprite?*"

"Maybe several somethings. They may take me back, Chris-person. I don't know. There's only now. This liberty's been a bitch. Let's go."

"What—take you back?" She'd met them at this station, she'd come, with what he overheard and what he guessed, with codewords and such she didn't show to customs. She *was* their access to a trade they had to have, that otherwise they couldn't find, couldn't access. A second, perilous grab at Capella's arm, as she turned away. "Have you told Austin this notion? Have you told him?"

"I'm not supposed to have told *you.* No. This is a confidence, Christian-person."

"*Christian,* dammit! And where do you get such notions? We aren't even *near* hyperspace."

Pale eyebrow quirked. Mouth pursed. "The presence. The spook that's in port. Is that solid enough for you?"

"*Can* you feel something?"

Capella had a fey, distracted look for an instant, as if she reached out at that moment, into something he couldn't, nobody could. But the eyes flickered and Capella drew in a sudden, unscheduled breath before she shook her head. "You can convince yourself of anything. No." She seized his arm and tugged him toward the frontage, and the bars. "I wish we'd see them."

"Who? The spook? This Patrick? —You think they're boarding, now?"

"I say if you find a small ship that is, you know his name."

"Well, *look,* for God's sake, look at the boards." He'd been occupied with Hawkinses and Capella wasn't, Capella wasn't concerned with *Sprite* or Hawkinses in singular or plural, he saw that now.

"I know two names. Because one is, doesn't mean the other isn't."

"You mean there could be a back-up in port? Tell Austin, for God's sake!"

"Austin knows there's danger. Austin's danger is Hawkins. Was, from when you let elder-brother take a walk."

"The hell!"

They'd reached the frontage. Almost the door, and Capella swung around on him, angry, astoundingly so. "Your *fault,*

Christian, *and* mine, I should have said, and didn't, it looked good, what you were doing, and it wasn't, it had flaws. It had flaws in *Christophe Martin,* it had flaws in assuming elder-brother's easy, it had flaws all over the place, and my looking for him was very hard, and very scared, Christian-person, so scared *I* made another mistake, and got attention from this damn spook, who isn't *ours,* do you follow me?"

Anger whited out half of it. But *ours* came through, touching on what he'd tried to understand. Ours. Theirs. Us. The Fleet. "Explain. Explain to me—ours, theirs,—who's *us?*"

"Mazian's, Mallory's, Porey's . . . the Fleet's pieces, the pieces that have their own partisans, their own spooks and their own suppliers . . . you work for Mazian, that's the truth. But not all do. Some ships are dead, Mallory turned coat, the rest . . ." Capella ran out of breath, and didn't find another immediately. "I'll tell you this. There's two needs here. There's *Corinthian,* wanting everything the same forever, and there's *us,* who can't make that happen, Christian, captain-papa won't understand that, but there's those that want me so bad . . ."

"Why? Because you can do what you do?"

"You might say. Because I know places."

"What places?"

"Places they want. Badly. —I can't let *Corinthian* get boarded. It's not in my own interest, you copy that? If the captain asks, —make him believe it. And we're running with guns live this jump. Take my side on that, if there's any argument on it."

It was crazy. He was up to his ears in the Hawkins business, he couldn't think about anything else, but Capella was telling him about waking up the guns they'd used once in his lifetime, about the ordinance Michaels maintained and serviced and kept viable, through all these ship-board years. It didn't happen. A chance encounter on a dockside didn't lead to live guns, when a crazy woman was trying to get them hauled in by port authorities.

But a spook had gone invisible . . . which could well mean some other ship at Pell was in an unannounced board-call at this very moment.

Hell in a handbasket, that was what it felt like. He *wanted* to break a Hawkins neck, and two or three others, but suddenly he was perceiving a threat that didn't give him time for that. Austin might not take it seriously. Austin had his mind on Hawkinses, on Marie Hawkins in particular. That was who was ruling *Corinthian*'s movements. Hawkinses had them going out instead of lying in port until at least they had the advantage of not being a target.

A genuine spook didn't carry cargo. It could overjump them, just traveling higher and faster in hyperspace. It had engines the power of which it didn't admit, and if it decided to beat them out to their next stop, hell, . . .

But Austin wasn't thinking down that track, no, Austin was busy with a woman who'd been threatening to kill him for twenty plus years, and who now wanted her son back. . . .

But Capella had said it when she came back from talking to Austin, and confessing to him what she'd stirred up . . . that Austin hadn't listened, damn him. Austin had known he could get Hawkins back, and *therefore* that became Austin's immediate problem, the one Austin daren't be caught in port with; and *damn* Austin and his whole elaborate joke . . . Austin wasn't going to listen to anything beyond that hazard. They couldn't even prove that Marie Hawkins was inbound, there being no reasonable prospect that a merchanter should leave its schedule for one lost crewman. Marie wasn't in charge of *Sprite*, and Austin was still running—*scared*, was what it amounted to, outright embarrassing to the ship.

And after Austin's cheap little piece of humor at his expense, *he* was the one who had to get his priorities straight, forget personal issues with Hawkins and cousin Saby Perrault, and listen to the ship's second navigator, who was trying to tell them they could get their butts shot off.

So it was up to him again, save their collective asses by doing what had to be done—talk to Michaels, tell their one-time gunner to dust off the simulator during system passage, lock himself in with it, and flip that armament switch when they went otherside.

Michaels would listen. Michaels wasn't the optimist Austin was, the hell with the regs about live guns at Pell.

He didn't want to die at twenty. Didn't want to go up in a fireball. Or, God help all of them, get conscripted aboard a spook.

"We're not on duty. Screw it all. Come on."

He was a willing abductee. Didn't want to deal with Saby, or Hawkins, Austin, or—least of all, *maman,* until he'd cooled down. Considerably.

They'd come in at the last minute. *Let* somebody head-count, and worry—if Austin wasn't blinded by Hawkins' reasonable, dutiful, *likeable* self.

Got himself a nice, desperate *reasonable* son, this time, hadn't he? Watch Austin turn on the charm. Austin had it to use. Austin used it when you made him happy and Austin was happy when you said 'yes, sir.'

Austin had won, with Hawkins. Austin had gotten his own way. Damned right Austin liked Hawkins.

Fool, brother! Go back. It's a trap.

—— *x* ——

"Go on!" Saby hissed, giving him a shove toward the lift doors. They were outside downside ops, on the main axis, the ring was still locked, the office the other side of the corridor was a steady traffic of check-ins, crew-cargo mass-check, stowage, and scheduling last half hour before undock . . . it could have been *Sprite*'s ops area—it didn't feel different, except the rowdiness of the crew coming on. Topside of the ring was where he had to report—the area where, considering the proximity of the bridge, and main ops, he was sure there was strong-arm security—wasn't territory he wanted to visit and Saby had to shove him again to get him into motion.

"It'll be all right," Saby said.

"Yeah," he said. They'd taken their time in ops. He hadn't unpacked. He'd gone down to galley and reported in, he'd talked to Jamal and Tink, and reported back to Saby before the time was up. All right, she said. All right. He'd *had* his dealings with Austin Bowe, all he ever wanted, and Saby could believe the man, but he didn't—didn't trust him a moment, an instant.

But he pushed the button for the lift, took a breath, told himself he wasn't going to panic at security up there or lose his temper with whatever happened. No matter what, he was going to control his temper, walk peacefully into Austin's office, let the man play his psychological games, and not react. Austin wasn't worse than Marie. He couldn't do worse than Marie— he'd no hooks to use, didn't know him, didn't own him the way Marie had, til he was, God help him, making love last night and thinking about Marie, in bed with Marie . . .

That was damn scary. Kinked. He had to ask himself . . .

"Just be calm," Saby said, when the lift door opened.

He walked in alone. Hangover and no sleep last night didn't help his stomach, either, as the lift shot up against Pell station spin. Bang, clang, and it opened its door and let him out.

Deserted corridor. No security. Camera, he decided uneasily; but he couldn't, at a glance, see where. The office number, Saby had told him, was number 1, in the first transverse short of the bridge.

No problem finding it. The vulnerable areas of the bridge were right in front of him, a handful of crew at their stations in the center and the near swing-sections . . . it gave him a giddy feeling, being that close to *Corinthian*'s unguarded heart, as if it was Austin's own challenge, Go ahead, be a fool, I'm waiting . . . could have talked to you downside. Or after undock. What's so damn urgent, anyway? What's so elaborate I have to come up here?

Fatherly repentance?

He pushed the entry request button.

The door shot open. Austin was sitting at his desk, writing something on the autopad.

And kept writing.

Damn psych-out, he thought. But Austin shot him an upward glance then.

"You want to come in?" Austin asked him, "Come in. Sit down."

He walked in, the door whisked shut, sealing them in, and he ebbed into the conference chair. Austin kept writing, while he waited.

And waited—but he gave up offence, since the civil invitation. A ship leaving dock was administratively busy. Frantically so.

And Austin *had* to see him right now? Not reasonable. Maybe it was important. Maybe something Austin really, honestly had to deal with.

Austin flipped the autopad off. Gave him a second, this time direct, look.

Drawled, "God, aren't *we* right out of the fashion ads. Designer this, designer that. Expensive taste. Can we afford you?"

Temper blew. "I figured I was paying," he said shortly. And revised all charitable estimates. Austin brought him up here to needle him and he didn't mean to back up—wasn't the way he'd exist on this ship, dammit, no way in hell.

"Who said you paid?"

"Stands to reason. What have I got, now? Ship-debt? A contract I'm supposed to have signed? My passport in the ship's safe?"

"Be polite. You were on *my* account."

That—was a surprise. He didn't know what it meant.

Austin just stared for a few heartbeats. Tapped the stylus on the desk. "I really," Austin said, "could have hauled you back."

"I've no doubt." He didn't want to be in Austin's debt. He preferred Christian's. Saby'd said, go to it, don't worry. Now he didn't know what she'd gotten him into.

"Saby said give you space," Austin said, and leaned back. "She said you'd come back. Funny thing, she was right."

"She's not stupid." He didn't want to think ill of Saby. Didn't want to think he'd been conned. Couldn't, in fact, believe she'd been head-hunting. "I hadn't a choice. You knew it."

"She said you were shy. Nice guy."

"Sure."

"She wants to bunk with you. I think she's crazy, myself."

Silence hung there a moment, and breath came thin and short. "Maybe." Another oxygen-short breath. Desperate thinking. "I don't think it's a good idea. She doesn't know me. Dockside and here is different."

"I'll tell you something. Nobody much tells Saby what she's thinking. Makes her mad."

He didn't know how to read Austin. He began to prefer the Austin who'd knocked him against a wall. Safer. Much.

"Look, you don't owe me. You don't give a damn. You know what my post is, you've got my papers, you're not going to put me anywhere near ops—*any* ops, because I'm good, when I want to be, and I can screw it, so let's not kid ourselves. Galley scrub's all you can trust me to do, that's all I want out of you, so just let me the hell alone, and let's not complicate anything."

"You're bound to be a problem."

"Yes, I'm a problem. I'll *be* a problem. I was *born* a problem." Shortness of breath made him light-headed, slowed things down, numbed the nerves. "Did you ever remotely think, maybe making a life ought to be worth at least as much thinking as taking one? Did it ever bother you?"

"You think of that last night?"

"I didn't have to think; I know I'm safe, right now, since before Viking, and it takes two, mister. *I* didn't get Saby pregnant, except by cosmic chance, and *two* sets of implants failing."

"She had the same choice. Saby did. Your mama did."

"So did you. And, yeah, so did she. You were out there looking for your personal immortality, she was, too, and, God save us, you got me, and here I am. Now what? Now where do we go?"

Austin was glumly sober for a moment. Then the mouth made a tight smile, and a laugh that died.

"You want an answer to that question? Or just an echo?"

"Is there an answer?" If there was one . . . he hadn't gotten it from Marie. Not from Mischa. Not from Lydia and not from the seniors in general. It didn't mean he was going to believe one from Austin. But he waited.

"You're going to say the hell with you," Austin said. "Still want it?"

"That the line you handed my mother?"

Another grim laugh. "I should have. No question. You're right about the immortality. Ships were dying. Every time you got to port, there were gaps in the schedules, the Fleet was going to hell, you couldn't get those numbers, but we knew. We were running supply. We had our network. We saw the wall coming."

"Damn Mazianni spotters."

"Suppliers."

"There's a difference?"

"Damn right there's a difference. The Fleet *paid* us for what we hauled. It wasn't even in our economic interest to promote raids on anybody—we knew they were conscripting, and we knew they wouldn't take any of ours while we were running their cargoes; but we knew which ships were raiding, too, and we didn't like going near them, let alone give them a way not to need us, does it take a thought? We didn't give them information. But where we got them legitimate supply they didn't *have* to raid merchant traffic. Safer for them. Faster. Left them free for military operations. We kept them supplied—there *weren't* raids."

It made some half sense. Easy to say. Unprovable, that they'd had any altruism in their trade. Unprovable, that they'd not sold out other ships at the going rate. Everybody said so. He didn't see anything to convince him otherwise.

"I wanted," Austin said after a moment, and quietly, "myself, to find a post in the Fleet. That was my ambition. But that year, ships were dying. *Africa* and *Australia* had turned to raiding commerce. Momentum was shifting to the other side. I hated

Union. I *still* hate Union. But that was the year I saw the handwriting on the proverbial wall, and, yeah, immortality figured in it. Wanting to leave something. Didn't know the kid was a firsttimer, those weren't the signals she gave off, or I wouldn't have asked her to my room. She was drunk, I wasn't sober, first thing I knew she hit me in the face, bashed me with a glass, I was bleeding, she got to the phone, and the station went to hell in five minutes. End of story."

"You didn't need to beat her up."

"See this scar?" Austin's finger rested on his temple. "I was bleeding worse than she was, your captain wasn't returning calls, they had the station authorities in it, my crew was trying to keep me out of station hands . . . yeah, some heads got cracked, three captains and three crews were at each others' throats—and, yeah, I was mad, I got mine, as time hung heavy on my hands, and since she'd told them it was rape, hell, I figured why not give her something to bitch about. I didn't hurt her—"

"The *hell!*"

"Physically. Let's talk about whose career was on the line, whose damn *life* was on the line, with Ms. Modesty screaming rape. I'll ask you who got screwed in that room, thanks."

"You could have walked out of there."

"Damn right I could, right into the hands of the station police."

"My heart aches."

"I was eighteen. I was nihilistic. My career was shot to hell, civilization was going down with it, nothing I did was going to last. Surprise, of course. Marie of course informed me when she got the chance—we have something in common, she said. And we do, matter of fact. Tenacious. Still mad. Hell, I don't cry foul. I respect the woman. Somebody did that to me, I'd track the bastard down, damn right. I wouldn't forget."

He could all but hear his heartbeat, under what Austin was saying. Could see his own life and his prospects in Austin's attitude, and Marie's.

"No forgiveness," he said, "anywhere in the equation. No regrets."

Austin shrugged. "I regret it's involved three crews who didn't ask for it. I regret my father put me in sickbay when he got his hands on me. Broke my arm, my collarbone, and three ribs. I am a patient man, you understand. He wasn't, the son of a bitch. But he ran a rough crew."

Austin, bidding for sympathy? Telling *him* he'd had it rough? Enough to turn a stomach. He *wanted* Austin to get up and hit him. Threaten him, do something else but bid for understanding. *He* wanted to hit Austin so badly he ached with it . . . but that wasn't the role he'd come to want, in this room, one more clenched fist, one more act of force that didn't do anything, didn't prove anything, except to a mentality that understood the fist and not a damn thing else.

He gave it a second thought, in that light. Maybe it would get him points. Maybe it was all Austin Bowe did understand. But he didn't hear that in the con job Austin was pulling, he didn't see it in the sometimes earnest look on the man's face . . . there was more to Austin Bowe than that, and hell if he'd give him a fight Austin had calculated to win.

"We all have hard lives," he said, Marie's coldest sentiment, and got up to walk out. "No, I don't want to bunk with Saby. She's got her own problems. I've got mine. Galley's just fine. Brig's all right. I like the door locked."

He thought Austin might pull the you're-not-dismissed shit on him. Might get up and knock him sideways, or lock the door.

"Marie's coming here, you know," Austin said, before his hand hit the switch. It stopped him cold, short of it, and he looked around at Austin's expressionless smugness.

"You don't know that."

"I know her. She'll be here—maybe three, four days, maybe on *Sprite*, maybe on something else. I'm surprised you're surprised."

"She can't. No way in hell." His hands had started to shake, he didn't know why. He jammed them in his waistband, trying to hide the fact.

Austin just shrugged. "We're out of this port. Glad you made it back."

"You son of a bitch. She's nowhere on this track. She wouldn't leave *Sprite,* no way she'd leave *Sprite.*"

Another shrug. "Take L14 for a berth. It's clear, nobody in there. You'll have to move some galley supplies, the bunk lets down, probably needs linens. Water lines need turning on. You're competent to do that, aren't you?"

"Probably," he said.

"You're permitted to Saby's cabin. The galley. The laundry. If I see your ass near an ops station, we'll discuss it. But you didn't want that, anyway."

"No, sir," he said, and the door opened, letting him out.

Marie wasn't coming here. He hadn't been that close to finding her, when he was loose out there. He couldn't have been that close.

The shakes got worse on his way to the lift. He had a knot in his throat that didn't go away on the ride.

No guard. No surveillance. He had a cabin assignment, not the barracks bunk he'd feared he might have, with hired-crew, who wouldn't go easy on a Bowe in disfavor, crew who clearly took orders from Christian—and not a bunk with Saby, which he was going to have to explain, downside, when the offer did explain why Saby'd so cheerfully shoved him topside to talk to Austin.

Saby just didn't know. Saby got along with Austin. And good for her. But he dreaded meeting her, when the lift door opened—and she was right by ops.

"Thanks," he said, uneasy, not wanting to have to explain, not comfortable meeting that clear-eyed stare of hers. "Thanks for taking my side. I—didn't want to involve you. I've got a bunk assignment, it's not that I didn't want the other—" A lie. "Just—I don't want you hurt."

"It's no problem, with me, there's nothing to worry about. . ."

"I don't want to worry." He wasn't doing well with the lie. His whole mind wasn't on it, and then was, and he knew it wasn't working. "I don't know what I think, all right? I'm not thinking real clearly right now. Too much input. Too many inputs. I just c-couldn't—"

"Tom." Saby took his face between her hands, rose up taller and kissed him, very sweetly, on the mouth. "Shut up. All right?"

"I didn't—" He wasn't doing better with his voice. Nobody'd ever kissed him that fondly, nobody'd ever forgiven him any least thing he'd done or not done or been suspected of thinking. Of a sudden his chest was as tight as his throat and his wits went every which way—suddenly everything good around him was Saby, Saby, Saby. Saby—who'd for some reason just kissed him, and for some reason didn't look like once was enough. He didn't know what to do. He didn't know what he was supposed to do next, or what had just turned inside out in him, so that a minute ago he could reason that he was infinitely better off in this universe without Saby and the next she was everything, absolutely everything worth living for.

"It's all right, Tom. Can I possibly write? Leave notes on your door? Messages through Tink, maybe."

"Don't *do* that to me! —I'm in L14, all right?"

"That's a damn closet!"

"It's home. It's my home." He snatched a retreating hand, held it as if it was glass. "I want a *place,* Saby, I want somewhere that's mine, I don't care how big it is, or what it isn't, I just want a place. But you can come there. I want . . ." He couldn't shape it. He hadn't a chance of the hope he had. He wasn't worth it. An instant ago, losing Marie had him shaking with panic and now he couldn't see anything but Saby. He told himself no, what he'd felt last night wasn't real—but now it was and Marie wasn't.

"Want what?" Saby asked, relentlessly, and squeezed his fingers. "I'm free tonight. My bunk or yours?"

"God. —Yours." He couldn't possibly subject Saby to a let-down bunk. He hadn't any sheets. He wasn't prioritizing clearly. "I just—"

"You're crazed." She stood on her toes and gave him another kiss. "PDA is positively against the regs, you know. Crew's coming in."

"Yeah. But the hell—" He gave her one back, the kind they'd shared in the night. . . .

Then a hand caught his shoulder, spun him—he thought instantly, life-long sensitivity about officers and public display—of some officer catching them; then in one split-second saw blond hair and saw Christian, before Christian's fist slammed his jaw, Saby yelled in outrage, and his back hit the wall panels.

He came off them for a grab at Christian, Christian hit him in the gut and then he landed one solid hit and another before Christian grabbed his shirt and they swung about, *bang!* into the echoing panels. Saby was yelling, some other female was yelling, futile hands were trying to drag them apart and then both females were trying to kick them apart while he was trying to keep a grip on Christian and get him stopped—minor hits on his back, minor kicks in the leg, which only let Christian get an arm free. Christian half-deafened him—

Somebody kicked him in the head, then in the ribs, kicked Christian too, for what he could figure, and a noise of male voices started yelling encouragement and laying bets.

He wasn't going to lose this one, didn't know what it was for, but he knew the stakes. He hit, he punched, he held on and tried to pin Christian flat while blows came at his midriff. He smelled alcohol. He heard Saby yelling for Michaels, for somebody, anybody, to get it stopped, but the bets were flying too fast. Christian hit him across the temple, he hit Christian in the jaw, then dropped an arm across Christian's throat and tried to keep him down, cut off his wind, end the fight, while Christian kept trying to batter him loose.

"Break it up!" somebody yelled. Male. Loud. Mad. "Damn you, break it up!" A hand grabbed his collar, a knee came up in his face, and from the deck, afterward, in a haze of pain, he saw Austin hauling Christian off the deck and up, Christian spitting blood and bleeding from the eyebrow.

"Mister," Austin said, shook Christian and shoved him against the wall. "Mister, you are drunk. Do you understand, you are drunk, reporting in?"

"The whole fucking *crew*—" Christian objected, and there was a crowd around them. Saby. Capella. Dockers, crew, all gawking, all suddenly melting away from the danger zone.

"The witnesses are your problem, mister," Austin said. "You did it. You fix it. Hear me? After undock and zone clearance. My office. Clean, presentable, and sober."

After which he let Christian go and stalked back into the open lift. The door hissed shut. The lift rose.

Tom blotted his lip with a bruised knuckle, felt whether teeth were loose. Saby touched his arm gingerly, meanwhile, trying to move him, but he stared steadily at Christian—he'd learned from the cousins not to turn his back. Christian stared back, mad, white, except the blood—Capella was trying to get him elsewhere, saying it was no good, it didn't matter, they had other troubles.

Finally it made sense to get away from the scene, let the business cool down. He walked off with Saby, left Christian to his own devices, went off to Saby's cabin and Saby's washroom, where he could clean off the damage.

He got a chance and he'd immediately done something to screw it. Didn't know all that he'd done, or why specifically Christian had gone for him, but he half wished Austin had knocked both of them sideways, at least not done that in front of the crew . . . it didn't make sense to him, except Austin didn't understand the impact of his actions—but Austin did. He'd no doubt of it.

He saw Saby in the mirror, behind him. Saw her looking upset.

"He's jealous," Saby said.

"Of you?" Talking hurt. Would. He rationed words.

"I brought him up," Saby said. "My aunt Beatrice is his real mama. She didn't want him, except the politics with Austin. I was ten. I did the best I could till I was, God, twenty-six and he was getting ideas. And I still feel responsible. —He *needed* a lesson this time, dammit, he has to get life figured— But things—got complicated last night, and then he walked up on us like that . . . I know what he thought: that I betrayed him, that I'd set him up—because I wanted you."

"Shit." He leaned an arm against the wall. Sniffed back what had been a nosebleed—thinking—no, feeling—what must have gone through Christian's insides. And he threw a glance at Saby, with a leaden foreboding that his lately-ordered universe was coming apart again. Couldn't last. Couldn't put together what so many screwed-up years had torn apart.

Complicated. Hell. Saby functioned for Christian as mama; and Saby's aunt, Christian's *maman*, hadn't wanted him? Another of Austin's little no-personal-protection accidents?

Damn him.

"Austin had to hit him, in front of the crew? And left *me* without a mark? What for God's sake does Austin think he's doing? The man can't possibly be that naive."

Saby hugged her arms across her, shook her head, and looked scared. "Christian screwed up. Christian knew it. Same rules—crew and hired-crew. You don't fight. At least—you don't get caught at it in lower main. Not when Austin's mad. And Austin . . . was mad."

"How'd he know I didn't start it?"

"A, Christian's an officer on this ship. It's his say, his resort to force. And, B, No question: he knows Christian."

Chapter Ten

—— *i* ——

GRAPPLES RELEASED—no take-hold had sounded, easy regulations on this non-Family ship, meaning crew was up and about . . . and, on his way from Saby's quarters, Tom found himself 10m short of the galley zone as that sound racketed through the frame.

He wasn't the only crew caught out—"Shit!" someone yelped. Crew around him started running. He made a fast sprint, along with twenty or thirty others, out of the hazard of lower main for the take-holds that lined the mess hall transverse—some in the corridor, some the other side of the divider, in the galley, in his case, far as he could get sideways, toward the galley counter, excusing himself past other take-holders, hand to hand clasp and a " 'Scuse me, thanks," as he slid past each individual, because you didn't stand loose for a second on this ship—no please and thank you and no warning when *Corinthian* moved, God help them.

Jamal had already clipped secure-sheets over the sink and the counter-top to secure his work area, and taken-hold at the bow wall behind the counter, which was the good place to be. Tink stood that side, too, massive legs braced, his shoulders against the wall and both hands, somewhat riskily, for a keypad/calculator . . . but the far side, the bow-side of the transverse, was about to be the deck, temporarily.

While his was about to become the ceiling. "Tink. I'm here." From two, three niches along the take-hold bar.

"Yeah.—Looks like." Tink made a grimace, seeing his face. "Ouch. How you doing?"

"I'm all right."

"You sure? You look like hell."

"I'm fine." He caught a breath. "Jamal, I need in the worst way . . . I need to make a call after undock. I've got sheets and such to find— All right to do?"

"You all right, kid?"

"Fine." Lie. Again. He was still out of breath, and dreading the shove. He wished he dared make the dash across—a couple of guys had risked it, and made it, but it was too dangerous on this ship. "Got some arranging still to do."

"Yeah, no problem," Jamal said. "But you stay out of—"

Bow-jets shoved *Corinthian* hard, and strained muscles he hadn't known he'd strained, located every bruise, up and down his arm and his ribs and back, before that burn abruptly redirected and added a nadir vector.

Tink grabbed a one-handed hold. Fast.

"Pilot's pissed," Tink said, rolling a glance overhead.

"At what?"

"You can't guess?"

About that time the shove came hard and fast.

"Shit!" someone said, as a pan escaped the sheet-restraint, hit the overhead and rebounded.

"Loose object!" Jamal yelled—they were inertial for the moment, jets at momentary shutdown, and things and people floated. "Damn her!"

Then, thank God, the passenger ring engaged, and added another component to further shoves from the jets. The pan settled. So did human feet, and hair and clothes.

There was swearing. There were sighs. Tink called across at him:

"We got a slow-go here at Pell. Lady Bea can kick our ass out, but we can't do more 'n one-point kips until we clear the zone, about thirty minutes out. How's the gut now?"

"I'll live. You think she's through up there?" He'd got the fact it was a woman at the helm. He heard the B, and it clicked into consciousness *who* was at the helm and why she wasn't happy. "God, I wish they'd announce moves."

"Pell's usually a three-burn . . ." a tech said from the take-holds down the wall, woman he didn't know.

And the third shove came.

"There we go. That's it. We're inert." But everybody stood still at the handholds until the siren blast.

Then the company left the walls, and he went behind the counter where the galley com-panel was, punched buttons for the universals of ship-com, the 01 that went to the captain's message file.

"Sir. This is Tom Hawkins. I urgently need to speak to . . ."

"*Austin.*" God, the thing had tracked him through the boards. "*What?*"

He'd composed a message. All the logic went straight out of his head.

"You apply the same standard. Me and my brother. Sir." His tongue went stupid. Breath caught in his throat and he swallowed. "Sir. He caught us breaking regs. He had some justice."

Silence from the other end.

"*It remotely strike you, Hawkins, that the captain might be busy?*"

"I'm sorry, sir, I was just trying to message the system."

"*About your policy assessments?*"

"Sir, —"

"*Where are you?*"

"The galley, sir. Sir, —I do want to talk to you about this."

"*Talk. Now. Fast. You're tying up channels.*"

"I mean I've got to talk to you in private. I'm on the galley-com, sir, I want to talk to you before you talk to—"

"Hawkins. I have a ship moving at 1.092 kips, exceeding Pell traffic speed limits, for which we have a 1k fine. I have a ship in count behind me and a caution on an inbound insystem hauler and two service craft, whose point-location is often a mystery unto themselves. Do you think we could postpone the personal business?"

"Yes, sir."

"Thank you."

Dead connection after that. He pounded the wall with his fist, thinking . . .

"Trouble?" Tink asked.

. . . Christian was going to walk into Austin's office, re-motely justified, and come out of there wanting to cut his throat.

Which wasn't smart policy, which wasn't what he wanted to live with, which wasn't the man he'd seen for about two beats when Christian was figuring out how and on what ship to dump him.

Say it right: Christian could have left him in that warehouse to freeze, and nobody would have found him. Christian, Saby had said it, had gone to a lot of effort to get him shipped out, never mind Christian could have walked him into a lot rougher situation than a ticket out of port and out of their lives. Christian was fighting for his place on this ship, was what Christian was doing. . . .

Beatrice didn't want him. *I* brought him up.

And he understood Christian in that light a lot more than he'd ever understand the man who'd raped Marie.

"Tom?"

"I need to check on something," he said. "Tink, cover me."

Maybe Tink wanted to ask. He didn't want to answer. He ducked down the straightway of the galley back toward lower main, where alterday crew was headed for the lifts.

He looked to find Christian anywhere in the traffic. He knew where his cabin was. He thought about going there. He checked near lower deck ops, and then at the nearby lifts, where the next shift was cycling up by the carload. He slipped into that lot, nervous, waited his turn, one trip after the other, then jammed into the car with the rest and stared at the level indicator instead of the faces around him. Crew stared . . . the cuts and bruises, it had to be, or the question what he was doing, going topside. "He clear?" somebody finally asked. And: "Think so," somebody else said. "—Mister, you got a clearance?"

"Appointment," he muttered, as the lift banged into its topside lock. "Captain's office." The door was opening. He wanted out. Fast. "Excuse me."

A hand caught his shoulder.

"Hold it, Hawkins."

He saw seniority in the grey hair. He said, "Yessir," and figured he'd just routed himself back in the brig. The guy shoved him against the wall by the lift doors.

"Appointment, is it?"

"My brother's supposed to be up here. I need to talk to him."

"Is that so?" The officer—Travis, the pocket emblem said—turned him back to the next arriving lift. "Right back downside, mister. *Stay* to lower decks."

Second lift opened. He faced, suddenly, blond hair, bruises, scowling face.

"Inside," the officer said, and jerked at him by the arm, sending him past Christian, into that lift. "Downside. Go. Now."

Hand propelled him inside. Christian dived in beside him, mad. The lift doors shut, on the two of them alone, and the lift sank.

"So?" Christian asked.

"I didn't want what happened. I'm sorry. I don't *want* to get in your way. . . ."

"You had a good time, you and Saby?"

"We—" He couldn't justify anything. Christian was looking for offense, and his face and his ribs were already sore. "We didn't plan anything. We ran into each other—"

The lift hit bottom. Crew jammed aboard, pinning them to the back of the car.

"I don't want another fight," he said. They were face-to-face against the back wall of the lift car as the door shut and the lift started up again. "I don't want to argue with you."

"Yeah. Keep your concern."

"He didn't do right. He wasn't *right,* lighting into you like that—"

"Just shut up, Family Boy. I don't *need* your damn condescension, all right?"

The door opened. The crowd in front vacated the lift. Christian shoved his way through and he tried to follow, but Christian turned around, furious, the other side of the threshold. "Get to hell out of my *life,* Hawkins!"

Shocked faces, around Christian. He'd started forward, to leave the lift. It seemed useless, then, with Christian opposed, to pursue anything with anyone in command.

Downbound crew flooded in, pushing him back against the rail. The doors shut, the lift went down and let out downside. The other passengers got off. He did.

Straight face-on into Saby.

"Tink said—" Saby began, and grabbed his arm as they worked their way outward, against the five or six upbounds trying to get in the doors.

He wasn't coherent. He waved a hand, made a helpless gesture as they got clear, back at the corridor wall. "No luck. Waste of time."

"I could have told you," Saby said. "Tom, let me talk to him."

"Not Austin. *Christian.* Damn him. Attitudinal son of a *bitch.*"

"Him, too." Saby made a flustered gesture and punched the

lift button. One car had gone. The other was downbound. "He's being a fool."

"You don't go up there!"

Saby turned around with a furious stare. "I'm going *up* there because this is my shift, and I'm late! —And leave it to me who I talk to!"

"It's my life, dammit!"

The lift arrived. Saby ducked in with a last few upbound crew. The doors shut. He stood there, having embarrassed himself, generally, having made a public scene with Christian, up and down the lift system, and disagreed with Saby, in public.

There was nothing but a shut door to talk to. There was nothing to do but walk back to the galley where he'd agreed to be. Forever.

Right now he wanted to strangle Christian. He'd blamed Saby. He'd blamed himself. He'd blamed Marie and Austin and fate.

But right now he saw only one person responsible for what had happened to Christian, and to him, and for the misunderstanding with Saby, and every damn thing else.

Wasn't Saby's fault she'd been drafted as surrogate mama to a jealous brat whose universe insisted every problem was somebody else's fault.

He slammed his fist into the paneling as he walked. It hurt as much as he remembered. He pounded it two, three, four, five times, until the corridor thundered and the pain outside equalled the explosion inside his chest.

Somebody put his head out of ops and ducked back again. Fast.

He hit the wall four more times, until his knuckles showed blood.

Nobody asked. Nobody came out. He got as far as the next traverse, with the mess-hall in sight, when the siren sounded, and the PA thundered, *"Take-hold, take-hold, long burn in one minute. This is your warning."*

He didn't run. He walked, deliberately, counting the seconds, down the mess-hall center aisle, made it to the comfortable side, the stern wall, this time, where Tink and Jamal were getting set.

"Fix it?" Tink asked.

"Waste of time. Waste of effort. Nobody listens."

Tink raised his brows. He remembered he was supposed to be seeing about bed-sheets. "Yeah," Tink said, and held out a bag of candy. "Lot of that going around today. Have one. Have two."

He did. His hand was skinned. He figured the knuckles would turn black. He ate the chocolate. Jamal had one, the three of them alone in a galley redolent of spices and, rare, expensive treat, bread baking.

The burn started, smooth, clean, steady, this time.

Mainday crew was the heavy load for the galley, the dockers, who seemed to keep whatever schedule they fancied—but figure that the horde would hit the galley hall for supper once the burn cut out. Sandwiches out to the working stations. Everybody to feed before they made jump.

Gentle burn. Reasonable burn.

"Easy does it now," Tink said. "Pell is the most reg-u-lated place in the ports we do. You sneeze and gain a tenth of a k in their zones, you got a fine. One k ain't nothing. Pilot knows."

"Runs in the genes," he muttered, while that 'ports we do' hit the conscious part of his brain, the assumptions he'd made, the questions he'd asked himself and not asked, because the routes were so laid down by physics and what points a ship could reach from where they were that he'd assumed Earth, Tripoint, and Viking. From Pell, they could make Earth, spooky enough thought, strange, overcrowded place. But that had been where *Christophe Martin* was bound. Christian wouldn't ship him where *Corinthian* was already going. From Pell . . . if they went really off the charts they could reach the Hinder Stars, the old bridge of stars the sub-lighters had used for stepping-stones out from Earth—shut down, now, dead,

. . . civilized powers couldn't keep the Mazianni out of them, and the Military had dismantled the stations.

So they said.

"Tink." He felt stupid asking, at this late date. "Where are we going?"

"Tripoint. Just Tripoint to Viking."

So mundane it shook him, after the giddy speculation he'd just made. He wasn't even sure he'd have believed it, if it hadn't come from Tink.

"Where's the Fleet connection?" he asked. It was just the three of them in the galley, Tink, Jamal, himself.

And a silence.

Then: "Tripoint," Tink said. That was all. The silence outweighed curiosity, reminding him Tink wasn't innocent. Saby wasn't. Nobody on this ship was. Now he wasn't, because he'd voluntarily come back aboard.

He'd been in a position, while he was free, to do everything Marie would have done—whatever it might have cost him. But he hadn't. Hadn't wanted to—thinking about himself. Then Tink. Then Saby, after which . . . he guessed now he was where he wanted to be, scared, lost—queasy at the stomach as the burn kept up, getting them up to the *v* Pell would let them carry in its inner zones.

And very, very lonely, just now. Cut off from everything and everyone he'd grown up with. From everything he'd been taught was right and wrong, good and bad.

Burn cut out.

"That's about 10 kips," Tink said. "Out *and* away from Downbelow's pull. We're outbound now."

"How long have we got? Days? Hours?"

"Four hours inside the slow zones," Jamal said. "Two meals to two shifts, fast as we can turn 'em, and all the resupply at the posts. You make coffee?"

"I can learn." He stood away from the wall, steady on his feet. Movement was starting down the corridor, a drift of mainday crew past the tables . . . "Serving line's not open yet,"

Jamal yelled out, which roused no complaint, but faces were grim.

Ship, he heard. People weren't happy, and it didn't have to do with the line not being open. While Jamal and Tink hauled the serving-pans out and settled them on the counter, he opened up the cabinet and got out the coffee and the filters, listening all the while.

Something about a ship following them.

Marie? he asked himself. His heart skipped a beat, two, recalling what Austin had said, that Marie might come here.

Then he heard another word. Mazianni. And he stopped cold, asking himself what in hell was going on, that *Corinthian* had to worry.

Didn't they supply the Fleet? Weren't they on the same side?

He looked at Tink. Tink looked grim, too.

"Aren't they friendlies?" he asked Tink. "What are they talking about?"

"Dunno," Tink said. "But, no, they ain't, all of 'em. Not by a long shot."

— *ii* —

"I DON'T FEEL SORRY FOR YOU," Austin said, for openers. "Not one damn bit. Am I going to hear you whimper, or what?"

"You don't get to hear anything," Christian said, and sank into the well-worn interview chair. "You're not interested. Do I get to go back to the bridge now? We've got a ship pulled away from dock. You might be interested."

"You have a seriously maladjusted psyche, Mr. Bowe."

"I have a seriously warped sense of values, captain, sir, that would indicate to me the captain might have advised me, rather than leave me and the second chief navigator outside the information loop. I hope you enjoyed your joke. I hope you enjoyed it a lot. Because thanks to our rattling around back there on

Pell docks, that's a Mazianni spotter behind us. That's a ship called *Silver Dream,* based at Fargone, if you haven't noticed before this."

"Let me recall how, also leading to this event, we had a deal with an Earth-bound ship that I didn't authorize. Let me recall . . ."

"Let me recall we're not talking about a personal matter. If Family Boy and cousin Saby want to screw each other blue in lower main, fine, that's their judgment, I'm glad they had a good time while we were turning the bars upside down and knocking on every door on Pell. So that's all right, they're in a room somewhere on your credit, thanks ever so much—but the burning question's still that ship back there. I'm sorry I blacked brother's eye, just for God's sake pay attention to what I'm saying."

"Attention? Did I hear the word, Attention?"

"Listen to me! Damn you, will you just one time listen to me?"

"Mister, I have the most shocking revelation for you. Your discoveries of the universe are twenty years behind mine, your insights and your wisdom do not overreach my own, your outrage at the situation does not outmatch mine, and I am moved at this moment to leave this chair and explain to you physically the same rules my father explained to me the week I made my own most egregious mistake, except that I swore that I'd lean a bit heavier on communication and a little less to the fist. *Which* I do, in consequence. —So what was it you had to say?"

"I said . . ." He fought for self-control. And quiet in his voice. "I said, We should lay back in Pell system, go slow . . . this guy's not hauling, I'll lay you money he's not hauling. He's certainly armed with more than the ordinary. Capella says . . . he's some different faction of the Fleet."

"Welcome to the real universe. Different factions of the Fleet. I'm amazed."

"Be serious, dammit."

"I am. Very serious. Decades of seriousness." Austin rocked his chair back, crossed his leg over his knee, folded his hands on his stomach. "Has it ever struck you, Christian, this fragmentation, this stupid factionalization of the Fleet that should have defended civilization, —says something about the human condition? That enemies are much more essential to our happiness than friends? That our rivals shape our ethics, and our failures define our goals? Seems so, from the business on our own deck. Screw Mazian. And Mallory. But what a miserable, *stupid* end it comes to."

"It's one damn ship out there! Quit talking about endings and give me some of that experience you claim to have."

"Scared, Mr. Bowe?"

"Screw you!"

"If you can't mate with it, eat it, or wear it, it's no good? I thought that was your philosophy. Maybe it can do something about the ship back there."

"Cut it out! You've made your point. Let's talk about that ship, let's talk about what to do—"

"Shoot at it, maybe? Or stall us insystem? I think that was Capella's advice. Fine for her. But not for us."

"You're running scared! You're more scared of Marie Hawkins than—"

"Than that spotter? No."

"Then, damn you, quit joking. I don't know when you're listening."

"You could ask."

"I could take it for granted, if you weren't such a bastard."

"Never take anyone's listening for granted. Children teach you that. Any other divine revelations? Human insights? Moderately wise notions?"

Christian set his hands on the chair arms, to get up. "That I've got things to do. I've had it. I'm through. I'm not listening, after this."

"Oh, give me some news. This isn't it."

"Damn you, pay attention to something but your ego! Capella says the other faction wants her—with the navigational data she has in her head. She's saying they'd go after us to get her."

"Ah. Information. Finally."

"So what are you going to do about it?"

Austin shrugged. "I'll let you know."

"What kind of an answer is that?"

"Exactly that. Go see to your own business. I'm offduty, you're on, good luck, good night, stay out of trouble. Meanwhile, consider that the woman you're sleeping with might just possibly have motives of her own."

"Oh, that's right, drive a wedge, plant suspicion—"

Austin rocked his chair back. "God, this is boring. Wake me when you have a thought."

"Damn you!"

"Still waiting."

God, he wanted to get up, walk out . . . he *hated* Austin in this damned, superior mode, this smug, condescending spite. He'd interrupted. He knew the pose.

"Father, sir, —*what* were you about to say?"

"Ah. About Capella? Her advice to stay in port . . . was better for her than for us."

"Because *we're* running from the Hawkins ship?"

"Because we can't keep this ship sitting at dock running up charges, boy, basic economics."

"Your real reason, damn you."

"Through putting words in my mouth?"

"Yes, father." Through clenched jaw. "Please."

"Because that ship is going to sit out there at Tripoint and wait as long as we can wait. Very simple. We can't avoid it. We can't outwait it. I'm afraid your friend Capella would like to stay at dock simply because there's a chance of a ship coming in that she can skip to, quietly, so when *Corinthian* does meet with trouble . . . she won't be on it."

"Forgive me, but I don't read her that way."

"I used to be that naive."

A biting remark was on his tongue. He didn't vent it. "Can we talk about the ship, sir? It's going to overjump us. I agree it's going to be waiting for us when we get there. It's going to read our entry shock and it's going to fire on it."

"Yes."

"Then what do we do?"

"If they know precisely where we're going, not damn much we can do. We hope that's not the case. We've got til our wave reaches them and their response, whatever it is, reaches us. We hope that's a long distance, that's what we do."

"That can't be all! They could be sitting right *on* our drop-point—"

"Why would they want Capella?"

"Because she knows a *lot* of Fleet drop points. Not just this one. Because they don't want to blow up the ship she's on."

"Possibly. Also—possibly because she knows the Tripoint drop and they don't. It's a lot of space to search, for something the size of a freighter. You can bet the dissident factions have tried to find it and you can hope they've failed. If they need her, we'll have whatever advantage she can give us. And she's not anxious to die. Or fall into their hands. So I do trust Capella—that she'll do what she does very well."

"So what do you want me to set up for you, on the boards? Any changes in config? In defaults, in display?"

"No. Nothing unusual."

"Dammit, this isn't a game."

"You've seen that. Good. This is not a drill. In the event of this actual emergency . . . we'll hand off thirty minutes before jump. Meanwhile, I need my nap."

"You're not actually going to sleep."

"I think so. I'll have my dinner. Catch an hour or so. See you. Good luck. Don't screw things too badly."

"God, I hate you."

Humor left Austin's expression, ever so briefly. And returned, like a mask. "You used to say that when you didn't get

your way. Sorry, this one depends on that ship out there. I say
again, don't screw it."

There was silence. He got up, slowly, and walked out. The
door hissed shut.

He stood outside, against the wall, for some few moments,
telling himself calm down, actually confusedly *sorry* about that
parting shot, for the way Austin had looked for half a heartbeat.
He'd never scored on Austin like that. Never gotten Austin's
real expression in an argument. In retrospect, maybe that was
what scared him. As if Austin was somehow and for a moment
wide open to him—as if, maybe Austin wasn't expecting to
come out of this mess.

But, hell, Austin had been in the War, Austin had shepherded
Corinthian through fire and mines and stray ordnance, only a
couple of times taken damage, Austin had gotten them out of
far worse, while he'd shivered inside the pillow-padded storage
bin where Saby hid with him, Saby swearing it was going to
be all right, the ship was going to move hard for a while, Austin
and Beatrice were doing it, don't be scared, Chrissy, don't be
scared—while Saby shivered, too, and half-broke his bones
when the *g*-force built, and you didn't know when it would
stop, or when it did, you didn't know why, or what could hit
you, or when.

Never forgot those years. The nerves had still been there
when he was sixteen, worse, maybe, that he'd only heard later
what was going on, never so that he could pin this sensation
to that movement . . . impressions all muddled up in a three-
year-old's memory, a five-year-old's terror.

For sixteen, seventeen years he'd been spooked by jump, by
the *g*-forces, by the whole feeling of a ship doing what a ship
did. But Capella had laughed him through his terrors, Capella
had snared him in other sensations, taught him to enjoy the
craziness, to see the dimensions as other than up and down and
falling. Austin was wrong about her—Capella had come to
him on the docks, not the other way around: he hadn't thought

of that argument against Austin's suspicions, he always thought of the telling ones after the door was shut.

He could trust her. Trust her with his life, absolutely.

With his half-brother—hell, cancel that. Don't think about it. Elder brother was stronger, faster, smarter, any adjective you wanted, he was also god-awfully clean-minded, noble, true, and honest. A thorough-going bore.

Dance, she'd said, light flickering around her, the music drowned in the drum-beat, the equation of a different space glowing below the bracelet, and no damn guarantee the enemies she was avoiding weren't going to walk through that door.

They'd been in mortal danger. He hadn't thought about it. Capella had been waiting for it. Wanting, maybe, a chance at it on the dockside, where her enemies were much more vulnerable.

Or . . . maybe keeping Austin guessing, whether she'd board or not. And making Austin know he might force her to board— but work for him?

God. God, he'd been blind. Focused on the wrong problem. Again. He had to get the pieces together, *had* to pull it out, if Austin was sinking into some self-destructive funk . . . Austin and Beatrice were feuding, you could feel it in the way the ship moved; the ship could lose more than trade, it could *lose,* out there in the dark, where if they didn't make that pick-up, they couldn't guarantee there'd be another. And if an enemy found that supply dump . . . they couldn't guarantee anything, either. Not even their getting out alive.

Capella sat on main crew, this trip. Had to. He was supposed to set things up . . . and no changes in routine, Austin said?

When they were running into ambush, and Austin knew it?

Had to talk to Michaels, that was what. Had to be sure that capped switch was thrown and the guns were up when they made the drop at Tripoint. Elder brother and that matter . . . didn't matter, in that context. A non-issue, until they got to Viking. If they got to Viking.

—— *iii* ——

RUMORS MULTIPLIED ON LOWER deck once mainday tech crew had hit the galley line in numbers, and the incoming detail gathered form as informants from various ops posts got together at the tables and fact and speculation intersected: Fact: the ship out there was *Silver Dream,* it was a closed-hold hauler, you couldn't tell whether or what it had in its holds. Fact: it had a large engine pack, which was always suspicious on a non-Family ship. Observation: Christian and the second chief navigator were uneasy about it, and: Speculation, were sure it wasn't hauling, and when they cleared the slow zones they were going to light out of Pell like a bat.

That much, Tom picked up just passing around the tables, refilling table coffee and tea pots. Heads were together, the galley was uncommonly quiet, voices were subdued and urgent. Dockers clustered apart from the techs, at their tables at the end of the galley zone . . . the questions in that corner were slightly different, no less urgent: What are we going to do, skip through the Point? And the answer: Can't offload. No way we can offload.

Somebody wondered, then, whether they'd still get their pay, in that event. The rest, apparently old hands on *Corinthian,* said Shut up, don't be a fool, being alive to spend it was the issue, and the captain would make it up, the captain never shorted you for what wasn't your fault.

Tom collected plates, grabbed them as fast as they emptied, folded up the tables and the seats, fast as he could. Heard names like Mallory, and Porey, and Edger, names of captains of the dismembered Fleet. Talk about ambushes. And a dump, whether *v*-dump, meaning whether they were going to slow down, or supply dump . . . it sounded like the latter. Rendezvous, of some kind? he asked himself.

"What do we regularly *do* out there?" he asked Tink. "Level with me. What's the ordinary scenario?"

"There's a place," Tink said, but someone came near, just

then, and Tink didn't feel comfortable talking, it was clear. Jamal frowned at both of them.

"Tink, get some help, that cart's ready for the bridge, Medical's ready to roll."

"Yeah, I'm on it," Tink said, grabbed a couple of offduty maintenance techs and dragooned them into cart-transport, while he folded tables and secured safety latches, wanting not to think about Mazianni weapons bearing down on them.

Mazianni operating at Pell, free and open, for God's sake? And following them out of port?

Where did they get undock clearance? Who assigned them dockers to get them out that fast, to follow *Corinthian?* Nothing fit with what he knew unless it was Mallory on their tail . . . but Mazianni didn't above all describe Mallory, who did operate out of Pell. Mallory was semi-legitimate. Had total station cooperation—it could be some ship working for her, and Pell authorities, to arrest them . . . or get evidence on them, but there were warrants for that, easier to do at dock.

"Tom!"

Tone of a man who'd been trying to get his attention. He looked at Jamal, blank of what the man had been saying.

"Hell, I'll get it," Jamal said. "No damn brain on duty anywhere. Stay here! Pull the delivery slips, check it off. If you screw up, Hawkins, somebody's without trank. Can you manage that?"

"Got it." He went back to the paperwork desk, laid Jamal's handheld on the communication plate, punched the requisite code for the deliveries, DDAT, to transfer, 1 plus T, no mystery in the software. The handheld registered File Complete, meaning it had read an end-of-file, —and a furtive, stupid thought sprang up. Stupid, stupid, stupid, he said to himself, system's guarded, all kinds of partitions. He looked longingly at that console, then, hell, shook his head and let it alone.

He'd done the checklist when Jamal came back with what looked like the stuff from Medical. Jamal took the list he'd vetted, left, with: "Stow everything behind doors. Don't trust counter-mounts. We don't know what we're into. Turn the water off, under the sink. Lock the drain down. You know how to do that?"

"Yessir," he said. Tink was still out on deliveries. He flipped the lever to dismount the mixer and the processor, stowed them below, secured oven latches, washers, cabinets, put the pans behind solid doors and latched them in. Got the water shut off, put the anti-vacuum lock on the drain. He'd never used one, but he'd heard about whole sections voided of air through a pipe breach.

Cast another, longing look at the computer. Looked at the door. Edged closer, then flipped it on just to see what program would come up.

Screen showed: MES>94.

He hit 01, keyed: *Your message software's a dinosaur. I could access. I didn't. T. Hawkins.*

Austin had a lot else on his mind. The whole ship rang with urgency. Stupid to do. Distracting to Austin. To . . . God knew who . . . but, dammit, things were happening up there he didn't have a clue to judge. He had skills he wasn't using. Somebody was after them, and he had to sit down here, being shot at, keeping pans from falling out of cabinets, getting rumors from the walk-ins . . . his stomach was in a knot.

It might make Austin *know* he restrained himself. Might get him at least access physically where he could access electronically. Software *was* a dinosaur. God knew what other was.

But, damn, no, ship was at risk. Wasn't a time for personal stuff. He ran a delete. Flipped the switch. Killed it.

Could be the militia after them. And here he was. Wrong side of Marie's quarrel. Wrong side of everything.

The ship was growing so quiet. He'd never heard anything the like on *Sprite* before they went to jump. On *Sprite* there were so many Family, there were so many kids running up and down, people yelling information at each other. Here . . . just quiet. Somebody walked outside the partition that divided the galley from general passage. Somebody shouted, far off in the ring. Somewhere, sounding sections away, a cart rattled. He made himself move away from the console, get to work, the last few table-seat units to fold up, thunderous, appalling crashes in the silence.

Jamal came back, started running checks on the cabinets. "You're L14."

"Yes."

"Left your stuff there. Trank and all. You ever get sheets?"

"I . . . no. I didn't." Sheets were the farthest thing from his mind. "I can do without. It's all right." In the crisis at hand, he regretted his protestations to Saby about his own quarters. Didn't want to be alone. Desperately didn't want to be alone, but he'd taken that position . . . didn't see how to talk to her now.

"Freeze your ass off," Jamal said. "I tossed some blankets in. Put your trank on the bunk. Sheets are down in Medical, you got to do that yourself."

"You didn't have to do that."

"Yeah, well, it's a crazy trip. Hope we see the other side of it."

Cart rattled and thumped somewhere, growing closer. Tink coming back, he thought, and Jamal said, "We're shut down here. You want to go get those sheets? I'll sign you out."

"Yeah," he said. "Thanks." Jamal was down furnishing his quarters while he was sneaking access on the galley computer. Didn't make him feel better. He went for the exit toward lower main, dodged Tink and the inbound cart.

"We done?" Tink asked cheerfully.

"Seems so," he said. He tried cheerfulness. It didn't take.

But Tink bumped him on the arm with a tattooed fist. "Hey. We're all right. Seen us sail through the damnedest stuff. Pieces rattling off the hull. We come through. We always come through. Can't scratch this ship."

"You been aboard that long?"

"Oh, yeah," Tink said. "You just belt in good. Hear? Hope

you secured those cabinets, or we'll have pans clear to Engineering."

He laughed a little. He truly wanted to laugh. "Yeah," he said. It made him feel better as he went his way down to Medical. Check out the sheets, yeah, pillow, too, got the blankets, already, sir, no problem, got the trank, yeah, I'm on the roster, I'm on galley duty, Jamal said he saw to it.

He got the sheets, he went to lonely L14 and checked out the accommodation. It wasn't quite a closet. It had plumbing. He remembered what Austin said about turning the water on. He tried it and it was off. But the outbound pipe needed shutting. He got down to locate it, found the cutoff labeled, and turned it.

The first of the acceleration warnings sounded, then. He banged his head on the cabinet getting out, his heart going like a hammer. He heard Christian's voice, at least he thought it was Christian: "We'll clear Pell slow zones in ten minutes. At that time we'll start our acceleration toward departure. We're releasing non-ops personnel to quarters to secure premises. Please secure all pipes and unplug all but emergency equipment. Area chiefs please check compliance and all vacant compartments. As you are aware, we have a follower. We do not know the ship's intentions, but we are on condition red alert. Double check all secure latches, secure all non-essential items."

Damn, he thought, palms sweating. Canned speech. Christian was reading—he couldn't be that calm and collected. But Christian had something to do besides imagine. He didn't. The walls seemed to close in on him.

"Be doubly sure of your belts. If you detect any belt malfunction, pad up with all available materials and secure yourself in the smallest area of your compartment. All personnel, review your emergency assignments."

There wasn't a 'smallest area.' The compartment was it. He got up off the deck and tested the belts. They worked. The emergency procedures all seemed unreal to him, more extreme than any drill he'd ever walked through, precautions against maneuvers he wasn't sure *Sprite* had ever had to make, at the worst of the War. They'd sat the bad times out in port.

Pieces rattling off the hull. Hell.

The door opened, without a by-your-leave. "Looking for a room-mate," Saby said.

He was glad. He was incredibly, shakily glad of that offer—welcomed Saby's arms around him, held to her as something solid, against the suppositions.

"Yeah," he said. "Good. Fine with me."

— *iv* —

"EVERYTHING IN PARAMETERS," Christian said, on the hand-off. Austin lowered himself into the chair, scanned the console, found the routine settings. "Anything else?"

The boy was always touchy. You never knew, unless you'd deliberately hit the button.

"No," he said. "Belt in, stay tight, this one's going to be interesting."

"We're going to skim it, right?"

Shoot right through Tripoint with no *v*-dump. Accumulate *v* at the interface and come into Viking like a bat out of hell. . . .

Certainly it was one solution. But they were loaded heavy. *Hell* of a mass.

"You run the calc?"

" 'Pella and I did. It's on your number two, all the options I figured. She says she can put it in margin. I say it's dicey."

"Very."

"They always short you in the cans. Absolute mass is 200k less. Saby says."

"That's nice."

"Nice. Hell." Christian was keeping his voice down, standing right by his chair. "What *are* we going to do? We're *not* stopping."

"Maybe."

"God in—"

"Shush, shush, shush, Mr. Bowe, a shade less emotional, if you please."

"You damn, grandstanding . . . _bastard,_ no, forget I said it, you haven't anything to prove to me, I know you can do it, let's just not try, all right?"

"I'm perfectly serious—as a possibility. I trust you calc'ed that with the rest."

"It's on there."

"It had better be. It had better be right, mister. Bet our lives it's right."

Christian's mouth went very thin. "Yes, sir," he said, and went forward, said a word to Beatrice, stopped for another to Capella, who wasn't standing down at shift-change.

Capella listened, frowned, nodded to whatever it was. Christian bent and, definite breach of regulations, kissed the second chief navigator on the forehead.

The second chief navigator grabbed his collar, gave him one on the mouth that went on. And on. Christian came back straightening his collar and headed, clearly, past, without explanation.

"Inspiring the crew?" Austin said.

"Just for God's sake _listen_ to her."

"Emotion, emotion. Get some rest."

Christian left. The sort-out of shift-change was mostly complete.

"You know," Michaels said, stopping by his chair, to lean on the arm and the back and deliver a quiet word to his ear, "the boy said, hit the sims, first thing; said, stay on 'em, said don't even ask you, just push the arming button last thing when we go up."

"Did, did he?"

"Whole list of orders, yours, his, identical down the line. Just thought you'd like to know."

He gave a breath, a laugh, couldn't say what. Michaels patted his arm, went on for a word to Beatrice. Felt all right, it did. There was hope for the brat, give or take what he'd stirred.

No way their tagalong was Mallory's. The Pell militia wouldn't chase you from Pell docks into jump. If Pell wanted you, you'd have hell getting undocked. They'd have agents out to blow something essential while you sat at dock, no question, they'd learned their lesson the hard way about quarrels with ships.

So, granted it wasn't the law, it was clearly a ship with a mission, and it was clearly on the Tripoint heading. If guesses were right, at worst-case, those holds were empty, and their lighter mass was going to give *Silver Dream*'s big engine-pack a hype to send it right past *Corinthian*. In terms of v, realspace negligible. In terms of position in space-time . . . ahead of them. Waiting for them, when hyperspace abhorred their energy-state out again at Tripoint.

But bet they wouldn't use nukes, not if they wanted to board and take the second chief navigator for themselves. They'd use inerts: simple mag-fired rifle balls, in effect—hoping to cripple *Corinthian*'s jump-capacity; and they'd have to launch those *after* they'd picked up the wavefront of *Corinthian*'s arrival.

"Nav."

"*Sir.*"

"Are you comfortable with what you have, with data?"

"*Yes, sir, more than adequate.*"

He keyed up the alternatives. Found the one he wanted. The supply dump. "Nav, receive my send. How close can you put us?"

"*Sir. May I talk privately?*"

"Come ahead."

Capella left her chair, came and leaned an elbow against his console. "Sir," Capella said. "If you want honestly to leave it to me, give me leave to dump at any point, I'll guarantee you best of two alternatives."

"What two?"

"We find this sumbitch far enough out we can make that

dump or close enough in we take my bet and skip through to Viking. We can dump down. Swear to you."

You looked in Capella's eyes when she was off duty, you learned nothing. You looked there now and you got the coldest, clearest stare.

"I believe you, second chief navigator. Are you saying leave that choice to you? *My* priorities involve the economics of this ship. Involve keeping a contract, with entities I believe you represent. Can you set us next our target, *if* our problem isn't within, say, three hours light? Can you assure me . . . we can stay emissions-neutral?"

"Hell of an accuracy, sir."

"Can you do it?"

Capella when that grin cut loose was the devil. The very devil. You didn't know.

"Maybe."

"I'd suggest you figure it, second chief navigator."

"You are one son of *a* bitch, captain, sir."

"Yeah. I am. How good *are* you?"

"Damn good."

"Then do it."

"Yes, *sir.*"

Never a way in hell he could have gotten that berth within the Fleet —point of fact, there hadn't been a way in hell he'd have wanted one, in his adult life, when they were losing ships faster than they could reckon what they'd lost, and attitudes inside the Fleet were responsible for that trend. He could still name a couple of the captains he'd have shot as soon as deal with, and the feeling was still, he was sure, entirely mutual.

He'd never truly known where Capella fit in that mosaic, until just now that he'd nudged Capella into action: Don't question me, second chief, just obey the order. And that straight look and that 'sir' out of their nameless navigator . . .

Satisfying, that he could get 'sir' out of this woman, who'd had the career that had slipped away before he was old enough to chase it, in any sense that the War could be won or that there was time left to reconstitute the old order. He'd seen nothing past the impending debacle, once upon the omniscience of his youth, seen nothing worth obeying or believing, fool that he'd been; and now his son was staring into another Götterdämerung, nothing of fire and fury, just a niggling increase of regulations—he could see that from where he sat, watching anachronism on her way to the navigation console.

He'd had his moral victory, maybe, maybe could slip out of this mess . . . maybe escape all the rest of the little regulation-generated disasters, so long as he lived, on a ship that had thrown in its lot with what was changing. Little ships couldn't get the profit margin, with the new regulations, couldn't keep ahead of the Family ships and the state-sponsored combines.

So what did a small-hauler do, but go on serving the ports they could, getting cargo where they could, even doing what obliged them to take personnel the Fleet dictated they take?

No way to refuse the honor, of course, no objection possible, and no assurance the divisions inside the Fleet weren't going to play out one day on their own deck, for interests a mere merchant captain didn't guess, and against opposition said captain might not find out about until it was too late.

Unless, say, the second chief navigator saw it, too, saw the same wall coming, and the same Götterdämerung.

Yes, *sir,* that word was, and he watched her settle in, all business, listened to her, on A-band, engage Beatrice, and tell Beatrice she'd have certain data, and she should trust it blindly, no matter how extreme it seemed.

Beatrice half-turned in her seat. He nodded. Beatrice settled back. So they were going with it. Beatrice would handle it. He had confidence, too, in the Fleet's gift—granted you knew which faction she belonged to.

— *v* —

ACCEL GREW HARDER, JOINTS POPPED. Fingers twined with fingers. Couldn't think of anything, not at this *g*-stress, just company.

"Want the light?" Saby asked.

"No. Dark's fine. I know who I'm with." Light just confused the eyes with here and now, and didn't solve what went on in the dark space.

Didn't silence Marie. She lived there, at the edge of jump. Like Rodman. Like Roberta R. Like the kids.

Just wondered . . . where they were going. What they were going to do.

"Tink says . . . back through Tripoint. Non-stop, I take it?"

Silence out of Saby for a few breaths. Her quarters. Her bed. Her fingers twitched in his. "We're hauling. Not light mass on this leg. My bet is, we'll deliver."

"Deliver to what?"

"Where we have to."

"Level with me. What do we haul? What are they after, this ship they're talking about?"

"Don't know. Don't know who this ship's working for." Another twitch of the fingers. "But while they're searching . . . we can move cargo. They can try to find us."

"That's crazed. You just dump it out there, or are we meeting somebody, or what?"

"Just a place. Spooky place. Dead ship. I don't like it. But stuff's waiting there for us. Always is."

"*Those* were the cans at Viking."

A moment Saby just lay still. "Yes," she said. "Sorry to say, that's what you found."

"Stuff they raided?" Indignation was hard, this close to the edge, under the heavy hand of acceleration. "That's your trade? Stolen goods?"

"Stuff from a long time back. Old stuff. It's the dates, the *dates* you don't want to question. Ships we deal with don't raid anymore. Don't want the attention. Long as we sell them food, medicines . . . import Scotch."

"And arms."

"Food. Medicines. Mostly food. Plants. Live plants."

"Live plants."

They maintained a separate silence a while, hands joined.

"That's the damned oddest thing I ever heard," he said.

"Truth," Saby said.

"I guess." Best offer he had. "If you say so—yeah, I believe it."

Chapter Eleven

Two hours twenty minutes. The whole difference. The whole . . . damned . . . difference between *Corinthian*'s system exit and *Sprite*'s entry, the height and depth of Pell Star system apart.

Nothing to do at that point but to continue on in, with *Sprite* running full-loaded as she was. Nothing to do but maintain a quiet calm, a sweetness to the offered sympathy of cousins and, of course, Lydia. Less likely . . . sympathy from Mischa, whose expression of regret had a certain lack of conviction, but Mischa had at least made the gesture.

"We tried, Marie. All we could do."

It *was* all they could have done, a heartbreakingly hard run through Tripoint, everyone on long hours and short food and sleep. Tempers had frayed, understandably so. And there had been recriminations about missing *Corinthian*.

Not from her. And they waited for her opinion. Maybe with bated breath.

Spirits aboard had picked up when their cargo sold during their run-in toward station, no languishing on the trade boards while the ship ran up dock-time, no waiting to sell this part and that lot of cans . . . Dee Biomedical bought the whole lot sight unseen, the publishing data-feed, the biomedicals, neobiotics, and biomaterials, with damage exceptions, which, Marie knew from her boards, there were none: every one of the cans came in registering, constantly talking to the regulation devices.

Not one can even questionable. And profit clear—Pell had *no* tariff on biomedicals of Cyteen origin, when Pell could get them.

Faces started to smile. People started to be pleasant to each other in the corridors. The seniors who'd been fuming mad about transshipping the government contract now thought that, of course, it had all been their idea.

But ship activity at dock? Pell didn't have that kind of information available to an inbound ship. Get it at the Trade Office once you dock.

Information on Thomas Bowe-Hawkins? His mother wanted to know?

Oh, there was a record of that. Listed with exiting crew on *Corinthian*. And listed with returning crew.

Somebody using Tom's passport, she thought, but she kept that to herself, and kept the information to herself until *Sprite* docked, grappled to, and opened its ports at 10 Green, where Dee Imports had can transports waiting.

Then she was off to the Customs Office so fast the deck smoked.

Well, yes, Tom's passport had been used. Well, yes, there had to be a credit record of transactions on station, but she had to get a court order. And, yes, they knew which agents had been assigned at *Corinthian*'s dock, and, well, yes, there was no actual regulation against an individual inquiry with the agent, although they didn't give out names.

Her pocket-com nagged at her. She ignored it.

"I'm his *mother,*" she said to the customs officer. "I have copies of his papers."

"The boy is over eighteen. By Alliance law, he's an adult."

"Do you have kids?"

"Look, Ms. Hawkins, . . ."

She didn't raise her voice. She made it very quiet. "This boy was out drinking when that ship cleared port. We're a Family ship. Check us out. I want to know does that passport, used exiting *Corinthian,* still have the right picture."

"You're asking if it was stolen."

"*Yes.*"

The agent vanished into inner offices. The pocket-com kept beeping. She thumbed it on.

"Yes, dammit!"

It was Mischa, asking did she need help.

"Not actually," she said, and flipped the display on her hand-held again, to market display, mere mind-filler, something to look at and think about before she went mad.

Mischa chattered at her.

"Yeah," she said, "nice. No, I don't need help. You're driving me crazy, Mischa. I'm busy here. All right?"

She thumbed the switch and cut him off. Didn't care what he was saying. The agent came back with a woman in a more expensive suit. "We're talking about a stolen passport?"

"This—" She laid the ID on the counter. "—is a duplicate of my son's ID. I want to know, does the agent remember this face?"

"Come into the office, Ms. . . ."

"Hawkins." She passed the counter, she sat in a nicer office, she waited. She drank free coffee and entered searches on the hand-held for low-mass goods, and sat there for forty-three minutes before the woman in the suit brought a uniformed customs agent into the office.

"Ms. Hawkins. Officer Lee. Officer Lee is the one that read the passport through at board-call. Officer Lee, this is the young man's mother."

The officer handed the ID to her. "I do remember him," the officer said. "He'd forgotten his passport. The captain came down to be sure he got ID'd. It *was* that boy, Ms. Hawkins, very well dressed, in the company of a pretty young woman and a man. Came up in a taxi. I thought then, that cost them. But the boy didn't act upset, except about the passport. Went right to the captain, he and the girl. They walked in together."

"How did he get out there without a passport?"

"Happens. He went out with a group, should've gotten it from the officer, once they'd cleared customs, but he didn't. Captain said he hadn't missed it til the board–call, and he panicked."

"This man with them."

"Rough-looking. Cheerful fellow. Drunk as a lord. Papers perfectly in order. Cook's mate."

"No visible threat."

The agent went very sober for a moment. "You mean was he drafted back? Didn't look to be. The young man spoke for himself, apologized about the passport, had a new haircut, clothes, brand new duffle, everything first class. Met the captain on friendly terms."

"Ms. Hawkins. Would you like to sit down?"

Out of nowhere a hand grabbed her arm. She didn't need support. She shrugged it off, took a deep breath, took out her wallet and managed to get the ID into the slot.

"Sit down," the woman said.

She did. The agent offered to get her water. She said yes. She wasn't through asking questions and they were distressed on her account, moving to get her whatever she wanted. "I want the credit record. If my son was on this station, I want to know who paid, where he slept. . ."

The woman looked doubtful. The damn com beeped again, and she cut it off, completely. "I have to know," she said. "This is my *son*."

"Just a minute," the woman said, and went somewhere. Officer Lee came back with the water and sat and asked her stupid questions, trying to distract her. She kept her calm, played the part. It was maybe thirty minutes before the woman came back, looking grim, and said there hadn't been any credit record, but that the young woman, the passport number he'd been with on customs exit, had run up big bills at the fanciest sleepover on Pell. Big bills at a clothing store. At Pell's fanciest restaurant. Dinner for two. Lot of drinks.

"I see," she said, a little numb, it was true. Maybe a little grey around the edges. But it did answer things.

"You might check station mail. He might have left a message."

"I have, thank you, Ms. . . ."

"Raines."

"Ms. Raines. Thank you very much." She shook hands. She was polite. She thanked Officer Lee.

She came to herself maybe half an hour later, in front of a shop window, and didn't know where she was until she looked at the dock signs opposite.

She had to get out of this port. She had to find that son of a bitch. Forget Tom. A nice-looking girl, fancy clothes, damned . . . shallow . . . kid. Probably scared, probably saw a cheap way out, just go along with it, wasn't too uncomfortable, he had a lot of money, *Corinthian* would give it to him, because *Austin* wanted to get to her. Austin wasn't going to drop the boy in any port, wasn't going to sell him out to the Fleet, no need. Tom had sold himself, for a fancy bed and fancy clothes and the best restaurants and a girl who'd do whatever it took to keep him and keep his mouth shut.

Damn him. You could see the boy's point of view. Easier to be courted than shake his fist in Austin's face and take the hits.

Easier to be let loose dockside with a pretty girl and more money than *Sprite* ever allotted its junior crew. Easier to be plied with lies and promises. Austin could be a charming bastard. A very charming bastard, give or take that the rough edge wasn't a put-on, far from it.

And give or take that the man's taste in bedmates ran to whores. That detail wasn't going to impact Tom's little bubble too seriously.

Hell!

She went to a bar. She ordered a drink, *not* her habit. She flipped on the hand-held, drank, and stared at the meaningless scroll of figures. She couldn't leave this port until they'd off-loaded. That was happening, as fast as the cans could roll out.

And that bastard on *Corinthian* was on his way back through Tripoint.

She'd *suspected* Tripoint was the dark hole where *Corinthian* pursued its private business, the off-the-record trades with God knew what agencies—it was a vast, gravitationally disturbed space, with no station to provide an information-flow: a dozen ships could lie there, silent, absolutely impossible to spot if you didn't know exactly where they were; ships could move, and the place was so vast the presence-wave wouldn't reach you for hours . . . you didn't know what might be watching you.

But *Corinthian* hadn't waited on this leg—they'd kited through and been gone by the time they'd come through.

Expecting trouble, it was clear.

Time-wise, *Corinthian* was in hyperspace now. A ship that followed them for the next month, real-time, would exist there right along with them until *Corinthian* dropped out again, and the vector was Tripoint. Again. Where *Corinthian* had business to do.

But *Sprite* couldn't catch them. The gods of physics afforded no chance to one freighter to overtake another with *Corinthian*'s head start—unless *Sprite* was running empty, with outright *nothing* in the holds when she went into hyperspace.

Tell the Family they were going back to Viking empty? That, having cleared one chancy low-mass, high-value deal at Pell, for which they'd had to dip into bank reserves, they were going to throw away everything they'd just gained at enormous risk—and run empty back to Viking-via-Tripoint?

No way. No way in hell. She could muster the votes against Mischa on the matter of the Pell run, because she could threaten the sure economic disaster of her quitting, against the promise of profit. She couldn't get anywhere in a vote by demanding a disaster.

She swallowed a mouthful of ice-melt and vodka and did a different-criteria search through the market.

Pell . . . was the gateway to Earth. To arts. To *culture.*

Books. Zero mass. Vids. Software. Distribution licenses. Always high-priced because ships bid on them. But ships only bid so much, usually scooping up what they could get without a fight, because it was a chancy market, riding local fads, and the willingness of some station-side promoter to take it off your hands where you were going . . . so if you were willing to gamble big that you knew tastes where it was going . . . ordinarily you could get it, the info-market being quiet, low-tension, not subject to big bids from ships that better understood the market for frozen foods and machine parts.

She took out her stylus, punched the keys you couldn't accidentally access with bare fingers, and money moved.

Data moved.

Data flooded into *Sprite*'s black-box info-storage. Permits, licenses. Credit. Text. Images. Patents. Two solid hours, while she sipped fruit-juice and vodka, of high-speed input—in which the info-market accelerated, picked up interest on some items—then hyped into a wild surge of activity.

She traded back some books, some vids, snapped up rights less useful to ships that didn't reach deep in Union territory: license to reproduce at Union ports and points further, exclusive rights down routes reachable from Unionside—prices ballooned as ships bid to get a speculative commodity they regularly dabbled in, rights they routinely bid on, ships and stationside interests battling each other for what somebody unknown was going for in huge quantities. The whole info-market soared as station-side speculators and automatic trading programs saw a rising price and a limited availability and went for it. Feeding frenzy set in, sent prices crazy. She sat it out for fifteen minutes and sipped her drink while the market computers registered a flurry of trades.

Four ships and one publishing house released major holdings

to profit-take on the market, she grabbed it all and resold, bought hand and fist on the panic, and the market dropped and rose and ticked into stability as the regulators slammed the lid on.

She keyed *Sprite* for departure at m2330h, then, scant time to get the Dee Imports cans offloaded and get the tanks filled.

After which, she turned on her pocket-com and told Mischa they were in count for departure in under twenty-four hours, beep everybody who was out.

"Marie," Mischa said calmly, *"where are you?"* Less calmly: *"—Are you in some bar?"*

"Noisy? I said 24 hours, Mischa, do you copy? We're bought up. We're going. I've made a profit just sitting here and logged us for departure. You can check the schedule board."

"Marie. We aren't loaded."

"Zero-mass. Publishing rights. Tons of publishing rights. We're bought and loaded. It's in *Sprite*'s databanks right now, didn't you notice that little light flicker? Every cent we have in credit. It's time-critical and I suggest we pull out the second the tanks are filled."

"Damn you! Get your ass back on this ship, Marie! Dump that infoshit back on the market, resell and get our money back! You're not pulling this!"

"Mischa, sweet, we've made money, as stands. There's been a modest little trade war in the last few hours and the market's gone under regulatory controls, now. There's really no way to make anything short-term under a regulatory, you know that. If we sell now, we sell at a loss. So we'd better make that schedule, Mischa. Dear. It'll work."

"This is going to a vote, Marie. Your post is going to a vote!"

"I'll call yours to one, too, sweet. Think about it. I've made us money in this port. I'll make us money where we're going."

"And where's that? What area's this damn infodump valid for?"

Mischa's grammar was going.

"Marie?"

"Cyteen, via Viking, via hell, brother. It's what we have to do. And speed counts. *Trust* me."

—— *ii* ——

WAVES UPON WAVES, SCARY climb into nothing and nowhere. Hand brushed Tom's brow. Voice, ever so far, whispered to him.

His heart started beating too fast. Colors flared and ran like dyes across his vision. It was Saby he was with. Saby's bed. He could feel her presence by him.

Feel the hovering presence, too, then a change in pitch of the surface he lay on. A finger brushed his cheek.

"You hear me, Tommy? No good shamming, I know you do."

"Leave me alone," he tried to say.

"Person's truly sorry, Tommy-lad." For a while the touch went away, and came back again. The universe quaked. Ran colors. Tilted.

"Stop it, dammit. Saby's. Saby's place, here."

"Yeah, sorry, Tommy-person. Didn't come to devil you. Came to be sure you were all right." Air whispered against his forehead. A touch followed. "Gets lonely, in the dark. Gets cold. You know it. They don't. You doing all right?"

"Yeah."

"My fault you waked. Sex'll do it sometimes. —And hell if I wanted Christian to ship you out to Earth—selfish me. I tried my best to warn you, Tommy-person, short of all the trouble you had. Tried to make you hear me. But you went out with him all the same. And now look. Saby's got you. I lost out again."

He felt the loneliness, and the cold. Then . . . just felt/smelled/saw the colors a while. And vast, terrifying silence. He tried to move, then. He couldn't feel things. Couldn't tell up from down. He leaned into space, flinched back toward solid limits, and thought he was falling.

Arms were there. Caught him. Hands showed him where level was. "Tommy-person," a voice said. "Sillyass. Easy. Easy. You took the trank. It's still in your system, and I can't watch you all the time. Break your silly neck, you will, or your nose. Lie still. Lie still. Enjoy it. Go with it . . . like sex . . . you got to go with it. You got to like it.—Deep breath. The willies will stop."

He lay still—he thought he was lying down, Saby lying near him, but whether it was light or dark didn't seem relevant to his eyes. He saw, somehow, or something like. The brain kept shifting things around or the walls truly ran in streams of color. Things just were. Couldn't see Capella, then shivered at a strangeness as her hand met his body.

"Where were you?" he tried to ask.

"Upside, mostly," Capella said. "The bridge. Everybody's cold, everybody's still. Don't worry, I won't touch you, just a sit-a-while, just a voice."

"Yeah," he said. He thought he could see and feel her, then, sitting on the edge of the bed, elbows on her knees, depressing the mattress.

"Yeah, well, once you start to, you know, be aware, the trank's real chancy. You're a little disconnected. Distances go down a tunnel, don't they?"

"Long. Long tunnel," he said, because it was. That very well described it. He was astonished and relieved that someone else could see what he thought was his own senses out of control. "Cold." He didn't remember walking. Didn't know where he was, just that he was on his feet in a wildly tilting universe, but Capella's hand found his arm. He was going to be sick, and then he wasn't. Was just lying on his bed trying to be steadily solid.

"Relax. Easy. I got you. I won't let you fall."

Two deep breaths.

"You can tell, you know. The ones that fight it. The ones that can hear you. More can than do, if you understand."

"Don't. Understand."

"Yeah. Easy. Don't know why it's cold. Metabolism, I guess. Maybe using up more 'n we take in. You'll drop a few kilos. Dehydrate. You got to drink, Tommy. Brought you a raft of the green stuff. Drink up."

Didn't want to. Wasn't tracking real well. But you learned, if somebody said drink, you drank, no matter the taste.

Didn't taste green. Tasted purple. Orange. Smelled blue. Stuff ran in front of his eyes. Colors made curls like water and oil in free-fall. Made you sick awhile. But it went away.

"Better?"

"Uh-huh," he agreed. It sounded reasonable. Anything would have gotten his agreement, echoing as it did, being color, and taste. It echoed on for a long, frightening while.

"We got a little problem out there," Capella said, after a long silence. He felt that sinking of the edge that told him most surely Capella was there, like a depression in space itself. "I think now there's maybe three of us. But the instruments are screwed, you can't tell, sometimes you get echoes off the interface, you see yourself. Lot of echoes in the sheet, sometimes from clear to hell and gone, you never don't know where they come from. Maybe not even human, who knows?"

"Don't understand."

"Ships, Tommy-love. Ships in the same relevance of space-time. When the Fleet would jump, several ships together, all space'd go crazy."

"Trouble?" He couldn't figure what she was saying. Couldn't figure if she was asking help. Couldn't stand up. "What do you want?"

"Talk. Just talk to me. Give me a voice, Tommy. I've heard the music too long."

He didn't understand about the music. But maybe that was what he heard, too, when he thought about it, you could call it music, a deep, deep sound, that went through the bones.

He heard it deeper and deeper. It might have been another time. When seemed irrelevant as where. Capella raked a hand through her hair, looked distractedly, desperately at the wall, the overhead, said, quietly, "Something's screaming out there. Hear it? Honest freighter passing, what it most sounds like, but I don't bet on it. We can fake ID, too, leastwise for a ship. So can Patrick. Sumbitch."

"Who?"

"Patrick. Mazianni spook. One of Edger's skuz, and Edger is not our friend. Chased us out of Pell, Patrick did, and this trading dump is lost to us, Tommy-person, no question he'll find it. Everything we can leave at Tripoint is loss—if not to him, to the cops: one or the other'll get it for sure. But, problem is, we can't leave the system without offloading—we unquestionably got to shed mass somehow—can't outrun this bastard otherwise. He's on us, and there's this very important little card . . . Shit, shit, *shit!*"

Shivery feeling. Like . . . things happened again and again, bump, bump, against the nerves, like the same colors, the same events, kept coming back, right through him, waves of sound bouncing off and coming back, off and back, heartbeat trying to synch with the waves, pressure in the ears, behind the eyes, in the brain-stem.

Touch came at his shoulder. Hard grip. Painful.

"Serious stuff. Tom. I want you to listen to me now, deadly serious. I want you to remember it."

Things came and went. Covers whispered. Bed tilted. Capella leaned close. "We dump down hard, and we're mass-heavy to start with. So you keep those belts on."

"Yeah."

"Dockers are going to earn their pay, now, no question. Unload fast as we can. I thought maybe we could skim on through, maybe make Viking, loaded as we are, but this sumbitch is good. He's on us, not overjumping, and we can't make it: if he adds his mass to ours in hyperspace, he can push us faster on the exit than we can brake with the mass we're hauling, that's what it adds up to—send us right to Viking and right into hungry, hot old Ep-Eridani."

"You sure?" Falling into a sun . . . wasn't how he wanted to go.

Colors came and ran in disturbed sheets. Space warped and twisted.

"Tommy, I've worked it every way I can think of and I can't drop us far enough out that we can do any damn thing but fall. He can stop, but us, with all the mass, one way we end up plasma and sunbeams and the other we go outbound with no fuel. Patrick-bastard's given me no choice."

"Shit. . ."

"No, now, listen, Tom. You listen. I got to drop us in solid at Tripoint, if I can fake him once. Use our mass to throw *him,* here. In one scenario, I won't throw him far enough and he'll be in our laps. In the one I want, we'll buy that time we need to dump mass. Depends on if Patrick reads my intention to drop us out, and if Patrick-bastard knows to a navigational precision just where that supply dump is. I *do.*"

Shook his head. "Can't do." Didn't like what he was hearing. Didn't know you could control anything in hyperspace . . . he knew there were things you could do right at the edge of jump or drop, but . . . this . . . God. . . .

"Bet our lives I can. Have to. Patrick's out there. And I can't wake Austin up to tell him how things in the universe have changed, you read me, Tommy-person? You got to read me, Tommy, pay attention."

"I hear."

"You got to tell Austin it's no doublecross. He doesn't trust me. And this time he's got to. This old hulk sits in the dark out there, you follow me? And it's got stuff inside for us to take and it's got loading racks we can offput stuff to, real fast."

"*That's* what those cans were, at Viking."

"Old, old cans, from the War. Salvage, legitimate salvage, if it didn't come from the Fleet. And ordinarily another ship comes to this old hulk and gets the cans we leave in trade, and takes our cans to somewhere else. But this isn't ordinary. Patrick's not our breed. You want to say Mazianni, Patrick's

Mazianni, no question, not Fleet, Tommy. Not our friend. He's a damn pirate, he'll have found our old hulk before we're done, he's armed a helluva lot heavier than he looks, and there's one way out of this thing—put a certain key in that old wreck and give it the right code and she'll let you aboard and credit your offload. Give her another one and she remembers things she's otherwise forgot. Got to have that card in the slot and that message input, Tommy. If Patrick comes at us, and he will, got to have that message input. Then that old hulk's our friend. Then she'll give us authorizations we got to have, bottom line, got to have to survive. There's a port we can go to, trust me on this."

What other port? he asked himself. Out of Tripoint there was Mariner, or Viking, cheapest vector out, or there was Pell, priciest, fuel-wise.

But he was following most of it. At least . . . the cargo part. The mass they had to get rid of before they came in at Viking velocity-high and fuel-short, aimed at the sun.

And he believed there was something out there dogging them in hyperspace: he *felt* something he couldn't explain.

But moral argument and promises of deliverance from a person he didn't half trust himself? Not so easy.

He felt Capella straighten his collar.

"Tommy-person. If I say on com, we got to move, we got to move. Tell Austin—if I was against him—I'd have switched keys on him. You know I could've, if he doesn't. I can open any door on this ship, pick any pocket right now. He's got that key I'm talking about. I'll give him the code that answers that son of a bitch out there, the way I said. If everything goes wrong—he's got to use it. Tell him so. Understand?"

"Chance this Patrick does know . . . where we're going?"

"We see in the dark, lover. But not that well. Even figuring that old hulk's on the Pell reach and the Tripoint perimeter . . . that's a lot of space to search, for a quiet object. No. Odds are absolutely on him not knowing, especially the way he's riding us. He doesn't want to lose track of us. And if he's any appreciable distance past us, hard-ordnance is impossible for him. Not impossible for us. We'll fire right down his tail. That's what I'll try to do, position us where we got that chance. But Austin's going to come out with everything screwed. Cargo screwed. Extra ship in the soup. Man's going to be real damn mad at me."

"Not your fault."

"Yeah. But, you got to understand, I'm on real short credit with him."

"Don't understand."

"Since Chrissy's stunt at Pell? Both of us are on Austin's shit-list. I want you to know this one more detail: this little card Austin's got? Austin's *got* to offload that mass, that's one, because we're loaded, and Patrick isn't; and he's got to feed the old wreck that keycard real fast, close as I'm dropping us. Austin doesn't know that. It's not a detail he's ever needed to know. Keeps the suppliers honest, you understand. Now he has to know. That key-card gets the hold to open, in the lock slot. But in the cargo console slot, with the right code, that old wreck can write to that key-card—and he's *got* to get me that authorization, he's *got* to use that codeword before we get out of here. But if happens he doesn't believe me—Tommy, if he won't input or if he takes me off that nav board, we are screwed. I've got to be on the bridge. Beatrice has got to take the next figures I give her. If the captain orders me off the bridge, I tell you, I'm locking-down the navigation computers."

"You can't do that!"

"Oh, I can do it, Tommy, I can do it, and Bianco can probably crack my lock, given an hour or so. But Patrick'll blow us to hell first. Austin will figure that part with no prompt at all."

"God, you're crazy."

"I've been accused of that. But you watch me not talk, Tommy-sweet. Austin can ask me, pretty please. Austin can do what I say." A hand brushed his forehead. "I just want somebody but me to know, if it happens. But, listen, if Austin's the man I think he is, he'll deliver that damn cargo. That card's his proof. His credit with the Fleet. Call it old-fashioned honor. I think they still use that word. He'll fight to keep it."

"How?" Consciousness came up for a moment. He saw her shadow against the running colors, solid mass, when nothing else was. Voices rang and echoed. Time might have passed. "I don't understand how you can do this. How. *Drop* us. Anywhere."

"Not much else you can control in this space, lover, just the power you can throw into the interface. Or dump off. Yeah, there's things I can do. Patrick-bastard's trying to hang back on me, not using the power he's got. It's an old trick, ride our wave and try to drop in behind us. He'd like to haul me down, but it's dangerous as hell, and say he can't do it without a gravity slope, so we're safe for the while. Besides, he knows I got to dump down anyway—and I know where and he doesn't. So when we hit the Tripoint slope, he'll expect I'll bobble the field and feint a drop. Wrong. I'll drop us for real, right out from under him. So if he doesn't read my mind, he's potentiating elsewhere. Same event-packet. Puts us time-wise near simultaneous, position-wise as far separate as I can fake him, the gods of physics know where: the variables are hell, and one of 'em's Patrick. *Wish* I knew if that ghosty freighter's an echo. If it's real, she'll come down, too. Just don't know where."

He was following it. Didn't want to, but he was—at least the part that said they were riding close with ships on entry.

Military stuff.

They didn't have to be boarded. Their own navigator was the breed an honest merchanter was most afraid of.

"Tommy-love, last warning, if Austin balks—h-a-v-o-c is the code he has to input to get us that authorization I need. Key-card in the cargo console slot while you input. Two should know that, down there. Tell him, if he asks, that Capella's not betrayed him." Mouth covered his. Hand went down his side. Gentle touch. "You're such an honest lad, Tommy-person. And there are so few. Go below when they ask for help. Saby'll take you. They'll need every hand they've got down in cargo and they damn sure won't want you up where the computers are. Remember what I've said."

"Huh?"

"Saby can get you down to cargo. I want you there. You just insist. G'night, lover. See you. See you otherside." Lips touched his again, passionately, deeply, gently. "Sweet, sweet dreams, Tommy."

Trank was worn thin. Didn't know long he'd waked, over all. Not long. Not often. Now he couldn't get his equilibrium. Couldn't rest, either, after the shadow was gone.

He lay there with sounds running through his brain, in the shifting chaos. Shutting the eyes didn't stop it. Colors kept going off, flashes, like pressure against the eyes. Thoughts kept going, turning back on each other, and he wanted to believe. Wanted to believe his night-walker was telling, however selectively, the truth.

Didn't know if it was scrambled logic, or if what you heard when the brain was flashing colors and rumbling with thunder that wasn't sound . . . had to stick in your head, and you couldn't discriminate what was lies.

Distances go down a tunnel, don't they?

Remember what I've said . . .

—— *iii* ——

SHIP DROPPED. LONG, long sequence. Body ached.

The whole of space seemed to bend.

Supposed to be a hard one, it was all right, it was supposed to be this way.

Then . . . he began to think it wasn't going right, that the ship was in trouble.

Something boomed through the hull. Vibration began—that experience didn't explain. He grabbed at Saby's hand, felt Saby's fingers bend around his.

He tried to keep his breaths deep and even. Dreams ran and

melted color across his vision. Memories of sound. Memories of a lingering, deeply erotic kiss, a touch running over his skin.

Boom. Thump. His pulse pounded

A moment of profound hush, the air gone numb.

Hydraulics worked, somewhere in the frame. Wasn't cargo. Couldn't figure . . .

Third loud boom. He'd never heard a ship sound like that on entry.

"We are here." A calm voice on com. Beatrice's, he thought, comforted by that icy competence. *"Stay belted. We are in docking approach. Essential movement only."*

It didn't seem real. "Can't," he muttered, thinking he must have passed out a while, lost some hours of time. "Docking? We can't be, this soon."

"We hit real close to the target," Saby murmured. "Pella's good. She always does this one." Her hand moved. He turned his head, making the whole universe seem to tilt. Saby had found the nutri-packs, he thought. He heard the rustling, reached to help her.

Pilot couldn't be better off. Trying to dock. The shakes crawling up a body's gut respected no occupation and no emergency, while Capella . . .

Dropping a ship straight into docking approach—couldn't do that, damn crazy woman . . . at Tripoint, no less, triple, unstable mass . . .

Computer lockdown.

Bloody hell . . .

Fingers were numb, on the seal of the packet Saby gave him.

Boom. Again.

Hands shook. "What *is* that?" he asked.

"That's us firing." Saby's voice was faint. Scared-sounding. "We fired once as we came out. Inertial-mass ordnance goes a major fraction of light, then. Whoever we're shooting at . . . for him to fire upslope, 's too far for his missiles, even internalpropulsions. He's got to hope we run into it. Seen this before, thanks. Don't like it."

Patrick, Capella had said—when had she said? —This Patrick, navigator. Like her. Another one that saw in the dark. Saw them—the way he'd seen—

Once you, you know, become aware . . .

Colors running. *Sound* coming at them . . . weaving back and forth, through bone and brain. . . .

Another volley.

Couldn't get the damn 'pack tube free. Hands trembled. Saby was beside him, trying to get herself collected. They were lying in a nest of spent nutri-packs.

Gets cold. Gets lonely. Tommy-love.

— *iv* —

NOTE ON THE PRESSURE-SLATE: propped up and braced against Austin's number one monitor, in an all-too-familiar hand: *I got us here. Spook rode us all the way, entrained a third ship of some kind, likely a light-armed freighter. Check screen. Sorry—Viking try was screwed, mass far exceeding brake with spook and freighter in packet.*

FYI: hulk is heavy armed and will fire if we don't provide keycard in airlock slot as usual within one hour from our crossing her perimeter, with firing in system. Always true. Now you need to know. If, arriving in her perimeter, we move any direction but toward her—she is not our friend. Maneuver or delay of approach not advisable. Patrick wants the key-card. May try to cripple, not kill. Respectfully, sir, suggest you not bet the ship on it. PS. You want Patrick's ass, you put card in the wreck's cargo console slot, input code HAVOC. Absolute necessity you do this or we don't leave. Meanwhile will lay course for next point. Must offload all cargo mass to reach. Safe port— distance 7 lights. Capella.

"Bloody *hell!*"

He shot a look toward Capella's station. Capella's back was turned. The second chief navigator was busy. Austin took a swallow, forced it down, stared at the nav screen that came up on his second monitor, first-formed data.

There *wasn't* any port out of Tripoint that lay at seven lights. Not Pell. Not Viking. Loaded, they *couldn't* do it. Unloaded, even, it was a stretch for *Corinthian.*

And where, for God's sake? What dark spot in the universe was the woman calc'ing jump for?

Meanwhile the ship was trimming up, under Beatrice's hands, with increasing jolts of the attitude jets.

Hard jolt. Stomach heaved. He grabbed another nutri-pack from the clip, ripped the tube out, sucked down a mouthful of copper-tasting fluid as navigation data arrived suddenly on his screen, first re-make since the drop.

Never got used to notes turning up out of the dark.

Didn't like unscheduled problems arriving out of it, either.

Three ships. *Corinthian,* near the Object, all right, and inbound. At distance, about 2 seconds light beyond them on their vector, *Silver Dream,* and at 1 second's remove—

Sprite.

Shit. —*Shit!*

"Michaels!"

"*Sir.*"

"That's *Sprite.*"

"*Just saw that. Dropped in front of us. Fifteen hour climb for their missiles. We're still all right.*"

A safe port, seven lights fucking distant? Off into the dark, to some Fleet refuge their navigator kept secret until now? A place no Union or Alliance optics had ever just happened to find, when optics had made a thorough scan of the edges of space?

"Nav. Why not Viking next?"

"*Wouldn't risk it, sir, if that freighter survives.*"

"Nerves, nav. Plot Viking, as an in-case."

"*Yes, sir. But if that freighter gets out of here, they'll report. They*

got a good position to see where we're working. Our cargo-site . . .
is blown, 'less they and Patrick both go to hell. And, sir, the Fleet
said when they sent me . . . there's a place you could go. I need that
little card validated, captain-sir, and I can take you there, safe and
sure. But I got to have the card. So does Patrick."

Give the bastard the card, was the thought in his mind.
Second chief's refuge at seven lights could just as well be a trap.
Crew taken. Ship confiscated for military refit. Rumor held it
still happened.

And Capella wanted to take them off into the dark, getting
them clear of this faction of the Fleet, while the other faction,
Capella's faction, was going to reward them with some damn
secret port for protecting a key-card to a hulk that, if they got
out of this, a freighter now knew for what it was?

Dammittobloody*hell* . . .

Not a chance, not a damn chance he'd heard all the truth
from the second chief yet.

And the *Hawkins* ship?

Firing was still going on, periodic *boom* as ordnance left
Corinthian.

Corinthian had fired at *Silver Dream* initially from a high-
energy point. Inertial-mass cannon-balls or self-propelled
nukes were equally deadly at that v. And they'd sent—were
still sending, at intervals—swarms of inerts after that ship.
Hindmost had the advantage in that regard.

Their inerts might equally well hit *Sprite*. The freighter had
shed all relative v, and they were close enough to be in danger—
he hadn't seen the fire-path calc'ed, but both *Sprite* and *Silver
Dream* had dropped late, beyond them.

Silver Dream had likewise dumped hard, then spent time
on an instant evasive maneuver, expecting those inerts to be
traveling up their backside, no question: the ship was a survi-
vor, to be this old in the game. Two seconds off from their
informational wavefront. Patrick knew where they were, no
question.

But even powered missiles weren't an option for Patrick to

use, not from a retreating vector at two light-seconds remove—
a single light-second or so past its target was worse luck for a
starship than a light-hour: *Silver Dream*'s stardrive couldn't
jump short enough to close the gap, Patrick's launch platform
was negative *v* relative to his target, and Patrick's only choice
now was a hard realspace run up to meaningful speed, with
Corinthian ordnance coming right down his path.

He had to reposition for his run in.

Meanwhile a noisy damn Hawkins freighter was flooding its
stupid *Sprite-Sprite-Sprite* ID out into the EM ambient because
Sprite didn't have a damn cut-off.

And *Sprite,* carrying a Pell-origin drift?

God, it was surreal. What *wasn't Sprite* hauling, that it could
have reached Pell and all but over-jumped them coming back
toward Viking again, until their collective mass snagged it into
system-drop with them? Low-mass cargo for sure.

Marie Hawkins' hate? Marie Hawkins' obsession?

He blinked, swallowed another metallic mouthful of liquid
and a shudder raced through his gut, maybe the nutrient, maybe
the realization of a ship full of fools and a handful of genuine
innocents sitting out there noisier than very hell, at a single
degree of separation from their position relative to the spook,
the spook maneuvering to bear down on them and consequently on *Sprite* as fast as Patrick could get here, God help the
woman, and God help her whole ship.

Sprite was a registered ID, on the ship-lists. The spook could
check her out in the flick of a key. *Silver Dream* could, maybe,
if Marie was lucky, decide that *Sprite* was a legitimate freighter,
just happening in, by some cosmic luck, and ignore it, like a
good, quiet spook.

Or the spook could figure it was *Corinthian* faking ID, or
that it was something else faking ID, and factor them into its
targeting decisions.

Ordnance from *Corinthian* should go right past *Sprite,* out
into the dark. The numbers showing now were a miss by an
absolute hair. Inerts or not, *Sprite* sensors should pick some-

thing up when that volley went past their bows. And *Silver Dream* might not be sure which ship it came from.

Figure it, Mischa Hawkins. Figure we're not firing at you. Read the ambient. Look out at the dark, you damn fool, just once in your life, look out there and ask yourself the right question.

There's fire coming the other way. Move the damn ship.

Burst from the trim jets. He snatched after another nutri-pack.

Get the ship into mate with their supply dump, yeah. They'd always dropped close. Capella was good.

Always made it well inside an hour. Put the card in, that was one thing. Always put the card in. It credited them, when they used it again, at Viking—along with the cargo always waiting for them here.

Capella had never mentioned that the old hulk had a kill-function.

Not your friend, hell.

But enter a code called HAVOC in that hulk, on their Fleet navigator's say-so, a code of that nature, into what she now admitted was armed, and she didn't tell you specifically what it did or where its hostile action stopped?

Not unless they had no . . . bloody . . . choice.

⚊ *v* ⚊

THE EMERGENCY SIREN WAS WAILING through the ship, Duran was on com, ordering *Sprite*'s kids' loft to take immediate emergency procedures, Paxton had been on a second ago saying they'd jumped short, nobody knew what the hell had happened, or why they'd dropped short of their intention, except a rough drop and then something going past them, so high-mass, meaning fast, that they couldn't figure what it was.

"Satisfied?" Mischa spared breath to ask her. "Satisfied?"

"Change coordinates." Marie pounded the counter above

Mischa's console softly with a clenched fist, tried to slow her breaths. A post-jump headache and an adrenaline overload didn't help. "Get us *down*, dammit. Get us up, get us out of the plane of fire."

"Somebody's back there," Paxton was saying, and Sully, helm, was yelling at Mischa, off-com,

"It was missiles, it's a heave-to order! It could be Military, one of them is bound to be the Military, chasing *Corinthian*— we can't go shooting at shadows, dammit!"

"Track point of origin," Marie said.

"We can't go firing—"

"Sully, just shut up!" Mischa, off-com himself. "I heard you! Get a point of origin!" Mischa was sweating. "Shut that damn siren off! God!"

"Hindmost is *Corinthian*," Marie said.

"*Corinthian, Corinthian,* I'm sick to death of *Corinthian,* I'm sick to death of Bowe, I'm sick to death of you and that damn kid! I don't want to hear about him, I don't want to hear any more of your damn ideas, Marie, just sit down and keep your mouth shut! You don't know anything about missiles, you don't know what you've stirred up, you got us into this mess, now, just get the hell back to your finagling damn deals and leave ops to people who know what they're doing."

"Mischa, —get us out of—"

Proximity klaxon went off. Marie looked up, stared at the screens, some of which flared red, winced, but it was less than the blink of an eye.

Whatever it was, second volley, had passed them into the dark.

"Where *is* he? Damn him, where is he?"

"They're not targeting us," Marie said. "We're still alive."

"They're firing at the Military," Sully said.

"Sully, for God's sake, — Marie, —shut *up!*"

"Mischa." Marie rapped the console, got a calm word in. "Take us out of plane. Now. Settle who and where later."

"Sit down! We're going on to Viking, we'll meet Bowe there, if that's what it takes. We'll do it where there's police."

"Viking's in the direction it's firing at, you damn fool!"

"I said sit down! We don't know where the hell we are. We've come down way out on the fringes, we have a navigational problem we have to solve before we complicate it with any—"

She brought her fist down on the console. "Shut *up*, Mischa, dammit! Saja, —Sully, plus 2 out of plane at 5 g's, count of five, *now!*"

"Set," helm said.

"Abort that, Sully, kill it!"

"Somebody better do something," Sully said.

Marie flung herself onto a safety bench and grabbed the belts. Shoved the catches closed.

"I'm calling a captaincy vote. Now. Saja. Sully. *Do it!*"

Ship moved. Hard.

— *vi* —

"Scared them," Mike remarked. Austin murmured a preoccupied yeah, and registered *Sprite*'s in-progress coordinate change as one problem down. Or up. At least not in line of fire. *Sprite* moved, sending its noisy ID out into the dark. *Corinthian* moved in EM silence, except the minor engines, passive scan only.

Figure *Silver Dream* was in motion, too, not in hard-scan range, but gathering realspace speed, off which her own missiles and inerts could be effective.

A Fleet renegade. Hope this Patrick didn't have an approach code that could let him dive inside the hulk's self-defined perimeter. Every klick he had to maneuver, every precaution he had to take to avoid it was an accuracy problem. And if he didn't know the hulk was armed—he knew *Corinthian* was; and had to assume that *Sprite* was.

And, mistake—but they weren't going to explain it—Patrick had to assume that *Sprite* was on *Corinthian*'s side, and had just maneuvered to fire up *Silver Dream*'s approach path.

Number two monitor had just gone live. A blinking blue circle framed a patch of what could look exactly like every other patch of starry space.

The Object was out there. That was what Bianco meant by switching him that black image, with the dot flashing in the center. Couldn't see it yet. Graininess of the image was equal to the dusting of stars equally dim.

Meanwhile . . . meanwhile . . . ask what *Sprite* thought it was going to do, with its little rail-gun, at one light-second.

Fire at them or fire at *Silver Dream,* who wouldn't believe protestations of non-combatancy.

Question who was in control on that ship, or what it was bidding for. And if Capella was right . . .

"Nav."

"*Sir.*"

"Does the Object take being fired toward?"

"*No, sir, it's real pissed if that happens. Recommend not.*"

Could guess that, all right. Hope the fool on *Sprite* didn't try it.

And maybe Patrick knew that, too, or suspected it, and planned not to fire but once. One heavy hit. Blow the hulk *and* them, together, the Mazianni's problem solved—if second chief was wrong and Patrick didn't have her head or that card on that high a priority.

A shadow appeared on the screen that targeted the hulk, now, frighteningly fast growth of a darkness against the dust.

Freighter. Years dead. Gutted. As good a warehouse as you could ask for, a cargo-handling rig as fast as a completely zero-g rack could afford, just hit the release when they came off the line and hope a rebound didn't come back at you . . . hellish enough, trying to rush the cans out.

Damn lunatic *Sprite* trying to shoot two-credit missiles at you the while. . . .

But the hands were good, and that cargo offload could be blinding fast, if you weren't worrying about fragiles—and most of what they were hauling wasn't, give or take the Scotch.

A few real high-mass cans. Steel rods. They were to worry about, when they were in motion. Inertial within the capacity of that rack, their mass exceeded can limits. Bitchy load even on a station dock, at their slow speeds. And a zero-g line tended to develop oscillations—*hell* dealing with that mass.

Hope Patrick made acquaintance of the inerts, head on, before he gathered v enough for shielding effect. It took far longer to dock and offload than it did to run those cans out into space . . . but inside the hulk's perimeter, with that card in, they had, according to the second chief, something she vitally needed . . . provided Patrick didn't also have codes to let him approach.

Damn lot of variables.

And Patrick's estimated position was shifting constantly now in the numbers on his screen. Patrick had begun his run—in longscan's primary estimation. That estimated v was coming up fast.

Couldn't fire dead ahead while you were putting on v like that—you'd run into your own ordnance. Patrick had to get off a passing or retreating shot. The EM bath that *Sprite*'s ID was sending out was no help at all. It echoed off solids, just like radar. Thank you, thank you, Marie Hawkins.

"This HAVOC code, nav, just what's it do?"

"*Sir, I think it'll respect the user. Nothing else. Damn sure nothing shooting at it.*"

"Hulk won't do that anyway, will it?"

"*Sir, I'm not need-to-know on that level.*"

Shit.

And the Hawkinses out there, ship full of fools.

Shit on them.

Beatrice wasn't talking. Not since drop. Probably was aware, but when Beatrice was working this particular bitch of an approach, she was in her own universe. The Object had no motion to speak of, but their two masses made one bitch of an impact possible, if they didn't soft-touch, and the Object didn't talk to you. Silent as any spook, always. Cold. Very.

Beatrice professed not to like it.

Like she didn't like sex.

Sudden slam from the engines. The screen suddenly showed an on-rushing dark spot. The blot on the stars rushed at the camera. Filled the screen, total dark.

Jolt. Stop.

The body had—gut-level, intellectual, rational functions to the contrary, and no matter how many times they'd done it—braced for impact.

"We have the Object between us and *Sprite,*" Beatrice announced calmly, then, smoothly as on station approach. "Touch in ten minutes. Do we believe nav, or what?"

"Thank you, helm. Yes, we believe nav, because we have no fucking choice."

He punched general com. "This is the captain. We have a very short window to offload. Enemy is in system, proceeding toward us from dead *v* at two seconds light. We will, however, offload to shed mass, and we are going to offload at all possible speed. We cannot afford mistakes. We have a narrow margin. Touch and dock in less than ten minutes. When the siren sounds, all hands, repeat, all hands, on-shift and off-, not at this moment at ops-critical stations, suit for vacuum and start cargo offload. We're going to tie down the brake levers, on both sides. We don't care if we dent the walls. I want volunteers for the release-station in the receiving hold. Hazard pay and hazard privilege both apply, and we hope the receiving equipment takes it."

—— *vii* ——

"I'M GOING," TOM SAID, still flat in bed, while trim-up went on. "Got to be at least an e-suit or something I can borrow. Saby, I swear to you. I grew up in the cargo office, I know the boards, I know the equipment. I've worked the line. I swear, I *swear* I won't screw it, I don't want to sit up here waiting to be blown."

He expected argument. But Saby didn't argue.

"Michaels has to be on the bridge. He's our gunner, he won't suit. Use his rig. I'm running Hold Technical. Just keep the cans off my neck."

Michaels. He remembered a man beaten.

Remembered why, then. Knew the rules, Tink said. Follow the rules. Ship was at stake. All their lives. Ship had its own logic. Forget everything else.

Remembered Michaels . . . saying, Kid's shaky . . . light duty . . .

Contact. Easy bump. Grapples activated, banged into lock.

Saby's belts clicked on that sound. So did his, and he cleared her path as she scrambled across—tried to help her up and threw a supporting hand against the wall, his own equilibrium not so reliable as he'd thought.

Saby didn't wait for amenities, opened the door and headed out, zipping what she'd loosed for comfort.

Crew and dockers in dress and undress thumped into the corridors at a wobbly, staggering run, generally in their direction, down lower main, knocking into walls, some of them, but going as fast as they could.

It was an eerie feeling, everybody running the same direction, like suit drill, but not drill, nothing now was drill. It was the emergency a spacer lived all his life trying never, ever to have.

The gang-up at the end of the corridor split in two directions, down the transverses, the mirror-image D blocks, where the suit lockers were—locker doors already powered open, from the bridge, suits open, helmets and harnesses suspended on their racks, a surreal gathering of human shells, crew already backing into them, sealing them in that drill a spacer could do drunk or asleep.

"Michaels!" Saby said, and shoved him at Michael's locker.

He turned, stepped into the suit backward, got his arms into the sleeves, sealed the front, kicked the release plate to bring the LS backpack and helmet down over his head and shoulders.

Seals clicked. Indicators and faceplate display flared on, confirming lifesupport and seals positive.

Came, instantly, that claustrophobic shortness of breath the suit gave him. It always got to him this way: he'd helped Marie in cargo, yeah, mostly from the ops boards safely upside—he never suited except in drills.

The borrowed rig smelled of disinfectant, of Michaels' use. The air he depended on came to him rationed by a regulator. The mass of the harness as it came free of the rack was an instant revision of body-space and center of gravity.

Another suited figure leaned into vision, adjusted something on his chest-link. SABRINA PERRAULT, the paint on the helmet said. With a decal rose. She bumped helmets.

"You all right? Com not working?"

"Yeah. It's working."

Stupid. He'd not turned his communications on. He'd sworn to her he knew what he was doing, and she knew . . .

"Channel D for private." She punched something on his shoulder. The channel indicator moved, near his chin. "Come on, expert."

She moved and he followed, at the shuffling, big-footed walk which ring rotation imposed on them, a lock-step sweating haste, back along the D-curve, toward the cargo lift as it opened.

They got in at the rear, jammed in as closely and as tightly as they could, fourteen, maybe fifteen suited bulks, before the doors shut and the lift jolted out of synch with the passenger ring.

Immediately after, one fractional pass of the ring about the core, the car banged into lock with the zero-*g* frame.

Automatic doors let them out on a dark hold. The cold of space froze their attending puff of humidified air into ice crystals in the spotty glare of the helmet lights. Hold lights flared on around them, illuminating loading machinery, racks, and tiers of cans that jammed their hold right up to the red line. A group of white-suited figures was going forward, down the still-empty cargo chute—he saw officers' sleeve patches on that lot. All around him, bodies moved, white, bulky, anonymous except for sleeve patches, non-com crew fanning out in silence along hand-railings, taking station out among the tiers of cans, ready to sort those racks out onto the main delivery track and secure the spent carriages when they came down the return track.

Saby grabbed his arm briefly, hit his chest with her hand and got his suit light on, illumination for the shadowed areas.

He wasn't tracking a hundred percent. The suit read-out wasn't in the familiar order in the chin-level display—he hadn't realized his light wasn't defaulted on; and crew knocked into them in their delay, making a gap in the line, hindering an already dangerous effort. A jump-queasy stomach and the beginnings of a headache argued he could easily become a worse problem, and he was determined not to be.

An enemy in the system?

Colors flashed, in memory. Sound wailed at them.

Got to have that card in the slot and that message input, Tommy. If Patrick comes at us, and he will, got to have that message input. Then that old hulk's our friend.

Sweat ran, a trickle down his face he couldn't wipe. He moved where Saby and the rest moved. Words echoed out of the dark in his skull, red and blue flashes smeared and ran while he hauled himself along on the hand-rail.

God, release the line brakes . . . The 4-meter cannisters, with the mass they carried . . . could probably survive the offload without bursting, if they were good, double-walled cans, no temperature-constant stuff—but Austin had called for hazard pay volunteers on the release end, and he'd seen first-hand what happened when a can broke under stress. He'd seen it happen to a ship on a station dock, brake lever accidentally jammed open. Can flew off, hit the deck, hit a support girder, killed one dockworker, sent fourteen to hospital—

"*Look out!*" came over his helmet-com. Somebody bumped him, passing down the line in a hell of a hurry. Didn't know who it was. He moved, out of breath, hand over hand down the rail that led along the can-track, trying to hit the rhythm Saby did, ahead of him—he was trying not to hold up the line behind them, because there was nobody in front, and he couldn't get his breath . . . colors washed across his vision. Remembrance of smell–taste–hearing, bone-deep sound, all but pain . . .

They were well past the hold lights, now. The can-track was a continuous-loop railing in the dim overhead, the exit-chute wall was narrowing around them, and light came as a scatter of patches where their suit lights picked out solid objects, a back-pack, a hand, a section of safety rail as they hand-over-handed into the absolute night of the chute.

Then the cargo check console materialized in Saby's chest-light, nobody manning it. Saby left the line, moved in with authority, threw the console switch that started the red motion warning strobing in the overhead . . . he hesitated, sailed off the hand-rail to clear others' way, and grabbed the console edge.

"*Run 'em out.*" That was Austin's voice over the com, on the general channel. "Get them moving, we're waiting up here."

Up here. Austin was forward, then, in the mate-up zone . . . that wasn't where the captain belonged, damn him. . . .

"*We got precious little time,*" Austin was saying. "*Shit's coming our way, but the sumbitch can't fire til he passes.*"

"*Cans are going to be all over that hold,*" somebody said. "*Damn free-fall billiards.*"

"*Yeah, yeah, best we can do, Deke, sorry, neat isn't in our capacity right now, we'll be real satisfied with out of here.*"

"*We got high-mass stuff in this load!*"

"*Deke, just watch the damn line—she's rolling!*"

Cans had started to move. Tom caught a look at Saby, lights from the console a multicolored constellation on Saby's mask

. . . busy and on a hair-trigger. Saby flipped other switches, engaging can-pickup robotics that moved the cans on their tracks way back in the tiers . . . he understood the board—he knew what process had just started; the carriages were picking up cans back there, sliding into the motorized track. The inspection brake at this console only slowed a can enough for the laser-reader to find the can customs-tags, and a deft hand to snatch off any remaining monitor plug . . . but then the tractor-chain caught the carriage and ran the can up to whatever rate of delivery the end-line brake was supposed to control.

If it wasn't latched down. Which left Saby's brake as the only regulator on a line not even designed for free-fall—God knew what motion the cans were going to pick up as they hit the chain. . . .

Stupid, stupid, *stupid* place to off-load, he said to himself, having the whole picture now, why crew had lined up along the exit track . . . human muscle, to keep those cans under control.

And no instructions . . . they'd done it before.

"You all right here?" he asked her. "You need help?"

"My job," Saby said. *"I got it. You know the board?"*

"Half-assed. I'm going on the line."

"You can stand back-up. Stay out of the track!"

Danger, then. Danger of a glitch in the line—crew forward couldn't do anything but help those cans across whatever inevitable bump in the track the mate-up with the other hold might make—never done a handoff to another ship, but it couldn't be a perfect mate—always a glitch-point, even with dockside. He moved, followed the hand-rail, knew he was heading for a potential accident-point, if somebody was going to lose a hand, once the walls narrowed—worst of all when the cans were in the mate-up, where carriages this side released and carriages the other side had damned well better be ready and adequate—

Can passed him, another, caught by the moving chain, then—he saw both sway as they whisked past him on the last tractor-section, into the cargo-chute's section, into the dark—didn't want any swinging, a swing started here could impact the side-rails, slow the cans, make a jam-up on the line.

He found a place to hang, wall at his back, safety rail between him and the track—a crewman was working there, and he joined in, met can after can with his gloved hands, until he hit a rhythm in the moves, move of his foot, move of his body—breath came too short at first, raw fear. Then he acquired a feel for the fractional degree and vector the cans tended to sway, and it became saner—the panic almost left him. He had wind enough; he heard somebody else breathing into an open mike . . . he thought it was Saby. He could hear the terse slow-up and speed-up orders to Saby's station from some officer forward in the chute, and fell into the rhythm until he all but forgot there was anything else in the universe but those cans coming faster and faster. Then something happened up ahead that shouldn't happen, the whole track shook for no reason. He couldn't hear it, but he saw the shudder in the cans—"Damn!" he heard over the com, and somebody else said: "Track's warping, she's shot a rivet, ease back, ease back."

Oh, *damn*, he thought, we're not going to make it; and Saby said:

"I got it slowed, I got it . . . Tom, get down there, get a look, tell me how bad."

He didn't ask—Saby didn't have eyes for what was happening ahead in the chute, the rig was stressed past design limits, and somebody on com was yelling at Saby to keep it rolling, dammit, keep it rolling, and giving orders to shunt tier five-c off to last-loaded, they'd run that set of cans out if the rig held and they had time . . .

Something in that load, he said to himself, something high-mass they weren't sure the equipment could take. He hauled himself along the hand-rail, along the outbound chute, as far as a section where the cans had picked up a hell of a bobble.

Cans were still coming past him. Guys were working ahead, damping down the motion with their hands and bodies, the same as they'd done higher up the line—you didn't know what kind of mass was coming at you in a given can, whether you were going to meet foam rubber or foam steel in a load. It was terrifying, but the receiving zone was yelling hurry up, speed up.

"Saby!" he said. "They got a hand-span swing at the rate you're sending 'em now, you copy?"

"*I copy. Get back here.*"

"I'm all right, do you copy?"

"*We got no damn time!*" somebody else broke in. "*Get on it, dammit, move it, move it up plus two, Saby, she'll take it—*"

That was an officer talking, by the sound of it, and he didn't belong on com. He found a space next to a big guy as the cans' delivery rate began to speed up—the several of them acting as living buffers to keep the cans moving steadily.

"*It'll be all right,*" came over his com, over somebody's hard breathing.

Didn't even know who the guy was until he'd worked up a total sweat and a can swung back, knocking him into the wall. The big guy sent the can on its way with a shove, and a one-handed reach met his grip as he rebounded off the wall—hauled him out of danger of the track, to a hand-hold he could reach.

Tink looked startled.

" 'S all right," Tom breathed, "I'm all right, Tink, thanks."

Wasn't time to talk. Cans were passing them, fast as nightmare, now. Oscillation at the warp-point had proliferated, and all he could do was keep one hand to the safety-hold, a straight-arm block to damp the motion in his area ever so little, next man to take a little more swing off, and on to the next, like assembly-line robots.

Couldn't let it stress the clamps. The track had already bowed under a mass-heavy can at too much *v*, no telling when another might come down the line—*hope* the crew in the hold were reading labels.

Oscillation grew worse. A can hit the wall, acquired a real nasty motion, slowed.

"*Hold it!*" somebody yelled. "*Got a hang-up, hold, hold, hold!*"

Cans bumped, all the way down the line. Tom hauled himself back, panting, shoulder to shoulder with Tink.

Then Austin's voice came on, and channel A's indicator flashed, general override. "*We're clear, we haven't got damn forever, Saby, let's get a move on.*"

The cans started to move again. Tom held his breath—one can had to nudge another into motion, all the way back from Saby's station, where she could let loose cans to the inertial line, that was all.

Bump, bump, bump, cans came out of the dark, nudging each other with a swing they had to damp, and the line moved, faster, faster, faster. He thought—nightmare flash—about that hostile ship out there . . . time lost, maybe fatal time.

He'd gotten the shakes into his knees, scared—exhausted, he wasn't sure.

Patrick, Capella'd said.

Patrick. Noise in the dark.

Runny blues and reds, sound that went through the bones . . . he couldn't remember. Except Capella saying, *A freighter screaming* . . .

He shoved at cans as they came, one after the other, the rack assembly moving uninterrupted, now, cans one behind the other, a moving wall of shadowed white.

Somebody screamed, on A, screamed, where official voices went back and forth. He heard Christian, then, somewhere, he had no idea where.

"*Just stay clear, stay back, it's all right. Patch it, patch! dammit, he's losing air—*"

"*Got it, got it. It's just his finger.*"

"*What's our time?*" somebody else asked, and Christian answered, "*Just do it, dammit. Keep your damn hands clear, we're one row to go.*"

Almost through. They could make it. Suddenly he couldn't get enough air, touched the air-flow regulator—but cans came in, bumped a slower can, set it in motion. Careful, careful, he

wished Saby, don't lose it, don't lose it—he ignored his short-
ened breath, shoved as cans passed, to the limit of his strength
and his grip on the hand-hold bar.

Bumping in the line had started another oscillation, cans
endangering workers along the walls—he flattened, had
enough room until the effect dissipated down the line. Cans
bumped one another, threatened another jam, and then
didn't—Saby was controlling the feed back there, finessing it,
best she could. . . .

"*Captain.* Sprite*'s moving this way.*"

Sprite's . . .

Moving.

"*Oh, . . . shit!*" Tink said.

He didn't know he'd moved, but he had, he didn't realize
Tink had made a grab for him, but he'd slung Tink's hand
off—didn't know where he was going, but he shoved with his
foot on a can and shot forward, the walls a blur in his vision
as he richocheted off cans, off the wall, grabbed for a handhold
where the railing climbed to the release zone. Brain caught up to
body, then—he wanted escape, wanted forward, where ship's
officers were, where Austin was, where the truth was, as much
as they hadn't told to him, who that ship was, that was coming
at them.

Bright lights now, vacant stretch of hand-rail, at the top of
the cans now, the cargo-lock mate-up area, cans bumping in
the guide rails, where the line started a process to shunt the
cans on *Corinthian*'s rails off into the mated rail in the other
hold—both cargo locks standing wide open, all the way into
the hulk they were dealing with.

Com D light was blinking. Saby wanted him. Maybe Tink
did. Breath was ragged. The suit regulator wouldn't give him
more oxygen.

Betrayal, then, Tink's voice, on Universal: "*All hands,
Hawkins is in Michaels' rig. —Tom, you got to get back here.*"

Save the ship. He knew that. He understood. Tink had to
get him.

"*Tom!*" Saby's voice. Saby couldn't leave her post. Wouldn't. Too many lives . . . "*Tom, come back, Tom, I need you! I need you, dammit!*"

"*Tom!*" Tink's voice, again, anguished. "—*Captain, he's coming your way! I can't catch him . . .*"

The whole ship wanted to stop him. In front of him, glaring light, *Corinthian*'s cargo-lock console, as he hand-over-handed toward the officers there.

"*Hawkins!*"

Christian.

He had no direction with the com. He scanned the 360° of helmet display, looking, but had no warning as someone snagged the back-pack, spun him around to rebound against the wall. "Son-of-a-bitch! What are you doing?"

He fended off the hold, but it wasn't only Christian, it was two, three of them, grabbing hold, starting an inertial tumble. They bumped cans, richocheted off to the wall of the chute, back again. A section of tractor-chain ground against his helmet, bump, bump, bump, until somebody hauled them out of it and anchored their collective mass along the rail.

"*Cut his regulator!*" somebody shouted. C. BOWE was the name on the helmet closest, the one with his hand on his oxygen supply.

He panicked, swung to free himself, claustrophobic as if the oxygen had already stopped.

"You lied to me," he panted, and struggled to get a hold on the rail. "You all fucking *lied* to me, you son of a bitch—*what ship, what's going on out there?*"

Someone else was yelling—he couldn't hear it; then "*Hold it!*"

Austin's voice. "*Hold it, dammit, that's high mass—brake on, damn you, cut it—*"

Something happened. "*Shit!*" somebody yelled, but he was still fighting for air, found an arm free and got a hold on the rail, as a jackstraw debris of metal rods flew everywhere.

"Brake! Brake! Can's ruptured—"

Crewmen were yelling, rods were flying everywhere, into the line, into the moving cans, rebounding. A piece slammed him side-on, knocked him against the wall with no surety his arm wasn't broken, but he got his glove to his regulator, tried to get the air-flow up.

"Patch!" somebody screamed—suit rupture—and nobody was watching him, they were shutting the cargo doors, far as they could with the racks mated, trying to stop the debris.

He couldn't breathe. He drifted, trying, with clumsy fingers, to adjust the external regulator. Last impact had thrown him against the cargo-lock console, piece of metal rammed right through the shelter wall and into the console board, more of the jackstraws in slower, entropic motion now, companions in his drift. He fended them, tried to calm his breathing.

"Austin!" he heard Christian calling. *"Austin, use your com, dammit!"*

"Captain was otherside," somebody said, *"in the other lock!"* and Christian:

"Shit, open the doors, open the damn doors!"

"Austin." That was Beatrice, somewhere. *"Austin, answer com!"*

"Yeah," came back, through heavy static. *"I got a problem."* More of it, but it broke up.

Crew were trapped over in the other hold—trapped with a ricocheting mass of steel—and he'd done it. *He* had. He caught a hand-hold, no one caring, now, no one paying attention to him.

"What's happened?" somebody asked, not the only voice. You didn't chat on Universal when an emergency was in progress, you shut up. He thought that last voice might be the bridge asking information, but nobody answered. He tried to, on general: "Can of rods ruptured." Air still wouldn't come fast enough. "Doors are shut, bridge—doors are shut, and that's my ship out there, dammit!"

"*Tommy?*" Capella's voice. "*Tommy, it's closing—it's* Sprite *and us both the sumbitch is after, —Tommy, d' you hear me? That's the truth.*"

Mind went scattershot, a dozen trails of logic—sounds in the dark, colors running—freighter, freighter screaming. . .

Capella, leaning close, whispering . . . touch of lips . . . saying . . . telling him. . .

"*Tommy, we got to have the card, now, Tommy . . . Austin's got to input. Hear? —Do it now, Tommy!*"

Limbs jerked, half paralyzed, moving to what he couldn't but half remember, just Capella's voice and the gut-hitting feeling that he might have been immensely, irremediably wrong in his instant assumptions, Marie's assumptions, beaten into him, dinned into him . . .

Not what he'd seen on this ship.

"*Where's Austin?*" the bridge was asking, and he listened sharp, wanting to hear, when somebody, a voice he'd heard before, answered:

"*Captain's caught otherside. The other hold. They're trying, Bea, they did an emergency close, and they got to jack the damn doors.*"

"*Shit,*" he heard, Capella's voice. "*Captain? You copy?*"

The outer cargo hatch had closed on the mated rails. Crew was jacking it open, using levers at either side of the doors, others trying to scrape past the doors and under the cans blocking them to reach the hulk's hold.

Tom slung himself that direction along the safety rail, no one stopping him on his careening course—was so shaken he strained his arm catching himself on the landing. But a man squeezed through ahead of him—he re-angled his body and hauled himself through, risking the LS kit on his back . . . felt it scrape as he entered the hulk.

His first sight in the hulk's cargo lock was loose cans, debris floating, white powder in clumps and clouds, adhering to surfaces, obscuring vision throughout the cargo chute.

He had no idea now what he was doing, except they were trying to get crew out past him, one man that could move himself, that tried to help his rescuers. White powder, God knew what, clung to his visor no matter how he wiped. Loose rods shot past, still potent with *v*.

Then a suited body drifted toward him along the stalled row of cans. He grabbed its arm, not able to see who it was, whether the man was alive or dead, or who it was—he wasn't moving, was all, and he hauled the man back to the cargo lock, through the whiteout of dust, and passed the man through the gap to the men on the other side—one life maybe they could save.

"Captain?" he was hearing on hail. *"Captain? Seven minutes. Closing fast."*

And a second voice, Capella's, he thought, desperate: *"We need that key-card. Look in the console key slot, Tom, somebody. Fast."*

He knew what he was looking for. He tried to go in that direction, when a rod bounced past, hit the wall noiselessly, ricocheted and vanished into the powder-storm. And crew hauled suited bodies past him, a man with a piece of iron through the torso, then one with a helmet gouged and splintered across the faceplate.

TRAVIS, the helmet said.

Only name he'd made out, on anybody. Wasn't Bowe. He found himself shakily relieved it wasn't Austin, as he grabbed a rail and tried to get along the wall.

A suited figure caught up with him in the obscuring dust. BOWE, the helmet said. C. Smeared with blood. Christian looked straight at him. He started to ask . . . where Austin was . . . and his com crackled with,

"Damn you, you Hawkins bastard, get out of there!"

A rod shot between them. Rebounded. Hit a can, ricocheted again, came back.

He was drifting, on a rebound. Grabbed something.

"Four minutes," he heard, in the ringing of his ears. *Motion alert,* was flashing in his faceplate. *"Get out of there,"* com said, male voice this time, *"Get out, now, we're screwed, leave it, leave it, leave it."*

And Capella's: *"Get the card, damn it!"*

His back hit the cans. He bounced off, saw a crewman near him, trying for a hand-hold, and he held out an arm, mindless free-fall reflex. The man grabbed him and he grabbed the rail as they grazed the wall in a conjoint tumble toward the bright light, spotlights all he could see in the white-out, except dark beads like frozen oil spatting against his faceplate.

He shoved off, dragging the man with him, grabbed the console rim and stopped their random motion as green seconds bled time away from him in the faceplate display. The man he'd rescued had hold next to him—crew had reached them, trying to pull both of them away; but the man shoved them off, shoved a card into the console they both clung to.

C. BOWE showed grey through the paste of white dust on the opposing helmet. He could see Christian's face, intent on the card, not on him.

Other voices on Universal sputtered with static. Somebody was yelling, *"Close the doors. Kick the cans clear! Shut the cargo doors! Fire window is forty-eight seconds—"*

Christian jammed the card down, firm contact, groped for the input slate and the electronic stylus scissor-jointed over it.

Wrote an H. A.

Hand shook, dithered in a fit of shock. V.

"O," Tom said, furious with his own spasm of shaking. Christian's hand wasn't making it. He grabbed the hand, forced a shaky circle. Shakier C. Son of a bitch, it wasn't just himself and Austin knew Capella's code.

Lights flashed. Display above the input said, in red letters: ENEMY IDENTIFIED.

TARGETING.

POSITIVE.

He flashed on *Sprite*'s corridors. Marie at her console.

But he believed Patrick was real, and Patrick was first on the old hulk's list. His voice in the dark said so.

While *Sprite* was out there. Coming toward them.

TARGET LOCKED, he saw on display, through a white haze.

FIRE INITIATED.

The hulk's frame shook. He felt it through the hand-grip. Stared at his brother's face, Christian staring at him.

Felt something pull at him, trying to pull them away. He held onto the console. But he saw suit lights then, coming around behind Christian, to take him away.

Christian went. But *he* wasn't leaving. Wasn't moving. No. Information was here. On *this* readout. It was all the truth he had.

"*Tom,*" Saby said. Hands tugged at him, failed to move him. "*Come* on, *Tom, dammit, it's fired, it's all we can do.*"

"*Tom.*" Tink's voice. A new hand pulled and he couldn't hold on any longer. His gloved hands lost their handhold, and they carried him back toward the doors, through the drifting white.

"*Tom.*" Capella's voice, then. "*Tom, Sprite is not, so far, a target, repeat, not, so far, a target.*"

"*Who's in command down here?*" he heard somebody ask, and Christian answer:

"*I guess I am.*"

"*Not yet.*" Another voice came faintly, scratchy with static. "*Not yet, you don't, kid. —Where's the damn hostile, can somebody find the hostile?*"

"*Fireball,*" came from the bridge, smugly. "*Any minute now.*"

Still couldn't get enough air. Tom let Saby and Tink pull him ahead, along the railing. He just breathed, his visor dusted over so the lights fuzzed.

"*There it goes,*" a female voice said. "*Austin. You copy? Got the bastard.*"

"*I copy,*" Austin said. "*Thank you, Beatrice.*"

He tried clumsily to adjust the air-flow. People talked to Medical, then, talked about broken arms and a suit puncture, one man dead. They said the cargo doors were shutting. But *motion imminent* had just gone off his faceplate display.

Nothing seemed real to him. Crew movement was all drifting now, leisurely. He heard Beatrice Perrault say,

"Evidently the robot respects a freighter ID. Or its direction, as nav believes. Sprite is, at any rate, sacrosanct. That gives us a new problem."

"Screw that," Tom said. New panic closed on him. Indignation. He shoved to get clear. "They're not attacking my ship." He couldn't break Tink's grip. He shoved the channel selector with his chin. *"Austin, damn you, that's my ship, dammit, that's my mother's ship—"*

"Put Hawkins in contact," Austin said faintly. *"Beatrice. Dan. Do it. —Tom."*

"Sir."

"That's a word I like to hear. We still have them outgunned, Thomas Bowe-Hawkins. Remember that. Tell mama hello."

"Yes, sir," he said.

"Stand by." Voice he didn't know. But after that:

"Go ahead, Hawkins. Talk them out of shooting. Or going away. The old hulk doesn't like either one."

Chapter Twelve

—— *i* ——

"Tom," Saja said, a face on the vid. *"Tom. Tell me again. Tell me why it's your choice."*

"Yeah, well, . . ." Breath still felt as tight as it had in the suit. "Dammit, tell Marie I want to talk. I'll tell her. All right?"

"She says, . . ."

"Yeah, screw what she says until she says it to *me*. Tell her get the hell on the com and talk to me. Now."

Silence, then. He sat there, on *Corinthian's* bridge, with Saby and Christian standing over him, and Austin sitting—a broken leg, four broken ribs and a broken arm, was Austin's tally, give or take. One man hadn't been lucky. Came of fools interfering with operations. Came of a mistake he'd never in his life forget.

But they'd delivered the last of the cargo. Austin insisted. Said he'd never failed a contract and he wasn't starting now. Flour and blood every damn where, iron rods floating all over the hold. Couldn't get that out of his memory.

Hadn't even realized his ankle was broken. He'd been that scared. That numb.

New image came on. Marie stared at him. He stared back, a light-second removed.

"*So?*" Marie said. "*You staying with* Corinthian?"

"Yes," he said. "*—Met a girl, Marie.*"

"*A girl.*" Marie snorted. "*You damn fool.*"

"Yeah. I know. But you'd like her, Marie."

"*Austin there?*"

That surprised him. That really surprised him. He looked at Austin. Austin turned his chair, reached across the board and put the aux com live.

"Hello, Marie. What can I do for you?"

While, across the bridge, missiles were armed and the scan was locked warily on *Sprite*.

"*Hello, Austin. You want him?*"

Austin shrugged. "Not my choice."

"*What do you want?*"

"To get clear. That's all. You speaking for *Sprite,* now, Marie? I hear so."

"*Damn right.*"

"Well, captain Hawkins, you're clear, you're free. My navigator says you could even cut a deal. I'll give you a password, in fact. Tell Miller Transship you want the deal I had. Whisper the word Tripoint. Somebody'll be in contact, if you're polite. Just sit at Viking and wait."

"*You're out of your mind.*"

"It's clean money, all legitimate salvage. Real old dates. And we're out of this route, for good. Got another offer. So it's all yours, captain Hawkins. Comfortable living. I do suggest you upgrade your armament, if you take the offer. And rig a cutoff for that damn ID."

"*Go to hell.*"

"Go to hell yourself, Marie. Love you."

"*Tom?*"

He punched the switch. "Marie. Yeah?"

Marie didn't say anything right off. Just stared. Punched a few buttons. Maybe the image-capture. It looked to be. He pushed that button on *Corinthian*'s board. Froze that look, that motion, for keeping, for the rest of time.

"*You stay out of trouble,*" Marie said. "*Keep yourself honest. Hear?*"

"You take care of yourself," he said. "Mama. You take care."

— *ii* —

DREAM OF A POINT OF shifting mass, three-body problem. Tricky spot, the navigators said.

Never been a star. Never could be. Complex motion, forever shifting, the third mass tending to widen the gap by very small amounts over centuries.

Navigators said the Point wasn't stable—said the close binary mass followed Sol on its strange course, maybe some ancient association with Sol and its planetary companions in the long-ago past, in their frantic pace across the long, long gulf Sol was crossing—all of human history in that passage.

And the third mass at Tripoint . . . was a newcomer, maybe swept up out of Pell, who knew? Scientists wrangled, nothing proved, nothing known for certain—they talked about probes, to reach down into the high-g depths of what might, almost have been a star.

Easy, most of all, to lose things in the triple mass. Easy to miss ships, easy to pick up the brown radiance of any of the three Points, blotting out all else that might lie behind it.

Tom could hear one deep sound, at least, going away from them. Sat there, while Saby slept the sleep that made hyperspace bearable.

Sprite was on its way.

So were they—to a Place, Capella swore, where there was cargo to be hauled, a place the Fleet had found, that they'd been supplying all along, but they'd not needed to know—until now.

Where? was the burning question in the crew. But Capella wasn't talking.

Said, the Fleet had never surrendered. They never would.

Said, Some things you got to take on faith.

Austin said they put up with her.

Christian said . . .

Christian said they could sell surplus crew to the Fleet, and older brother should watch his step, and not screw anything really essential.

They made one seven-light jump, toward the place they were going.

Arrived, not at Pell, or Viking, but at another dark mass and a fuel dump.

So where they were going now was far, far from places they knew . . . he didn't know of any two-jump that lay on ordinary routes.

Some Mazianni hideout, it might be. Austin was still worried, he caught that, in things he'd overheard. But rumor had always said the Fleet had places nobody knew.

Mostly, he regretted Pell. He wanted to go back if only once, wanted to recover that time with Saby. That walk in the spacefaring forest. He wanted to see a rainstorm, even from water-jets.

Saby had kept the leaf safe for him. He sat on the bed looking at it . . . you could sit a long time, in the strangeness of jump-space. He hadn't duties. Computers weren't reliable right now. It was the interface the ship engaged. Time wasn't. Logic wasn't. Colors and sounds came and went.

The music, Capella called it. He heard it. At least . . . it sounded that way.

A shadow arrived in his vision. How long and when didn't matter in this space. Capella was there. She sat down on the bed. He folded the leaf back into its paper safekeeping.

"More of those," she said.

"What, more of those?" Sometimes, with Capella, you had to start in the middle of conversations.

"Where we're going," Capella said. "More of those."

"You're not serious."

"Absolutely. Always. Well, sometimes. But this is true, Tommy." She reached out, patted Saby's foot. " 'Scuse. Sweet dreams."

"Forests?" he asked.

"Might be."

"Can't be."

Capella shrugged. Tucked her knee into the circle of her arms. "All that Earth was," she said. "Will be again. Six more jumps."

"Six. My God."

"There'll be fuel dumps. We'll be fine." Capella looked at him sidelong, tilted her head and looked at the overhead as if she could see through it.

Maybe she could. He was still discovering things.

"Do we come ever back from there?" he asked. The territory beyond was dark to him, a complete, uneasy unknown. Except, suddenly, the idea of forests. Green. Damp. Alive.

"I've been there," Capella said. "Truth is, —I found this place."

"You?"

"Heard it, in the dark. —D' you hear that?"

Something. He wasn't sure. Felt it, more.

"What was it?"

"Dunno," Capella said. "There's things you can't explain. Keeps you wanting to go again. Listen. Listen to it. There's a whole universe out there."

He did listen, for a long while. Capella went away again. The whole ship was theirs. Visit any cabin. Open any door. No one knew.

Forests, the woman said.